Y0-CAR-890

DESIRE'S CAPTIVE

"Stop fighting me, damn you!" Derek hissed, grabbing Lauren by the shoulder and rolling her onto her back. "I'm not going to hurt you!"

"Do what you must, but don't lie to me!" Lauren shot back furiously. She tried to roll onto her side to push Derek off, but he was too heavy and much too strong.

"I know you don't trust me," he said, his face just inches from hers. "What you've got to understand is that I don't trust you, either."

"I'll fight you to the end!" Lauren hissed.

He took Lauren's face between his palms.

"You use your mouth to curse and threaten," Derek whispered, looking deep into her eyes. "Perhaps you should consider more tender uses for it." Then his mouth descended on hers. . . .

HEARTFIRE ROMANCES

SWEET TEXAS NIGHTS (2610, $3.75)
by Vivian Vaughan

Meg Britton grew up on the railroads, working proudly at her father's side. Nothing was going to stop them from setting the rails clear to Silver Creek, Texas — certainly not some crazy prospector. As Meg set out to confront the old coot, she planned her strategy with cool precision. But soon she was speechless with shock. For instead of a harmless geezer, she found a boldly handsome stranger whose determination matched her own.

CAPTIVE DESIRE (2612, $3.75)
by Jane Archer

Victoria Malone fancied herself a great adventuress, but being kidnapped was too much excitement for even Victoria! Especially when her arrogant kidnapper thought she was part of Red Duke's outlaw gang. Trying to convince the overbearing, handsome stranger that she had been an innocent bystander when the stagecoach was robbed, proved futile. But when he thought he could maker her confess by crushing her to his warm, broad chest, by caressing her with his strong, capable hands, Victoria was willing to admit to anything. . . .

LAWLESS ECSTASY (2613, $3.75)
by Susan Sackett

Abra Beaumont could spot a thief a mile away. After all, her father was once one of the best. But he'd been on the right side of the law for years now, and she wasn't about to let a man like Dash Thorne lead him astray with some wild plan for stealing the Tear of Allah, the world's most fabulous ruby. Dash was just the sort of man she most distrusted — sophisticated, handsome, and altogether too sure of his considerable charm. Abra shivered at the devilish gleam in his blue eyes and swore he would need more than smooth kisses and skilled caresses to rob her of her virtue . . . and much more than sweet promises to steal her heart!

Available wherever paperbacks are sold, or order direct from the Publisher. Send cover price plus 50¢ per copy for mailing and handling to Zebra Books, Dept. 3460, 475 Park Avenue South, New York, N.Y. 10016. Residents of New York, New Jersey and Pennsylvania must include sales tax. DO NOT SEND CASH.

ROBIN GIDEON
Pirate's Passionate Slave

ZEBRA BOOKS
KENSINGTON PUBLISHING CORP.

To Tim and Tina,
for good friendship,
and to Rick and Shane,
for marshmallow noses.

ZEBRA BOOKS

are published by

Kensington Publishing Corp.
475 Park Avenue South
New York, NY 10016

Copyright © 1991 by Robin Gideon

All rights reserved. No part of this book may be reproduced in any form or by any means without the prior written consent of the Publisher, excepting brief quotes used in reviews.

If you purchased this book without a cover you should be aware that this book is stolen property. It was reported as "unsold and destroyed" to the Publisher and neither the Author nor the Publisher has received any payment for this "stripped book."

First printing: July, 1991

Printed in the United States of America

Chapter 1

1817

"What's wrong with you men? Why won't you fight?" Lauren Masters demanded, her ebony eyes darting from the approaching pirate ship to the frightened faces of the seamen on the ship *Miss Malaki*. She had boarded the schooner six days earlier with her chaperon, Miss Nichols, who was asleep in their cabin.

Lauren watched in horror as the sails were set loose, the fluffy white canvas collapsed, and the ship drifted to a stop. It was inconceivable to her—a Masters from head to toe—simply to give up without a fight, but that was exactly what the crewmen of *Miss Malaki* seemed ready to do.

As a mixture of anger and fear fought within her breast, Lauren rushed to Captain Disner, who stood like a statue at the edge of the cruiser, watching the rapidly approaching ship through a collapsible telescope.

"Captain, I order you to command your men to fight!" Lauren demanded, as only a wealthy young woman accustomed to giving orders could "What's wrong with them?"

Captain Disner finally turned from the spyglass to gaze on Lauren. She saw the defeat reflected in his old, weathered eyes, and although it saddened her, it did nothing to soften her resolve.

"If we fight them, they'll surely kill us all. Maybe if we give them what they want, we'll be spared," he whispered, shaking his head wearily. "Everyone who sails these seas knows what the Jolly Roger means." He nodded toward the three-mast clipper now less than a hundred yards away. It flew the white skull-and-crossbones against a black background, the universal flag of seafaring outlaws. "If we give up—simply give up—then we might be alive tomorrow."

"You're an idiot if you think that!" Lauren seethed. She turned on her heel and rushed starboard to get a better view of the oncoming pirate ship. Like everyone else aboard, she had heard the legend of *The Unholy One*. It was supposed to be the fastest, most heavily armed ship sailing the seas surrounding the Virgin Islands, and its captain and crew were rumored to be cutthroats without a shred of human decency or compassion. Lauren doubted the rumors were entirely accurate (on principle she had grave doubts about *all* rumors), but under the circumstances it was only prudent to believe they were. Throwing themselves to the mercy of a gang of pirates seemed nothing less than suicidal. If Lauren could convince crewmen from *Miss Malaki* to fight back, they might die in battle, but at least they would not have gone down without a fight. With Masters blood flowing strong and true in her veins, it was simply impossible for her even to consider surrendering.

Lauren strode from one white-faced, frightened seaman to the next, searching for someone who was willing to fight at her side. But following their captain's orders, the sailors all refused. Several passengers

6

appeared willing to fight, but judging from their stylish dress and the way they held themselves, Lauren doubted the elderly businessmen and the one fiesty old woman who said she was not afraid to die could muster an effective defense against cutlass-wielding pirates bent on destruction and domination.

Lauren felt the panic build inside her, intensifying with every second, and she fought it. This was a time when cold, levelheaded logic was needed, if there was any chance at all of saving herself and any of the others aboard *Miss Malaki*.

"Where do you keep your weapons—your rifles?" Lauren demanded, taking a young sailor by the collar of his shirt, shaking him as he stared as though in a trance at the sight of the pirates, who were now just seconds from boarding the ship.

"In the captain's locker, miss," the young man replied, trembling visibly. "He keeps 'em locked up with the liquor an' the ale." His eyes darted from Lauren's to those of the first of the pirates boarding the ship. "Don't fight 'em, miss. That's *The Unholy One,* an' anybody fights them winds up feeding the fish."

If there was one emotion Lauren hated above all others, it was the feeling of helplessness against forces that influenced her life. She had always railed against anything that had power and control over her. But as she watched the unwashed, grim-faced pirates board *Miss Malaki,* Lauren realized she could not fight the invaders alone and without weapons. Whether she wanted to or not, she would have to follow Captain Disner's advice—and hope for mercy.

The leader of *The Unholy One* was clearly distinguished. He stood back, away from the long plank that was being thrown from one ship to the other as a makeshift bridge. He was of medium height, extremely broad shouldered, and squarishly built. His curly hair was copper red and closely cropped. His beard, too, was cut short, so that Lauren couldn't distinguish where his hair ended and his beard began. In his right hand he held a heavy, curved cutlass; with his left he gestured as to where he wanted men to go, or at those he wanted apprehended. His face wore a thin-lipped sneer of contempt, and Lauren believed without doubt that this man, rumored to have wantonly slaughtered many who had fallen under his cannons, lived up to every gruesome tale.

On *Miss Malaki* the crewmen stood by silently, their hands at their sides. They were capable sailors; they were not soldiers. They knew how to fight hurricanes and look to the skies to guess what weather was forthcoming; they did not know how to fight men, or how to anticipate the actions of men who killed for greed and pleasure.

A dozen passengers were screaming in horror, men as well as women. Lauren watched as an old man was knocked to the deck by a pirate, then kicked savagely in the stomach. Apparently the old man's offense was that he hadn't appeared frightened enough to suit the pirate. The redheaded leader shouted his encouragement at the violence.

Lauren shook herself from her stunned torpor and dashed toward the huge wind tunnel, which funneled fresh air below deck. She squatted behind it, partially hidden, too curious not to watch the widespread carnage that was happening around her.

A second man appeared beside the leader. He was strikingly different in both appearance and demeanor. Slightly over six feet tall and quite slender, he had the wiry, well-muscled body of a panther. His clothes, unlike the soiled, ragged, threads of the leader, were immaculate: a waistcoat of midnight blue silk, a white silk shirt tucked into dark, tight-fitting trousers, and

8

knee-high, shiny black boots. He had fair hair and gaunt cheeks, and even the sixty feet that separated him from Lauren could not mute the piercing quality of his blue eyes. His nose was prominent and slightly hawkish, and his chin was faintly clefted. He wore a long cutlass with an ornate handle inside a sheath at his left hip. He appeared disdainful of the violence he saw, and this struck Lauren with a strange force that made it difficult for her to take her eyes from his face.

Two dozen pirates had boarded *Miss Malaki,* most crossing over on the narrow plank, some swinging over from ropes. The vile blood-lust of the pirates fed upon itself and the violence intensified. As Lauren watched in horror, one pirate cut a man down with his cutlass for no apparent reason whatsoever. Lauren's stomach turned and she was afraid she would be sick. She averted her face, closing her eyes and whispering a silent prayer for a quick and merciful death when her time came.

A booming voice—Lauren instinctively knew it was the redheaded man's, though she'd never before heard him speak—cut through the rising din. "Kill the old wench! She's too old and ugly to be of value to me!"

Lauren did not want to see what carnage she knew would come, but she could not prevent her eyes from opening. There on the deck not ten feet from her was the elderly, white-haired woman who had been willing to fight against the invaders with Lauren. The woman was on her knees, her small fists clenched in anger, her arms crossed over her head. A pirate stood above her, slowly pulling his cutlass far back for a lethal swing.

"If she spills one drop of blood, you will spill a thousand!"

The oath was issued quietly, yet it carried deadly authority. The man's words hinted at an English accent—Oxford educated, was Lauren's guess. Lauren

9

saw it was the fair-haired, well-dressed man she'd noticed earlier. In his hand he held his saber, with deadly steadiness, pointed at the pirate's chest.

"She ain't no good to us!" the pirate spat, angry that he had been denied the thrill of an easy kill, angrier still that he had been threatened with death by someone he obviously feared.

"Then let her be," the tall Englishman said, his razor-sharp saber unwavering.

A high-pitched scream drew Lauren's attention. She spun around in time to see a young woman not much older than herself being caught by three pirates. The men hoisted the screaming woman up onto their shoulders, carrying her toward the aft of *Miss Malaki*. Lauren could guess what fate awaited the woman, and the thought of it sickened her.

Lauren's concentration and concern were on the young woman, so she did not see the three pirates approach her. Before she knew exactly what had happened, she was grabbed by the arms and hauled to her feet. The scruffy, lusty-eyed pirates pushed Lauren back until her shoulders struck the bulkhead.

"No-o-o!" she screamed, trying to claw the eyes of one of the men.

Before she could do any damage, Lauren's hand was grabbed and her wrists were pinioned against the bulkhead. She tried vainly to kick the closest man in the groin, but he side-stepped the move, allowing her foot to glance harmlessly against the outside of his thigh. He moved between her legs, kicking her ankle so that he could move in close, between her thighs. He shoved his grimy fingers inside the velvet bodice of Lauren's gown, balled the fabric in his fist, and savagely ripped her décolletage down the front, nearly to her navel.

"N-o-o-o!" Lauren screamed again, fighting with all her might against the three foul-smelling pirates who

tore at her clothes and intended to use her cruelly to satisfy their base, violent lusts.

It was getting out of control. Lord Derek Leicester York stood on the deck of *Miss Malaki,* his eyes darting right and left, trying to see which vicious scene he might be able to control, cursing once again the cruel fate which had led him inexorably to *The Unholy One* and now to *Miss Malaki.*

He saw one of the men, a young and particularly savage pirate named Bones, grab a woman by the hair. Bones was slender to the point of emaciation, extraordinarily savage, and determined to rape the woman.

Derek rushed to the man and grabbed him by the shoulder. He touched the tip of his saber to Bones's ear.

"You'll never live to finish," Derek said, adding an ounce of pressure to add lethal emphasis to his words. "I promise you that."

Bones released his hold on the woman's hair. He turned toward Derek, pretending not to notice the sword pointed squarely at his throat. "Your day will come, and when it does, I'll be there to feed your guts to the sharks."

"You'll be shark dung long before me," Derek replied.

Before he could say more or in any way comfort the woman who had fallen to her knees and was crying hysterically, the sound of a young woman's scream, followed by *"N-o-o-o!",* cut through the air like cannon fire, alerting Derek to the continuing danger. He spun toward the sound and saw the loveliest young woman he'd ever spied being pinned against the bulkhead by three men. A moment later the woman's bodice was torn in two, revealing her full breasts beneath a silk chemise.

"Stop!" Derek shouted, his boots clicking against the wooden deck as he hurried to prevent yet another soul-stealing tragedy.

"She's ours, you English bastard!" one of the men said, brandishing a sharp dagger.

"Release her," Derek said commandingly. "I claim her for my buyer!"

"A pox on your buyer! He can have her when we're finished!" The pirate stood his ground, his courage fueled by lust and the captive woman's extraordinary beauty.

"Perhaps . . . perhaps, good man," Derek said coolly, "but before he meets his maker with the pox, he will have that woman. And if my guess is correct, he will be the first to have her. If my buyer is *not* the first, her value goes down, and then *you* will answer to Captain Gregor for the loss of profit."

Derek sensed that he had finally inspired fear in them. At the mention of Gregor, all three pirates suddenly lost interest in their young captive. Gregor's cruelty was legendary, and every man on *The Unholy One* had witnessed the keelhauling of mates who had defied him. No man had survived a keelhauling, and the corpses were fed to the sharks.

"I claim her now," Derek continued, still holding his weapon steady on the man's stomach. "Leave before you task me further."

The hatred he saw in their eyes was a frightening thing, even though Derek was not a man who frightened easily. These men would kill him, given the chance. Derek knew and accepted this. He could only hope that he would be off the ship before they had the chance to exact their cruel revenge. Until he accomplished what he needed to, his concerns for safety had to be put aside.

"Th-thank you," the woman said quietly, pulling her

12

bodice close to hide herself. "They would have killed me."

"Killing you wasn't what they had in mind," Derek said, wishing that she wasn't so attractive, knowing it was her beauty that had put her in such jeopardy. "What's your name?"

"Lauren." She would not give him her last name.

"If you do as I say, I might be able to help you," Derek said, his blue eyes fierce, brilliant, anxious. "If you fight me, there's nothing I can do. Do you understand?"

Lauren looked at him, doubt showing plainly in her eyes. She didn't trust him at all, and this burned into Derek's heart. There was a time when people he'd never spoken to before trusted him; now, upon meeting him, they were afraid for their lives.

"Come on," Derek said, knowing there was nothing he could say that would assuage Lauren's suspicions. "I'm getting you out of here." He grabbed Lauren and began pulling her through the chaos toward the passenger cabins.

"Where are you taking me?" Lauren braced her feet, resisting. He may have saved her from being raped by three foul-smelling cretins, but she doubted that his actions were motivated by anything other than self-interest.

"Stop fighting me! I haven't time for it!" Derek hissed through clenched teeth, squeezing her arm cruelly, sure that he was bruising her. "Stop it, or you can try your luck with those fine men I just fought off!"

The threat hit home. Lauren's eyes glared daggers of hatred at Derek. "You'll never enjoy it," she promised in a whisper.

For a second Derek closed his eyes and cursed himself and the strange fortunes that had brought him to *The Unholy One*. She thought that he had saved her only so that he could rape her first . . . and worse yet, Lord Derek York knew that nothing he could say or do would change her mind.

"Come on," he said harshly, his eyes darkening with anger. "If you do what I tell you, maybe you'll be safe and maybe you won't. But if you resist me, you'll not have a prayer in hell."

And this is hell, Lauren thought as she allowed the tall, well-dressed pirate to lead her below deck to where the captain's quarters were.

Derek found the place quickly enough. The two rooms were being ransacked by four young men who searched for the riches that every captain was rumored to carry, though few did. They had just broken open a small chest and were fighting over an old watch, the only valuable in it.

"Get out of here," Derek said, holding Lauren in one hand and his deadly saber in the other. "Take what you can carry, then leave. And you—" he nodded toward the youngest man—"stay outside the door and make sure nobody comes in here in my absence. Should this woman leave, or should anyone enter, I'll have you keelhauled."

"Even if Captain Gregor wants in, sir?" the young man asked.

"Especially if Gregor wants in!"

The pirates exchanged looks. The Englishman was the only man aboard *The Unholy One* who dared call Gregor by name without using his title. They all hated Derek, but they also feared him, and his curved saber had been used to settle arguments before—with fatal results.

"Stay here and lock the door," Derek said when he was alone with Lauren. "I've got to go on deck and do what I can."

Lauren didn't say a word. She could guess what evil

things he had to do, evil things he planned to do when he returned to her. A shudder went through her, and she pulled her bodice together more tightly, sitting on the edge of the captain's bed.

"Just stay here," Derek said when it was clear that Lauren wouldn't respond to him. He left the captain's quarters, saw that the boy was standing guard just as ordered, then headed for the deck at a run, hoping he could keep the·murder and mayhem to a minimum.

Chapter 2

When the door closed behind Derek, Lauren buried her face in her hands. She wanted to cry, but somehow she couldn't. Instead she cursed herself for having taken the trip to the Virgin Islands, she cursed her lousy luck, and she cursed all the decisions she had made of late.

It had actually started a year earlier, when Lauren had been swept off her feet by the practiced, seductive words of a much older man. She was twenty at the time, still a virgin, wondering if she would ever find a man who could meet her standards.

Then along came Richard. He was very attractive, smiled often, had a clever wit, appeared financially well off, and, best of all, treated her like a queen.

"I do believe I'll love you all my life," he said on their second chaperoned outing. "It's not merely your beauty, which is so exquisite that I cannot take my eyes from you, but your spirit as well. Lauren, can't you see that we are made for each other, *destined* for each other?"

She had waited too long to hear those words to prevent the tears from pooling in her large brown eyes. When he held his arms out to her, she slipped into them and delighted in the warmth and comfort she felt with her head against his shoulder. She didn't care that the few kisses they shared did not make her spirits soar, as she had been told they would when she kissed the man of her dreams. And when during that embrace his hand came up to cup her breast, she did not swoon with pleasure. Rather, Lauren felt a little disappointed the night Richard wanted more than a warm embrace, which had seemed to satisfy him before, and was as much physical comfort as Lauren required.

Although Richard did not exactly talk about his plans for marriage, Lauren did not resist telling her parents that she had found the man with whom she would spend the rest of her life. Richard was an honorable man, wealthy and industrious, and he would provide a good home for her. His holdings, combined with her own considerable wealth, would furnish them with everything they would need for their life together. The love was there, Lauren said . . . and it really didn't matter that her life with Richard would not have the consuming passion that her parents had. Michael and Sharon often locked themselves in their large, well-appointed bedroom at their estate in Virginia and did not come out for hours, with only the warm sounds of merriment and the muted sounds of passion to warn family and servants that they were not to be disturbed.

Lauren's father, a protective man who knew Lauren's vast holdings were a prize any gigolo would find hard to resist, had had Richard investigated. He found out that Richard was not the wealthy man he claimed to be, and what's more, that his unsavory past included two wealthy wives who he had either divorced or simply left after stealing most of their money. With an effort to control his anger, and restraining himself from giving the lout the beating he deserved, he forbade Lauren from ever seeing Richard again.

Defiant of anyone—even her beloved father—who told her what she could and couldn't do, Lauren rushed to Richard to confront him with what she'd learned. Richard denied everything, and though Lauren was suspicious of the denials, the sincere and tender look in his eyes made her doubt he was the heartless monster her father had described.

It was that night, in defiance of her parents and against her better judgment, that Lauren succumbed to Richard's seduction. The experience was not horribly painful—Richard was not exactly a man of heroic proportions—but neither was it in the least satisfying. When it was over, Lauren felt slightly fouled by Richard's perspiration on her body, and empty of any sensation of being joined to him in body and soul. Immediately after making love, Richard excused himself to wash, then refused to cuddle with Lauren, which was what she desperately wanted.

Deep within her a little voice had tried to warn Lauren that Richard was not what he appeared to be. That was why his kisses did not make the blood warm in her veins and his caresses did little to ignite the dormant passion within her bosom. A dark, foreboding gloom overcame her, and though she battled with her doubts, she at last did her own investigating into Richard's past. When she discovered the irrefutable truth—that Richard was a liar, opportunist, and bigamist—she rushed to her parents in tears and cried her heart out.

For six months she cursed herself for her foolishness. Then, when Michael and Sharon prompted her to get on with her life, she decided to travel to St. Thomas Island to research imported products for Masters Enterprises—the trip would be the perfect balm for her troubled, healing heart. Although they had grave doubts about Lauren travelling so far away, her parents employed a Miss Nichols to chaperone Lauren, and they watched *Miss Malaki* set sail for tropical waters.

"A curse on all men," Lauren whispered, lifting her head out of her hands, forcing away all thoughts of the past. She worried about Miss Nichols and could only hope that her chaperone was safe in the cabin they shared.

She could not worry about what had been, or about the reasons she was being held captive aboard a ship swarming with pirates. The only thing that mattered to her now was freeing herself and Miss Nichols and as many of the other passengers as possible.

Lauren began rummaging around the captain's quarters. The pirates had been thorough in their search for valuables, and virtually everything the captain had once had neatly stowed away was now strewn over the floor. A cutlass would do nicely, a dagger even better. If she couldn't find either, she'd use a club of some sort.

Lauren was powerfully built for a woman, her muscles strengthened by hours of horseback riding, and by participating in the athletic pursuits that her family encouraged. But she was still no match for Derek. He was at least six feet tall, she guessed, a half-foot taller than her; in a face-to-face fight he would easily defeat her. But if she could club him when he returned—and she had no doubt that he would, and knew what would happen to her when he did—then she just maybe had a chance to escape the captain's quarters, steal one of the dinghies, and row off toward St. Thomas to alert the authorities.

She wasn't sure how far away from St. Thomas they now were, and she didn't bother to ponder the odds of being able to steal a dinghy without being noticed. Her father always said that any task, however great or small, must be attacked one step at a time. With this in

19

mind, she determined that her first obstacle was the tall, handsome, but apparently ruthless pirate who went by the name of Derek.

Lauren picked up the leg of a chair that had been broken by the marauding pirates. The leg was round, smooth, solid. She held it in both hands, raising it high above her head, then brought it down with all her might against the mattress.

Yes, this should work nicely against the Englishman's skull! she thought, pushing away her fears of what vicious things Derek would do to her if she failed to render him unconscious.

Derek stood toe-to-toe with Gregor, looking the shorter, but much more powerfully built man in the eyes. The contempt between them was thick, deadly, and undisguised. Since Derek had boarded *The Unholy One* two weeks earlier, Gregor had resented his very presence, especially since Derek continually tried to keep his men from killing passengers on the ships they captured.

"I want that wench!" Gregor spat, his knuckles tightly gripping the haft of his cutlass.

"I have claimed her for my buyer," Derek replied easily, though his senses were ready for an attack by Gregor. "There are many other women for you to take, if that is your inclination."

Gregor laughed, but it wasn't a friendly sound. "And what is it you think I want to do? Ha! Of course I tend to take her to my bed!"

"If you do that, you will decrease the lady's value. That would not please my buyer, nor would it please the man you answer to. Profit is what this venture is all about, isn't it?"

Gregor's teeth were clenched. A muscle twitched in

his jaw. Derek saw that Gregor wanted desperately to withdraw his cutlass and thrust it into his heart—or worse, stab him through the stomach for a slow, hideously painful death. If Gregor went for his cutlass, Derek would go for his own revolver, and he was confident that if they crossed swords, he could cut the pirate down before his own blood was spilled. But to draw Gregor's blood would destroy any chance Derek had of discovering who controlled Gregor's nefarious activities. If Derek was ever to find his beloved sister Amanda, who had been kidnapped three months earlier, he had to find out who Gregor sold his captured women to. This alone kept Derek aboard *The Unholy One,* and kept him from ending Gregor's vicious reign of terror running a white-slave operation on the high seas of the Caribbean.

"There are many women," Derek continued, a half-smile curling his lips. "I want so few for my employer. Why must we argue about this particular one? Why let something so trivial as a woman come between us in this profitable partnership?"

"We ain't mates," Gregor hissed, uttering the words holding a promise of death. "Don't you ever forget that, Englishman." Gregor turned on his heel and stormed away, unsheathing his cutlass as he went.

Derek turned away and breathed a sigh of relief. He had saved one woman. But his protection of Lauren and his refusal to give her to Gregor would assuredly cause the death of someone else. Whenever thwarted in his ugly wishes, Gregor always took his frustration out on someone, unleashing his cutlass to spill warm blood. Derek could not protect everyone—indeed, he was lucky enough to protect a small handful—but the realization that he would inadvertently cause someone's death weighed heavily upon him.

Whatever valuables could be found were taken from

the passengers and cabins on *Miss Malaki* and brought to the coffers of *The Unholy One*. The women young enough to be sold as slaves were thrown into the brig, while other women were temporarily claimed by various pirates. Young men who were strong and could work were put into a separate brig. Old men and women were deemed to have no value to Gregor, and many of those were summarily thrown overboard.

Derek did what he could to prevent the killings, carefully treading the fine line between exerting what authority he had and usurping Gregor's.

Three hours later, the darkness enveloping him, Derek made his way below deck. The guard he had posted outside the captain's quarters was still there, though Derek could see that someone had brought him rum, because the young man was quite intoxicated.

"On my ship, I'd have you court-martialed for drinking on duty," Derek said disgustedly as he dismissed the guard.

"This ain't yer ship, Mr. Derek," the young man said with a drunken grin, badly slurring his words.

Derek fixed the boy with a look, and the young man hurried off to join his mates in the foul pleasures that Gregor encouraged after ransacking a ship and taking women prisoner.

Lauren heard the sound of Derek's voice just outside the door. The hours she had spent waiting for him to return had sharpened her senses. Crouched behind the door, holding the chair leg tightly in both hands, she waited to make her move. The room was enveloped in darkness, but Lauren's eyes had adjusted to it. If Derek's weren't, he would be momentarily blind, giving her a considerable advantage. If she waited for

22

him to close the door before she struck, her chances for success were greater.

The door opened and Lauren's heart stopped beating. She held her breath, every muscle in her body tensed and ready.

"Lauren, are you still in here?" Derek asked, taking a step inside the room, leaving the door open.

Lauren was too anxious to delay. She leaped to her feet and brought the makeshift club down with all her might, aiming for Derek's head, praying that the blow would be lethal.

But Lauren immediately realized her prey's reflexes were superlative. He bent his knees and snapped his head to the side, partly avoiding the blow. The chair leg glanced off the side of his head and smashed into his shoulder with jarring force, dropping him to his knees as he raised his hands to block a second blow.

Lauren did not wait to strike again, choosing instead to run. Derek moved too quickly—like a cat, she thought—for her to risk fighting him. She was out the door and in the dark hallway in an instant, her slippered feet almost silent against the hard wood.

Lauren had run hardly twenty paces when she rounded a corner and ran square into the arms of the young man who had stood guard outside her door. He was with three of his comrades, passing a tin cup back and forth. On the floor at their feet was an uncorked keg of rum.

They grabbed Lauren before she had a chance to escape, pinning her between them. Cruel hands groped her, tearing at her already ripped bodice, further exposing the plentiful swells of her breasts. Their sadistic laughter sickened her, and the rank smell of their rum-soaked breath assaulted her as much as their rough, mauling hands.

"Stop it! Leave me alone!" Lauren shouted. She managed to free one hand, and she raked at the eyes of the closest man. She missed his eyes but managed to scrape bloody slashes down his cheeks. To her horror the man only smiled.

"You'll pay dearly for my blood!" the man hissed, his hand shooting out to take Lauren by the throat. "We know just how to take the fight out of a wench like you!"

Lauren looked at the young man who had stood guard outside her door. He was so young, and his face belied an evil soul. "Please, won't you help me?" she asked, unwilling to believe that such a young man could be so heartless.

The youngster only laughed, tossing his head back on his shoulders. He wiped away excess rum from his chin with his dirty sleeve. "I'll help you get rid of your clothes, m'lady. Is that help enough for you?"

To end any doubt that he meant what he said, he took Lauren's tattered gown in his hands and yanked savagely. Lauren's exquisite gown, designed in Paris and made in Italy, ripped down the center to her waist.

"Easy men," Derek said, swaying slightly as he approached the foursome, holding his saber at his side, the gleaming blade pointed at the floor. "Damaging her clothes is excusable; damaging her flesh isn't."

Lauren couldn't believe she was actually happy to see Derek. His voice had a strange effect on the men, and on her as well. Although he spoke in a conversational tone, his words carried all the authority and power of a shouted command.

"C'mon, Mr. Derek, 'ave a 'eart," the oldest of the four pirates said. "We won't mark 'er up. Yer buyer will never know the diff'rence."

"*I'll* know the difference, and I don't like cheating my employer." Derek moved within a couple steps of

24

Lauren, staying back far enough so that he could use his weapon, if necessary. "Release her to me. I'll pay the four of you handsomely for catching her."

The oldest pirate shook his head slowly, his eyes glittering menacingly with lust, hatred, and rum. "That ain't good enough, Englishman. I got rum and I got a wench. I ain't got no need for money."

"You've also got your life, but unless you do what I tell you, you won't have that." Derek felt a trickle of blood run along the back of his ear into the stiff white collar of his silk shirt. He cursed Lauren for clubbing him, hoping the blood didn't show; these scoundrels would pounce on the slightest sign of weakness. "Enjoy your rum. Enjoy enough of it and you'll have no want for a woman."

The pirate laughed loudly. "I ain't never been that drunk in my life, Englishman! I'm a man through and through! Drink has never unmanned me, and it never will!"

"I've heard that boastful talk from better men than you," Derek said softly. Though his saber was still pointed at the floor, he twisted the haft slowly in his hand, drawing attention to it. "And the name is Derek. *Mr.* Derek, to you, sailor. If it's a problem for you to remember that, perhaps I can give you something to help your memory . . . like a blade through the knee, for instance."

The men backed away from Lauren in unison, releasing her arms. She immediately pulled together the tattered remains of her gown to hide her breasts.

"Come with me," Derek said to her, his heated gaze showing appreciation of her beauty and fury at her behavior. Once out of earshot, he hissed, "And don't give me another moment's trouble, or I'll give you back to those men. My buyer might *not* know the difference."

25

The words were ice in Lauren's veins, and a shudder of revulsion swept through her. She fought against a rising tide of fear that made her want to fall to her knees and beg for mercy. But what mercy could she expect from a rogue—a pirate—like Derek? She straightened her shoulders, held her head high, and said defiantly, "Is it back to the captain's quarters, or do you intend to defile me here so that your friends can watch your pathetic attempt to prove your manhood?"

"To the cabin," Derek answered, taking Lauren by the arm, pushing her along. "I enjoy my privacy."

Chapter 3

The door to the captain's quarters had been broken when the pirates stormed *Miss Malaki,* so Derek had to prop a heavy teakwood steamer trunk against it to keep it shut and prevent unwanted intruders from getting in. It wasn't much protection against the legion of evil that roamed the decks of *Miss Malaki,* but it was the best he could do under the circumstances.

He turned to study Lauren, who sat on the bed, watching his every move with eyes that missed nothing. She had beautiful eyes, Derek noted, big and brown, wide spaced, and clear. He also saw suspicion, contempt, and defiance in their brown depths. He gritted his teeth in frustration.

"I'm not going to rape you," he said softly.

Now that the immediate danger had been removed, he felt quite weary, and the throbbing headache that she'd provided—courtesy of a chair leg—had returned full force.

Derek peeled off his jacket, revealing the fine white shirt and the self-styled, custom-made sheath that carried a stiletto-bladed dagger under his left arm. He poured water into a small basin, rummaged around until he found a cloth, then applied the damp cloth to the lump on his head.

"Thanks a hell of a lot, by the way," Derek said with a groan, pressing the cloth against the wound. He had stopped bleeding, but the collar of his shirt was sticky with blood. "You nearly killed me."

"I wish I had," Lauren replied in a whisper.

"And what good would that have done you?" Derek felt his anger rising. He fully understood this young woman's contempt for him, but that didn't make it easier to accept. "If it hadn't been for me, you'd still be with those jackals. And believe me, the odds weren't in your favor. When they were done with you, others would have joined in the fun."

"Others like yourself, no doubt."

"That's not my idea of fun."

Lauren made a sound of incredulous contempt, turning away from Derek, but not so far that she couldn't observe his movements from the corner of her eye.

His raging headache aside, Derek found he was begrudgingly becoming more and more fascinated with her. In the face of impossible odds, held captive against her will, she was still fighting, still defiant. He leaned against the chest of drawers to give himself a moment of undisturbed thought.

What the hell am I going to do with her? She's too beautiful to be set free, but I'll have to fight constantly to keep her. I can't fight the entire crew of The Unholy One and find my sister as well!

He swallowed an oath of frustration, pressing hard enough against the head wound to increase the pain, which he welcomed. Pain would prevent him from having libidinous thoughts . . . or so he hoped. He tried to keep his eyes from Lauren, aware of the effect she had on him, but his will was not great enough.

She was, even by his high standards, stunning. Her hair was as black as a raven's crown, falling in loose waves around and over her shoulders. Her profile was strong, her full, sensual mouth pressed into a grim line, her chin tilted slightly upward as though in preparation for battle. Her velvet dress had been destroyed by the calloused hands of cruel pirates, and earlier Derek had seen the fullness of her breasts within the form-fitting silk chemise. In profile, the sensually rounded contours of her bosom were even more noticeable, and the effect on Derek was profound, even though he had spent his adult life surrounded by attractive women.

Derek watched as Lauren fiddled with the few buttons that remained on her gown, modestly trying to close it.

"I'm not going to rape you, I said." There was a harshness in his tone because her beauty had conjured up softly enticing, sensual images that he knew could never be possible with a woman who saw him as the devil incarnate.

She turned slowly to fix her gaze upon him. "Yes, I know, you've told me. I've been told lots of things by men . . . enough to know that men have a marked propensity for lying—especially to women!"

Derek chuckled softly, a little surprised that this woman clearly had received at least some formal education. "Marked propensity? I can't argue with that." He rinsed out the cloth, then reapplied it to his head. The bleeding had stopped, and the swelling appeared to be decreasing slightly. He felt compelled to draw Lauren into a conversation, hungry to know more about her, which was unusual—Derek did not normally talk much with anyone. "What's your name?"

"I already told you."

"Your last name."

"What's yours?"

She'll give up nothing without a fight, Derek thought with no small amount of respect. And though he hadn't even told Gregor his last name, he said, "York. Derek York, at your service." He kept his title to himself, sure that even if he told Lauren his full name and title, she wouldn't believe him.

"I'm Lauren Masters."

"American?"

She nodded. Derek studied her closely, seeing the almond hue of her skin, wondering what her parentage was. She could be part Indian, he thought, but that didn't seem likely. She was well educated, and judging from the cut and quality of her dress, also financially well off. During his business trips to the States, Derek had discovered that the native Americans were treated abysmally and didn't enjoy great success in the thriving country, so the color of her skin surely must have come from somewhere else.

"It's late," Derek said at last, dropping the cloth into the rust-colored water in the washbasin. "We'd better get some sleep." He took a step toward the bed but stopped when he saw Lauren's body tighten and the muscles in her shoulders flex in preparation for a fight. "I told you I wasn't going to rape you. I don't *do* that sort of thing."

"But you've got nothing against murder, and you allow your men to rape." Lauren laughed hatefully. "I could more easily believe the serpent in the Garden of Eden than the tales you tell."

Derek stepped forward until he was directly in front of her. It had been a long and hideous day, and he had fought hard. He had done all he could to keep the carnage to a minimum, and the effort had taken a

30

terrible toll. "If you fight me, I can't protect you. Why can't you understand that?"

"Go to hell!"

"I'll tie you up if you persist."

"And I'll scream my head off!"

This time it was Derek's turn to laugh contemptuously. "And what good will that do? Do you really think you'd be the first woman tonight to scream? Do you really think any of the monsters roaming the ship give a damn if you do, or will come running to your aid?" Derek spun away from Lauren, searching through the rubble to find something to bind her hands and feet so she could not steal his dagger as he slept. "I'm tired, Lauren! Tired down to the marrow of my bones! Before the month is out, there's a very real chance Gregor is going to kill me, or send his men to do the killing, and right now I just can't let it happen, do you hear? I've got something I must accomplish, and I can't let you or Gregor or anyone or anything stand in my way."

Derek's frustration and anger had worked into a fever pitch, and when he turned back to her, holding the severed sleeve from one of the captain's shirts and the pull cord from the porthole curtain, he saw the abhorrence she felt for him glittering bright and unconcealed in her eyes.

She fought him just as he knew she would, and her physical strength was surprising. It was much more difficult to pin her arms behind her back and bind her wrists with the cord than he'd anticipated, and compounding his anger was his body's response to wrestling with such a beautiful opponent.

"Fight me no further, you bloody wench, or I swear I'll strike you!" Derek hissed, grabbing her by the shoulder and rolling her onto her back. Her gown had

31

opened further during the struggle, and the vision she presented—her heavy, round breasts rising and falling with her rapid breathing, straining against the pale, ivory-colored chemise—made his heart race.

True to her nature, Lauren refused to place her feet together for Derek to bind them with the shirt sleeve. She fought him like a wildcat, kicking with all her might, until her feet were tightly bound and she was helpless.

"I know you don't trust me," Derek said, pushing Lauren until she was at the very edge of the bed, her shoulder against the wall. "What you've got to understand is that I don't trust you, either. And the only person whose standing between you and those murderers and rapists is me! Now before you try to kill me again, I want you to give that some thought."

Derek removed his saber, pulled the dagger from its sheath, then lay on the bed beside Lauren. He stretched out, and though everything in him—every instinct and every reflex honed since puberty—screamed for him to take this lovely woman into his arms, he just closed his eyes, holding the dagger in his right hand.

"Sleep now," he whispered. "Tomorrow could be an even worse day than this one."

Lauren could not sleep. She tested the rope around her wrists every few seconds, but there was no give to it. She kept waiting for Derek to roll over, rip the clothes from her, and rape her. She lay waiting tensely, wishing for death rather than defilement, but his breathing soon became steady, and she knew he'd gone to sleep.

He's tired, she thought. *Surely that is the only reason he hasn't satisfied his cruel lust with me. In the morning he'll finish what the others started.*

She turned her head to look at the face close to her own. She saw the blood on the collar of his shirt and felt good that she had injured him. At least his victory over her would not be without some loss of blood on his part.

Looking at him, Lauren thought how horribly unjust it was that such a handsome man should be so evil, and she contemplated why some men go bad and others do not. Derek York seemed intelligent, and he certainly was handsome and physically fit. He had so many traits in his favor—why would he sail on *The Unholy One?* True, he had saved Lauren, and she had seen him save the life of an old woman the pirates had wanted to kill for no reason other than that she was old and of no value to them. Did that mean Derek York was a decent man? Not necessarily . . . even the most evil of men have soft spots—vile murderers had been known to love puppies and children.

As these questions bounced around in her head, Lauren, quite by accident, slipped into a shallow, uncomfortable sleep.

Derek awoke before dawn as he always did, without a move except to open his eyes. The revolver was still in his right hand. He waited a moment, collecting his senses, listening for activity on the ship. He heard nothing except the sound of Lauren's shallow breathing beside him.

In sleep, she had rolled toward him to relieve the pressure against her wrists from the bindings. Her mussed ebony hair spread over her shoulders, strands resting against her soft cheeks, touching her lips. Derek felt a stirring within him, a low stirring that he wanted to pretend was a normal morning reaction for a man, though he knew it was triggered by Lauren's warmth and powerful sensuality.

33

He eased himself out of bed, careful not to awaken her. On her side, her breasts rested one against the other, which made them look even more voluptuous. The top two buttons of her chemise had come unfastened, as well as the very bottom one. Derek idly counted the ten tightly spaced ivory buttons, pretending he was only curious, knowing in his heart that he was unable to take his eyes from her.

Tentatively he touched the wound behind his ear. The swelling had gone down further, and his headache had disappeared. A smile curled the corners of his mouth. In all his life he'd never met a woman who battled against impossible odds as Lauren had. She had the fighting spirit in her, a flame which burned brightly, drawing Derek to its heat. Perhaps other men liked their women docile, silent, and subservient, but not Lord Derek York.

"If I want something to sit at my feet, I'll get a dog," he had once told his father, when the topic of his continuing bachelorhood had once again arisen. Derek's father scoffed at the comment, muttering that Derek was a damned fool.

Where did a woman who can afford fine silk undergarments and an exquisite velvet dress learn to fight the way she did? She seemed like a pampered princess, but was she?

It was a tantalizing question, and Derek wondered if he would ever know Lauren well enough to learn the answer.

He used his dagger to cut through the shirt sleeve that bound Lauren's ankles. The moment her feet were free, she lashed out at him, her heel just missing his jaw.

It astonished her that he had moved away from her kick. She had pretended to be asleep and was certain

34

she'd caught him off guard, but his reflexes were still fast enough to prevent her from delivering a devastating blow.

Lauren pulled her knee up to try for a second strike, but Derek leaped upon her, pushing her knee to the side to protect himself, and slid between her thighs. Lauren knew the only reason he would untie her ankles was to spread them . . . and she also knew what he intended to do next!

"Stop fighting me, damn you!" Derek hissed, stretching himself over Lauren's supine body, his face just inches from hers. "I'm not going to hurt you!"

"Do what you must, but don't lie to me!" Lauren shot back furiously.

She tried to roll onto her side to push Derek off. He was too heavy and much too strong, and her struggles only caused her dress to slide higher up her thighs. Derek's pelvis was now pressed against her own, and not even their combined layers of clothing prevented his heat from seeping into her. She felt the warmth of his chest and the steelish muscles beneath the silk shirt against her bosom, compressing her breasts. Fear had hardened her nipples, and they now seemed irrationally responsive to touch.

"Get off me!" Lauren whispered.

"Not until you promise to stop fighting me," Derek replied with a small grin.

He had, as claimed, never forced himself upon a woman, and he fully intended to go to his grave without ever committing that reprehensible offense. But he was a man, and was by no means immune to the sensations provoked by wrestling with Lauren, feeling her ripely voluptuous body writhe beneath him, embraced by the erotic allure that wrapped about her like an aura.

35

"I'll fight you to the end!" Lauren hissed, then tried to bite Derek's face.

He tossed his head up to avoid her teeth, then took Lauren's face between his palms to push her back down on the mattress. His manhood was straining against the snug confines of his trousers, throbbing with life, aching to be buried in the warm entrance that was so close. Derek twisted his hips unconsciously, rubbing himself against Lauren, and heated tendrils of pleasure coursed through his veins, making him steelishly hard.

"You use your mouth to curse and threaten," Derek whispered, holding her face more gently now, looking deep into her eyes. "Perhaps you should consider more tender uses for it."

He did not really intend to kiss her, and Lauren certainly hadn't intended to provoke him into defying his own standards of conduct. When she watched his face come down, she closed her eyes, determined to be passive and unresponsive. She knew that she could do nothing more to prevent the inevitable, and she couldn't control what actions Derek decided to take—but she could control herself, and that would save her soul. She would close her eyes, let her mind drift, and wait until Derek was finished with his foul deed. Only then, when he was finished and sated, would she pull her mind and body together again.

That, at least, was Lauren's intention.

Instead of the bruising, brutish kiss she anticipated, Derek hardly touched her lips with his own. He placed several light kisses upon her mouth, as soft and gentle as the touch of a butterfly's wings. This surprised her, and she was still thinking how sweetly Derek kissed when the tip of his tongue traced a warm, moist outline around her mouth, gently—not demandingly—seeking entrance.

36

Despite her intentions, Lauren relaxed slightly. Instead of squeezing her eyes tightly shut, she let her lashes merely rest against her cheeks. The warm, moist tongue slipped between her lips, and almost unconsciously she met it with her own. A delicious, drowsy warmth came over her as her tongue touched and then entwined with Derek's, She felt the subtle movements of his body, the strength in his lean hips against her thighs, the smoothness of her silk pantalets being pressed tightly against her most intimate area by his weight, the beating of his heart against her breasts.

A soft moan escaped Lauren, the sound coming from deep within her as the kiss evolved from tender and experimental to probing, inciting. Incipient passion came to life within Lauren, unprecedented and mysterious. She opened her lips wider, allowing Derek's tongue to probe deeper, almost inviting its more intimate exploration. Unconscious of her own movements, she raised a knee, sliding her thigh against Derek's hip, enjoying the texture of his body against her stocking-sheathed flesh.

How long the kiss lasted, Lauren could not guess. When her mouth was finally free, though, the assault on her senses was not over. Derek kissed her cheek, then her neck, his teeth nipping softly at the golden flesh, followed immediately by the slippery warmth of his tongue.

"I won't hurt you," Derek whispered. "You've got to stop fighting me."

The words brought reality back, and with it came the awareness of where she was, who she was with, and what she was doing. Her hands were still at the small of her back, her wrists tied together with an ungiving cloth cord that would be there until Derek decided to free her. She had allowed her defenses to lapse momen-

37

tarily, but Lauren was determined that her weakness was only a fleeting aberration that would never happen again as long as she was in Derek's company.

"I don't want to fight with you, so please stop fighting with me," Derek whispered, his breath warm against the moist spot on Lauren's silken throat that he had just kissed. The timbre of his voice conjured up images in Lauren's mind, created a deceptive mirage of seduction, and she fought against them.

She turned her face toward the wall, catching her lower lip between white teeth, biting down to silence a moan of pleasure.

Fatigue has weakened me, Lauren thought. *That's why I'm responding this way. If my hands weren't tied, I'd claw his eyes out.*

It was self-delusion, and Lauren knew it. She could not understand why her body reacted to Derek when it never had with the only other man who had ever been close to her.

"Will you stop fighting me?" he asked, his words spoken softly in the dark room.

Lauren did not reply. Derek kissed her throat again, moving slowly downward. She wanted to demand that he stop, but she didn't trust her own ability to speak the words dictated by logic and decency. She willed herself to remain silent and motionless, to feel nothing at all. She would not give this foul pirate the satisfaction of knowing that his cruel lovemaking had hurt her. Since such actions had never before given her any pleasure, she was unconcerned with giving up something of herself, of masking an inner emotion she had never experienced.

"Just . . . stop . . . fighting," Derek whispered, adding a light kiss to Lauren's scented flesh after each word.

She felt Derek slip off her, removing his weight, and for an instant she assumed that her cold demeanor had at last brought some sense of decency to him. She was quickly disavowed of this errant notion when she felt the ivory buttons of her chemise being slowly unfastened by his long, graceful, and clearly experienced fingers.

Derek unfastened the last button and sighed with appreciation. He felt oddly like an adolescent, as though the experience of having a beautiful woman in his arms was once again new and mysterious. The pale cream color of the silk chemise set off Lauren's darker flesh to perfection. With her chemise fully unbuttoned yet still concealing her breasts, he could see the rounded, taut inner swells of her bosom, and the sight made his arousal throb painfully, aching to be freed from its constraints.

Very slowly, as though he was unwrapping a fragile present, he peeled the chemise away from Lauren's breasts. His breath caught in his throat at the sight. The aureoles were dark brown, and in the center of each an erect nipple stood up proudly. Derek wanted to believe that Lauren's nipples had grown erect with passion, but reason told him that she would react the same way to fear.

"Look at me," Derek whispered, slipping his left arm beneath Lauren's head. He needed to look into her eyes to know if she was fighting against the passionate feelings of her body, or if she was fighting against the revulsion she felt at his touch. Shakespeare had written, "'Tis no art to read the mind's construction in the face," and Lord Derek York was a believer in the Bard's wisdom.

He waited for her to turn her gaze his way, but she remained motionless, her eyes closed, her face turned

39

toward the cabin wall. In a slow, lingering fashion, Derek traced circles around her breasts with his fingertips, lightly touching the heated, silken surface of her skin. Resting on his elbow, he looked down at Lauren, seeing the concave stomach and the outline of her ribs beneath the heavy swells of her breasts. He should, he knew, leave her alone. She had already been through enough trauma in the past day to mar a lifetime, and Derek didn't want himself included with those she considered her tormentors. But his inner strength, his willpower, was not great enough to make him remove himself from the chamber, or even to make him take his eyes away from Lauren for a second. With a low groan of acceptance of his own weakness, Derek watched his hand, as though it had a life of its own, slide upward from her stomach to cup one taut-crested breast.

Lauren tried to control her breathing, but it was impossible. The tingling sensation that went through her at Derek's touch sent shivers through her, and even she couldn't pretend that she was shivering with revulsion.

This is evil, she thought. She tested the cord around her wrists once more. The pressure of the rope against her tender skin reminded her that she was helpless against her captor, and as such, not responsible for what happened to her.

Derek was whispering that he wanted to look into her eyes. She would not give him the satisfaction of seeing her fear. *Take me if you want,* she thought, *but don't make me look into the eyes of my defiler!*

He kissed her throat again, his lips warm and moist. The caressing hand which manipulated her breast and made her heart pound so furiously must surely belong to the devil himself. If not, why did her body respond as it did? Why did Derek's touch make her heart pound

40

and her blood sizzle when it never had before?

"I hate you," Lauren said suddenly, whispering the oath as much to reaffirm her desire to feel only contempt for Derek as for his ears.

"You don't hate me; you mustn't fight me. I am your protector—I swear it!"

He's a liar! Everything he says is a lie! she thought. She felt the tip of Derek's tongue circle her breast. When his lips surrounded the erect tip, pulling more of her breast into his mouth, Lauren trembled, and her breath seemed caught in her throat. The heated mouth created a warmth within her own body that was frightening in its intensity and triggered a mystifying pressure within her, a tightness down low.

His mouth went from one breast to the other, his tongue circling the erect bud before pulling it between his lips. Lauren shivered, biting harder on her bottom lip, hoping vainly that the pain would conquer the illicit, sensual enchantment caused by the heated wet lips that tugged and sucked skillfully on her breasts.

Stop it! Stop it! Stop it! Lauren's mind screamed, but the words died somewhere between her brain and her tongue. She could not force the words from her throat, though she knew they had to be said.

Derek raised his head from her bosom. The sun was just coming up over the horizon, he noted, casting a pale glow over the chamber. He could see Lauren better now, and the sight of her, her breasts moist and glistening from his kisses, her shapely legs spread slightly, encased in expensive dark stockings, exposed to mid-thigh . . . it was much too much stimulation for a man of his avaricious desires to ignore.

He closed his eyes for a moment, searching within for the strength to leave Lauren now, while he still had not gone thoroughly beyond the limits of gentlemanly

41

conduct. But just as before, he found himself unable to prevent his hand from straying over Lauren's satin-smooth flesh. He inwardly cursed himself, hating his weakness, then dipped his head down to taste once again the sweet, responsive flesh of Lauren's golden breasts.

Lauren felt moist inside, at the juncture of her thighs. She realized that this was how she was supposed to have felt before, in those few clumsy, inauspicious sexual encounters with Richard. This was how her body should have responded, but it had not. And now, with the dawning awareness of what pleasures her body was capable of feeling, she battled with a deep, pervasive guilt, since the man causing this pleasure was the last man in the world she should feel anything but hatred for.

She felt Derek's fingertips against the inside of her thigh, very near the top of her stocking, inching closer to the center of the inner heat of her being.

"No," she whispered, afraid of the touch, yet anticipating it.

"Yes," Derek replied, raising his head briefly from her breast.

When at last he touched her, the shock was like a strange current jolting through her, powerful in its intensity. Lauren arched her back, turning slightly toward Derek, pushing her knees further apart. The contact of her smooth, silk pantalets against the heated petals of her femininity was blinding in its depth. Back and forth, up and down, Derek's fingers pressed with just the right amount of pressure to create volcanic feelings that bubbled and simmered deep within Lauren's soul.

She was aware of each touch individually and collectively. Sharp teeth nipped at the aroused tip of her breast, then a slithering tongue smoothed over where the teeth had been, fueling the flames of passion. Derek's fingers moved skillfully at the juncture of her thighs, touching her heated flesh through her undergarment, his hand never actually making contact with the burning center of her womanhood, yet in its avoidance increasing her pleasure in lewdly and wildly erotic movements.

A silent scream was caught in Lauren's throat as a white-hot fire burned through her. She arched her back, raising her rounded hips to press herself with wanton abandon against the damnable hand that had stolen her better judgment. The shuddering, unprecedented release of pleasure jarred Lauren, rippling through her in a series of spasms that made her tingle from head to toe.

And when at last the spasms ended and Lauren had slumped to the mattress, guilt overwhelmed her. She rolled away from Derek, clamping her knees tightly together around the hand that remained there. Her pantalets were moist, clinging wetly to her flesh, a reminder of sinful pleasures that she instantly regretted with every fiber of her being.

"See?" Derek said in a passion-hoarse whisper. "I want to cause you pleasure, not pain."

"Leave me," Lauren replied, squeezing her eyes tightly shut against the tears that burned to be shed. She felt betrayed and confused by her own body.

"I could more easily prevent the sun from rising than leave you now."

Derek continued to cradle Lauren's head in his left arm. With his right, he reached down to his trousers, tugging at the belt, intent on freeing his engorged arousal, which had been ignored for too long already.

The moment he had unbuckled his belt, a woman's

high-pitched scream cut through the morning air. The distinctive voice of Gregor followed immediately with, "Throw the old hag to the sharks! They need breakfast as much as we do!"

Derek had gone so quickly that when Lauren was left alone it took her a couple seconds to realize it. She squirmed on the bed until the skirt of her gown was to her knees, but no movements could return her chemise and bodice to modestly cover her breasts.

He'll come back for me.

It was a dreadful thought for Lauren. She closed her eyes, fearing what would happen when Derek York returned for her. She wondered, too, what had just happened to her, and none of the conclusions she came to gave her any solace at all.

Chapter 4

Derek heard the splash of a body hitting the water, accompanied by the raucous laughter of the pirates, and he knew he was too late to save the old woman. He rounded the upper deck in time to see Gregor slapping several of his men heartily on the back, and the sight of it made nausea well up inside him.

"I've told you before that I do not want prisoners executed unnecessarily!" Derek hissed through teeth clenched in rage.

"And I told you before, you English bastard, that I don't give a rat's arse *what* you want!" Gregor hooked his thumbs into the wide belt surrounding his waist, holding the scabbard and saber. He rocked back on his heels, his gaze locked challengingly with Derek's. With his men surrounding him, Gregor had no fear of Derek, and he would not let the intruder bully him in any way. "Now what have you got to say about that?"

Derek's gaze went from Gregor to the men surrounding him. They all wanted a face-to-face confrontation, he knew. The crew of *The Unholy One* were waiting for the chance to draw their deadly daggers and spill his blood, and perhaps one day that would happen—but it wouldn't be this day.

45

"You may be captain of this ship, but you aren't captain of your destiny," Derek said quietly. "Whether you like it or not, we both work for other men, and our fate is held in their hands. It is your job to find ships, and it is my job to select the best women from those ships for my employer's stable."

Gregor snorted, hawked, then spit on the deck of *Miss Malaki*. Seeing Derek's face twist in a look of disgust, Gregor laughed. "And how many wenches does that man need, anyway? You've already got nine slaves on the island, and one locked below."

"That's ten women that your employer will be handsomely paid for. Don't forget that, Gregor. Your employer will keep you alive only as long as you can show him a profit."

Gregor withdrew a dagger from its sheath and picked at the grime beneath his fingernails. He did not like the turn the conversation had taken; he wanted his men to see him as their supreme commander who answered to neither man nor God.

"I allow myself to be paid for the work, that is true, but do not think that I am unhappy with the arrangement. When it no longer suits me to be paid by another, I will change the winds and sail in whatever direction I choose."

"So you say," Derek replied, smiling bitterly. He had planted a seed of thought in the pirates surrounding Gregor; he could tell they now looked at their captain in a slightly different light. "But you are assuming that your master is willing to let you live if you decide you don't need him. You may be assuming wrongly, Gregor. Don't forget that." Derek looked at the pirates, taking each on in turn. "Don't *any* of you forget that."

Gregor's bearded scowl darkened, and his face turned red. "Someday, Englishman, I'm going to cut your tongue out and make you drown in your own blood."

"When I've purchased enough women for my employer, we'll see who will kill whom. Until then, I see no need to listen to your impotent threats."

Gregor bellowed with false laughter. "Are you saying I'm not a man, Englishman? Who are you to talk? You've got that dark-eyed lass in the cabin below deck, and you claim to save her for your buyer. You have said he pays a premium for virgins. She spends the night with you in a cabin, and you don't touch her. So tell me, Englishman, which of us is a man?" Gregor howled again, and his men joined in the laughter. "Does he sound like a man to you, mates? Or maybe he's a liar, and he's just keeping us from having a taste of his wenches?"

"I'm not a rapist," Derek said quietly.

"He sounds like a limp man to me, Cap'n!" Bones shouted gleefully. "Or maybe one o' them that likes only boys!"

Derek walked away, feeling the perspiration on his body cooling. The confrontations with Gregor were becoming more frequent, the hatred in them more volatile. He did not know how much longer he could continue to listen to Gregor's insults, to keep Gregor's hatred at bay, as well as save as many of the unfortunate souls as possible who came under the deadly cannon sights of *The Unholy One*.

Would he find the identity of the man behind Gregor's reign of kidnapping and piracy before the inevitable, final confrontation occurred? If he did find out who that mystery man was, would he be able to track down his sister, Amanda? Was she even still alive?

The questions haunted Derek. He tried to push them from his mind and concentrate on the tasks at hand, but it was difficult. Compounding his problems were distracting thoughts of Lauren, who never strayed far from his consciousness.

What he had done—touching her, kissing her, exploring her body while she was unable to defend herself—was unforgivable. It mattered little to his guilty conscience that he had not assuaged the burning ache in his own loins. The issue was not that she had responded to his touch; she shouldn't have been touched by him at all. When he had first set eyes on Lauren, he'd realized that her beauty was too great to be ignored. If he did not claim her, Gregor would take her, then pass her off to his men as a reward for some particularly atrocious deed.

Derek thought of returning to the cabin but quickly discarded the idea. His blood was still too fevered for him to trust himself in her company. When his blood had cooled and he once again had faith in his ability to control his desires, he would cut Lauren free. Until then, he watched the pirates as they busied themselves transporting valuables from *Miss Malaki* to *The Unholy One*. The women who were to be sold as slaves were herded past Derek, and he turned his eyes from them, sickened at what he saw, angry that he could not save more of them from a hideous life of sexual tyranny and slavery, unable to take any satisfaction at all in knowing that he had saved ten young women from that fate.

Lauren was on her knees on the bed, peering through the porthole. It was difficult to make out all the words that were being spoken, but she gathered that Derek had done what he could to prevent Gregor and his men from killing captives they felt were unsalable. It was obvious to Lauren that Derek York was not really one

48

of the crew of *The Unholy One,* and that contempt for him ran high among the regular crewmen, and especially with Captain Gregor.

Lauren had witnessed Derek challenging the pirates several times now, threatening violence and risking his life for the benefit of people he did not know. This behavior seemed so contradictory for a man who had willingly sailed aboard *The Unholy One* that Lauren was increasingly mystified.

What secrets did Derek York harbor? Why would a man who apparently hated violence and murder associate with pirates who regarded cold-blooded murder as sport and brutal rape as nothing more than a conqueror's due?

And in the end, just before Derek walked away from Gregor, why hadn't he told them of the sexual liberties he'd taken with her? From all Lauren knew of men, they seemed only too happy to talk of their sexual conquests, real or imagined. Though Lauren hadn't overheard everything, she understood the pirates had challenged Derek's manhood, questioning whether he liked women at all. Lauren had felt the hard length of his arousal pressing against her, so she knew that he found women—or at least *her*—sexually attractive.

When Derek walked away from Gregor, Lauren spun around, sitting again on the edge of the bed. Her heart accelerated as she prepared for Derek's return. She wished there was some way for her to close her chemise to hide herself, then cursed angrily. What difference would it make? Derek would only unbutton the chemise again, if that's what he wanted to do.

Feeling frustrated with her inability to defend herself effectively, certain that Derek would return shortly and force himself upon her, wildly confused about what had happened with her own body and why she had seemed to turn inside out when Derek's hand had

49

ventured below her skirt, Lauren waited . . . and waited . . . and waited. . . .

It was three hours before she heard his footsteps. When Derek stepped in, she noticed for the first time the fatigue that pinched his eyes, sensed the faintly worried, haunted quality that had escaped her notice before.

He looked at her, pulling the stiletto dagger from its shoulder sheath. "Turn around," he said.

"If you're going to cut my throat, at least have the courage to do it while I face you."

"Do as I tell you. I'm in no mood for an argument."

Lauren twisted on the bed, closing her eyes, waiting for the cold blade to touch her. It never did. The cord binding her wrists was sliced cleanly in two. Before Lauren turned around to face Derek again, she quickly buttoned her chemise and pulled the torn bodice of her gown together.

"We're leaving," Derek said with a finality that warned Lauren any confrontation would be met swiftly and severely. "If you value your life, you'll do everything I tell you, and you'll not get more than five steps from me until you're safely locked in my cabin aboard *The Unholy One.*"

"What good is a life that's not free?"

For a moment their gazes held. The haunted quality that Derek tried to hide was fully revealed for only a second before the invisible veil of invulnerability was again pulled down around him. "I'll do what I can," he said quietly, an inner torment tearing at him. Then he added gruffly, "Now don't ask me any more questions I haven't got the bloody damned answers to!"

Derek looked at the captain's cabin, taking in the destruction. He shook his head slowly, as though answering an unspoken question.

"I've got a cabin that you should find comfortable,"

50

he said quietly, his tone distant and distracted. "It's clean and orderly, anyway. Soon we'll return to port. I can't promise what will happen after that, but I'll do everything I can to ensure your safety and comfort."

"What port will we sail to?"

Derek gave Lauren a look. She saw his distrust of her as he weighed telling her. "It's a pirate's port. Besides St. Thomas, St. John, and St. Croix, there are over a hundred small islands in these waters. Most of them are uninhabited and even unnamed—at least by Europeans. There's a small port and a village that's being used by Gregor. I'm sure there are others, but this one I'm familiar with." He shook his head slowly, sadly, his voice deepening. "That's what makes them so bloody dangerous. My queen or your president could send every fighting ship at their disposal to these waters and they'd never catch *The Unholy One*. It's too fast, and Gregor knows these waters too well. An armada would only end up sailing in circles, chasing ghosts, ripping out their hulls on submerged rocks or beaching on sandbars."

"I see," Lauren replied, her voice as soft as Derek's. His attitude toward Gregor confused her more than ever.

"No you don't . . . but that doesn't matter now. Come, Miss Masters, it's time for us to leave."

Lauren held her gown together as they left the cabin. She remained close to Derek, not fighting the hand he put at her elbow. Though the betrayal of her body to his touch and kiss was still clear in her mind, she realized that Derek was a lesser evil to the other pirates. At least there was only *one* of him.

On deck, Lauren heard the distinctive sound of Gregor's booming, sadistic laughter. When she saw what had caused the laughter, she gasped in shock. Gregor had Captain Disner on a plank stretching out

51

over the blue expanse of the Caribbean. Captain Disner's hands were tied as he stood at the end of the plank, facing *Miss Malaki*.

"Jump, you yellow seadog!" Gregor bellowed, laughing heartily with his men beside him. "The fish are hungry! The sharks await you!"

Lauren turned her face away, hissing to Derek, "Can't you do anything about this?"

"No," Derek replied, anger and sadness in his tone. "He's the captain. Gregor believes that he should be the only captain in these waters, so he always has the captain of the ships he attacks walk the plank. It's his charming way."

Gregor's laughter cut through the warm morning air, and despite the balmy weather, Lauren shivered. She had not known that men were capable of such evil.

"Jump, you swine, or I'll cut you in little pieces and chum the waters with your liver!"

Lauren heard the splash, and she knew that Captain Disner had, without begging for mercy, jumped. Her heart swelled in sorrow for the man, and she couldn't help thinking that perhaps the captain's fate would have been different if only he'd chosen to flee from *The Unholy One* instead of giving up without a fight. Surely dying in battle was less ignominious than walking the plank.

"Let's go," Derek said, taking Lauren's arm firmly in his grasp, guiding her toward the bridge between the ships. "The men are looking at you. The more they look, the more they'll want you. I can't keep them at bay forever."

Silently, Lauren followed Derek onto *The Unholy One*. He took her directly to his cabin, which she noted was small and not particularly well appointed. It reminded her of a small, clean, but unremarkable hotel room.

"What's going to happen to the people aboard *Miss Malaki?*" she asked when the cabin door was closed and locked.

"The sails will be stolen. The ship will go wherever the tide and waves take it. Those alive will remain alive as long as what little food and water Gregor leaves them holds out. If they're lucky, another ship will find them and rescue them. If not . . ."

Lauren shivered at the thought. Though she worried about piquing Derek's temper by asking too much of him, she needed to know the whereabouts and safety of her chaperon.

"When I left, I had a woman with me . . . my chaperon, Miss Nichols. I haven't seen her since you attacked." Lauren bit her lip, cursing herself for her choice of words. She waited for Derek to exact his discipline, fully expecting him to slap her, or worse. When he didn't, she moistened her lips and searched for the least offensive words she could. "Is it possible that you can find out what happened to her? I didn't know her very well, but she looked after me faithfully during this trip."

"I'll see what I can do," Derek replied coldly. "Stay here now. We'll be under sail soon. Don't unlock the door for anyone but me. Is that clear?"

"Yes," Lauren said, and then as an afterthought, added, "sir."

"Wrong title," Derek growled, then left the cabin.

And what the deuces does that mean? Lauren mused as she threw the bolt, locking the door after him.

Amanda York's eyes were open wide, their clear blue depths reflecting her deep terror. She wrapped her arms around her knees as Aldon Mitchell crossed the room, her gaze never leaving him.

53

She could not remember how long she had been held captive. It seemed like years, though she knew it was actually only a month, give or take a week. Keeping track of time was impossible for the unwilling members of Aldon Mitchell's private harem.

"Fetch me some wine," Mitchell said, issuing the order in his usual fashion to no one in particular. He didn't care who did his bidding so long as his whims were met instantly.

Amanda looked at the girl next to her. Neither moved. Amanda waited another second, then got to her feet and rushed to where the wine was kept. She poured some into a large gold goblet encrusted with gems, then brought it to Mitchell, her head bowed respectfully.

He took it from her and sat in his chair behind his desk. Open before him were his ledgers, the critical records he scrupulously kept concerning his rapidly expanding empire. Though he had originally hired Gregor and outfitted *The Unholy One* to plunder valuables from passing ships, he was discovering that white slavery was extraordinarily profitable.

"Sit," Aldon said. Amanda sat at his feet. This pleased him. He enjoyed having women at his feet when he went through his books.

Amanda knelt, resting on the backs of her heels. She had been told it was the position Aldon preferred. After her capture, she had refused to bow to Aldon or do the things he demanded of her. Her punishments had taught her that it was easiest and safest just to do what she was told. If she defied him, she was punished; if she swallowed her pride and simply obeyed his commands, she didn't have to feel the lash of the leather strap Aldon was so fond of using.

With her eyes cast down, Amanda listened carefully. She heard the pages of the ledger being turned and the occasional sounds of approval or displeasure that he made deep in his throat. These were always good signs, signifying he was thinking about his money rather than about pursuing more physical pleasures.

"My pets, you cost me plenty," Aldon said quietly. "Just the same, I suppose you're worth it. You give me comfort and pleasure, and in this world, that is as much as any man can hope for."

Give? Amanda thought incredulously, biting her tongue to keep the hot words of anger from spilling out. *We give you nothing! You take what you want and pretend that we give it willingly, you contemptible beast!*

"I swathe you in the finest silk shikars and mitars, do I not?" he said, referring to the traditional clothing of the island. "It is a worthy expense, though. All of you look so becoming in fine silk."

Amanda turned her head slightly, glancing at Chantell, a young girl from France, who had been abducted at the same time. Chantell had had as difficult a time adjusting to the indigenous clothing as Amanda had, and Chantell's anger was reddening her cheeks and neck. While hardly moving a muscle, Amanda silently warned her friend to remain calm. Provoking Aldon's anger drew his wrath, and when aroused he was prone to lash out at all of the captive women in his private harem rather than at just the one who had angered him.

Aldon Mitchell sipped his wine and leaned back in his chair, letting his eyes roam over the six women in the room. Each was young and lovely and quickly becoming well trained. They represented the most attractive women Gregor kidnapped, and they would reap a heavy profit when he sold them to the wealthy, white businessmen from Africa, Brazil, and Peru. With each shipment of women, Aldon personally inspected the "catch," as he called it. He took the most beautiful and spirited women for himself, keeping the captives between three and six months. When he was finished with them, he'd trained the women to be dutiful slaves who followed their master's wishes without question. The extra time it took to train the women provided Aldon with the chance to sample their charms. He broke their spirits and trained them in a fashion that was fundamentally no different than training a pet dog, and in the end they sold for five to ten times the normal cost of other attractive slaves.

Aldon let his eyes roam freely over Amanda. She was frightfully young, and her youth and beauty had charged his blood. Her hair was the color of morning sunlight, he thought, and her eyes as blue as the Caribbean, especially when she was angry and harbored thoughts of defying him. Slender and petite, her body aroused him, and her skin was as smooth as the silk that now clothed her.

"You're a fiesty one, aren't you, my love?" Aldon asked, tapping her knee with the toe of his boot. She didn't look up, and that drew a chuckle from him. He was certain that if she did, he would see the anger and defiance in her clear blue eyes. If he saw that, then he would have to punish her, and he didn't feel any sadistic need at the moment to take a strap to Amanda or any of the other women.

Aldon finished his wine and pushed himself to his feet. Wealth was putting extra pounds around his middle, and though this made him less nimble, he was proud of his expanding belly. It proved he was successful.

"I'm told a new shipload will arrive soon," he said. "Mayhaps I'll bring you some new companions." He laughed suddenly, tossing his head back and patting his

56

protruding belly. "Be ready, my sweets, my blood will be heated after I inspect the new catch! I'll have need of you, that I will!"

He left the room, continuing to laugh. Amanda York closed her eyes and prayed that something foul and deadly would strike him down before he returned.

Chapter 5

Derek settled himself in the rowboat and tried to ignore the contempt of the men around him. *The Unholy One* had dropped anchor six hundred yards out to sea, and the only way to the small village and port was by rowboat. Gregor had left in the first one, and as his men rowed toward shore, Derek found it difficult to keep from watching his progress.

Perhaps this time Derek would be lucky enough to follow Gregor surreptitiously and see who he met with. Would Gregor go immediately to his employer, or would he stop at the ale hall, *As the Crow Flies,* to drink himself drunk and brag to his mates of his latest conquest at sea, then find a willing wench to spend the evening with? That was how Gregor usually spent his first night upon returning to port, and Derek was hoping that it would be different this time. Each passing day heightened Derek's fear that he would not find his sister, or that when he did, the trauma would have destroyed the soul of the fiery young woman he'd grown up with.

As the rowboat made its way toward the village, Derek's thoughts turned from his sister to the young captive he'd left locked in his cabin. Guilt bit into him as he thought about the things he had done only the day before. It was unconscionable for him to touch her, he knew, but he had been unable to keep from kissing her, from letting his hands explore the sweet hills and valleys of her extraordinary body. Her mouth was soft, her lips enticing. Derek wanted to dismiss his actions as unintended and unavoidable—after all, he was only a man—but he could not. A lifetime of training in gentlemanly behavior prevented such ready and self-serving excuses.

Gregor's boat reached shore fifteen minutes before Derek's. True to form, Gregor went to *As the Crow Flies.* Derek followed but kept his distance. He was not welcome at Gregor's table, or at any other table, for that matter. It wasn't until he bought a round of rum for a small group that he was invited to sit, and only then was it possible for him to not stand out so prominently.

The pirates' thirst was extraordinary. Derek tried to drink as little as possible. This was definitely not the time to let his mind get addled by rum. But as so often is the case with men, when one drinks, the demand is that they all drink. To do otherwise is to invite scorn and scrutiny, neither of which Derek could afford if he was to follow Gregor to the man who bought the women captured by *The Unholy One.*

After having poured an astonishing amount of rum down his throat in a very short time, Gregor grabbed one of the serving girls, pulling her onto his lap. She squealed with delight, lightly slapping at him as he tried to kiss her. Derek saw Gregor's hand tighten around the woman's wrist so hard that her hand turned red. Gregor pushed her off his lap and began pulling her toward the small rooms in the back. The woman no longer laughed and giggled with delight; now she was terrified, and Derek's heart went out to her. There was nothing he could do to stop Gregor—nothing short of killing him, that is, and that would only result in his own death, which wouldn't help Amanda at all.

"I have drunk my fill, good men," Derek said, intentionally slurring his words to make it appear he was more intoxicated than he really was. "So I bid you all farewell."

The men laughed drunkenly, slapping Derek on the back and punching his arms. It took all of his resolve to keep from lashing out at the cretins, and his hatred for them rose a notch.

"Ain't yer got no stomach for rum, you lily-liver?" Bones asked sarcastically, hitting Derek's biceps once more.

"Not like you," Derek replied, smiling falsely, rising to his feet.

"Sit an' drink, Englishman! Sit an' drink, or I'll slice open yer belly so you can fill it up again with rum!"

Derek dropped a gold coin onto the table. It drew the greedy attention of the men. "Drink enough for both of us," Derek said, swaying exaggeratedly for effect. "This should help the cause."

It took a second gold coin for him to bribe men to row him back to *The Unholy One*. He wanted to return before the sun set, as long as it was clear that Gregor would be of no use to her this evening. Leaving Lauren alone on the ship was dangerous. With enough rum in their bellies, the men still aboard *The Unholy One* might find the courage to break down the cabin door and take what had been denied them. Saving Lauren from them was about all Derek had accomplished during his quest thus far, and he was determined to keep his victory intact.

* * *

Lauren was startled by Derek's return, and when she smelled the rum on his breath and saw the liquor glaze in his eyes, she felt something inside her sink. She had thought he would be different from the other pirates in this respect, and his intoxication disturbed her more than she wanted to admit.

"I see you've been working hard, as you said you would," she said caustically, holding her bodice together and eyeing Derek cautiously.

Derek was taken aback by her anger. It was easy for him to forget that she had every right in the world to hate him to the marrow of his bones. She had, he noticed, used his brush, and her ebony hair gleamed healthily, falling in loose waves around her shoulders, glowing in the dim light of the kerosene lamp. The rum in his belly may have dulled his thinking, but it did not alter the course of his thoughts or diminish the impact of Lauren's physical charms on his senses. She was as alluring and insolent as ever. He wondered if he had the strength to lie beside her in the bed they shared without touching her. It was an accomplishment he had achieved last night; he doubted whether he could do it again.

"Well?" Lauren demanded. "Did you find out anything?"

Derek went to his washbasin and splashed his face with cool water. He toweled his face dry before replying, "I'm sorry to say that Miss Nichols was not spared. I am truly sorry, Lauren. I had nothing to do with her death, and if it was possible for me to prevent it, I surely would have."

The words hit Lauren hard. She had not known Miss Nichols well—the old spinster was someone hired by her parents to chaperone her—but that did not make her death any less significant.

"So many deaths," Lauren whispered, looking down, feeling warm tears fill her eyes. "Needless, senseless deaths."

"I am sorry." Derek looked at Lauren, wanting to take her into his arms to help comfort her, knowing that if he did she would resist. In her heart, he was at least partially to blame for Miss Nichols's death; she would not seek comfort from a murderer. "I also checked into the whereabouts of your belongings. Your cabin was completely cleaned out. Everything that you owned was distributed among the men to use as gifts for the local women. Gregor kept your jewelry."

Lauren grinned ruefully. "My dresses are now traded for sexual favors." She looked up, and her eyes were cold and hard. "At least those women are given something for their trouble. It's more than I can say for myself."

Derek turned away from her, his hands clenched into fists. He did not wish to fight with her—not tonight, when he had drunk more than he should—but she seemed determined to provoke him, to rile him into anger.

"Have I raped you?" Derek demanded, his back to Lauren so that he wouldn't see her beauty or be affected by her charms. "Last night—did I even touch you?"

"N-no," Lauren quietly answered. "That was last night."

"Yes, you bloody fool, that was last night!" Derek hissed angrily, spinning to face her. "But tonight will be different!"

Her reaction to the threat doused any desire in Derek. He had caused her fear, and it was impossible for him to be aroused by a woman who was frightened of him. He had intended to spend the night in his chambers aboard *The Unholy One,* then transfer

62

Lauren to his rented hut on the island in the morning. But he couldn't risk being confined with Lauren in such close quarters a second night—her voluptuous sensuality was too threatening. At his island hut there was more room to separate them.

In short order Derek got together a crew to row them to shore. The pirates protested the extra work, and a third gold coin was withdrawn from Derek's leather pouch. The money was as much as the men made in a month, and though they disliked Derek and particularly disliked following his orders, the money was persuasive. Lauren protested when Derek began tying her wrists, and only the threat that he would tie her wrists and ankles and let the pirates carry her aboard the rowboat otherwise—their dirty hands groping her along the way—made her give in to the demand.

When they reached the village, the bacchanalia was still going strong. Men stared wantonly at Lauren, who followed Derek with quiet resolve, the rope binding her wrists held by Derek to show everyone that she was his property and was not to be trifled with.

Derek's rented hut was set away from the main village. It was a single-room structure, like most on the island, made primarily of rough-hewn bamboo with a thatched roof. Inside there was only a mattress and a fine cedar chest.

"Is . . . is it possible for me to bathe?" Lauren asked after Derek had freed her wrists. "I feel dirty."

Derek's gaze held Lauren's. Did she mean that his touch made her feel unclean? It was yet another haunting question that he didn't like to ponder. When he said nothing, Lauren offered a half smile and shrugged. "It's a small thing to ask, isn't it?"

At last Derek returned her smile. "Yes, I suppose it is." He went to his cedar trunk, which contained everything he'd left London with. He found a fresh bar of soap and handed it to Lauren. "There's a small cove not far from here. You'll have privacy there."

Lauren took a single step toward the door, then stopped, pivoting sharply to face him. "But you'll be there," she said accusingly.

"Yes, I'll be there. But it'll be just me. If you can't accept that, then you can go without your bath." Derek took Lauren's hand in his, looking down into her eyes, hoping he could win at least some small measure of trust from her. "I'll keep my distance. It's dark. I can't let you out of sight because you'll run away, and if you do that, you'll only get caught again. If Gregor catches you, you can guess what will happen. You've seen what he's like, haven't you?"

Lauren nodded, casting her gaze down. Yes, she knew what Gregor was like, and the threat that he posed, but she also knew what Derek York was like . . . and the threat *he* posed, which was, in its own way, much more enticing and dangerous than any other she had ever known.

"Wait, I've got something for you." Derek rushed back to the cedar chest and tossed open the lid. He reached down past his tailored silk shirts and a fine twill jacket to remove two pieces of shimmering white silk. "Wear these," he said, handing the cloth to Lauren. "With that dark hair and skin of yours, you shouldn't stand out *too* much if you dress like a native."

Derek knew it was a lie. Lauren would stand out, would draw the attention of men no matter where she was or what she was wearing. Not even a gunny sack dress and unkempt hair could hide her beauty effectively enough to prevent men from stopping and staring appreciatively at her.

Lauren looked at the soap, recognizing its marbled blue and white color. The soap was made by Foxbury Limited of London; it was the same expensive soap

64

that Lauren's mother preferred. Another layer of mystery surrounded Derek York, and once again Lauren wondered who he really was and why he would have any association with the felonious crew of *The Unholy One*.

The cove was a half mile from Derek's hut. It was small and shallow, the curving landscape providing a natural barrier against winds and high waves. Pausing at the waterline, Lauren looked at the water and thought how, if circumstances were different, this could be a haven for her, a secluded, contemplative spot she could call her own.

"Can you swim?" Derek asked, cutting into her thoughts.

"Yes. Very well."

"Good. I'd hate to have you drown on me."

Lauren sent him an annoyed look, but there wasn't much vehemence in it. "Don't worry," she said quietly, turning away from him to see the moonlight shining on the water. "I'm afraid I'll be your captive for at least a little while longer." She took a step to the side, moving further away from him. "Now, if you'll excuse me, I'd like to bathe. You promised you'd give me some privacy." She waited for the sound of Derek's footsteps in the white sand. When they didn't come, she issued a long-suffering sigh that was loud enough for his ears. "Don't worry. I won't drown myself . . . at least not until I'm absolutely sure there's no way for me to escape."

"That's honest," Derek said, pleased with her unbending refusal to passively accept the conditions of her captivity. He took several steps back, his eyes never leaving Lauren. Wrapped in the softening glow of the moonlight, she was more beautiful than ever.

Lauren knew he was watching her. She could feel his eyes upon her as she unfastened the buttons at her sleeves, then slipped the gown around her waist and pulled her arms free. She shoved the gown past the swell of her hips and stepped out of it, then kicked off her slippers. Her heart started pounding harder, and she could feel her pulse throb against her temples as she removed her stockings, chemise, and pantalets. Naked, her face flushed with embarrassment, she picked up the soap and rushed into the water, not wanting to give Derek any more time to look at her than was absolutely necessary.

Lauren went in until the water was above her waist, then dipped beneath the surface to wet her hair. She rubbed the comforting soap into her hair. All her life she had used the fragrant and gentle Foxbury soap, and the smell of it now brought back memories of her childhood in Virginia.

The sand against her feet was smooth, and Lauren dug her toes into it, giggling softly as it tickled her arches. It was easy for her, waist-deep in the warm Caribbean, soaping her arms and shoulders, to completely forget that she was not alone. She soaped her back as best she could, enjoying the feel of having clean skin once again. It wasn't until she heard the faint splashing of footsteps in water that her reverie was broken. She wheeled around, crossing her arms to hide her breasts.

"It seems like you need some help washing your back," Derek said in a conversational tone, a half smile on his face as he approached Lauren, as naked as the day he was born.

Lauren turned her back to him, her heart pounding against her ribs. She knew he had no sense of decency—he'd already proved that beyond any reasonable doubt—but still, she'd never suspected he'd just disrobe and walk into the water with her.

"You said you'd give me some privacy!" Lauren said hotly, accusingly. "I thought I could trust you."

"I'm just trying to help. I saw the difficulty you were having washing your back." Derek moved close behind Lauren. The water barely came over the tops of his thighs. The proximity to Lauren in all her freshly soaped, naked splendor had been too much to keep him on shore. "Hand me the soap and I'll get those places you missed."

"Please leave," Lauren whispered. She couldn't see Derek, but she could feel his presence close to her. It was difficult arguing with a man she couldn't look at, and though she didn't want to think about it, she couldn't banish from her mind what she had seen when he was only knee-deep, walking toward her. "You promised . . ."

"I lied. What can I tell you?" He placed his hands lightly on Lauren's shoulders. "Hand me the soap."

Lauren tilted her head back to look up at the moon. Why did this have to happen to her? What had she done to deserve such hideous luck? What would happen if she refused to comply with Derek's demand? He had kept his hands from her last night . . . but that was last night; tonight could be a different story. . . .

"Please?" he asked quietly, reaching over her shoulder.

I shouldn't, Lauren thought as she placed the soap in his hand.

"I know it's difficult for you to trust me. In your position I probably would think the same," Derek said, beginning to massage a thick lather of soap into Lauren's shoulders. He pulled her hair together, then placed it over her shoulder to completely bare her back to his ministrations. "But you must try—just *try,* that's all I'm asking—to believe that I really mean you no

67

harm. In fact, until we can get you away from this island, you've got to consider me your one and only protector."

"I can protect myself," Lauren said defensively.

She fought against the soothing warmth that was seeping into her veins. Derek's hands working over her shoulders, neck, and back, all slick and soapy, felt positively heavenly. She kept her arms crossed over her breasts, part of her still unwilling to accept the illicit pleasures that she knew Derek was capable of igniting . . . but part of her craved the complete abandonment to physical pleasures that had taken over her senses.

"Sure you can," Derek replied with sarcastic good humor.

"I can! If I had a rifle I'd have shot you before you ever boarded *Miss Malaki.*"

"I believe you. I do," Derek replied in that tone that said he did not believe her. "Now raise your arms. You want to get clean, don't you? There's no telling when we'll be able to bathe again."

"No!" Lauren said, getting angry, hating Derek's easy dismissal of her ability to defend herself, having no intention of letting him touch her any longer.

"Okay, then perhaps you'd like to repay the favor by washing *my* back?"

Having him touch her was less loathsome than having to touch him, Lauren decided. Very slowly she uncrossed her arms, extending them straight out from her sides. "I hope you're enjoying yourself," she whispered through teeth clenched in anger.

Derek chuckled softly. *"You're* the one who's being treated like a pampered princess, not me!"

Why did he have to turn around everything she said, and in such a fashion that there was always at least a little truth to it? He infuriated Lauren as no man had.

He started with her left hand, soaping it, washing each finger before moving on up to the wrist and forearm. Lauren closed her eyes as a heady sense of well-being came over her. She knew she mustn't give in to the feeling, but she had been through so much hardship lately that it seemed unreasonable not to accept some small measure of comfort when she could. Derek's soapy fingers kneaded her forearm, then her biceps. The tension that had gripped her almost every waking moment since her capture slowly and inexorably slipped away. Then she felt his hand and the bar of soap at her underarm, and incongruously she started to giggle. She brought her arm down sharply, trapping Derek's hand.

"Ticklish?"

"Yes," Lauren admitted, then forced the smile from her lips. There was nothing humorous about this, she sternly reminded herself.

"Well, you've got to get clean. Extend your arm. I'll be quick about this."

I must be completely out of my mind! This man's touch should not please me! she argued to herself.

It astonished Lauren that she did as she was told. It wasn't easy to keep from laughing as Derek soaped one underarm, then the other as he worked his way across her body. When he was finished, Lauren bent her knees, sinking until the water was around her neck to rinse off the soap.

"Now the legs," Derek said.

"No!"

"Yes."

"You're insane!"

"Perhaps, but that's not the issue here. The issue is cleanliness."

"You're insane *and* a liar!"

"Think of me as a faithful servant just trying to do his duty."

"You're a dog!"

"No, a man."

"That's worse!"

Derek laughed, and despite herself Lauren joined him. The water level was at her navel. She refused to turn and face Derek, and she wouldn't walk into shallower water with him. With no other acceptable options, she bent over, extending her right leg up behind her.

"Well, that's a start. A little inefficient, but we all do what we have to do," Derek said. He moved the bar of soap over her calf, smiling as she tread water with her hands to keep her head above the surface.

The position was a little ridiculous. In her mind's eye, Lauren saw herself as a bizarre, naked ballerina, balancing precariously on one foot on a stage in New York. The image brought laughter bubbling forth, and that was all it took to make her face go under the water.

Derek held Lauren's foot a moment longer than was necessary, and she completely lost her balance. When he released her, Lauren came up sputtering and angry.

"You did that on purpose!" she accused, pushing the wet hair away from her face. "Why do you always have to be such a lout?"

She glared angrily at him for a moment before noticing the direction of his gaze. He was looking at her breasts, now fully exposed to his scrutiny. Lauren crossed her arms instantly, her anger growing.

"I think I'm clean enough," she hissed.

The tantalizing little game they'd been playing had gone on long enough, and it was becoming increasingly dangerous. Derek York might not be as murderous as

70

the pirates he sailed with, but he was still a man, and as such, he had limits to the control he held on his desires. Though Lauren had heard Gregor accuse Derek of not liking women, she knew it wasn't the case at all.

Though the water was up to Lauren's stomach, it was only at the top of Derek's thighs. In spite of her anger, Lauren couldn't resist looking at him, taking no small amount of pleasure in what she saw. His shoulders were quite broad, and his chest was well formed. He had almost no hair on his chest at all, and his muscular pectorals were clearly defined. Beneath that his ribs were visible, the sinewy muscles in his stomach like corded rope. Her eyes went down to the gently lapping surface of the water, and she blushed crimson when she realized where she was looking, though the moonlit water prevented her from seeing what had piqued her libidinous curiosity.

"Can we go in now? I'm as clean as I'm ever going to get."

In a smoky tone, his hooded eyes unreadable in the moonlight, Derek replied, "You're clean, but I'm not. Isn't it time to return the favor and wash *my* back?" He extended his hand with the bar of soap. Lauren backed away, afraid he would try to grab her. "Don't be selfish, Lauren. I was nothing if not gentlemanly when washing your back."

"I'm rapidly learning to despise your sense of logic," Lauren replied, shaking her head slowly, amazed that she wasn't more angry than she was. Derek tried to hand her the soap again. "Turn around, *then* hand me the soap."

Chuckling, Derek turned his back and extended the soap over his shoulder. "Consider this a sign of trust. No telling what you'll do with my back turned."

"If I had a weapon, I would seriously consider the

possibilities," Lauren muttered loud enough so that Derek could hear. Her words only brought another infuriating chuckle from him.

He put his arms out, and Lauren paused a moment to continue her perusal. The muscles in his shoulders were as finely sculpted as a statue's, and from behind, the narrowness of his lean hips was even more apparent. His physique reminded her of her brother's, but seeing Phillip when they went swimming as children had never elicited the sensual response that Derek's physique provoked.

Angry with herself for taking any appreciation at all in what he looked like, Lauren began soaping him, feeling the firm suppleness of his muscles beneath the skin. She bathed him just as he had bathed her, first his back, then his arms, and if her hands lingered a little longer than necessary when kneading the soap suds into his biceps or strayed toward the front of his body when washing the small of his back, she tried to convince herself that it was an accident, and that she was only doing what her captor demanded. But in her heart she was painfully aware that the first time she had lost her better judgment with Derek, it was when he had touched her, and this time, as the inner warmth of burgeoning passion heightened the sensitivity of her skin and triggered an internal pressure, she knew her aroused state was caused by touching him, by exploring the steelish muscles and the smooth skin of his back, shoulders, and arms.

"Now the front," Derek said, turning slowly.

Lauren's breath caught in her throat, but she did not back away, and this time she did not cross her arms to hide herself.

Chapter 6

A low, throaty groan came from Derek when he looked at his young captive. With her face tilted up to his, he felt a strong urge to kiss her as he had before, exploring her mouth with his tongue, savoring the special taste of her. His gaze went slowly down to her breasts, which were high, large, and round. Derek's arousal hardened, and he struggled against the urge to force himself upon her then and there, plunging himself into her selfishly, concerned only with his own satiation.

"The front," he said, his voice hoarse. He placed his hands very lightly on Lauren's shoulders, moving a half step closer to her. "It's important to finish what you start."

And what does that mean? wondered Lauren, battling with the warring emotions within her heart.

She looked at her right hand, which held the soap, and noticed that she was trembling. Almost as though she was in a trance, she brought the soap to Derek's chest and began rubbing it lightly over him. She lathered his chest, and when the white bubbles were thick and trickled down to his stomach, Lauren began rubbing him with her left hand as well. Her fingertips

73

found his nipple, and when she rubbed it with the pad of her thumb, Derek moaned his approval.

She could feel his heated gaze upon her breasts, which felt taut as they swayed slowly with the movements of her arms. Lauren never allowed herself to look up into Derek's eyes, afraid of the desire she knew was reflected there, afraid, too, of the passion that must surely show in her own eyes.

"You are a mystery to me," Derek said, finding it difficult to make his tongue and lips work properly to form the words. "You fight like a wildcat, and yet you are so passionate, so feminine. You want to give yourself to me, yet you fight me at every step. Funny thing is, you fight yourself, as well."

"I have no choice," Lauren whispered, only half hearing what Derek was saying. She was watching her own hands explore the rippling muscles of Derek's hard, flat stomach. "I must fight. I am a Masters, and we fight whenever we are threatened."

"I am no threat to you," Derek said, his hands sliding down from her shoulders to the upper slopes of her magnificent breasts.

"Yes, you are—you're the greatest threat I've ever known," Lauren replied truthfully.

Derek's touch heated her blood. Suddenly aware of what she was doing, and of how close his hands were to the sensitive crests of her breasts, she took a step back, unaware that she was moving into shallower water. When Derek followed, she took several more steps.

"I . . . am . . . not!" Derek said, following Lauren, his strong heart hammering with desire. Taking another step toward Lauren brought Derek into shallow water, exposing his hotly throbbing erection to the cool night breeze.

"Oh!" Lauren gasped, seeing the full extent of Derek's passion for her.

The sight of him was frightening. She was no virgin, but her single experience with a man had not prepared her for the length and breadth of Derek York's fiercely aroused manhood.

She stopped her retreat. Her legs felt weak; her knees trembled beneath the water. As Derek walked slowly toward her, the soap dropped from her hand into the water with a splash. Numbly she looked down at the dark water.

"Forget it," Derek whispered, stepping up to Lauren. "I own the company. I can get a thousand more." He touched Lauren's slender chin with his fingertips, raising her face to look down into her eyes. "You are the most spectacular woman I have ever met, Lauren . . . the most exquisite woman I have ever known."

She moaned as Derek's face came down to hers. She tilted her head back further, inviting his kiss. And when his mouth touched hers, she eased her tongue between his lips. Her palms flattened against his hard, soapy stomach before sliding around to his back as the kiss deepened. When she felt the warmth of his body against the tips of her breasts, the pleasure was so intensely physical that she pulled him closer.

The long, hard length of Derek's arousal was trapped between them. Lauren felt him throbbing with desire against her, the rigid, searing scepter almost burning the flesh of her stomach.

He's too big . . . he's too much man for me! a frightened inner voice warned her.

She ignored it. As she kissed Derek, sliding her tongue against his, writhing against his body to rub her breasts against the muscle-corded surface of his chest, she realized that the hour she had spent with him in the water had been a languorous exercise in sensuality. Just being close to Derek, both of them naked in the moonlight, had slowly and inexorably aroused her; the caresses had put the finishing touches on the seduction. Lauren was frightened, but she knew she could not back down now. She doubted Derek would let her deny him; what's more, she knew beyond a certainty that the feverish cravings of her own body would not let her.

"My lady," Derek whispered, his hands pushing between their bodies to cup her breasts, now slippery with soap from his body. "You make me tremble like a boy."

His lips went from her mouth to her neck, and Lauren tilted her head to the side to facilitate the kiss. Derek caught her nipples between forefingers and thumbs and pinched lightly, sending a jolting, electrifying passion radiating through her. Shifting her position subtly, Lauren rubbed herself against the heated shaft that pressed demandingly against her stomach. He was so large! In spite of his size, Lauren knew she was ready for him. The touches, the deep kisses and whispered caresses, had all worked their magic on her senses.

"I want you," Derek sighed. He slipped a hand around Lauren, cupping her buttocks, pulling her tighter against him to feel the delicious warmth of her satiny flesh against his manhood. "I need you, Lauren!"

In a haunting realization, it occurred to Derek that he wanted Lauren for more than just his sexual pleasure.

Lauren slipped her arms around Derek's neck, pushing her fingers through his sandy blond hair. She pulled his face down to hers, kissing him hungrily, demandingly, giving herself completely to the ravishing sensation that stripped away shame and fear and doubt. Derek's strong hands cupped her buttocks, and he pulled her up as she wrapped her legs around him, locking her ankles together at the small of his back.

Though Lauren was not a small woman, Derek held her easily. She clung to him, trembling with desire, a hunger in the core of her soul burning with an emptiness that she had never before known, and which she instinctively knew Derek could satisfy.

He lowered her slowly. The conical tip of his mighty phallus touched her, its searing heat making Lauren gasp. Once again she vaguely wondered if it was even possible for Derek to enter her, but this doubt vanished when he lowered her further and she felt herself opening to his strength.

"Ohhh!" Lauren gasped, her fingers laced together behind Derek's neck, her muscles suddenly relaxing as he pushed deeper and deeper into her, simultaneously filling her and consuming her.

Derek lowered her slowly until at last he was completely buried within her. Lauren's head sagged back on her shoulders. To feel Derek inside her, motionless except for the fevered pulse which raced through the shaft, was the most exquisite sensation she'd ever known. With a cry of surprised ecstasy, Lauren squeezed her eyes tightly shut as incredible convulsions gripped her, searing spasms that made her tighten around his invading phallus. She cried out her pleasure, her legs suddenly straightening, only Derek's hands and his manhood holding her in place as she writhed mindlessly in the throes of an ecstasy she had known only once before.

Derek felt her tightening around him. He had waited so long for this to happen! Though he usually had great stamina and the ability to control himself during the sexual act, he felt himself slipping away, a passion named Lauren dissolving his aloof reserve. When she finally opened her eyes, tilting her head to look at him with eyes filled with wonder, he raised her hips, then lowered her again, concerning himself at last with his own passion.

"I cannot . . . control myself . . . with you," Lauren whispered, locking her ankles together once more to assist Derek. The movement of him sliding inside her, filling her so completely, was a dangerous elixir. This man, this sensual, mysterious man, must not be surrendered to . . . but she could not do anything but give in to him.

Lauren watched the passion spread across Derek's handsome countenance, transforming his features. He raised and lowered her with slow but quickening speed. She watched the muscles in his chest and upper arms moving, flexing and relaxing as he carried her weight, and the sight of it made her shiver.

With a muffled groan, Derek pulled Lauren to him, embedding himself fully within her. She wrapped her arms around his neck, pressing her breasts against his chest, her cheek against his.

"Derek!" she gasped, her lips next to his ear.

Hearing her say his name passionately was more than Derek could take. Squeezing her tight, he released his passion in a torrent of ecstasy.

Lauren unlocked her ankles and slid down Derek's body. When he slipped out of her, she issued a soft moue of disappointment. She leaned into Derek, her breath coming in deep, ragged gulps.

What had she done? Had that really been her, Lauren Masters, who had done those terrible things?

"I-I think we'd better . . . get to shore," she whispered, trying to slip out from the circle of Derek's arms. Her passion fulfilled, she now wanted to distance herself from him. He was too dangerous to be near. He made her feel things and do things that were not like her—at least, not like the Lauren Masters she thought she knew.

She started for shore, but Derek caught her hand. "Don't run away from me now," he said quietly. He dipped his head to kiss her forehead, then softly kissed her mouth. "I think we need to talk."

"Whenever you talk, I end up doing things that I shouldn't," Lauren said truthfully, defensively. Some things were too good to be true, and she was beginning to believe that Derek's touch was one of those things.

Lauren grabbed for her clothes, but Derek stopped her. "Wait until you're dry. You're not cold, are you?"

Lauren shook her head. It was a warm evening, and the breeze would soon dry her. It was modesty, not warmth, that made her go for her clothes. The intimacy they had shared had passed, leaving behind a delicious afterglow of newfound passion and a niggling sense of embarrassment and guilt.

Derek shook his head, spraying water in all directions. Lauren laughed and did the same, showering Derek, who chuckled in return at her playfulness.

"Sit," he said, reclining in the thick, green grass beyond the edge of the white sand.

Lauren did as instructed, but she turned to the side for modesty and crossed her arms over her bosom.

"You're always hiding yourself," he chided. "You don't need to do that. I love looking at you."

"Perhaps, but I don't love being looked at." Lauren kept her face averted. Derek was casually stretched out on his side, and if she allowed herself, she knew she would caress his golden body with her eyes. She did not

79

want him to know the effect his body had on her, even when she was doing nothing more intimate than looking at him.

"So you say . . . so you say," Derek replied. He pulled a spear of grass from the ground and nibbled on it. "In time, if we are at all lucky, you will learn to love having me look at you. I'll teach you that."

The confidence in Derek's tone annoyed her. She felt a sudden need to take something away from him, to let him know that he wasn't as superior as he seemed to think.

"You weren't the first, you know. There was someone else," she whispered, hoping it would displease him. Men, she had been led to believe, considered themselves grand victors when they deflowered women.

"I know. Are you still with him, or didn't things work out?"

Lauren turned her gaze upon Derek, perversely hating him for not getting angry at the news she'd just imparted. "That's not any of your business!" she spat.

"No, it's not." Derek's voice became softer, more tender and less teasing. "Did he hurt you?"

Lauren hunched her shoulders. She didn't like thinking about Richard, and she didn't like talking to Derek about him. It surprised her when she heard the sound of her own voice. "He hurt me, but not physically. He pretended to be someone he wasn't, and I believed him. He didn't hit me, if that's what you're asking."

"Men can be real bastards," Derek said quietly, wanting to take Lauren into his arms to comfort her. He knew that if he tried to hold her she would misread his intentions and he'd end up doing more harm than good. "Sometimes it's necessary for a man to pretend to be something he isn't."

"Like you?" Lauren asked, the question escaping her lips before she had a chance to silence it.

"Yes, like me."

"What are *you* pretending to be?"

Derek looked into Lauren's eyes for a moment, thinking that he had never before known a woman quite like her. It was unusual for him even to consider opening his heart and telling his secrets to a woman, but somehow that didn't seem so heinous with her.

"I'm pretending to be a pirate," he said at last. "I'm not happy about it, but for now it's necessary."

A silence developed between them. Lauren waited as long as she could, wanting Derek to clarify his statement. When he didn't, she said with a trace of malice, "Yes, and you're pretending so well that I truly believe you *are* a pirate. Only a pirate would sail with *The Unholy One.*"

"Listen to me," Derek replied quickly, his own anger rising though he thoroughly understood Lauren's distrust of him. "I wish and pray with all I hold dear that every man aboard *The Unholy One* goes to court, is given a fair trial, and then is hanged! I hate them all— Gregor especially. I live for the day the world is rid of that bloody bastard, and if I have my way, I'll be the one to put an end to his life! But for now, until I've done what I set out from London to accomplish, I've got to go along with Gregor and the rest of them. I don't want to, but I have to."

"Why?" Lauren demanded, part of her still horribly convinced that he was a pirate, like the murderous Gregor.

"I can't tell you why. I can only ask that you believe me."

"Give me something more than words to believe, and maybe I will."

81

With a huff of frustration and anger, Derek bolted to his feet. He grabbed the shikars and mitar and tossed them to Lauren, then quickly began putting on his own clothes.

Lauren looked at the two pieces of fine white silk. They were both rectangular, one considerably larger than the other, each with two long, slender tails at the corners of the material. Even the larger of the two was much too small to be a toga, so she had no idea how it was to be worn.

Derek dressed quickly, then turned toward her again. Naked, her body bathed in the glow of the moonlight, Lauren's image gripped him powerfully, and he cursed himself because he knew she could never trust him completely. Nothing he could say would change the fact that she had been kidnapped and that she saw him as her kidnapper. She was the most enticing woman he'd ever known, and her fiery spirit delighted him. He was as yet unwilling to admit that she was the woman he'd been waiting for, but the possibility was there, and it gave him no peace of mind.

"Let me help you," he said, moving closer.

Lauren spun, turning her back. The curve of her hips and heart-shaped buttocks was an aphrodisiac that played havoc with his senses.

"I can do it myself," Lauren replied with soft malice. "I don't need your help."

"You've said that before, and you were wrong then, too." He took the larger of the two silk pieces from her. "Now this is called a shikars. You wear it like this."

Lauren wanted to protest, but did not. There wasn't much fight left in her after the exhilaration of lovemaking. Derek wrapped the cloth around her hips twice, then tied the long tails at the upper edge to secure the shikars like a shirt.

"And this is called a mitar," Derek continued, taking the smaller piece of silk from Lauren. A vein pulsed at his temple, and he felt his blood heating at Lauren's nudity, but he sought to control his own desires. "You wear it like this."

The mitar came under Lauren's arms, then criss-crossed over her breasts and was tied at the back of her neck. When Derek finished, Lauren adjusted the silk around her breasts, surprised to find the garment quite comfortable. The clothing did, however, completely expose her stomach, and she felt more than just a little indecent with just one layer of silk covering her breasts.

"That's how the natives dress," Derek explained, taking a step back to inspect his handiwork. He had seen many women wearing mitar and shikars, but none looked like Lauren. None had her aristocratic face, or her rapturous curves. "You'll blend in with them a little better wearing that. It's a good thing you don't have blonde hair, or you'd really stand out."

Lauren wondered if Derek preferred blondes to brunettes, and if he was greatly disappointed that her own tresses were ebony black.

"Come on, let's get back to the hut," Derek said, picking up her discarded European clothing. "We'd better get some sleep."

Lauren followed Derek back to the hut, wondering if their lovemaking had meant anything at all to him. She was certain she had aroused him, but she also knew that his arousal wasn't enough. She wanted more from their joining than just his lust. After Richard, Lauren had promised herself that she would never again be duped by the persuasive lies of a dishonest man. The thought that she had again been foolish enough to believe softly spoken lies twisted insidiously through her.

He forced himself upon me. I had no choice. I'm his captive . . . and I'm lying to myself. . . .

"Lauren, what's wrong?" Derek asked, slipping his arm around her waist as they walked.

"Nothing. Nothing at all." She quickened her stride to move away from his arm. "Just leave me alone."

Chapter 7

The morning sun coming through the window hit Gregor full in the face. He groaned, blinking, turning from the torturous morning light. He felt the bed beside him and was disappointed but not surprised that the waitress had left him sometime during the night.

He rolled onto his back and placed a hand over his eyes. Even through his lids the light was painfully bright. His head pounded, and his stomach felt like the time the ship's rum supply had run dry, so he drank liquor he'd distilled himself. He nearly died from the experience, and his stomach had never been quite the same since.

He tried to think of the previous night's activities, but the vague memories didn't bring a smile to his face. The waitress loved to flirt with her customers when she was at the tavern and felt she was safe. The flirting provided extra income from the sailors who adored her and thought her laughter and smiles were the genuine article. Her laughter never stopped until she realized Gregor really wasn't going to take no for an answer.

It bothered Gregor that she'd refused to kiss him and made no attempt to pretend she was having a good time while he was atop her. When he was finished, he rolled over, grabbed a jug of rum, laughed heartily, slapped the waitress on the behind, and said that he was just joshing, that he meant no harm. The waitress said she understood, and had taken no offense . . . but a veiled hatred behind her eyes promised Gregor that someday she would get even with him for what he'd done.

Gregor doubted she'd waited more than two minutes after he'd fallen asleep to leave his room.

Very slowly, groaning with pain, Gregor pushed himself to a sitting position at the edge of the mattress. He folded his legs beneath him and rubbed his eyes. His hangovers were getting more painful, he thought. It was also taking more and more for him to get drunk, and more for him to get sexually aroused.

It was just bad rum, that's all. I'm not getting older. Not yet. I'm as much a man as I ever was. . . .

It was a comforting thought, and Gregor eagerly embraced it. What he needed was someone special, a woman who was different from all other women . . . these thoughts led naturally to the dark-haired woman with the vuluptuous body who had been taken when *Miss Malaki* was stormed.

Gregor hadn't been able to see everything that the woman had to offer—what was it Derek had called her? Lauren?—but what he had seen, with her torn bodice and her straining chemise, was enough to make his blood sizzle.

Thoughts of Lauren led annoyingly to thoughts of the Englishman, Derek. Gregor loathed the man, and only Derek's apparently limitless wealth, which was being funneled to Aldon Mitchell, kept him from letting his natural instincts—to kill the bastard—have free rein.

That damned Englishman! He took the best-looking women for himself, and he wouldn't even share them! What difference could it make if the women were with a few men from *The Unholy One* before they got sold to Derek's buyer? And even if Derek was concerned only with getting the best slaves for the money, that still didn't account for Derek's infuriating habit of stopping the men when they wanted only to have a little fun by killing passengers too old and weak to be of any value.

Gregor rubbed his face, fighting the aftereffects of the alcohol. Today he was scheduled to show Aldon Mitchell the new captive and get paid for his services. Aldon would expect him to be sharp and mentally alert. He didn't trust Aldon and suspected that if he was anything less than completely sober for their meeting, Aldon would find some way of swindling him.

Getting unsteadily to his feet, he thought that today he would ask Aldon Mitchell when he would be allowed to kill the Englishman.

Lauren's first conscious thought was that there was warmth beside her, and the warmth was good and comforting. She snuggled closer to the coziness, pressing her cheek against Derek's naked chest, sliding her knee along his thigh to rest closer to him.

So peaceful . . . warm . . . safe . . . peaceful . . . with Derek. . . .

It was the fuzzy awareness of Derek beside her that brought her fully awake, and with consciousness came the realization that she lay naked and in his arms, and had done so through the night.

She began to get up, easing away from Derek, and he stirred. "It's okay," she whispered. "Go back to sleep. I'm not going anywhere."

Derek smiled sleepily, and Lauren breathed a sigh of relief. She needed a few moments to think, to sort out the bizarre direction her life had taken, to figure out what to do in the immediate future.

87

Finding the shikars and mitar near the mattress where Derek had discarded them shortly before they'd made love again, Lauren wrapped the garments around herself, tying the knots especially tight this time.

The knots might provide some protection against Derek's advances, Lauren thought with grim determination. *I don't seem to have the strength to deny him.*

Lauren tried to put her hair into some semblance of order, found she couldn't and abandoned the task with an angry huff. She wanted the brushes she had in her cabin. She wanted her own clothes, which were tailored for her and were more modest than those Derek had provided. She wanted to be home in Virginia with her mother and father and her sweet nanny, all of whom doted on her every wish. She wanted to be anywhere but on some tiny island in the Caribbean, in a small hut with a man she knew as Derek York, but who she was certain she hardly knew at all.

Looking at Derek's sleeping form, she smiled. Derek was at rest, and for the first time since she'd met him, he did not have that haunted aura, nor did he exude the intense vitality and virility that overwhelmed her senses. Asleep, he was just a man—more handsome than others, to be sure, but still just a man, and as such, easier for Lauren to see in a clearer, more logical light.

Which Derek was the *real* Derek? The pirate who sailed with *The Unholy One,* and captured women to be sold as chattel to satisfy the fetishes of wealthy men? Or was he a good man relentlessly caught up in something ugly, something larger than himself that was deadly enough to frighten him? Had it been circumstances beyond his control that put that haunted look in his eyes? Or was he merely an evil man, unwillingly tortured by the guilt of a past, present, and future of his own making—a past littered with the bodies and souls of victims whose only crime had been that they were weaker than the bloodless killers aboard *The Unholy One?*

Derek opened his eyes and Lauren briefly met his gaze. It was disturbing the way he awoke—not moving, just opening his eyes, instantly alert without any foggy transition. She turned away from him, walking to the uncovered opening in the hut's wall. In the balmy Caribbean climate, no windows were necessary.

"Good morning," Derek said. Lauren kept her back to him as he pulled on his trousers. "Did you sleep well?"

"Yes . . . fine."

Derek looked at her, liking what he saw. In the white silk, she was a vision of loveliness. The memories of last night's lovemaking came back to him forcefully, making him grimace. Had he forced himself upon her, or just seduced her? And if he *had* seduced her, did she really have any chance? With an effort, Derek pushed the thoughts aside, not wanting anything to mar the powerful memories of holding her against him as they stood in the waist-deep water, plunging himself deeply into her until his passion erupted with such force that he was left weak and breathless.

He reached for his saber and dagger, then stopped himself. He wanted to believe that Lauren posed no real threat. Her lovemaking had been real, not contrived, not the frightened act of a woman wanting only to please her captor.

"We'll have a long day ahead of us," Derek said, rising, moving closer to her, drawn to her. He removed his hairbrush from his trunk and brushed his sandy blond hair straight back. "Maybe today I'll get lucky enough to find out who is behind Gregor."

"What do you mean?"

"I want to find out who Gregor sells his women to."

Derek tightened up inside. He shouldn't be telling Lauren these things. She had no need to know, and telling her put him in jeopardy. Still, he felt a strange need to confide in her, at least sometimes.

"Why is that important?"

"Let's just say it's important to me and leave it at that." Derek moved close to Lauren. "Would you like me to brush your hair?"

"No!" Lauren said sharply. She took a step away, but Derek followed. His closeness made her feel warm inside, but it also made her nervous and jittery. "It's not necessary. I can do that myself."

"Of course you can, but isn't it nice having someone do things for you once in a while?" Derek placed his hand lightly on Lauren's shoulder. He smelled the freshness of her body and the fragrance of the Foxbury soap. He felt a low stir within himself and was amazed at the power she had over his senses. "Relax now and let me brush your hair. After that, I'll make us something to eat. By the way, can you cook?"

Lauren ignored the question. She knew how to cook over a campfire, but not in a kitchen. Her family often went on hunting expeditions, living in tents and cooking their meals over an open fire. When they were at the Masters mansion in Virginia, there were cooks to handle such chores. She thought it best to keep this information to herself. If Derek knew that she came from a wealthy family, it could further jeopardize her chances of escape. Ransom was a possibility she could not ignore.

Without getting his answer, Derek slipped his finger under Lauren's ebony, wavy hair and smoothed it over her shoulders. Then, very gently, he began brushing the tresses, starting from the ends and working his way upward to ease the tangles out.

"You've got lovely hair," Derek said in a tone barely above a whisper. The sound of it caressed her. "So soft and shiny, gently wavy . . . lovely."

Lauren's eyes closed as she felt the tingly sensation against her scalp. Her mother had brushed her hair a thousand times, and so had her nanny, but it had never felt like this. No man had ever brushed her hair, and Lauren felt herself relaxing slowly as she luxuriated in the gentle strokes of the brush.

"That feels nice," she whispered, tilting her head to one side so that Derek could draw the brush along her temple.

Her dark hair was a stark contrast to the white silk mitar. Derek looked at the knot at the back of Lauren's neck, remembering the glorious breasts that would be exposed to him if he'd just untie that knot and let the mitar fall away. He stifled the urge, knowing her trust in him was still too fragile to withstand much deceit or forwardness on his part. But, this understanding did not prevent his body from reacting to Lauren's innate sensuality, and as he brushed her hair in a slow, lingering fashion, his manhood burgeoned, straining against the fabric of his trousers, pulsing with renewed vitality.

"What's . . . what's going to happen to us?" Lauren asked quietly, her eyes closed. She was unaware of the impact her beauty was having on Derek. It bothered her a little that she had said "us" instead of "me" but she continued anyway. "Why do you stay with Gregor and *The Unholy One* when it's clear you're nothing like them at all?"

Derek swallowed dryly. He wasn't at all sure he could make his mouth work properly to voice the answer. As he pulled the brush through Lauren's hair, smoothing it over her shoulders with his palm, his passion escalated. Each pass with the brush, each touch of his hand against her hair, was a caress to his senses that could not be ignored.

"Won't you answer?" Lauren asked dreamily, tilting her head to the other side to invite Derek's touch. "I promise I'll never tell anyone what you tell me."

"I just don't know if I actually have an answer. Not an easy one, anyway." Derek cleared his throat. His hands, he noticed, were trembling slightly. His confined phallus pulsed with need. "All I can really tell you is that I don't want to be a part of *The Unholy One,* and I pray with all my heart and soul that I'll see the day each and every crewman comes to justice."

"But doesn't that include you?" Lauren hardly heard what Derek said. The tingling sensations that had been concentrated on her scalp had slowly traveled through her body, heightening her sensitivity from head to toe.

"No, it doesn't," Derek said, a harsh edge creeping into his tone. "I can't expect you to believe me, I know, but I am *not* a crewman of *The Unholy One.*"

Lauren turned slowly, spinning within the circle of Derek's hands. She looked up into his clear blue eyes and said honestly, "I want to believe you. I just don't know if I can."

"Try . . . please try," Derek whispered.

She heard the brush land on the dirt floor behind her. His hands came slowly around to cup her face tenderly.

He's going to kiss me. If I stop him now, before this starts, I'll have the willpower to deny him. I won't give in to him if I just stop him now. . . .

Lauren could not put the thought into action. She tilted her head back as Derek bent down, and she uttered a low, throaty purr when their lips met. He kissed her softly, his lips barely touching hers, the tip of his tongue nudging between her lips, his fingers lightly caressing her cheeks. Lauren placed her palms against his stomach, her heart racing with excitement as she felt the warmth of his skin. Her hands roamed upward, and she explored his small, round nipples, drawing a groan of pleasure.

Derek's hands slipped around her head, the fingers sliding under Lauren's hair. He pulled her close, his kiss deepening, heightening in intensity. His tongue pushed deeply into her mouth. Lauren curled her tongue around his, shivering with the building passion, knowing that she was doing something terribly wicked, but not caring. Notions of right and wrong, of what she should and shouldn't do, were slipping away from her, and she bade them good-bye without a second thought.

"I can't keep from touching you," Derek whispered hoarsely, pulling back to look into her dark, sultry eyes. "I try. I truly do. But I can't stay away from you."

At that moment, Lauren didn't care if his words were nothing more than beautiful lies. She wanted to feel desirable, needed to feel as though she was special to Derek, special in a way that he had not intended and perhaps even didn't want. When his hand slipped down to cup her breast, Lauren moaned softly and leaned into his palm, forcing her breast to fill his exquisitely kneading hand. He caught her nipple through the sheer silk mitar, pinching softly. Pleasure spread throughout Lauren like molten gold in an ornate cast, and she opened her mouth wider, inviting the erotic exploration of his tongue as the fire of desire burned hotter, searing away the last vestiges of guilt and trepidation.

He lifted her and carried her to the small mattress, placing her down gently, his mouth never leaving hers, then stretched out beside her, sliding an arm around her waist to pull her against him.

"We . . . shouldn't," Lauren said with some difficulty, turning her face away. His moist lips had found a particularly sensitive spot on her throat, and when he kissed her there, Lauren purred contentedly, despite the teachings of her youth, which said such a union out-side of marriage was inherently wrong. "We mustn't, Derek. Please . . . last night was a mistake . . . a mistake we mustn't let happen again."

"Last night was beautiful, and this morning will be even more beautiful."

Derek tried to untie the mitar at the back of Lauren's neck, but she had knotted it too tightly. Hesitating only a moment, he eased his fingertips beneath the mitar and pushed the confining silk upward, freeing her breasts. He looked down at her, issuing a rumbling sigh of appreciation at the extravagant wealth of her body.

Lauren looked into his eyes. Blue as sapphires, they were hot and glittery, touching her in a way that was almost physical. To her surprise, she saw her own hand at his cheek, and when she pulled his face down to her breasts, Lauren realized that she was as incapable of denying herself as Derek seemed to be. As the warmth of his mouth suffused her breast, his tongue circling around the sensitized tip, she trembled on the mattress and surrendered herself once again to the enigmatic Derek York, praying silently that his caresses were honest and that his life with Gregor and *The Unholy One* was all a hideous lie.

Derek felt her acquiescence, and he promised himself that this time she would feel things she had never felt before. She would know first-hand sensa-tions that she had never dreamed possible. The night before, when he had raised Lauren high and then thrust himself deep into her, he could tell he had not been the first man she'd ever known. And if he couldn't be the first, he *could* be the best . . . and maybe, if the fates and the gods were with him, her last!

He feasted on her breasts, taking unbridled delight in

the way she responded to him. Though his own desire was escalating with each passing moment, Derek willed himself to be patient. Lauren had given up a part of herself—had entrusted him in a way that she hadn't planned—and because of this, he felt indebted and responsible.

"Let me pleasure you," he whispered, his hand slipping between the folds of her shikars to bare her satiny thighs. "Just give yourself over to the feeling, and I'll take you where you've never been."

The fingertips tracing widening circles at the inside of her thigh had the force of a tidal wave. Under Derek's gentle insistence, she parted her legs, then cried out softly, arching her back, when he touched the center of her desire. In an oddly disconnected way, she felt his tongue follow the line of her ribs. She pushed her fingers through Derek's hair, unaware that she was guiding him downward, oblivious to his intentions, conscious only of the tantalizing fingertips that probed gently, caressed with consummate skill.

"Relax, and let me take care of you," Derek whispered, his breath cool against the moist, heated petals of her femininity.

He kissed her, his tongue darting inside, and Lauren cried out sharply. She half sat, pushing her elbows beneath her to look down. What Derek was doing was shocking, terribly wicked . . . and wickedly exciting.

"Lie back," he said, his eyes burning with luminous passion. His eyes held Lauren's as he reached for her breast and took the nipple between his fingers, then kissed her intimately again.

Lauren shivered as she fell back on the mattress. She had thought she knew all there was to feel, all there was to do with Derek, and now she realized that her journey of understanding had only just begun. His tongue was like a serpent's, and with it he ignited a fire within her that made her heart race uncontrollably and her body tremble as though she was freezing to death. The sensations carried her higher and higher. The pressure within her became unbearable, just as it had before, only this time it was even stronger. And just when Lauren was sure she could accept no more of the probing kisses that electrified her nerves, Derek slowed his caresses and prolonged the inevitable.

"Don't stop! Please, I'm begging you, please don't stop!" Lauren cried out, her eyes squeezed tightly shut.

Sure at last that he had accomplished what he'd set out to, Derek turned the full force of his erotic abilities on Lauren. Within seconds she was screaming—literally screaming—as the white-hot waves of her culmination coursed through her.

When she was finished, Lauren lay immodestly on the mattress, the folds of her shikars opened to expose her thighs and above, her mitar pushed above her breasts. She felt she should make some attempt to cover herself, but she lacked the strength to make the effort.

She felt Derek pull away. She wanted to reach for him, but she did not. If he was intent only on pleasing her, as he had been the very first time in his cabin when he showed her what wonders lay at the end of stimulation, she could accept that, though a part of her wondered why he would be so selfless.

Through her thick, dark lashes, she watched him stand, then remove his trousers.

My God . . . he's too big for me!

Lauren knew it was an irrational thought. Hadn't she made love to him twice already? But last night when her body had twice opened to accept him, it had been dark. Now in the light of the morning there appeared to be even more man. Fear curled within her as Derek knelt on the mattress beside her.

"Wait . . . I don't know if I can," she whispered.

"Of course you can," Derek said, easing his knee between Lauren's, stretching out above her. "Don't be afraid. I can make the magic happen again. I promise."

"I don't believe your promises."

Lauren shivered as he entered her slowly, in one long, breathtaking thrust. She twisted her arms around his neck to hold him close, to feel the beating of his heart against her. She heard him say, "Yes, you do," and she hated him just a little because she knew he was right.

Chapter 8

While the lovemaking rejuvenated Derek, giving him renewed energy and spirit, it had just the opposite effect on Lauren. She wanted to do nothing more than remain on the small mattress, her head on the pillow, her forearm shielding her eyes from the sun, enjoy the warm post-lovemaking sensations.

"Come on, sleepyhead, we can't stay in this hut all day," Derek said upon returning from the small clay stove situated a safe distance from the hut. He was cooking the morning meal of turtle eggs, with portions fit for a king—or for a man who had worked up a healthy appetite.

"Do we have to leave now?" Lauren mumbled, unwilling to move a muscle. It seemed unnatural that Derek was full of energy, and it seemed wholly unnecessary that they should have to do anything this early on a morning that was, at least for Lauren, unique and very special. "What's the rush?"

Each passing day reminded Derek of how little progress he had made in finding his sister; each passing day made him wonder what horrors his sister had lived through the night before . . . if, in fact, she was still alive.

"It's important," Derek said at last, his tone harsher than he'd intended. "Let's leave it at that."

He saw her body stiffen as she turned toward him, propping herself up with an elbow. She had modestly rearranged her mitar and shikars, but she was still a frighteningly beguiling vision to behold, even after Derek had explored every inch of her body and tasted her secret places, even after thoroughly satisfying his own burning lusts.

He knew that he had hurt Lauren by speaking so harshly. She wanted to be held and spoken to softly, to be reassured that what had happened between them was not just crude, physical need being unleashed and satisfied. Derek was conscious of all this, yet he knew he mustn't give Lauren the comfort she wanted. It wouldn't be in her best interests to love him, or even like him too well, and Derek was determined that he wouldn't endanger Lauren any more than was absolutely necessary.

A silence formed between them that didn't end until Derek dished up the food he had prepared. On several occasions he had tried to strike up a conversation, but Lauren's one-word responses had cut him short. She felt cheated by Derek's brisk energy and his harsh statement that they couldn't spend some quiet time together.

Finally Derek felt he had to say something to mollify her.

"I'm sorry if this hasn't turned out the way you wanted," Derek said, pushing turtle eggs around his plate with a fork. "I know things have been rather hard on you, but you've got to believe that I don't want to make them any harder. I've just got—"

"Yes, I know, you've got something important to accomplish," Lauren cut in sharply, her chocolaty eyes growing even darker as her hurt evolved into anger.

99

"Of course, you can't tell me what this important thing is, can you?" Lauren stood and looked down at Derek, who remained sitting cross-legged outside the hut. "You ask an awful lot, Derek . . . and you *take* even more!"

Derek bolted to his feet, knocking the wooden plate to the ground and spilling his food. He strode past Lauren so quickly that she flinched, fearing that he would strike her. He returned a moment later holding a length of rope.

"I can't argue with you all day," he said, moving intimidatingly close to Lauren. "Put your hands together."

"No!" Lauren hissed, hating the thought of being tied up again, fearing that horrible sensation of being helpless.

"Do as I tell you, damn it! I haven't the bloody time to argue with you!"

Lauren looked up into Derek's steel blue eyes. She saw the resolve in his soul, saw the determination that would not be bent or swayed. Slowly, not taking her gaze from his, she placed her hands together.

"I have to do this," Derek said as he looped the rope loosely around her wrists, then tied it, leaving a long end trailing down to the floor. "If I don't tie you, it'll draw suspicion, and I can't afford that. Don't move your hands too much. I don't want anyone to see how loose the rope is."

When Derek looked away for a moment, Lauren tested the rope. True enough, it was looped so loosely around her wrists she could get her hands free in less than a minute or two if she really tried.

"Where are we going?" she asked, mystified at Derek's latest behavior.

"To the village. There are matters that I must see to."

"And you intend to drag me around with you, like a dog on a leash?"

Derek fixed her with a stare. "As a matter of fact, yes. The alternative is to tie your hands and feet like I had to do the last time I left you. Of course, if I did that, then there wouldn't be anything I could do—or you could do—to prevent Gregor or one of his men from just walking into the hut and having his way with you." He leaned down so that his face was very close to Lauren's. "So the choice is yours. Do you want to come with me and be led around like a dog on a leash, as you so indelicately put it, or do you want to have me tie you up so that you can't move at all, and leave you in the hut?"

Lauren looked down at her hands, hating the sight of the coiled rope, hating all the things that she had so little power to control.

"I'd rather go with you," she said softly. "I won't be any more trouble. I promise."

Derek turned and began walking along the winding path that led to the pirate village, holding the rope as Lauren followed close behind.

"You're not trouble to me, really . . . I just didn't expect to find you. You weren't in my plans," Derek said, speaking so softly that, with his back to Lauren, she could barely make out the words. "I'm tired of all this bloody damned fighting! When you fight me, I take my fear and anger out on you. I don't mean to, but I do."

Lauren sensed that Derek was telling her something that he'd never thought he would, and it mystified her. *Who is this man?* she thought once again. *Why does he say one thing and do just the opposite? How can he make love to me one minute, then not trust me the next?*

At this time of morning, the village, with a population of just under a hundred, was rather quiet. To Lauren's amazement, numerous pirates lay passed out beneath the trees, sleeping off their drunken stupor in the morning sunlight. She wrinkled her nose at the sight of the dissolute men. The thought that one or more of these smelly, unwashed cretins might have raped her sent a shudder rippling up her spine.

Lauren wanted to ask Derek questions—where they were going, what it was he hoped to accomplish—but he never slowed his pace or turned around to look at her. Seeing his broad back made her remember how her hands had explored him, feeling the muscles beneath the skin, digging into his smooth, pale flesh with her fingernails when her passion had reached its peak. Had she left any marks on him? As Derek stoically continued his stride, Lauren hoped she had scratched him deeply, and that his skin would always carry her marks.

The small village had two taverns, and Derek went to the larger one—the sprawling, one-story—*As the Crow Flies*. To Lauren's surprise it was already open for business. Looking through the open front doors, she noticed that several of the stools at the long bar were already occupied by pirates from *The Unholy One*.

"I want you to stay out here," Derek said, his voice low so that he couldn't be overheard. The village was awakening, and men were making their way sleepily toward the tavern for their morning elixir of rum. "Don't talk to anybody. If anything happens, scream your bloody head off and I'll come running."

"Why can't I stay with you?"

Derek gave her a look. "That's not a place for a

woman. Besides, I'm not going to be in there long. I've got to ask some questions, then I've got to check on some . . . some other matters, and I don't think you should be with me for that."

Lauren didn't appreciate Derek's secretiveness. When she looked inside the tavern again, she saw several women. One of them was extremely young—younger than Lauren by about three years—who wore a blouse she'd left unbuttoned; it nearly revealed her small, firm breasts completely. The shocking sight was made even more disturbing when she realized that the patrons hardly paid the young woman any attention at all.

"There are women in there," Lauren commented dryly.

"No, there aren't—the women in there are professional companions for the sailors. They're not women in the way you're a woman." Derek glanced right and left to see whether anyone was looking, then took Lauren's bound hands lightly in his own. "Please, don't argue with me. Stay here quietly and keep your eyes and ears open. Let me know what you hear. Please?"

She heard the sincerity in his voice, saw it in his sapphire blue eyes. She wanted to believe him, but he had to give her something more than just words and empty promises.

"What am I supposed to be listening for? I can't be any help to you unless you confide in me."

A pirate, walking zombielike and holding his head as though afraid his skull would split in two if he released it, staggered past them. Derek immediately dropped Lauren's hands. As the pirate moved past her, he looked at the ropes around Lauren's wrists, then over at Derek. He grinned crookedly, showing a mouth missing most of its teeth. "That should keep the wench in line, matey!"

Lauren flushed with anger. Didn't Derek see how he was humiliating her with the rope? Couldn't he see how he was scarring her soul with this inhumane treatment?

"I'm sorry," Derek said, reading Lauren's thoughts. "It's necessary for now, but it won't always be this way." He took Lauren's hands in his own again, squeezing reassuringly. "If you hear anyone saying anything about women being sold as slaves, and where they are taken, or anything like that at all, try to remember *everything*. I'll be back for you as soon as I possibly can."

Lauren watched in horror as Derek tied the loose end of the rope around the trunk of a slender palm tree, tying her up like a horse to a hitching post.

"Do you have to leave me here? Can't you leave me somewhere less . . . public?"

Derek shook his head. "The more people around, the safer you'll be. By now all the men from *The Unholy One* will recognize you and know I've claimed you for myself. One of them might want to do something, but they'll never risk it if they know that sooner or later I'll find out."

"The word you're so artfully avoiding is rape, correct?" The defiance in Lauren's eyes shone bright and clear as her hot gaze bore straight into Derek's.

"Yes. That's why it is so important that you do everything I tell you. You're so beautiful, Lauren . . . so beautiful . . . and what you don't understand is that your beauty puts you in great jeopardy. To make the situation worse, there isn't a man aboard *The Unholy One* who doesn't despise me, and who would love nothing more than to take what's mine."

The conflicting words made Lauren's head spin. Derek was telling her how beautiful she was, but his words somehow lacked the effect that a compliment should have. She wanted to scream that she wasn't *his*—at least, not in the way Derek made it sound. She was Lauren Masters, an independent young woman, and she wasn't owned by anyone, not now and not *ever!*

Angrily, Lauren replied, "Fine . . . I'll be just fine. Go and do whatever it is you have to do. I'll see what I can see."

Derek whispered tenderly, "Lauren . . ."

"Just go! You're always in such a damn hurry, so why aren't you hurrying?"

A moment later Derek was inside *As the Crow Flies.* Lauren sat at the base of the tree, adjusting her mitar and shikars to hide as much of herself as possible. As men walked past her on their way into the tavern, they made lewd comments on how she looked and what they'd like to do to her. At first Lauren looked them in the eye, challenging them, hating them. Then, as she realized the futility of her defiance, she learned to keep her eyes down. It wasn't as painful that way. Then, when she heard the ugly, lustful things the men said about her, at least she didn't have to look at them and attribute the words to an unshaven face and unwashed body.

Mirabell was happy to see Derek. Though she had only talked to him a few times, she could tell he wasn't like the other men aboard *The Unholy One.* He was always neatly dressed in expensive European clothes, he treated her politely, and occasionally he favored her with a smile that warmed her blood.

"Good morning, Mr. Derek," she said with a smile, intentionally leaning forward with her elbows on the bar, her blouse opening enough to show her petite

105

breasts to him. When she saw Derek's eyes flick down-ward, she wondered once again why he hadn't asked to sleep with her. "Can I get you one?"

Derek didn't want a drink so early in the morning, but he knew it wouldn't look manly for him to abstain. If he didn't imbibe to excess along with the other pirates, it would be one more thing that drew their suspicion and animosity.

"Sure," he said, wondering if he would even be able to swallow the rum at this hour, and cursing himself lightly for looking at Mirabell's bosom.

She returned a moment later. From the color of the rum, Derek could tell it wasn't the standard rum sold at *As the Crow Flies*—Mirabell had tapped into some-one's private stock of good liquor. He reached for his money pouch, but she stopped him quickly, reaching over the bar to place a hand on his arm. "This one is from me."

Derek smiled, his gaze holding Mirabell's for a moment. He wondered what her heritage was. She had caramel-colored skin that was smooth and clear, dark brown hair lightly flecked with red, and a long, slender, aquiline nose. Clearly, she was of mixed heritage, but Derek couldn't tell whether her parentage came from the United Kingdom, Belgium, Holland, or the United States.

"Where did you get the blouse?" Derek asked, breaking the look that had formed between them. "A gift?"

Mirabell frowned. "From a man . . . just a man." She hoped Derek wouldn't be disappointed with her, though she was certain he already knew she occasion-ally slept with men for money.

"You should button it up," Derek said, feeling pro-tective toward her, wishing there were something more he could do for her. She seemed so young to him, so innocent, though he knew she wasn't. "These men don't deserve to look at you."

Mirabell quickly buttoned the blouse. It was much too large for her, and it hung down to where her shikars wrapped about her trim hips.

"Is there anything else I can do for you?" Mirabell asked, hope in her voice.

Before Derek could answer, a man several stools down growled, "If you ain't gonna drink that, pass it down! Cain't you tell good rum when you see it?"

Derek turned slowly to see who had addressed him. The pirate, in his forties, though looking much older from years of drinking, had bloodshot eyes and a trembling hand on the cutlass at his side. He was suffering from a foul hangover. A week earlier Derek had had harsh words with the man.

"I'll drink it when I choose," Derek said quietly, noticing that all conversation in the tavern had stopped. He could almost hear the men asking themselves: is this the morning the Englishman gets run through?

"If you weren't such a land-lovin' lilly boy, you'd 'ave been done with 'er by now! If you cain't take no enjoyment in the good things this life 'as to offer, step aside an' let those who do 'ave it."

Without taking his eyes from the pirate, Derek picked up the glass of rum, tossed it to the back of his throat, and swallowed the contents in a single gulp. The liquor burned his throat, even though it was excellent rum; the taste of it so early in the morning nearly made him gag.

"Now be silent," Derek said quietly, glad to hear that other conversations had again begun. "You're disturbing my morning drink."

Ten minutes passed before Derek again felt confident that none of the men were listening to him and

Mirabell. He leaned close to her, and when she placed her tiny hand lightly on his forearm, he did not move it.

"You hear everything that happens here, Mirabell, and that's part of the reason why I'm hoping you can help me."

"You need only ask," she replied in a hushed tone, indicating that there was absolutely nothing she wouldn't do for Derek—in or out of the bedroom.

"Have you heard anything of where the women are taken after they're brought here?" Suspicion flashed in Mirabell's eyes, but Derek had gone too far to back down now. "I'm looking for someone special. I think she might have already been sold, and I'd like to buy her back from whoever bought her. I'm willing to pay a fair price . . . any price, actually."

Mirabell's eyes were soft, showing an inner hurt that she tried to conceal. "Am I not a special woman for you, Mr. Derek? I can treat you better than any other girl. It is true. You can ask. . . ."

The words died away, and Mirabell looked down.

Yes, I can ask any of the men, and they'll be only too happy to tell me how good you are to them in bed, won't they, nice gentlemen that they all are, Derek thought savagely, angry not at Mirabell, but at the cold reality that made it necessary for her to sell her body and her youth just so she could feed and clothe brothers and sisters she kept tucked away on another island.

"I know you'd treat me well," Derek said at last. "But this woman is . . . she means something special to the man I buy for. It isn't that she's more beautiful than you are. No girl could be."

Mirabell nibbled on her bottom lip thoughtfully, wanting Derek, yet not knowing what approach she should take. "I may have a girl's body, and be a girl in years, but I have a woman's knowledge, and I know what will make you happy."

"Yes, I'm sure you do." Derek felt the gnawing in his stomach, hating this moment, cursing himself for letting Mirabell go on when he knew he could never give her what she wanted. "But this special woman, she's not for me."

"I could be for you? Maybe someday?" she asked. Derek nodded, and Mirabell's broad smile tore deep into his soul. "If you are looking for a woman who has been sold already, I do not know if I can help you. But if she is waiting to be sold, then perhaps she is with the others on St. Lucifer."

"St. Lucifer Island? Where is that?"

"South of here, south of the little island of rock that has no drinking water."

Derek knew of it. While aboard *The Unholy One* he had seen it from a distance, noticing its beauty, and asked a sailor about it. The island was, at least by Europeans, unnamed, and unpopulated. Without potable water, its beauty could be enjoyed only from afar.

"Thank you, Mirabell," Derek said. He reached for his money pouch, and though she protested, he pushed a coin into her palm. "It is the least I can do."

"Perhaps someday I can do something for you," the girl whispered in a rush of words, astonished at the money that had been given her. She would be able to feed her brothers and sisters for several weeks with the single coin.

"Perhaps," Derek replied, getting to his feet. He had no intention of ever sleeping with Mirabell, but he thought it best to avoid saying anything.

Derek left through the back, resisting the urge to check on Lauren. If he saw her, he'd want to talk to her; they would only argue once again. He just wasn't ready for another fight with the strong-willed woman. As he made his way down the weed-infested road that led from one village to the next, he thought about Mirabell and wondered if there was any chance for him to get her and her family out of this hellish place after he found and rescued Amanda.

Two hours had passed since Derek had left Lauren tied to the palm tree, and in that time she had experienced no end of humiliating insults. She could easily untie the rope from the tree and walk away, or even more easily work her hands free. But Derek had warned her that she mustn't do that, and at least for now, Lauren was willing to believe that following his orders was in her best interests.

She wished now that she hadn't stood and looked into *As the Crow Flies*. To see Derek with that young girl with the open blouse had fired her jealousy. She didn't want to admit she was jealous, but she knew she was. And there was no doubting his soft, sincere expression while he and the girl talked, their faces intimately close. In the end, when he gave her a coin, what was that for? Services rendered from some recent assignation? Lauren couldn't deny the possibility, especially since the girl obviously wasn't overly modest—not if she could walk around wearing an unbuttoned blouse.

Was the coin for something the girl was supposed to do later?

Lauren tried to force those thoughts from her mind. It did her no good to speculate on what Derek was doing or had done. Everything about him was a mystery . . . especially his ability to make her body come alive under his touch.

Her thoughts of Derek came to a jarring halt when Gregor and another man stopped in front of her and looked down at her with undisguised lust.

"She's a looker, ain't she, Cap'n Gregor?"

"Aye . . . a looker she is." Gregor hooked his thumbs into his thick leather belt and thrust his pelvis forward, drawing attention to it. He chuckled when Lauren quickly turned her gaze away. "The Englishman shouldn't have it so good. He wants me to believe he ain't puttin' it to this little whore, but I know better."

"What ya say we 'ave a bit o' her, Cap'n Gregor? Mr. Derek won't never know the diff'rence."

Lauren got quickly to her feet. She didn't need to deepen her humiliation by allowing them to look down on her literally as well as figuratively. Feeling their eyes devour her body made her feel sick inside.

"We might at that, good fellow," Gregor replied after several seconds. "That Englishman thinks his money can buy him every wench that tickles his fancy. Maybe it's high time we showed him otherwise. . . ."

The two laughed softly, enjoying the anger they saw in Lauren's eyes, becoming aroused by her hatred, her fear, and her beauty.

"Mr. Derek sure puts 'er in fancy silks," the pirate commented quietly. "But then, 'e keeps all his whores dressed up fine an' pretty, eatin' all that fine food an' livin' like fairy princesses."

All his women? How many women does he have . . . besides me? Lauren wondered, wanting to ask the question, but knowing she mustn't say a word now. Gregor was looking for a reason to flout Derek's wishes, and she was afraid saying anything to him at all would give him the cause he was looking for.

"Aye, mate, that he does," Gregor said, rubbing his belly, looking Lauren up and down. "If we took off her silks, we wouldn't even get them dirty, would we? And I know for a fact that Derek's gone to inspect his wenches." Gregor chuckled softly. It was a hollow, lifeless sound filled with suppressed violence. "I just got back from the Big House, an' the Big Man says I've got to put up with Derek a while longer. Just a while, though . . . then I can do with him whatever I want."

"When the time comes, can I have a piece of him, Cap'n Gregor?"

Gregor turned, patting his friend on the shoulder. "Of course you can, matey! You can cut out his liver and fly it on the flag pole, and when I'm done with this wench here, you can have her next. How's that sound to you?"

"Like an 'onor, Cap'n Gregor! Like an 'onor, indeed!"

"Good! But first you can buy your captain a drink!" Gregor shouted with a laugh, and the two men entered *As the Crow Flies* after final lustful looks at Lauren.

Chapter 9

When the women saw him approach, they all stood and rushed to the side of the large bamboo cage, all wanting to talk to Derek. Seeing their desperation sickened him; they weren't truly happy to see him because they thought he was a good man; they just considered him less of a monster than the men who guarded them.

"Afternoon, Mr. Derek," the guard said. He stepped aside to let Derek pass, knowing from past experience that the Englishman would want to talk privately with his slaves.

Derek paused a moment just to look at the nine young women. They were the prettiest of all the captives that had been taken by *The Unholy One,* and he'd demanded they be placed in his custody because he knew it was the most attractive women who suffered the worst from Gregor and his crew.

The women didn't appear to have been beaten, but Derek knew how deceiving looks could be. Whether the guard had taken sexual liberties with them was something he couldn't be sure of.

"Good afternoon, ladies," he said at last. It was hideous to see their smiling faces behind the bamboo cage that Derek had had specially built. It had a roof to keep out the rain and the sun, but no walls for privacy. "How have you been?"

They all began to speak at once. Derek held up his hand and they stopped talking instantly, each one frightened of making him angry, of displeasing him in any way.

"Have you had enough to eat?" he asked. "Have you been treated well?"

Sue Ellen, who at twenty-seven was the oldest of the captives, spoke for all the women. "Sometimes he makes threats," she said, gesturing in the guard's direction. "He says that if we don't do something for him, he won't feed us. But he never follows through with his threat. He just says it to frighten us." She glanced over to the guard, then back to Derek. "He says he's not scared of you, but we know he is."

Derek digested this information. He would like to hire a new guard for the women, but to do that would further alienate his present guard, and though the rogue threatened the women, he hadn't acted on his words.

"He hasn't let anyone in the cage? Hasn't touched you?"

Sue Ellen shook her head, sending her tangled blonde mass of hair swirling around her shoulders. Derek made a mental note to bring a brush for the women the next time he checked on them.

"Have you heard anything about where the other women have been taken?"

Again Sue Ellen shook her head, though now a guarded look came into her eyes. "We haven't talked to anyone but the guard, sir."

"Best to keep it that way." Derek opened his watch. It was past noon. He had been away from Lauren for three hours, and her welfare was weighing on him. "I've

114

got to leave now. Don't talk to anyone if you can help it. If you hear anything, let me know. Try to keep your spirits up. I'll see you again just as soon as I can."

"Yes, sir," Sue Ellen whispered. "We will."

Derek walked away from the women, finding it difficult to believe that there were actually nine women in a cage—a bamboo cage that he had commissioned.

With any luck, he could soon put them all on a boat, sail them to the United States or Cuba, and set them all free. With any luck . . . just as soon as he found his sister and set her free . . . if she was still alive . . . if this whole sordid charade wasn't in vain . . . if Gregor didn't kill him first. . . .

Lauren was astonished at what she'd heard since Derek had left. Men talked in front of her as though she did not exist. To them she was a slave, a piece of property who couldn't hear or see or think. This attitude allowed them to say things in front of her that they would never say in front of Derek. Lauren was repulsed by their attitude, but she realized that being seen as unthinking chattel did allow her to garner helpful information.

Men often stopped to just look at her, and Lauren pretended she wasn't aware of how their eyes undressed her. They spoke of Derek in tones that varied between open contempt and thinly disguised fear. The pirates all wanted to force themselves upon Lauren, but none was willing to take the risk of facing Derek's revenge.

Gregor had stayed in *As the Crow Flies* for three hours. When he came out, he swayed slightly and his eyes gave away how much rum he'd consumed.

"There's the wench that heats my blood!" he bellowed, to no one in particular, "lookin' as bewitchin' as ever!"

Lauren, leaning against the tree, looked away from Gregor, but listened to everything he said. Of all the foul men she had come in contact with since the *Miss Malaki* was overrun, Gregor was easily the foulest of the bunch, and the one who most readily sent icy fear racing through her veins.

As he moved closer, she smelled the rum on him, and the foul stench of stale perspiration. She wrinkled her nose, sniffing in disgust. It brought a wide smile to Gregor.

"You don't like me, do you, Lauren?"

He spoke her name slowly, lewdly, somehow making it sound very ugly. It was the first time he'd called her by name, and the sound of it coming from him was nauseating.

"I could make you like me. Women *always* like me after I bed them."

She knew she shouldn't say anything, but his arrogance was too enraging. "You stink of rum and sweat," she said calmly, though her heart was racing. "Do you really think any woman would be happy to be close to you, much less share a bed with you?"

Gregor grinned crookedly, stepping very close to her. "No woman has ever talked to me like that before," he whispered, his fetid breath assaulting her. "I like spirit in a whore. It pleases me." He reached out to take a thick tendril of Lauren's ebony hair between his callused fingers. "I'm not a shy man. I could take you right here and let me mates watch while I do it."

A deep male voice answered, "No, you wouldn't, because you know I'd kill you before you even got started."

Gregor spun around to see Derek standing at the front of the tavern. He wasn't holding his saber, but he had his hands pushed inside his jacket on his hips, opening the garment enough to show the dagger and

116

sheath beneath his left arm. The implication was unmistakable.

"If you were alive, maybe you'd stop me," Gregor said tautly. "*If* you were alive."

"Didn't the waitress you raped last night satisfy you?" Derek goaded. "Or maybe the rum had taken the wind from your sails."

Lauren watched Gregor's bearded jowls flex as he gritted his teeth. The look in his eyes said he wanted to torture Derek before he killed him. Then the look softened, as though he'd thought of something that pleased him greatly, and he issued a short, harsh laugh. "I can bide my time, Englishman. She'll still be pretty a week from now, or a month from now. She'll be pretty long after you're dead."

Gregor reached up to paw Lauren's breast, and in a move of blinding speed, Derek pulled his dagger and cocked his arm, preparing for the lethal throw. No one doubted he would hit his mark with the dagger. "Your hand will never touch her," he whispered.

Gregor laughed, turned away from Lauren, and walked away. Lauren breathed in deeply, suddenly aware that she hadn't breathed at all since Derek had arrived on the scene.

"Did he hurt you?" Derek asked, sheathing his weapon as he moved close to Lauren.

"No," she said. It wasn't the truth, of course. Gregor's words had hurt her, just as the words of all the taunting pirates had hurt her. But still, being hurt emotionally was not as bad as being hurt physically.

"We're going back to the hut. I imagine you're famished by now."

Lauren followed him, trailing behind like a pack mule, resisting the urge to say how much she hated being led by a rope.

It won't always be like this, she thought with fleeting

hope. *Derek promised me it wouldn't. On the other hand, what good are Derek's promises?*

Lauren had spent her entire life surrounded with all the creature comforts money could buy. Her Virginia home had thirty-six rooms, and her own bedroom suite consisted of three large connecting rooms. When she returned to the small hut that Derek had rented and felt an overwhelming sense of security and joy in being there, it was an odd revelation.

"What's wrong?" Derek asked when they returned.

"Nothing . . . why?"

"You had the strangest look on your face when you came in." He quickly removed the rope from Lauren's wrists and began to rub the skin lightly with his palms, looking for some sign that the rope had blemished her flawless flesh. "I'll bet you're starving. I'll fix you something right away."

Lauren sat on the mattress, folding her knees beneath her. It was a pleasure to feel doted on, especially by a man like Derek. He was such a mass of contradictions—one minute hard-edged and dictatorial, the next worrying whether the rope had hurt her and hurrying to meet her needs. She wondered if there would ever be a time when she would truly understand all the mysterious, intriguing facets of him.

They ate a meal of cut fruits. It wasn't the hearty meat-and-potatoes fare that Ida, Lauren's nanny, would have prepared, but it was delicious.

Lauren thought of Derek's "other women," and she wanted to ask him directly about them. Being direct, she had found, was almost invariably the best way of getting what she wanted. But she had seen Derek withdraw into his shell, pulling the walls of secrecy around

118

him, so a more circuitous approach seemed preferable.

"How was your day? Did you find out what you wanted?"

Derek shrugged, turning away from her. "Mind if we eat outside?" He picked up his plate without waiting for an answer. She followed him outside and they sat with their backs to two large trees, facing the breeze that blew in off the ocean. "I found out a few things, but not very much. There's a small island called St. Lucifer. I'd like to explore it."

"What you're looking for might be there?"

"Maybe . . . it's a long shot at best. The odds aren't very good at all, and I can't think of any way of improving them."

Lauren smiled at the poker metaphor. She had spent hours playing poker with her brother and sisters, and sometimes even her father. Her mother said it wasn't good to learn poker— especially not for a young girl— but her father taught the girls anyway, using the opaque excuse that it would teach them something about mathematics. There were times when Derek sounded much like her brother, and she wondered if the two would ever know each other, and if they did, whether they'd become friends or enemies. She suspected that whichever it was, it would be an extreme. That was just the way Clayton and Derek were.

"I heard the men talking," Lauren began, not much liking the memory of her morning and afternoon. "They talked openly in front of me. They don't see slaves as people, so they had nothing to fear."

"I'm sorry for that," Derek said softly.

Lauren nodded to acknowledge the apology, then continued. "I learned something that could prove helpful. They talked about a big man—that's what the men

119

all call him, the 'Big Man.' And he lives in what they all call the Big House. Apparently he's the man behind Gregor. That's my guess, anyway."

"You don't suppose that—"

"—the Big Man lives in the Big House, and they're both on St. Lucifer?"

For a long moment they looked at each other, contemplating the question. Lauren was the first to smile, then Derek followed suit. It was one of the few honest smiles she had ever seen him give, and it warmed her soul. She reflected that he should smile more often, and she found it difficult to remember that he was responsible, at least indirectly, for her capture, and her continued enslavement.

"Do you know where St. Lucifer is?" Lauren asked, feeling the excitement build within her, though she had little knowledge of what Derek had planned, or what his unspoken "mission" was.

"Vaguely. Enough to give it a try."

"Give *what* a try?"

Derek smiled again, reaching out to place his palm lightly against Lauren's cheek. "It's probably best I don't tell you. The less you know, the safer you'll be."

"Don't give me that nonsense! I want to know!"

Ignoring the insult, Derek said, "You've done magnificently, darling. You've accomplished more in a single afternoon than I did on my own in three weeks."

Lauren tried to stop the words from escaping, but they were too quickly spoken. "I wouldn't say you haven't gotten anything. You had that waitress mooning all over you."

Derek took his hand from her and leaned back against the tree, his eyes roaming her face, his gaze cool.

"Mirabell is different," he said in a low voice that dared Lauren to challenge him. "She's doing what she

120

can to survive in this living hell, and for that I have a great deal of respect. I can't say I wouldn't do the same thing if I were in her shoes . . . except that she's so poor that she doesn't wear shoes."

Lauren was taken aback somewhat by the force of his words, but she refused to be cowed by him. She put her foot out toward him and wiggled her toes. "If you'll pay close attention to what's attached to my ankle, you'll find that it is a foot. You'll also notice that on that foot is nothing but skin. My own."

"Don't be sarcastic."

"If you'll pay even closer attention to what's around you, you'll notice that the only people on this island who do wear shoes are your shipmates from *The Unholy One.*" Her tone steadily grew hard and angry. "The local population doesn't wear shoes, Derek. If you want to find out what's actually happening here, you've got to stop thinking like an Englishman. You're not in your blessed, *bloody* London anymore!" Lauren drawled the word *bloody* with a thick British accent, trying to annoy Derek, and succeeding brilliantly.

She leaped to her feet, her hands clenched.

"You and your damned silly English pride!" she hissed, staring down at him with dark eyes that glared daggers. "You want my help, but you won't tell me what you need help with! And then, even though I accomplish more in an afternoon than you have in God only knows how long—you've admitted that yourself—you still refuse to tell me anything significant. Now what in God's name are you doing?"

Lauren watched as his stern countenance dissolved into a smile. At first she thought he was laughing at her, and that only exacerbated her ire, but before she let loose a second volley of vitriol, he placed his hands up placatingly.

"Lauren, I give up! You win," he said, grinning,

121

shaking his head slowly, amazed that he should even consider telling her anything. "Sit down and relax. You've got to have a cool head or none of this is going to make any sense to you."

She sat, arranging the shikars around her legs, unaware of how attractive she looked in the waning sunlight. She felt the quickening of her heart, the hard beat of her pulse, and for the first time she honestly felt emotionally drawn to Derek.

"I'm looking for someone very important to me. She was on a boat captured by *The Unholy One*. I suspect she's been sold into slavery." He looked toward the sea, fighting the doubts that plagued him. Lauren looked at his profile, at the long, slender, Romanesque nose and the solid line of his jaw, and thought him an astonishingly handsome man. "I can't stop until I find her." He pushed his fingers through his sandy blond hair. The unconscious gesture of fatigue was more emotional than physical, and her heart went out to him. "She's the reason that I've been sailing with *The Unholy One*. I'm staying with them just until I find her, then I'm going to do everything in my power to put an end to Gregor once and for all."

"Who is she?" Lauren asked in a small voice, frightened by the answer she might receive.

"My sister."

The audible rush of Lauren's exhaling made Derek close his eyes. *She's glad I'm not looking for my wife,* he thought guiltily. *She may not trust me, but she has feelings for me, just as I have for her. And if I were any kind of gentleman at all I'd find some way of sending her somewhere safe. If only I didn't have Amanda to worry about, if only I didn't have Gregor wanting to cut my throat, if only. . . .*

"Tell me what you're thinking," Lauren said, interrupting Derek's torturous thoughts.

"Nothing. I wasn't thinking anything at all."

"You can stop lying to me."

Derek looked at Lauren, and she saw the walls come up to lock her out. She would learn nothing more from him, at least not now. Perhaps later, she might find out about the women Derek had hoarded away somewhere; she might find out who Derek really was, and what his life was like away from Gregor, white slavery, and the Virgin Islands. Would she ever know Derek when he wasn't haunted by nightmares? The questions tugged at her thoughts and denied her the peace of mind she sought.

Derek rose, looking out to sea. He said softly, "When the evening comes, I'll leave. If St. Lucifer has what I'm looking for, I'll be back for you and we can leave this place."

"I want to go with you," she replied, a chill running through her at the thought of the dangers Derek would face alone.

"No."

Lauren looked at him then, hating him for his stubbornness, astonished with herself at being so concerned with his safety.

I don't want to be alone. I want to be with Derek and face his battles with him, at his side, she thought.

Chapter 10

They hadn't said a word to each other for hours. Lauren stayed outside the hut, watching the waves lapping against the shore, thinking about Derek and wondering what it was she really knew about him. All she knew for certain was that she didn't want him to go to St. Lucifer. Whatever was meant by the Big Man and the Big House, it could only mean trouble, and no matter how capable a fighter Derek was, he would surely be outnumbered.

She sat and she worried, and she cursed Derek often for being stubborn and pigheaded and just plain infuriating.

"Stay inside while I'm gone," he instructed as he strode to the doorway.

Lauren flinched at the sound of his voice. She'd been so deep in thought she hadn't heard him approach. She looked at him and briefly wondered if this sort of espionage was new to him, or if he was an old hand at it. Derek had exchanged his frilly white silk shirt for a dark blue one beneath a black waistcoat. In dark clothes from head to foot, it would be harder for anyone to see him at night.

"You're leaving?" Lauren asked, unable to resist asking the obvious. Derek nodded. "And you won't let me go with you?"

"It's too dangerous," he explained.

"Too dangerous for me, but not for you. I'll pretend that isn't an insult." Lauren looked away, afraid for Derek's safety, afraid of her growing feelings for him. The sound of harsh, drunken male laughter from the village drifted through the trees. The men were close, and an idea hit Lauren with such pleasing clarity that she had to fight to keep from smiling. "If you leave me alone, I'll be defenseless against those men, if they come for me. You know that as well as I do. Gregor . . . he wants me. He wants to take something from you, too . . . and I'd hate to be raped as some twisted act of revenge against you." She looked up at him, secure in her logic. "I'd actually be safer going with you than staying here—don't you agree?"

As Derek hesitated, the raucous laughter broke out again, closer than before, and someone shouted, "We need a wench!" Derek gritted his teeth in anger, then looked down at Lauren, wondering if there was some way she could have orchestrated such an incident.

"Very well, you can come with me, but I'm warning you now: you'd better not slow me down. We've got a lot of ground to cover; keep up with me and don't complain."

"Yes, sir," Lauren replied, her smile radiant in victory. "I won't be any trouble at all."

"I've heard that kind of nonsense before," Derek muttered angrily.

They set off while it was still dusk, and by the time they'd made their way through the trees and over the rise, night had fallen. On three occasions Derek reached inside his jacket to feel the smooth handle his flintlock pistol. He hoped he wouldn't need it tonight. This was to be nothing more than a reconnaissance mission similar to those he'd operated in India, and later in Africa, during his military service. If all went well, he would find out where Amanda was being kept and then devise a foolproof plan to free her.

Derek tried not to think about Lauren being with him or about the danger he was putting her in. A dozen times he thought about giving her his dagger and telling her to return to the hut. With the dagger she would be more than a challenge to a drunken pirate. But there was always Gregor to consider: Gregor wanted her badly, and knowing that Lauren was his "property" made her all the more appealing to the renegade pirate captain.

They broke through the trees and stepped onto a long, white expanse of sandy beach. Derek stopped to see where Lauren was and nearly bumped into her because she was following so closely. He accidentally stepped on her foot, but she nimbly danced out of the way before he put all his weight down on it. He noticed that she was barefooted, and a pang of guilt bit him.

"How are your feet? Sore?"

Lauren shook her head. "I like it. As a child I was always the first one in the spring to take my shoes off. Mom and Dad and especially Ida were always yelling at me to put on my shoes. Ida said it wasn't right for a young lady to be outside without her shoes on, but I didn't care."

Derek looked at her, thinking she must have set the young boys' hearts fluttering. And what would her protective parents think of her now, dressed in sheer white silk, barefooted, traveling with a man who, was ostensibly, a pirate? He pushed the thought from his mind and tried hard to ignore how attractive she was in the pale light of the half-moon.

"The first thing we've got to do is find a rowboat," he said, more gruffly than was necessary, not at all happy with himself for noticing Lauren's loveliness at a time like this. "I figure we've got eight good hours of darkness. After that the odds start getting bloody awful."

"If we split up we can cover more ground," Lauren replied. "You go that way and I'll go this way. We'll meet here in thirty minutes."

Derek's brow furrowed. He was not accustomed to working with a partner, and he certainly wasn't used to taking orders from a woman. He surprised himself when he didn't protest, and nodded in agreement.

Twenty minutes later, Derek heard Lauren call to him. Instinctively, protectively, he drew his dagger and sprinted toward her voice. Without fifty yards separating them, he had little trouble spotting her; the shimmer of her white mitar and shikars was alarmingly visible.

I should have given her something else to wear. That white silk is too visible. Too late now . . . curse it, I should have never taken her along!

Derek slowed to a trot when Lauren called out to him again, and he could hear only happiness in her tone. As she drew closer, he watched the rise and fall of her heavy, round breasts within the mitar, and how the shikars had split with her long strides to show much of her legs. He felt an immediate stirring within him and cursed himself for the hundredth time that day for wanting her.

"I found a little boat," Lauren said, her face flushed with excitement. "It's just down around that bend. It's big enough for both of us—there are oars and every-thing!"

The boat had been made by one of the locals; it was shaped like a canoe. It had a long outrigger on the starboard side for stability in rough waters. Long and slender, it would cut cleanly through the water and not be difficult at all for Derek and Lauren to move along.

They pushed it into the water, with Lauren in front. Derek took his oar and began stroking, impressed by Lauren's skill.

"Just keep her headed toward that small island straight ahead," he whispered, knowing how well voices carried over the water. Stealing a boat from a poor islander was ignominious enough; getting caught would be doubly reprehensible. "If my guess is correct, St. Lucifer is right behind it."

"There it is!" Lauren hissed excitedly when the ominous outline of St. Lucifer became visible, bearing straight ahead. She dug her oar deep into the water, pulling even harder than before.

"Ease up," Derek said, keeping his voice down, even though they were too far away to be overheard. "I don't want you to be exhausted when we get there. There's no telling what kind of reception we've got waiting for us."

It had taken over two hours to reach St. Lucifer. By Derek's vague estimation they had traveled eight or nine miles. The return trip, with a northern wind behind them, would be much faster.

Derek watched Lauren from behind as her arms and shoulders worked to pull at the oar. He found her full, curving figure and robust spirit entirely *too* attractive, and irresistibly feminine. Watching Lauren from behind, he couldn't understand what he had ever found

128

stimulating in the white-skinned debutantes with their too-slender bodies never touched by the sun . . . and probably not by any man, either.

St. Lucifer was little more than a mile long and half as wide. On the western end the terrain rose steeply upward and was nearly impassable. Heavily wooded, with thick underbrush, it lacked any source of potable water, except for what rainwater was caught and stored.

"Where would you guess the Big House is?" Derek asked.

Lauren glanced at him, hiding a smile. Derek had seldom asked for her opinion, and she was pleased at the respect it implied. As she rowed toward the dark shoreline now less than a hundred yards away, she let her first instinct guide her.

"I'd say over there, to the left. High enough to be away from high seas, but deep enough into the woods to be protected from high winds. If the Big House was built up over there, at the highest point, it would be more difficult to carry supplies back and forth."

Derek mulled over her theory, liking it more than he wanted to admit. A thousand different things about her pleased him, and this was just one more to add to the list.

"Let's go with it," Derek said at last, whispering again as they approached the island. "Find a smooth place where we can beach and hide the boat."

They landed safely and covered the boat with branches and palms. Derek threw the last branch onto the boat, then turned toward Lauren. "It's odd," he said, speaking softly. "I've done a lot of crazy things in my life, but I've always done them alone. I can't figure out whether I'm in more danger because you're with me, or if I'm better protected."

"You're better off with me," Lauren replied, shocked at Derek's openness. It suddenly made her feel uncomfortable, and she turned away. "We'd better get started. Any idea at all what this Big House is supposed to look like?"

"None at all. I'm not even sure it exists. *You're* the one who heard about it."

"You were right about the odds being terrible," Lauren whispered.

Lauren did not believe in luck. Her father had warned her about superstitions and how deleterious they could be. "Anyone who believes in luck is a fool," was Michael Masters' gruff appraisal. But when Derek and Lauren skirted a small cluster of huts and broke through a stretch of dense undergrowth, they stepped into a clearing. There incongruous with its rustic surroundings, stood a huge, opulent mansion. "Papa, you were wrong—there really is luck."

"What?" Derek asked, confused by Lauren's whispered comment.

"It's nothing . . . just a word to my father, that's all."

Derek shook his head, muttering, "Lauren, if I live to be a thousand I'll never understand you."

The Big House lived up to its name. Two stories high and more than a hundred feet long, it was a lavish display of wealth that outdistanced anything Derek had seen on the islands with the exception of the few mansions belonging to Britishers on St. John and St. Croix. As he studied the mansion intently, he noticed there were no lamps burning inside and no sign that anyone within was awake.

"You're sure you won't stay out here as my lookout?" Derek asked.

"Positive. I'm going in there with you." She gave him a teasing smile. "I've got a vested interest in your success. The quicker you free this lady of yours, the quicker you'll free me."

Derek wanted to say that she wasn't really his captive. He wanted to tell Lauren that as soon as he possibly could, he would sail her far away from all this madness and she would never have to see him again. But instead he gave her a tight-lipped grin, stepped out from the trees in a low crouch, and headed for the Big House.

They entered through a curtained window. Once inside, Derek drew his pistol and thumbed back the hammer. The metallic sound of the gun being cocked gave Lauren a start. He smiled reassuringly at her, patting her forearm. "It'll be fine, don't worry. I'm not going to hurt anyone."

Unless you have to, Lauren thought, and quite suddenly this daring little game was no longer enjoyable and the dangers they had walked into tightened around her.

"Let's split up," Lauren whispered. "We'll meet back here in an hour. If we get separated, meet me back at the boat. If I'm not there by sunup, go on without me."

Derek grabbed Lauren's arm and pulled her to him, crushing her body against his. His mouth came down over hers in a hard, feverish kiss that surprised her, taking her breath away.

"Be careful," he whispered, his lips brushing against Lauren's as he spoke. "And don't you worry, I'll never leave this island without you. If anything goes wrong, you give a yell and I'll come running, and God help any poor soul who gets in my way."

"You just worry about yourself. I can take care of—"

"I've heard that before," Derek said crisply, cutting Lauren short. "Be careful—I mean it."

He turned away from her and stepped out of the

room, moving on silent feet, leaving Lauren to wonder about the significance of the unexpected kiss.

Lauren looked around the room. It was apparently a storage room. Linens were piled high on several racks along three walls. Alone now without Derek and his deadly weapons to ward off evildoers, she felt droplets of nervous perspiration form at her temples. She brushed her hair away from her eyes impatiently, wished that she had her special gold-and-ivory combs, which had been stolen, to keep her hair in place.

She had no idea where to start, or even what to look for. Derek had told her a little of his plans, but even his most loquacious discourse fell short of full communication.

The first room Lauren checked harbored a sleeping old man. His beard was long and white, and in sleep he looked very frail and old. He *couldn't* be the Big Man the pirates from *The Unholy One* had spoken of with so much fear and respect. Lauren moved on.

The next room held an older woman, sleeping on one side in a small bed, and two children in a bed against the opposite wall. *Servants,* Lauren surmised. *Dozens of rooms in this place, and the servants still have to double up with their children.*

One of the children pushed himself up on an elbow and looked at Lauren through sleepy eyes. "Angelina?"

Lauren put on her best smile, even though she was scared to death. "Shh! Go to sleep, now," she said in a soft-stern voice, praying the child's mother wouldn't awaken. "You shouldn't be up so late."

The child curled up beside his brother, pulled the light cotton blanket up around his shoulders, and obediently closed his eyes. Lauren shut the door and breathed deeply several times to calm herself. That had been a close one. Had the child awakened his mother all hell would have broken loose.

Lauren continued on, making her way through the first-floor rooms, not finding any of them very promising. She wondered where Derek had chosen to begin his search. She kept thinking that he moved very quietly for a big man, and she wondered if his father had taught him that, just as Lauren's father had taught her and her brothers to walk quietly when hunting game for the dinner table.

The last room before the narrow, circular stairway that led to the second floor of rooms looked promising to her. There was a small table with several thick books piled on it. She stepped inside, made sure she saw where the candle holder and matches were, then closed the door. Once the door was closed, the room was enveloped in impenetrable darkness. Blindly, Lauren walked with her hands out, taking mincing steps, mentally judging the distance she had to walk before she came to the candle. In her mind's eye it was easy to picture the candle. With a minimum of fumbling she struck a match against the desk top and lit the candle, bathing the room in a soft yellow glow.

Excitement grew thick and heated within Lauren's breast. She was scared, but she was also excited. She felt more a part of the action than ever before. Her family, the famed and powerful Masters, had faced some formidable enemies over the years. Those fights, some taking place on the legal battlefield of the courtroom, and some settled in a more direct but less civilized fashion, had always excluded Lauren. Her parents, against her wishes, protected her from such things.

She still wasn't absolutely certain whether Derek was truly a decent man trying to take down an evil man, or an evil man trying to rid himself of an enemy. That question could be answered later . . . for now it was enough for her to know she was doing her best to find information that might hurt the Big Man and free innocent young women who, like herself, had fallen prey to Captain Gregor.

She pulled the nearest book across the table and paged through it. Thankfully, it was written in English. Lauren scanned it quickly, saw nothing that directly implicated the buying and selling of women, then read it a second time more carefully. The ledger contained nothing more interesting than an inventory of the foodstuffs required to run the household. Apparently all the food consumed by the residents needed to be shipped to the island.

She replaced the ledger and picked up a second one, angling it so that she could read more easily in the thin light of the single candle. This one contained information on items of value sold at auctions. Lauren's heart began racing, thudding against her ribs. The "items" sold had a corresponding mark beside them, and on one she read *"Miss Malaki."*

This was the log that might prove the Big Man was behind the pirating by *The Unholy One!* If the Big Man was engineering the sale of valuables taken from the *Miss Malaki,* then it stood to reason he was also behind the sale of the unfortunate women taken from the *Miss Malaki!*

Lauren was just closing the ledger, intent on stealing it for further perusal later, when the door opened and the white-bearded old man she had seen sleeping stepped into the doorway. Wearing a tattered nightshirt, he looked at her through sleep-bleary eyes.

"Who are you? What do you think you're doing?" he asked in a gravelly voice. He sounded more confused than angry.

"I . . . I was just going through the records for food expenditures," Lauren said quietly, praying the lie

134

would work. "I was told they didn't match as they should."

"You're new here, aren't you?" The old man's eyes went over Lauren appraisingly, as though he was judging the quality of a horse at auction. "Why aren't you one of Mr. Mitchell's women? It pays better than being a servant."

Mitchell? Lauren wondered. Her hands were trembling, so she placed them beneath the table, out of sight.

"I don't know," Lauren said finally, afraid that the old man would begin to question her story if the conversation went on much longer. "I was never given a choice." A thought struck Lauren, and before she could let fear overwhelm her, she said, "Maybe the Big Man doesn't want me."

The man's face creased into a grizzled, weary smile. "I can't believe that," he said, his eyes once again assessing her, straying down to her rounded, taut mitar. "But as long as you're new here, let me give you a warning: If Aldon Mitchell ever hears you call him the Big Man, being a part of his harem will be the last of your worries. He'll give you to those barbarians aboard *The Unholy One,* and when they're done with you, if there's anything left, you'll get sold to some monster from Peru or Bolivia." The man grimaced at the thought. "No woman ever comes back from that. The Bolivians . . . they don't appreciate a beautiful young woman. They like to inflict pain, young lady."

"Yes, sir," Lauren replied in a whisper. "I'll heed your advice and show Mr. Mitchell only the utmost respect."

The old man grunted his approval. He didn't like Aldon Mitchell in the least, and he knew what horrors the women of his private harem went through. At first

135

this had bothered him greatly, but over the years he had developed an attitude where he didn't much care what happened to the women so long as they weren't from the islands and he didn't know them personally.

"I just wished I could be informed before they make changes around here," he muttered, as much to himself as to her. "What's your name?"

Lauren, flustered at being discovered, could not think of a suitable lie. "Lauren," she blurted out.

"Well, Lauren, go to bed. You can do your work in the morning. And remember, if anyone wakes Mr. Mitchell before noon, he takes a whip to them. You're skin is much to lovely to be marred by a whip."

The old man turned away from the door, leaving it ajar. Lauren sighed, stunned that she had actually gotten away with her ruse, frighteningly aware that she had been discovered, and that if the old man had been fully alert, her answers would have triggered more questions and her feeble lies would have been discovered.

She was thankful now for her dark hair and the color of her skin. Wearing the native attire had made it possible for her to pass herself off as a local, at least to the sleepy old man. If she'd had blonde hair, the alarm would have been sounded the moment he spied her.

Lauren picked up the ledger, blew out the candle, and left the room, carefully closing the door behind her silently.

She was standing outside the door, wondering how much time had passed since she'd first entered the Big House, when she heard a cry of alarm—high-pitched, yet definitely male—come from down the hallway. A moment later there was the sound of another male voice, the grunting thud of a fist being slammed into a soft stomach, and then the sound of a body falling hard to the floor.

Boot heels pounding against the wooden floor let Lauren know that Derek was making his way down the stairway at a dead run. Not waiting for instructions, she sprinted down the hall, heading for the linen storage room where they had entered.

"Run, damn it, run!" Derek screamed from behind.

Lauren leaped headlong through the open window, landing on the ground hard and losing grasp of the ledger. She got her knees beneath her, grabbed the ledger, and glanced at the window just in time to see Derek, with one leg in the house and one leg out the window, pull the pistol from his waistband. He shot into the darkness. Though Lauren could not see what he aimed at, she knew his bullet had hit its mark.

Oh, God, we're going to die! Lauren thought as she scrambled to her feet and began running.

Chapter 11

Derek's ears rang from the gunshot. He watched the thickly muscled man slam against the storage room wall from the impact. Even though the slug had struck him full in the chest, the man tried to raise his flintlock to shoot Derek. A second later the bare-chested young man slumped to the floor, his weapon still held tightly in his dead hand.

Derek tossed himself out the window, paused a moment, then looked inside. A second bodyguard, a dark-complected native like the first one, raced into the room. He held in his hands a short-barreled blunderbuss. Derek aimed through the window and fired. The bodyguard fell atop his friend and did not move.

Wheeling away from the carnage he had left behind, Derek saw Lauren ten yards away, facing him, holding something large and square in her hands.

"Run, God damn it!" he shouted, taking off.

Lauren turned and ran, but Derek could tell that the object she carried—in the moonlight it appeared to be a thick book—slowed her pace considerably, keeping her off balance as she shifted it from one hand to the other.

"Just keep going," Derek said when they reached the

treeline. Lauren turned off the narrow road and headed into the cover of the forest, instinctively doing what Derek wanted. "No matter what happens, just keep running."

Derek stopped at the treeline, kneeling to keep himself concealed. He looked toward the Big House in time to see lamps being lit within it. Several bare-chested, strong-bodied men raced out through the front doors carrying pistols and rifles. Paid to protect the Big Man, they were out for blood. He had already killed two of them, and they would want revenge. Their employer would no doubt make their lives a living hell as well, since they had allowed an armed intruder into his residence.

Derek raised his pistol, sending a quick shot in the general direction of the bodyguards, unsure if his bullet reached its target. All he hoped to do was slow down his pursuers long enough for him to elude them in the tangled jungle undergrowth.

In the tense darkness he almost ran into Lauren, who stood waiting for him to catch up. He cursed. "Go!" he hissed.

They ran at a steady pace, zigzagging through low-hanging branches and around trees. Derek could hear Lauren's breath coming in gulps, and he knew that the additional burden of the book—for he was now certain that that's what she carried—was taking a heavy toll on her.

"Drop it," he said, jogging behind her. "It's not worth it."

"It's . . . a ledger . . . for sales," Lauren panted. She shifted the book from her left hand to her right, then settled on carrying the book directly in front of her, using it to help block the branches that cut at her arms, shoulders and face.

"Drop the God damned thing!"

"We need it!"

They ran for twenty minutes without stopping, Derek always staying behind Lauren, afraid that one of the bodyguards would cut loose with his rifle. The bullet, he hoped, would strike him before Lauren. He wanted to take the ledger from her, but to do that would tie up his hands, and they were needed now to steady his pistol, the only real defense they had.

Derek stopped to hear how close the bodyguards were. Lauren, no longer hearing the pounding of his boot heels against the ground behind her, also stopped. She moved beside him, breathing deeply, feeling the muscles in her thighs, calves, and arms ache with fatigue.

"They're still with us," Derek whispered, his head cocked to the side to hear better. "I can't tell how many."

A male voice cut through the early morning air, shouting something indistinct in English, with a thick Danish accent. He was from St. Thomas, where many Danes had settled. A second voice followed, this one with a British accent.

"Five or six," Derek whispered, trying to gauge the location of the voices. The thick foliage and trees distorted the direction of the voice, and Derek clenched his teeth in anger. He looked at Lauren, seeing the small cuts on her forearms and shoulders. "I'm sorry I got you into this. I should have left you at the hut."

"I would have followed you," Lauren replied, clutching the ledger as though it were an irreplaceable work of art. "I wouldn't have let you go alone."

"How much further can you go?"

Lauren tried a smile, which pulled up the corners of her mouth but never quite hid the anxiety in her eyes. She knew what price she would pay at the hands of her captors if they were caught.

"I can go just as far as I have to," she said with glib confidence.

"You're a damn good woman, Lauren. The bravest I've ever known," Derek replied. "Keep heading this way," he said, pointing in the general direction of the stolen boat. "I'll stay behind you."

Sometimes Derek couldn't even see her as she hurried ahead because it was so dark, the moon occasionally hidden by thin clouds. At other times the silk shikars and mitar were so clearly visible that he could not understand how she could ever hope to remain hidden. Three times gunshots rang out, and Derek knew that the pursuers, who had split up in their chase, were shooting at each other. He also knew that there were at least ten men in the hunting party. The Big Man, Derek noted wryly, must have many enemies to need that many armed bodyguards surrounding him.

Lauren came to a stop so quickly that Derek hit her from behind, knocking her to the ground and sending the ledger flying. She gave him an annoyed look.

"What's wrong?" he asked in a rush. "Why stop?"

"Because I can't walk on water," she replied.

He grinned, helping her to her feet. He had been so concerned with what was behind them that he hadn't noticed they'd reached the shoreline, and that only miles of ocean lay ahead. He peered out at the water. From what he could judge, they were far south of where they had hidden the boat. If they took to the beach, the going would be much faster, but they'd also be more visible.

"Catch your breath, then we'll move out," Derek said, looking at Lauren, wondering how much stamina she had left. "We'll be out of here and on the water in no time. Then they'll never catch us."

The fatigue was etched into her face, though she tried to hide it. She studied the shoreline. "If they break

141

through the trees north of us, we'll be cut off from the boat." The first slender hint of sunlight was showing to the east. Once dawn broke, their chances for escape, particularly on the water, were dim. "Damn . . . oh, damn, time's running out."

"We'll make it," Derek said. He took Lauren's hand in his and squeezed it. With more confidence than he felt, he added, "Don't worry, I won't let them catch you. Just stay as close to the trees as you can. That silk reflects light like a mirror."

Lauren looked down at her shikars, then uttered an oath. Aside from the fact that the once flawless white silk was now torn in several places, and smudged and dirty in many more, it shone eerily in the thin moonlight.

"Let's go," Lauren said, new fear taking root inside her. She looked at Derek. With his dark clothes, the most visible part of him was his sandy blond hair. Picking up the ledger, Lauren prayed it was worth taking along. If she and Derek learned nothing of real value from it, the failure would be compounded by the agony she was feeling now.

They had hardly taken twenty steps in the white sand when a harsh cry rang out. "I found the woman!" the Dane shouted. "Over here! She's over here!"

Lauren dived into the trees, hearing Derek's strangled curse of frustration. Though he had been right beside her, only Lauren had been spotted, and she knew the reason.

"Go on ahead," Lauren said. "They've spotted only me. You can make it past them."

Derek shook his head, his eyes glinting with anger. "I'm not going without you," he said, his tone low and tinged with anger. "I got you into this mess, and I'll get you out of it."

Lauren looked at Derek, wishing it wasn't so dark.

Then she could see the azure blue of his eyes, see the intensity of his spirit.

"It'll be easier for you without me. I'm slowing you down," she continued in her most reasonable tone.

He grabbed her arm and hauled her roughly to her feet. "I haven't got time to argue with you!" he hissed, bending over so that his face was very close to hers. "Stop arguing with me and let's bloody well *go!*"

After that, Lauren never uttered another protest. She followed Derek, tracing his footsteps through the heavy vegetation. There was a trail through the trees, but they didn't dare use it. Mitchell's bodyguards would undoubtedly have it staked out. Their travel toward the small canoe was slow and laborious. On occasion they heard a shout from one of their followers, but not a cry that they'd actually spotted their quarry. Usually they shouted because they'd seen a shadow move, or noticed one of the many night animals that prowled the small island. Lauren could hear the bloodlust in the tone of the men when they shouted.

Her heart raced, especially when she was crouched beside Derek, hiding in the bushes as a two- or three-man patrol went by. When they were on the move, making their way slowly but relentlessly toward the canoe, she felt more relaxed. At least when she was moving she was doing something, she was taking action. The breathless waiting, the don't-move-a-muscle hiding . . . that was what made her heart pound in her chest and her pulse pound deafeningly in her ears.

"We're almost there," Derek breathed softly, his lips touching her ear as he spoke. "The boat's over there." He pointed beneath the thick tree limb at an unidentifiable shape twenty or thirty yards away.

Lauren squinted in the darkness. She could see a difference in the outline of the shadows, but she couldn't really tell if the formless object represented the hidden canoe. She was astonished that Derek had made his way through the unfamiliar jungle-like terrain—and at night!

They heard footsteps and froze. Lauren was certain her heart was pounding so hard the pursuers could hear it. The whisper of Derek's dagger being withdrawn from its sheath deepened her horror. The footsteps drew closer. Derek handed Lauren the dagger, then put a finger to his lips.

Lauren held the dagger and was vaguely surprised to see that her hand was steady, her grip firm and confident. The thought of using violence—bloody, lethal violence with a knife, the crudest and most primitive kind—sickened her, but she knew in her heart that she could not shirk it. It could be that more than just her own life was counting on it—it could be Derek's as well.

The footsteps were very close now, almost close enough to touch, it seemed. They stopped, and then the Dane said, "The woman is wearing wedding white; ain't seen the man."

An English voice replied, "Sure it's just one man?"

"Naw. Just one woman though. I got a good look at the wench a while back." He chuckled softly, and Lauren felt ice flow in her veins. "She'll be sorry she sent me on this chase and disturbed my sleep—that she will! I'll spread her out like a Christmas dinner!"

The Englishman, whose tone was more businesslike, replied, "You can satisfy yourself with her later. Let's just catch the bastards. They've been staying to the thick and away from the clear, so let's move inland. And watch your arse, my friend. We've got two good men dead already."

"The wench will pay for their deaths with her blood,"

144

the Dane promised quietly.

"Sun'll be up in an hour or two. Then we'll make easy pickings of 'em, if we don't catch 'em sooner. Just keep watch for the white. That's what you'll see."

"Aye, sir. Aye."

The footsteps moved away, and only then did Lauren realize that she had been holding her breath. When Derek started to rise, she caught his sleeve, tugging him down so that he was kneeling beside her again.

"They know we're staying in the trees," she whispered, leaning so close to Derek that her bosom touched his shoulder. She handed him the knife, holding it by the blade. He pushed it away.

"You'll need it if they catch us."

She held it out to him again. "Give it to me in a moment. I've got an idea."

After he took the knife, Lauren hesitated, took a deep breath for courage, then set the ledger down and reached behind her neck, quickly unknotting the mitar. She looked down, averting her gaze from Derek's, then removed the garment. She dropped it on Derek's thighs, then unknotted the shikars and removed that, too, feeling hot embarrassment redden her cheeks. She was thankful that it was dark enough to prevent Derek from seeing her nudity too clearly.

She steeled her nerves, picked up the ledger, then took the dagger from Derek. "Okay, let's go. We'll stay as close to the water as we can. They're not looking for us there."

Derek unbuttoned his shirt and shoved the silk mitar and shikars inside, then buttoned it again. Despite the gravity of the situation, he was grinning, and Lauren wanted desperately to slap the grin from his face.

Keeping very low, they reached the shoreline. Lauren stayed behind Derek, clutching the dagger so

145

tightly her hand began to throb. She had made the right decision in removing her luminous clothing, but this knowledge did nothing to prevent guilt from swamping her. No excuse, she knew, would make her parents understand why she was running around naked on an island ironically named St. Lucifer.

They crossed the final thirty yards at a steady trot. They removed the obscuring branches and pushed the canoe into the water. Without a word they paddled into the darkness, the canoe and outrigger cutting cleanly through the water.

Derek pulled hard on the oar, propelling the canoe further from St. Lucifer. He often checked the island over his shoulder, squinting to see if anyone had spotted their escape. No cry of discovery came, and after traveling five hundred yards he was quite certain they were in the clear.

On the eastern horizon the first pink rays of dawn were staining the sky. In an hour, anyone on the beach would be able to see for miles across the blue expanse. They had a bit further to go before they were truly safe.

As he pulled on the oar, he turned his attention to the courageous, naked woman in front of him. He watched her shapely arms and shoulders working as she paddled with long, powerful strokes. Her hourglass figure, unencumbered by clothes, ignited a spark of desire deep within him.

Don't think about her now! he commanded himself. The curve of her hips, her exquisite buttocks, the shadowy suggestion of her breast . . . the pull on Derek was stronger than any fear of capture. The desire to take Lauren there in the canoe increased, causing Derek's misbehaving manhood to grow uncomfortable within the tight confines of his breeches. Angry with himself, he took the mitar and shikars from his shirt.

A second before he was about to speak, Lauren laid

146

her oar across her thighs. She placed an arm across her breasts and turned slightly to look over her shoulder, extending a hand.

"My clothes, if you please."

He had been about to give them to her, but Lord Derek Leicester York quite suddenly changed his mind.

"What if I don't please?"

Chapter 12

"Give me my clothes, or I swear to God I'll cut your heart out!" Lauren said, grabbing the dagger on the floor of the canoe between her feet. Though she held the knife threateningly, the violence never reached her rich brown eyes.

"In a minute," Derek said. "Let me see that book you stole. If it was important enough for you to lug through the forest all night, I'd better have a look at it."

Lauren almost gave him the book. Her hand was on its way toward the ledger when she stopped and, smiling, said, "We seem to have reached an impasse. I've got the ledger and you've got my clothes."

Lauren knew she shouldn't be taking so much pleasure in this teasing banter. The frantic run for their lives through the darkness, the trees scraping her arms and legs, the sound of violent men pursuing them with murderous intent—it had all terrified her and reinforced her image of the fragility of life; it had intensified the preciousness of pleasure and happiness. She had never really wanted to feel anything positive toward her captor, Derek York. It had never been her intention to see anything good in his character or his looks.

But many things had been happening to Lauren lately that were never in her plans, and this was something she was unwilling to accept. The run for their lives, for their freedom, was at least temporarily over, and Lauren was left with energy and excitement that had to go somewhere. Right now it was turning toward the golden-haired, muscular man with the teasing grin and the cool blue gaze that swept over her with appreciative intimacy.

"Are you going to just sit there looking at me?" Lauren asked, her grin broadening.

"It's not the worst way I've ever dawdled away my time."

"Someone might see us . . . we'd better keep moving."

Derek looked around, a stone-serious expression on his face. There was nothing but miles of blue ocean in all directions. "No, that doesn't seem likely."

"If I come at you with this dagger, there won't be anyone here to protect you." Lauren twisted the knife in her hand, her gaze pointed, locked with Derek's. She turned a little more toward him, keeping one hand across her bare bosom. "You would be helpless . . . completely at my mercy."

Derek actually did want to see the book Lauren had stolen. He'd waited so long for any sign at all of where his sister might be that it was impossible for him to understand why he wasn't now demanding—actually *demanding*—to see whatever clues existed concerning the whereabouts of his captured, enslaved sister.

"Give me my clothes, Derek," Lauren continued. She turned more toward him, now almost directly facing him. Her heart was pumping, and for the first time she was acutely aware that she wanted to be with Derek right there, in the middle of the ocean, in an old canoe they'd stolen.

"Give me the book."

She twisted toward Derek and let the dagger slip from her hand. It dropped to the floor of the canoe with a *thunk!* Derek's eyes went to the dagger, and when they came back up to meet Lauren's, she had removed her hand from across her bosom. She saw his blue eyes darken with burgeoning desire. His desire for her heightened her own already rapidly accelerating passion.

"We made it," she said in a breathy whisper, her tone husky, ". . . I knew we would." She slipped onto her knees, inching her way toward him, feeling the heat of his gaze upon her. Her nipples had hardened, growing erect and tight; the warmth and moisture in her groin was a now familiar response to this man, and she welcomed the sensation. "I knew they wouldn't catch us. I knew you wouldn't let them hurt me."

Derek tried to speak, but he couldn't get his mouth to form the words. He knew that, with kisses and touches, he could make her want him; her slow advancement, so obvious in its intent, so gracefully sensual, was the most erotic feeling he'd ever experienced. His other partners had always been passive, playing the role of the seduced, never the seducer. In his blueblood English society, Lauren's behavior would be considered, even by the most jaded of men, entirely wanton and unacceptable. But at this very moment, Derek realized this woman was not like any of the women he'd ever known, ever heard about, or was ever likely to meet. Suddenly all the old rules had to change; they simply didn't apply to the bewitching Lauren Masters.

As she moved ever closer, Derek felt, rather foolishly, like a speechless teenager embarking on his very first voyage into the sexual realm. When Lauren carefully knelt on the floor of the canoe and pushed his knees apart, Derek sucked in his breath with an audible gasp. He set his oar aside, every instinct screaming at him to take Lauren into his arms. But a tiny, curious voice in his head whispered that he should wait and experience what would happen next.

"My family wouldn't approve of you," Lauren said, her gaze darting from Derek's face down to the swollen length of his phallus straining against his dark breeches. She inched closer. Her hands slipped up his thighs. She moistened her full lips with the tip of her tongue. Her throat felt tight, and there was a burning sensation within her. Lauren felt powerful and in control, and it was an exhilarating sensation. "If you really want to know the truth, I don't think I approve of you, either. But right now, that doesn't really matter, does it? Right now nothing matters but you . . . and me . . . and us . . ."

"The book . . ." Derek managed to say, his tone strained, his hands white-knuckled as he gripped the sides of the canoe.

". . . will still be there when we're finished."

The vixenish purr that came from Lauren's throat was a sound she had never made before, and it surprised her. It was a confident sound, and though all her friends back home thought she was sure of herself at all times, being the aggressor with Derek—the seducer—was not something that made her feel confident.

He reached for her breasts, unable to restrain himself. Lauren caught his hands before they reached her and placed them once again on the sides of the canoe. She did not know how long her confidence and courage would last, but she knew that if Derek touched her, she would lose control, just as she always did whenever he touched her, and that was something that she didn't want. Not yet, anyway.

Derek swallowed, his hands squeezing the rough-

151

hewn sides of the canoe. "Lauren, what in the bloody hell are you doing?"

Impishly, she gave the answer she'd always given her parents when, as a child, she was doing something she shouldn't: "Nothing," she whispered, the tips of her fingers inching up his thighs.

She was looking into his eyes when her palm ran over the prominent bulge in his breeches. She felt the heat, the hard virility trapped inside. She squeezed him, and his eyes fluttered momentarily as a wild pleasure coursed through him. Lauren purred, beginning to enjoy this new sense of power, the control she had in this spine-tingling, leisurely encounter with him. She squeezed him again and felt his manhood throb powerfully, pulsing with his life blood.

Her hands slipped upward, away from the object of her desire, over the hard, flat surface of Derek's stomach and chest until she reached the top button of his shirt. She never took her gaze from his as she slowly, with calculated leisure, opened the buttons of his shirt.

Lauren pushed her hands inside his shirt and jacket, exposing his chest. She couldn't completely remove his shirt without allowing him to remove the dagger sheath, so she abandoned her quest, thoroughly pleased with the expanse of sinewy muscle and pale skin now revealed. With some effort she tugged the tails of his shirt from his trousers and unfastened the last of the buttons. Derek's body was flexed, the muscles in his arm, chest, stomach, and thighs knotted with suppressed tension.

"Your hands aren't really very callused," Lauren said softly, in a casual tone that belied the racing of her heart. "But you're body is hard . . . hard and lean, like a working man's body. Why is that?" She blushed when

152

she wondered whether Derek knew she was talking about *all* of his body and not just one particular part of him.

She wasn't really interested in the answer, and she didn't get one. Lauren repositioned her knees beneath her and leaned forward to kiss his chest, then move higher to kiss his chin. His beard stubble was prickly against her lips. She decided she liked it; it gave him an earthiness quite different from his fine silk shirts and his magnificently tailored jackets.

Derek started to reach for her, but once again Lauren stopped him. She returned his hands to the sides of the canoe, kissing his throat as she did so. As she arched her back, the tips of her breasts brushed against Derek's stomach, sending a shiver through her.

"You're such a handsome man," Lauren commented softly, leaning back to sit on her heels.

She opened Derek's shirt wider, letting her eyes roam over him appreciatively. She scratched his nipples with her thumbnails and felt Derek tense.

There was no getting away from what had to happen next. Lauren looked down, seeing the thick length of Derek's masculinity straining against his breeches.

She thought she should know everything about Derek, but as her hands fumbled somewhat clumsily with his belt and the buttons of his fly, Lauren realized that she really didn't know Derek's body very well at all.

He raised his hips invitingly. Lauren hesitated, her confidence vanishing at the implicit request, but returning as quickly as it had left. She tugged down his breeches and undergarment, and he sprang free. *He's so big,* she thought, realizing this fact yet again. Lauren swallowed dryly, unsure, quite suddenly, if she could continue.

153

She placed her hands lightly on his hips, looking into his eyes. "Don't stop," Derek whispered. "Please. . . ."

She touched him very tentatively, with just her fingertips. Derek groaned; his phallus twitched. He tried to speak, couldn't, then sighed. Lauren took him in her hand, feeling his heat, the fierce, raging hardness of his desire. . . .

"Beautiful . . . body," she whispered, testing him with her hand. She leaned forward, kissing his chest. "Beautiful . . . man!"

She flicked her tongue over his nipple. His phallus leapt in her hand. Leaning forward to kiss his mouth, Lauren felt the firm tip of his manhood brush against the smooth inner slope of her breast. Emboldened by his obvious pleasure, she rubbed his solid phallus back and forth over the tips of her breasts. To Lauren, it seemed a wickedly erotic thing to do. The feel of his searing hot maleness against the sensitive tips of her breasts made Lauren's desire, her anticipation of fulfillment, soar to heady levels.

Lauren had intended to do more, to experiment with this object of desire that had propelled her into a world of ecstasy that she had not realized existed until she met Derek. She had wanted to take her time, to peruse him, touch him, taste him, explore the mysteries of his body, just as he had explored hers. But when she cupped her breasts, trapping Derek's arousal between them, he groaned and lifted her bodily onto his lap.

"Now!" Derek hissed through clenched teeth, his large, strong hands at Lauren's waist, raising her, guiding her onto his lap.

She felt him enter her in one long, thick plunge. She tossed her head back wildly, feeling the ends of her jet hair tickling the sensitive flesh of the small of her back. With a primitive, abandoned cry of ecstasy, she

154

impaled herself upon him, shivering with desire as he pulsed hotly within her.

"Kiss me!" Lauren cried out, pushing her fingers through Derek's hair, hugging his face to her breast, demanding, now, the delirious sensations he had taught her to crave.

Chapter 13

Amanda hugged her knees to her chest, trembling with fear and hope.

The gunshots had woken her from an uneasy slumber. At first she wasn't even certain that it had been gunfire that had shattered her sleep. The following shots, and the cries of anger and excitement coming from the direction of the Big House, let her know that perhaps—just *perhaps*—her prayers had finally been answered.

Something was happening—precisely what, she could not say. What she did know was that Aldon Mitchell, the devil incarnate, was not as all-powerful as he wanted everyone to believe.

Something is happening! she remembered.

Huddled at the window, peering into the ebony night, Amanda found herself conjuring up several scenarios to explain the gunfire. Each one culminated with her brother Derek rescuing her from her imprisonment.

Unfortunately, she had no certain way of knowing if it really was Derek causing all the commotion. Since her capture, Amanda had no source of information other than Aldon Mitchell, and the other women in his private harem who had been captured after her. But she believed, as only a sister who adores her brother can, that Derek would eventually come for her. It was this belief that had strengthened her through her ordeal, that had kept her heart strong and her spirits from deflating entirely.

She had been at her lowest emotional point, and had even contemplated suicide earlier that day. Now, with the haunting echo of gunshots piercing the night, her hopes soared and she felt truly alive for the first time since her capture.

Something is finally happening!

Whatever that something was, it couldn't be good for Aldon Mitchell, and whatever wasn't good for Aldon Mitchell must surely be good for her, and for the rest of the captured women he had.

"Can you see anything?" Amanda asked Chantell, the only other woman in the room who had the courage to go to the barred window and look out.

"No."

"It's Derek . . . it must be."

"Who's Derek?"

"My brother."

"How do you know it's him?"

"Because he wouldn't rest until he found out what happened to me. By now my family has to know that our ship was overtaken by *The Unholy One.*" Amanda took Chantell's hand and squeezed it, trying to give her friend some of the confidence that she now felt flowing in her veins. "I know Derek. I knew he'd come for me, and this is the proof that I've been waiting for. It's like a dream come true."

Chantell scowled. She had been a captive too long to hope for miracles. "I don't believe in dreams," she said under her breath, then crawled from one mattress to the other to get to her own sleeping spot. "Go to sleep now. Whatever is happening out there doesn't include you, and you'd best be happy it doesn't."

"Yes, it does . . . I'm *sure* of it."

"Don't get your hopes up. It only makes it harder when you get knocked down again."

Amanda refused to allow Chantell's cynicism to affect her; it was only a matter of time before Derek showed up to rescue her.

Curling up on her mattress, she silently prayed none of the gunshots she heard would find their way to Derek. When Amanda was a child, she had seen Derek as her invincible big brother; as a young adult, she now knew that nobody—regardless of title, wealth, or even luck—was invincible.

Aldon Mitchell was in high dudgeon, and looking for an outlet for his rage. His home—his *sanctum sanctorum!*—had been violated. There were two corpses piled in one room with blood all over the floor, and nobody had any answers as to what had happened or why. He had checked his valuabies and nothing was missing . . . so what the hell had happened?

"We'll get 'em next time, sir," the Danish body-guard said, standing at casual attention in Mitchell's office. "You can count on it."

Mitchell looked at the Dane, and the look alone silenced the man. Mitchell had hired the man because he was particularly savage, and his loyalty could be bought rather cheaply, so long as women and rum came with the deal. Beside the Dane was the English-man, who was sometimes capable of savagery, but who was not innately savage.

"Let me see your gun," Mitchell said. The Dane pulled the weapon from his belt, handing it handle-first to Aldon. Aldon sniffed the muzzle and guessed that it had been fired once or twice. "You fired two shots and didn't hit anything. *Hmm* . . . I wonder if I can do better."

The Dane's brows pushed together in confusion. "Sir?"

"Do you think I can hit anything with your gun?"

"I suppose, sir. Depends on the target."

Aldon Mitchell calmly raised the pistol and fired a shot point-blank into the Dane's chest. The young man crumpled to the floor without a sound. The acrid smell of cordite permeated the room. The Englishman's face paled; he was convinced that he was about to be executed as well.

"That man failed to do what I paid him to do," Aldon said calmly. "Furthermore, he said he'd get the intruders *next time. There won't be a next time.* " Aldon handed the weapon to the Englishman, looking the frightened bodyguard straight in the eye. "There won't be a next time. Is that understood?"

"Perfectly, sir."

"Get this garbage out of my office, and clean up the mess."

"Yes, sir. I'll handle it personally."

"You do that. And this is your last warning. If anything like this ever happens again, you'll be the one lying on the floor."

Aldon turned away from the Englishman and walked to the window. He had already completely dismissed the Dane from his thoughts. That was a problem that no longer existed.

"Round up the local women," Aldon said softly. "You say she looked like a local?"

"We didn't get a good look at her, sir. Dark hair, though, and wearing clothes like your ladies wear."

"Make sure none of the wenches have escaped," Aldon said. "If none have, I want every woman on this island who even vaguely resembles the woman who came here last night brought to me for questioning." He turned toward the Englishman and there was death in his eyes. "I want answers, and you're going to get them for me. I want them before the day is out . . . understand?"

"Aye, sir. If the women of this island know anything, they'll tell me. And if they don't . . . they'll wish they did."

Aldon Mitchell nodded his approval, then left the room. He would check for himself to see if all of his private stock of women were still with him. If they were, then he would take pleasure in their bodies. That might soothe the raging desire to spill blood that burned in the pit of his stomach.

Aldon Mitchell slipped off the seat of the two-wheeled carriage. He took a moment to adjust his white linen jacket and made sure the crease in his trousers was perfect. He always dressed immaculately as a sign to others that he was a special man deserving of special treatment. His carriage—the only one of its kind on any of the small islands—was also a sign of his stature. There were, of course, plenty of horses and carriages on the major islands of St. Croix, St. John, and St. Thomas, but on all these small islands, his lacquered black carriage and coal-gray mule marked him as a man of distinction.

He needed to feel special this morning. His home had been violated, and the perpetrators hadn't yet been caught. He wouldn't rest until everyone responsible for the incident was dead.

"Master, we await you," the old eunuch said, bowing low as Aldon approached his lavish second home on the island of St. Lucifer. This wasn't as large as the Big

House, but it was still considerably larger than any other island domicile. It was here that Aldon kept his private harem, and with the exception of an occasional hour or two of bookkeeping concerning the buying and selling of stolen goods, he never worked when he was at the harem house.

A runner had been sent ahead to warn the servants and eunuchs that the master would soon arrive and that he was not in pleasant spirits. The attitude of the servants was even more obsequious than usual. Aldon wordlessly passed the eunuch without a second glance.

He went to his pillow room, the largest in the house. It was strewn with pillows and mattresses for his comfort and libidinous convenience. Inside, four women awaited his arrival, all dressed in the finest silk mitars and shikars money could buy. Aldon paused and looked the women over, deciding that he wanted his satisfaction privately, not in public. His first thought was to go for Amanda, the pretty blonde one, but he discarded this thought. Though she no longer protested his advances, she didn't show the enthusiasm he desired.

"You, come with me," Aldon said in a deep baritone, pointing a finger at Chantell, the attractive French girl. He knew her sexually uninhibited ways were a ruse, a role that she played for him like an actress on a stage, but she played the role with skill, and if he closed his eyes he could make himself believe he was really as skilled as she said he was.

Chantell rose without hesitation, her eyes downcast. He took her hand and led her out of the pillow room into his private bedroom. There, just maybe, Chantell could make him feel all-powerful, special in a thousand different ways, perhaps even godlike.

* * *

Derek studied the ledger, sure he hadn't missed anything on the first and second readings, but too desperate for news concerning his sister's whereabouts to allow any chance for error.

He sighed, running his fingers through his hair. No matter how many times he read the ledger, he still wouldn't find anything indicating Amanda York's whereabouts.

"Find anything?" Lauren asked softly. She had watched the look of disappointment spread over Derek's face, but she had to ask.

"Nothing . . . not a damn bloody thing about her."

"I'm sorry—truly I am."

"It's not your fault. You tried, and the truth of it is, you've gotten more than I have. *I* was the one who alerted the guards, not you."

Derek closed the ledger, then tossed it into the water.

"We'd better hurry," he said, picking up the oar. "News travels fast between the islands."

Gregor was in a bad mood for the simple reason that Aldon Mitchell was in a bad mood. The boat from St. Lucifer arrived early in the morning, while Gregor was still nursing his hangover, and it hadn't been good.

It was always bad to have Aldon Mitchell angry. The Big Man had a way of venting his anger on anyone who happened to be close by, and Gregor was often too close to escape punishment, even if he had had nothing to do with what ignited Aldon's anger.

He paused as he silently moved toward Derek's hut, watching, listening carefully. When he heard nothing, he approached the hut and looked through the window opening. Derek lay on his back on a small straw mattress, with Lauren's head cradled in his left arm.

Gregor smiled, thinking, *So he's been spreading her thighs after all!*

Gregor pulled his cutlass from its scabbard and went to the door. He quietly stepped inside the hut, not wanting to awaken Derek. Having the upper hand on the arrogant Englishman was something that happened so rarely, he was determined to make the most of it.

The sound of a flintlock's hammer being brought back to firing position stopped Gregor. Derek's right hand was beneath the light blanket that covered him and Lauren. Derek hadn't moved a muscle, hadn't opened his eyes. Gregor wondered if he'd actually heard the threatening sound or merely imagined it. He took another step.

"Your next step is your last step," Derek said, his eyes still closed. His tone was almost friendly, as though he'd just said "Good morning" instead of issued a threat.

"I knew you were keepin' the wench all to yourself," Gregor hissed, wanting to rush forward and run Derek through with his cutlass, but knowing he'd never make it without catching a bullet for his attempt.

"Okay, so now you know. That doesn't change anything." Derek opened his eyes and looked at Gregor. He moved the gun, tenting the blanket so that there could be no doubt that he had the drop on Gregor. "She's mine. Only mine. I don't like sharing my women, especially not with the likes of you." Derek eased his arm out from beneath Lauren, resting her head gently on the pillow. He rolled away from her, keeping the loaded flintlock ready in his hand. "What are you doing here?"

Gregor sheathed his cutlass. Another time he would use it on Derek. He could be patient for now. "It's pay-up time. You've got a cage full of women you've been promising to pay for. The man's coming for his money now."

"I want to meet him."

"Nobody meets him. I told you that."

"I still want to meet him." Derek got to his feet, nodding toward the doorway. He guessed that it was about noon, and he didn't want to disturb Lauren's sleep. "Outside."

"One o' these days you're going to give me one order too many," Gregor whispered menacingly.

"One of these days you might be right, but it won't be this day. Outside . . . she had a long night."

Derek saw the expression on Gregor's face turn from anger to lascivious curiosity about what Lauren had been doing all night to make her sleep past noon. He wanted to take Gregor by the throat for his thoughts and throttle him.

I've got to get her away from all this. I can't keep Gregor at arm's length much longer, Derek thought with dark certainty.

He waited until Gregor finished with his usual insults and vague threats. When he was nearly finished, Gregor added, "The price of your wenches has gone up. It'll be double."

"I thought we had an agreement."

"We did, but we don't now. And for that one inside, it'll be triple."

Derek's expression never really changed, but he knew he was in trouble. His purse was not bottomless, and he doubted he had enough money left to pay twice the amount for the nine women he had locked away in the bamboo cage. Which of them would he have to set free to be sold into slavery? The thought of it was appalling.

"If that's the way you want it, I can't argue with you,"

164

Derek said calmly. In his days in London he had negotiated hundreds of deals, and last-minute changes and demands were nothing unusual. But this time he didn't have a battery of attorneys working on his behalf, with a sound legal system to strengthen his position. "But you won't get a single crown until I see the man I'm paying." Derek grinned crookedly. He was bluffing, and he aimed to make the most of it. "And while we're at it, I want to see the rest of the stock. My client has quite an appetite for women. Maybe I want some of the women I've passed up."

"You can forget it, Englishman!" Gregor hissed, his hand tightening on the haft of his cutlass. "The Big Man don't see nobody."

"Fine. Then the deal's off." Derek fixed Gregor with a cold blue stare that said he meant every word. "How happy do you think your so-called Big Man is going to be when you tell him he hasn't made a single sale? If I can't have all the women I need, I'll find them somewhere else. It's all or nothing, Gregor. Make your play."

"You're a son-of-a-bitch!"

"I'm a *rich* son-of-a-bitch, which is much, much better than being a *poor* son-of-a-bitch," Derek replied softly, moving closer to Gregor, forcing the shorter man to look up. "You've made your grandstand play by upping the ante; I've made mine. Let's just hold our positions and see which one of us gets his stones cut off by the Big Man, shall we?"

Gregor's face turned as red as his beard. "Someday, Englishman . . . someday *soon!*"

Gregor stormed off. Derek sighed and let his shoulders droop for a second. He had called Gregor's bluff, and now there was no way of backing out from the commitments he'd made. The moment Gregor thought Derek couldn't afford to pay for the women was the moment Derek's life was no longer protected by his bluff.

"And just how many women *do* you have stashed away, Mr. York?"

Derek turned to see Lauren standing in the doorway, a cross look on her face, her arms folded tightly over her chest. She wouldn't listen to reason, Derek suspected. Her posture told him as much.

"Too many," he answered, wondering if there was some way to send for more money from his London bank.

"Were there too many women before you acquired me, or was I the straw that broke the camel's back, so to speak?" Lauren's words were thick with malice and betrayal.

"It's not what you're thinking."

"You're a liar, Mr. York. A handsome liar, a skillful liar, but just the same, a liar." Her eyes were hot with scorn for the man whom, in the early morning hours of that day, she had seduced. "It's been quite a few hours since you've had me. Is it my turn to satisfy your lust again, or are you going to have one of the other women you've *acquired* satisfy you?"

"I've never touched them . . . not a one!"

Lauren's brows raised above dark, mocking eyes that concealed the hurt she felt. "Oh, I see—am I supposed to be flattered that you decided to have me? Of course, it must have been easy for you, me being tied up and all. You knew that sooner or later I'd get tired and forget the kind of monster that you are, and that before I really knew it you'd be taking my clothes off." She made a soft self-derisive sound. "I played it just as you knew I would, didn't I? Just one more silly little naive wench who closes her eyes and pretends that if a man makes love to her he must love her."

"Shut up!" Derek hissed, closing the distance

166

between them. He grabbed her by the arms and shook her hard. "Don't talk that way! Don't you *ever* talk that way about yourself, do you hear me?"

Lauren looked at him blankly. There was no fire in her eyes, no intensity . . . just a sad, resigned, dull glaze that tore at Derek's insides.

He pushed her into the hut, his anger rising.

"What difference does it make what I think or say?" Lauren asked. "It's only what you want that counts. That's why you haven't told me what you're really doing. Did you think I'd believe that story about searching for someone? Actually, I did—for a while." She pushed Derek's hands from her arms. "So you're going to buy all the women Gregor has captured, huh? Do you think you're man enough for what, twenty women? Thirty women? And this man that you buy for—is he man enough to handle all your castoffs? Will I like him? Is there anything special I should know about him before you give me to him?" She laughed at herself mockingly. "What difference does it make? I'm sure he'll teach me the things in bed that he likes, just as you have."

"Nobody is ever going to touch you, damn it!" Derek's hands clenched into fists of rage. He hated the way Lauren was talking about herself. The thought of any man touching her filled him with a fury that was frightening in its vehemence, and this revelation did not sit easily with him; he had never before concerned himself with a woman's past or future sexual partners. "Nobody . . . ever!"

Lauren went to the mattress, stretching face down on it, cradling her head in her arms, not looking at him.

"I'm going to get a little more sleep, if that's all right with you. If I've got bags under my eyes from lack of sleep, I won't be worth as much on the auction block, will I?"

167

Staring at her back, Derek cursed himself hatefully. Lauren had overheard his conversation with Gregor, and although it had destroyed his credibility with her, Derek knew he mustn't confide in her. He had already endangered her too much. The more he told her the greater the danger was, so even though he knew she hated him for the misconceptions she now believed, he could do nothing to convince her of the truth.

A plan began to take shape in Derek's mind. Though still vague and wholly unformed, it offered the chance to *act* against circumstances rather than *react* to them. He didn't want to leave Lauren alone—there were a thousand things that could happen in his absence, and none of them were for the better—but he saw no other way around it. He would wait until she was asleep, then make his move.

Chewing on his lower lip, Derek watched Lauren's gentle movement as she breathed, hoping she would be asleep before long.

Chapter 14

The homecoming of Phillip Masters, eldest son of the Masters of Virginia, with his young bride Angela and their son, Michael Nico Masters, was a joyous event. Phillip had been in Greece for nearly three years, and even the normally taciturn patriarch of the family, Michael, was ebullient in his affection at the reunion.

"Such a baby! Such a beautiful baby!" Ida, the elderly black nanny, purred, holding the child in her heavy, maternal arms. Silver tears dribbled down her rounded cheeks. To the rest of the world, Ida was just a slave nanny, but to the Masters, she was the aunt or grandmother they'd never had.

Always perceptive, even under such happy conditions, Phillip saw tension in his father's eyes. Something was wrong. As soon as he could, Phillip politely pulled his father into the library and closed the door behind them.

"What is it?" Phillip asked, pouring brandy into snifters as Michael sank his long, lean body into a leather chair near the unlit fireplace.

"It's Lauren."

Phillip groaned, and Michael shot him a look.

"Before you say 'What now?' let me remind you that

you were once young and impetuous," Michael said.

His headstrong younger sister was always getting into trouble of one kind or another. But his father was right: Phillip had caused his parents a fair amount of worry and sleepless nights, but now that he was married and had a family, his roustabout days were behind him. It was easy to forget what it was like to be young, single, and with few responsibilities.

"What's she done now? It's not that creep she thought she was in love with, is it?"

Michael shook his head. "He's finally out of the picture, thank God. She wanted to take a trip, do something to get him out from under her skin. At first your mother and I didn't think it was a good idea, but you know how determined and persuasive Lauren can be. She didn't let up until we gave in."

Phillip grinned broadly, and his face was a picture-perfect replica of his father's thirty years earlier. "Lauren always *could* twist you and Mama around her little finger." He chuckled at his father's cross look. "I guess some things never change."

"She wanted to do something for Masters Enterprises. She had a plan to open up markets in the Virgin Islands. It actually made a lot of sense—"

"Lauren made sense? Business sense?"

"—so your mother and I gave her permission to go. Ida is too old to take such a trip now, so we hired a chaperon to attend her."

Phillip sat down in the chair facing Michael's. Not even brandy could numb the cold stab of apprehension that was slowly spreading in his stomach.

"And?" Phillip nodded. It was always difficult to get his father to say much of anything, and urging him on most often got precisely the opposite response, but curiosity and fear were becoming stronger with each passing second.

170

"We haven't heard from them for some time now." Michael sipped his brandy, his eyes staring off into space, his mind contemplating all the possible courses of action he could take to find his daughter. "It doesn't surprise me that Lauren hasn't sent us a telegram. She's never been good at keeping in touch with us. But Miss Nichols would surely send us word."

A muscle flexed in Michael's lean cheek. He sipped his brandy, then chewed a knuckle for a moment before continuing. "Something has gone wrong. I can feel it in my bones."

"Let's take a boat and go down there, Papa. Hell, we've got the men, and we've got the money to do it. We'll turn the islands upside down and shake them until Lauren falls out."

Michael shook his head. "Not yet. If we go to the Virgin Islands and nothing is wrong, Lauren will know we don't trust her. You know how proud she can be. Things between Lauren and myself have been . . . strained . . . since that gigolo."

Phillip didn't bother to tell his father that Richard really wasn't a gigolo. An opportunist and a bigamist, certainly, but no gigolo. And though Phillip now saw himself as a respectable businessman, husband, and father, he was thinking about tracking down the man who had broken his sister's heart, and repaying him with a broken nose, and maybe a broken arm or two.

"What can we do now?" Phillip asked, his voice low.

"Wait. At least for a while longer, we just wait." He issued a half-smile, and pride showed clearly in his eyes. "I'm glad you're home again. I've been needing you at my side."

"Angela and I will stay until we get this mess straightened out. Don't worry, we'll have Lauren back in no time."

Michael nodded, saying with only a little conviction,

"She's probably lying on a beach somewhere with twenty servants catering to her every whim and wish, sipping cool wine and nibbling on fresh strawberries. . . ."

They spent several hours in stony silence. Lauren lay on the thin mattress, her face to the wall. She was pretending to sleep, but Derek knew she wasn't, and Lauren *knew* that he knew.

The conversation between Gregor and Derek kept chanting over and over in Lauren's mind.

The facts were all so very simple . . . and so very damning. Derek had many women that he intended to buy. He had said as much to Gregor. If he couldn't buy all the women he needed from Gregor, then he would simply go elsewhere. To Derek and Gregor, women were a commodity, *things* that were bought and sold at whatever price the market dictated.

I'm not a thing! I'm a woman, and you can't treat me like this! she thought, furious.

This angry thought gave Lauren no comfort, because it was immediately followed with: *Yes, you can, you bastard. Money is the only law here. If you've got money, you can do whatever you want.*

A hundred times she saw herself back in the outrigger canoe, naked, moving toward Derek, touching him, wanting to please him. She saw herself responding to his touch, willingly abandoning everything her parents had tried to instill in her.

In all her life she had allowed only two men to touch her. One left her feeling cold and violated; the other had made her feel more alive than she'd ever dreamed possible. But in the final analysis she knew she'd actually been violated by both men. She'd been deceived, lied to, and used. Derek would one day

172

sell her to the man he worked for, and then he would find another woman gullible enough to believe his lies.

It was all quite devastatingly simple.

"I'm leaving," Derek said suddenly, cutting into Lauren's torturous thoughts. "I'll be back later. Don't go anywhere." Lauren turned to him, her eyes filled with mistrust. He placed his dagger on the ground near her. "I'll leave this with you. If anyone comes while I'm gone, don't try to talk your way out of trouble—just use the knife. It's all that these men understand."

"Where are you going?" Lauren bit her lip. She hadn't intended to ask Derek anything, since he probably wouldn't tell her the truth anyway, and it really shouldn't matter to her what he was going to do.

"I want to talk with Mirabell. Maybe she's heard something that will help us. There's bound to be some backlash for what we did last night. I've also got to see Gregor." Derek pulled his pistol from his belt, checked the load, then returned it to his waistband. "Just stay here until I return. And you might want to get back into your own clothes. The less you look like you did when we were on St. Lucifer, the less chance there is that someone will recognize you."

For long moments their gazes locked. Lauren thought of Mirabell and how pretty she was, and how any man would be attracted to the slender girl who tended to the drinking desires of the pirates at *As the Crow Flies* with a blouse she left unbuttoned.

"Have fun," Lauren said with quiet malice.

She received an angry look from Derek, but nothing more. He left her alone in the hut, unbound, the dagger on the ground beside her.

I don't care if he wants to make love to Mirabell. I don't care what he does or doesn't do, because he means nothing to me at all.

173

Another inner voice amended immediately, *Yes, you do!*

Lauren spent five minutes alone in the hut feeling sorry for herself. After a few minutes, which was all the time she had allotted herself for useless emotions, she bolted to her feet and stripped off her shikars and mitar, then grabbed the torn and dirty dress she'd been wearing aboard *Miss Malaki* when it was overtaken by *The Unholy One.*

The bodice of her gown was ruined. The buttons were missing, and even if she did put the gown on, it wouldn't do very much to hide her bosom. Angrily she tossed the gown aside and threw open the lid of Derek's steamer trunk. She felt like a thief going through his possessions, and the feeling did not sit well with her.

Derek's stolen my pride, my dignity, my passion . . . that gives me the right to steal from him, she thought.

She removed a navy silk shirt and dark trousers. The night before, she had been spotted because she was wearing white silk. It was a mistake she wouldn't make again.

The trousers were tight at the hips and loose at the waist, and she had to roll up the cuffs several times. She used the dagger to cut the rope that Derek had used to bind her wrists, and used it for a belt. The shirt was baggy on her, the sleeves way too long. Uncomfortable with nothing beneath the shirt, Lauren put her mitar back on, then replaced the shirt, rolling the sleeves up to her forearms.

The outfit would have to do.

The moment it was dark enough, Lauren left the small hut. Stepping outside, the lethal little dagger clutched in her hand, she felt an overpowering sense of freedom. This was the first such moment she'd had since the capture of *Miss Malaki.* Lauren breathed in deeply, unsure of what she intended to do next, certain only that whatever the night held in store for her, she would be taking charge of her own life instead of waiting and hoping for some faceless, unseen hero to come to her rescue.

At first she started toward the village. The urge to know what Derek was doing with Mirabell was strong, but she resisted it.

To hell with him! He means nothing to me, she thought, trying hard to convince herself it was true.

She found a narrow, winding path through the trees and began to follow it. Wherever she was going, it was away from the hut Derek would return to, which meant that it had to be in the right direction.

The sudden rumbling sound of male conversation and laughter made Lauren's heart leap in her chest. She ducked behind some trees. The three men, who passed a bottle of rum among them as they walked, passed without noticing her. When they were far enough away for safety, Lauren stepped back onto the trail and continued her aimless journey.

She saw the glow of the small campfire first, the flickering light eking through the dense foliage. Instead of making a wide arc past the possible source of trouble, something compelled her to continue forward cautiously. What she saw made her stomach turn.

The women, nine of them, were in a bamboo cage. The man who guarded them held a bottle in one hand and a cutlass in the other. He was saying something to them, speaking in tones too low for Lauren to hear. He waved the cutlass often, weaving a little on his feet.

Like animals . . . those poor women are caged up like circus animals. . . .

Lauren squeezed the hilt of the dagger. Could she use the knife against the guard? She had seen so much violence lately . . . could she resort to similar violence, even for a greater good?

A sickening feeling came over her as she imagined what it would be like to use the dagger on the guard. She closed her eyes and shook her head.

She tucked the dagger into the rope belt at the small of her back, then began crawling on her hands and knees, searching for a rock. The first rock she found was much too heavy; the second wasn't large enough to have the impact she would need. She found a tree limb that had been cut to a three-foot length, apparently for firewood. Lauren held the limb in both hands, testing it, swinging it a little up and down. Yes, she thought, this will do the trick. She remembered striking Derek over the head aboard *Miss Malaki,* and the memory brought a grim, humorless smile to her lips.

The guard was still talking to the women when Lauren moved closer. She could hear now what he was saying, and the suggestions he made to the women sickened her. She wondered whether the dagger and not the club was what he really deserved.

She approached him slowly, from behind. The guard continued his foul, obscene dialog with the women. The more Lauren heard, the more she knew that she could go through with whatever violence was necessary to subdue him.

She was twenty feet from the guard when the first woman noticed her. Lauren pursed her lips, indicating she needed silence, but that didn't prevent the young captive from clutching onto her friend's arm and gasping in surprise.

The guard reacted to the warning, but his reactions were slowed by rum. Lauren made her move, leaping forward, rushing at a dead run, raising the club over her head with both hands.

She issued a warlike scream, a piercing, instinctive battle cry, and it shocked the guard as much as her presence. Long accustomed to cowed, frightened women, he looked at the onrushing woman in men's clothing as an aberration, something to be ridiculed, not something to be frightened of.

The club was lancing downward with crushing force toward the man's head when he finally realized the full extent of Lauren's threat. If the guard hadn't raised his cutlass in a blocking move, he'd have been instantly knocked senseless.

His cutlass prevented the club from hitting him, but he was knocked savagely to the ground by the force of the blow, his cutlass stuck deep in the wood. He tried to wrench his cutlass free and in doing so nearly pulled the club from Lauren's hands.

"What's wrong with you, wench?" he demanded, twisting on the ground, dislodging the blade from the wood. Lauren stumbled toward him. He reached for her and nearly caught her long, ebony hair.

Lauren stepped back, her heart pounding, holding the wood tightly in both hands. She had hoped to make quick work of the man; now she had a fight on her hands that she wasn't certain she could win. She pulled the club back over her shoulder, preparing to swing; the guard held the cutlass out in front of himself, ready to jab it straight forward. He was grinning, and Lauren knew he had much more experience at fighting than she did.

"Come on, wench!" the man taunted, poised on the balls of his feet for balance and mobility. The rum made his bearing wobbly, but he had been drunk often enough to not be thoroughly disoriented by the influence of the rum. "Come an' git me! I won't hurt you! Come on an' try!"

Lauren inched closer. She had to get close enough to use the club and somehow stay out of range of the deadly pointed tip of the cutlass. She wanted to drop the club and run—run for her life and save herself, abandoning the women in the cage. Perhaps she would have even done that if she hadn't heard the cheering of the women captives and thought about what their lives must be like, living in a bamboo cage with this foul man watching over them, saying filthy things to them.

Rum and Lauren's beauty had made the guard impatient. He wasn't interested in killing this crazed, stunning woman who wore man's clothes; he wanted her alive. All he had to do was get the club from her, then wrestle her to the ground.

He smiled. It would be easy. And once he had her on the ground, the pleasure would be immense.

He rushed her this time, sure that she would swing at him with the club, sure that he would block the swing with his cutlass. He *knew* that this was what she would do, and that he would get inside the arc of her swing and get his hands on her.

For a split second, when the guard had moved past the outward range of the club, he thought, *This is too easy!* Then the woman, instead of swinging for his head as anticipated, swung for his leg. He tried to get his cutlass down in time to block the move, but he failed; the club came crashing down with brutel force against the outside of his knee.

His leg buckled. The guard screamed an animal sound of rage and pain. He was still screaming, raising his cutlass to put an end to this madwoman's life, when she spun completely around and the club slammed into his jaw, just beneath his ear.

He didn't even groan as he pitched forward, face down in the dirt.

Lauren knelt near the man, touching his neck. She could smell the rum on him and it sickened her. But no amount of hate she had for the man could make her wish him dead, and when she felt his pulse—faint, but steady and regular—she breathed a sigh of relief.

The women were all talking to her at once. "Get the key! The key's in his pocket!" was the most common refrain.

Lauren patted the man's trouser pockets, then his shirt pocket. She found the long, oddly shaped skeleton key there and brought it to the gate of the cage. The lock was rusty, and it took a moment before Lauren could work the corroded tumblers free.

She looked at the women as they streamed out of the cage, thinking they were all attractive, all half-mad with fear.

"Is any of you named Amanda?" she asked.

A young woman with waist-length red hair and frightened, pale green eyes replied, "I will be Amanda if you want me to. Just don't lock me up again and I'll be anyone you want."

"Don't worry, I'm getting you away from here. Nobody's ever going to lock you up again," Lauren replied, though she had absolutely no idea of what to do with the freed captives now.

A woman who introduced herself as Sue Ellen knelt near the unconscious guard, inspecting him. For a moment Lauren thought Sue Ellen would take the cutlass and kill the man, but instead she just muttered a curse under her breath.

"You should have killed him," Sue Ellen said quietly.

The rest of the women began talking to Lauren, and Sue Ellen said commandingly, "Quiet!" Eight women were instantly quiet. Sue Ellen looked at Lauren and asked, "Now where do we go?"

Lauren hadn't planned for this to happen, but she sensed that the women needed leadership from her. She picked up the cutlass, her mind spinning in confusion, looking at each of the women in turn, giving herself a few precious extra seconds to think.

"I know of a cave where you can hide," she said,

remembering a small cave that she'd run across the previous evening, when she was searching for a canoe to steal. "You can stay there, at least for a little while."

The pretty redhead whispered, "We'll never make it. They'll find us somehow."

"Stop that!" Lauren snapped, her dark eyes fierce and frightening. "I don't want to hear such talk! If you think you're already defeated, then you will be." Lauren moved closer to the girl, looking her straight in the eyes, saying with a biting tone that brooked no dissension, "Just do exactly as I tell you and you'll get away from here. You'll be free . . . but only as long as you *believe* you'll be free." And then, remembering something that Derek had told her long ago, she added, "I can't help you if you fight me."

The young redhead lowered her face, blinked away tears of relief, and nodded.

"Let's go." Lauren started away from the empty bamboo cage and the unconscious man, hoping she could find her way back to the cave, having absolutely no idea what she would do once she got the women there—if she got them there at all. "Follow me, and don't make a sound," she cautioned.

Even Sue Ellen, who was not one to take orders, did exactly as Lauren said, sensing the young woman's confidence, drawn in by her innate, natural sense of leadership.

Chapter 15

Derek felt icy fear tingling in his veins. The guard sat near the small fire, holding his head in both hands. His jaw was swollen, distorting his features and slurring his speech, though the rum certainly contributed to his lack of diction.

"Where did they go?" Gregor demanded, his hulkish body towering over the guard. *"Where,* damn you?"

"I told you, Cap'n Gregor, I didn't see where they went." He looked up at Gregor with eyes that pleaded for understanding. "I was at my position, jus' like Mr. Derek paid me to be, and then I get hit from behind! I didn't see nothin', nohow!" It wouldn't be at all acceptable to admit being bested by a woman, so the guard left that little detail out.

"You didn't see a thing then?" Derek asked, moving beside Gregor.

"No, Mr. Derek, I didn't see nothin'!"

Derek walked away, trying to think of who could have freed the women. The guard had no idea how long he had been unconscious, so there was no way of knowing how far away the women could already have gone. Derek was certain of only one thing: The women were now in much more danger than they'd been in in the cage, where the threat of his retaliation kept the pirates at bay.

"You stole the goddamn wenches!" Gregor hissed, his round, heavy face crimson with anger as he approached Derek. "You stole the whole lot of 'em, and I'm going to cut your liver out for it!"

"Don't be a bloody fool! If I *did* steal them, where the hell would I put them? *You* run everything on this island. Even *I* can't get off the island without you providing the boat." Derek had never seen Gregor quite so angry, and he wasn't at all certain he could delay the inevitable showdown between them. He stood ready to go for his dagger. "Maybe you freed them yourself," Derek continued, taking a new tack. "You upped the cost of them. Maybe you're trying to get even more money for the women, and this is all just part of your ploy."

Gregor growled, the animal-like sound grating through yellow, clenched teeth. He held his dagger in a huge, tight fist.

"There'll be no payment to you until I get all of those women back in the cage—safe and sound . . . and untouched." Derek stared hard at Gregor, unsure of what leverage he now had over his nemesis. "You don't get one crown from me until they've all been returned."

"And *I* say you *stole* the wenches!" Gregor twisted the dagger in his hand. "Maybe if I start cutting pieces off you you'll tell me where you had 'em put."

Derek knew that if he reached for his dagger or cutlass, the talking would be over with and the bloodletting would begin. Even if he *did* kill Gregor, he couldn't kill every pirate from *The Unholy One* who happened to be on the island. Gregor's crewmen wouldn't stop looking for him until they got him . . . and killed him.

"Why don't you stop making idle threats and put together a search party?" Derek suggested in a faintly condescending tone. "This island isn't that big. You've got enough men to find them. Without the women, you don't get paid . . . and how long will it be before the Big Man decides that maybe someone else can handle your job better than you have?"

Derek saw the implications of the escape registering in Gregor's brain. A mixture of dread, hatred, confusion, and rage distorted the pirate's features. Spinning sharply, Gregor yelled, "Get the men together! I want every inch of this island searched! I want every wench brought back to *me* before morning!"

"I've claimed the women," Derek said, moving closer to Gregor. If the women were taken into Gregor's custody, he couldn't protect them. "They're mine, and I don't want you or your men touching them."

Gregor smiled wickedly, smug with power. "They ain't yours, Englishman, until you pay for them, an' like you say, you ain't paying for anything you ain't got!"

Lauren was sitting at the edge of the mattress, dressed again in the white native clothing, when Derek returned to the small hut. Her eyes were bright with excitement, her face flushed from exertion. Upon seeing him she leaped to her feet and started toward him, stopping only when she noticed the grim expression.

"What's wrong?" she asked quietly. She'd never seen Derek look quite so haunted. "Have you found your sister? Has something happened to Amanda?"

"Everything has gone awry." His troubled mind quietly registered that Lauren was unaccountably winded from exercise, but he was too obsessed with the beautiful young women now free and roaming the island to question why Lauren was out of breath.

"Those I am trying to protect are in far greater danger now."

Lauren moved close to Derek, standing behind him as he poured red wine into a goblet. She wanted to comfort him, put her arms around him, and reassure him that everything would be all right, but she sensed that she couldn't scale the emotional walls that surrounded him.

"I don't understand," she said in a whisper. "I thought you needed to find your sister."

"I do . . . but some lunatic released the women from their cage. If I'd found Amanda earlier, she might be out there with them, being tracked like a fox by the hounds, running for her life."

A chill passed through Lauren. "What are you talking about?" she asked slowly and quietly. *"What* lunatic?"

"We don't know . . . anyway, it's not important for you to know."

Lauren placed her hands lightly on Derek's broad shoulders as he sipped his wine. She felt a twinge of anger at him—once again he had casually dismissed her from his troubles . . . but this time she was afraid she was the cause of them.

Derek took another sip of wine and closed his eyes briefly as he inhaled deeply to compose himself. "What are you so happy about? Tell me, Lauren. I need some good news to cheer me."

Lauren's voice was steady, despite her apprehension. "I left while you were gone. I wanted to help you find your sister, so I went out on my own. I didn't find her, but I found other women. They were in a cage. A beast of a man was guarding them, taunting them. I couldn't just leave them there. I hit the guard with a club and set the women free." Derek turned slowly, his silvery eyes burning, his sensual mouth now a thin,

184

cruel slash across his face. "They were being treated like animals!" Lauren rushed on, seeing the rage build in Derek's face. "I had to do something! I couldn't just leave them there!"

"You fool! You bloody damned fool!" Derek spun away from Lauren, tossing the expensive, gem-encrusted goblet to the floor. He took several steps, needing the distance from Lauren to quell a mounting urge for violence. "Those were *my* women you set free! *Mine!* Where have they gone? Where did you take them?"

"Your women, Derek? I thought all you hoped to accomplish by being with *The Unholy One* was the rescue of your sister."

"If I can protect others without endangering Amanda, then that is what I will do! I am honor bound as an English gentleman to do no less!"

Gentleman? Lauren made a derisive sound. "I set them free!" she said in a low voice that rang of triumph. "They were slaves in that cage—*your* slaves! Now they're free women, and God willing, they will stay that way!"

Derek rushed to Lauren, taking her forcefully by the arms. She saw the rage in his soul, but she did not back away. Her ebony gaze locked with his. She was certain now that all Derek's words had been nothing but attractive lies, wrapping around an ugly truth. He was a white slaver, just as she had first suspected. He now had but one captive—her—and Lauren was willing to sacrifice her freedom to save all the others.

"You fool," he hissed again, staring down at the spirited young woman who had the cursed ability to enrage him as no woman had. "You put those women in greater peril than you can imagine. I had claimed them for myself because they are young and lovely and therefore would be the most abused by Gregor and his

185

crew. In that cage they were safe from Gregor's men, who knew I would cut them down like the rabid dogs they are if the women were touched. Now I have no claim on the women, and if they are found—*when* they are found—they will suffer in ways you cannot imagine."

The impact of Derek's words hit her with staggering force, and for a moment her knees shook. She might have fallen if his hands hadn't been holding her by the biceps.

"I wanted only to help," Lauren whispered. "As God is my witness, I wanted only to help."

Derek chose his words carefully, his anger making him hurt Lauren with his tongue so that he might not hurt her with his hands. "On this island there is no God, and good intentions get you nowhere. You've turned those women loose in hell."

Derek's grip on her arms slackened. Lauren stepped away from him, her mind spinning. "I know where they are," she said softly, devising a plan even as she spoke. "We can get them all back."

"Where?"

"A cave I found the other night. I took them all there."

Derek rubbed his eyebrows, pleased beneath his anger by Lauren's courage and audacity, even though the end result was possibly disastrous. "You'll be the death of me yet," he said, strapping his saber around his lean hips.

Lauren smiled at the comment, but her happiness was short-lived. She believed that in freeing the women she had openly endangered them further—she had no doubt about it. What she did not entirely believe was Derek's claim that he had caged the women only to protect them from the ravages of Gregor and his men. Was his volatile anger the result of losing nine of his most beautiful slaves? Or was he truly concerned with the welfare of the women?

Until Lauren knew the answers, she knew she could never trust Derek, nor take any pleasure in his embrace.

Derek remained near the window of the hut, his face impassive, his eyes cold and hard. He had been there for three hours, silent, unmoving, staring at the man hiding in a thicket of trees not far away. Lauren's gaze remained on Derek, never moving from him. She could feel his lingering anger, sense the betrayal he still felt toward her for having freed the caged women.

Lauren hugged her thighs tighter to her chest, her chin on her knees. *It's unfortunate that he's so good looking,* Lauren thought as she studied his profile from across the room in the darkened hut. *I might not have been so affected by him if he was an ugly man—ugly like Gregor.*

It was Derek's continuing anger that convinced Lauren that he was indeed guilty of being a white slaver. Lauren had freed the women, and now Derek would lose the commission he'd had hoped to make from their sale. It *had* to be money—and the loss thereof—that had made Derek so angry. In the three hours since Derek had returned and said such cruel words to her, Lauren had gone through a hundred possible explanations in her mind over who and what her "captor" really was. Her worst fears were the only ones that withstood her internal cross-examination. As much as she wanted to believe otherwise, she finally had to admit to herself that she had lost her heart to a dishonest, evil man.

Derek rubbed his eyes. Fatigue was etched deeply on his face.

"Why don't you get some sleep?" Lauren asked softly. In the dead silence of the hut, her voice seemed unusually loud. Derek looked at her, saying nothing, his expression unreadable. "I know you're angry with me. You probably even hate me. But right now none of that matters."

"What *does* matter to you?"

Lauren couldn't hear the faintest hint of affection in Derek's words. If he hated her, there was nothing she could—or *should*—do about it now, she told herself with flagging conviction.

"It matters to me that those women not get caught by Gregor's men."

Derek nodded, his eyes cold as ice. "Apparently you've changed your opinion of me."

"No. You're just the lesser of two evils. One bad man is less heinous than a dozen bad men."

Derek smiled wryly, without humor. "That's honest."

"Why don't you get some sleep? I'll keep an eye on the guard out there. If he goes away, I'll wake you." Derek looked at Lauren as though weighing her words. His doubts further irritated her already raw nerves. "I *promise* I'll wake you. You won't be any good to anyone if you're dead on your feet."

Derek nodded, and without a word, stretched out on the mattress and cradled his head on his forearms. "Keep your eyes open. If anything happens, if anything changes, wake me right away."

He was asleep in seconds. Lauren took Derek's position, but after confirming that the ill-concealed guard was still on duty, she paid more attention to the handsome man sleeping only a few feet away.

Lauren thought of the women and what they must be going through. Were they still in the small cave, keeping quiet and staying put until she returned for them, just as Sue Ellen promised they would? Or had fear gotten the best of their better judgment, making them search for a boat to take them far away somewhere—anywhere? Had Gregor's men already found them?

When she looked out the window again at Gregor's sentry, she saw that he was now leaning against the trunk of a tree, his head slumped to one side in sleep. A smile creased her mouth as she stared hard into the shadows, watching him intently. When she was certain he was asleep, she moved away from the window, unsure of what to do next, knowing only that she had to do *something*.

She knew what she should do, of course—awaken Derek.

But in her entire life Lauren had seldom done what she was supposed to do.

On graceful feet she crept to Derek's clothing chest and silently raised the lid. She needed to get out of the white silk shikars and mitar if she was to make her way to the cave unseen.

She found a second blue silk shirt with long tails in front and back that came down to mid-thigh. It would do nicely. It was not as modest as she would have liked, but that was a minor consideration compared to everything else she had endured in the past few days.

She stuffed her discarded shikars and mitar into Derek's steamer trunk and carefully closed the lid. He still hadn't moved. When she checked the window again, she saw the sentry's body sprawled in the shadows.

Lauren waited at the doorway, searching the shadows for the second sentry. She knew if she was caught by Gregor's men, Derek would be powerless to stop them from taking whatever they wanted from her.

Don't think about that now, she reminded herself. *Think only of succeeding!*

She stepped outside . . . then ran like the wind, her

bare feet silent against the grassy trail winding through the trees.

Something isn't right.

The unconscious thought brought Derek awake instantly. Without moving any more than necessary, he rolled onto his side and withdrew his dagger.

What's wrong?

He looked to the doorway where Lauren was keeping watch on the guard—but she wasn't there. He looked around the small, dark hut. She could have fallen asleep, curled up in a corner somewhere, too angry to sleep beside him on the mattress.

"Lauren?" he called softly, but got no answer. He sat up, holding the dagger tightly in his hand, now fully awake, his senses alert. "Lauren? Are you here?"

Curses welled up inside him. She was gone! The bloody woman had *left* him!

A bitter smile curled the edges of his mouth. He shouldn't have been surprised that she'd *escaped,* which was the appropriate word for what she'd done. She believed he bought and sold women, saw her chance to get away from him, and left—no, *escaped.*

The heavy weight of responsibility pulled at Derek's soul. Now she, too, was in as much danger as the women she had freed from the cage. The thought of Lauren being trapped by Gregor, being mauled by his foul hands, sickened Derek.

He raced to the door. The sentry was there, standing beside another man. He listened carefully, hearing something about Gregor and what he would have done if he'd caught the sentry sleeping. The first sentry patted his replacement on the back, said he owed the man a drink, then headed toward the village. His replacement sat cross-legged against the tree. In the

190

moonlight Derek watched him bring a bottle to his lips.

I never should have gotten close to Lauren, Derek thought bitterly. *I let what's between my legs do my thinking instead of what's between my ears, and now she's in worse danger than ever! I'm not one bit closer to finding Amanda. Damn me to hell and back! If Gregor or any of his men so much as messes Lauren's hair, I'll kill them . . . I'll kill them all.*

In a blinding realization, Derek knew that he hadn't simply "gotten close" to Lauren, he loved her as he'd never thought he could love any woman. She considered him the worst enemy she could possibly have; she could never truly love or trust him; and unless he found her before Gregor's men did, he would never be able to live with himself.

With the deadly dagger in his right hand and the cutlass in his left, Lord Derek Leicester York stepped into the night, walking quietly toward the sentry. He had no idea where Lauren might have gone, but he had to find her before Gregor's men did . . . or die trying.

It went easier than Lauren thought it would. Only once did she hear anyone else moving about in the night, when three pirates from *The Unholy One* passed her along a path. One carried a torch, and all three talked in loud voices, alternately complaining about the job they'd been given by Gregor and bragging about what they would do to the nine women when they found them. As before, Lauren hid in the underbrush until they'd passed.

She found the beach and went straight to the spot where she and Derek had parted to search for a canoe. From there she found the cave without making a wrong turn, even though it was very dark, and the moonlight was dimmed by thin clouds.

"I'm back," Lauren whispered, standing several feet from the mouth of the cave. "It's just me. Don't get nervous."

Sue Ellen stepped into the entryway, a haggard smile on her face. "I knew you'd come back for us. The others were getting scared, but I told them not to."

Lauren clasped hands briefly with Sue Ellen, then stepped into the dank cave. The women sat huddled against the far wall. Lauren wrinkled her nose at the smell of stale saltwater and the stench of decaying sea vegetation. She wondered why she hadn't noticed the smell before.

"We've got to go back," Lauren said as the women gathered around her. They protested in clamorous unison, and Lauren put up her hands to silence them. "You've got to trust me," she continued. "Derek's not a bad man. He had you in that cage so that you'd be protected from Gregor and the others. Derek didn't mistreat you, did he? He didn't abuse you or let you go hungry, did he?"

"He sails with *The Unholy One* and puts us in a cage," a woman said in a hard-edged voice, slowly shaking her head as she spoke. "That ain't sounding like a good man to me! Now you want us to just go back to him? Have you lost your mind, or just changed sides?"

"I haven't done either," Lauren continued, knowing she had to lie if she was to protect the women. "Derek's a good man! He's only trying to help you! If you come back with me, he *can* protect you. If you don't, Gregor surely will find you, and you will all wish you *were* back in that cage!"

For ten minutes the argument went that way, with Lauren not really believing that Derek was a good man, but sure that she would never get anywhere by claiming that he was the lesser of evils; the women pro-

192

claimed that death was preferable to continued enslavement. Sue Ellen, Lauren noted, had stepped away from the group and said nothing, listening intently to what everyone else said.

"I say she's lying! Lying like a dog! She's been sharing Derek's bed, and that makes her no better than he is! She was the one who got us out of the cage, and now she wants to put us back in it. What kind of sense does that make?" The most insistent of the women looked at Lauren with ill-concealed contempt. "She's Derek's whore, nothin' more and nothin' less. What good is the word of a pirate's whore?"

The words bit into Lauren's soul. Was that how these women actually saw her—as Derek's whore? She didn't like the accusation.

"I'm telling you the truth," Lauren said. "Whether you believe it is up to you. But if you *don't* do what I tell you, you'll get caught, that I can promise you. Gregor's men won't stop looking until they find you. You'll *never* be free until you leave this island, and I don't see any way for you to sail away from here without a boat. Do you have a boat? One big enough for all of you? And if you did, do any of you know how to sail it? Where would you go? How long has it been since you've had food or fresh water?"

Sue Ellen stepped forward, elbowing her way through the women to stand beside Lauren. "I believe her. Everything she's said so far is true. We can't hold out forever, and if we stay in this cave, we'll die of thirst and starvation. If they're going to sell us, they'll have to take us somewhere else eventually. Maybe then we can escape. Without a boat, and food and water, we haven't got a prayer. I'll take my chances with Lauren and Mr. Derek."

"Maybe you've got an eye for Mr. Derek yourself?" The women looked hard at Sue Ellen, then at Lauren.

193

"I'm sure he'll like bedding the two of you. Men are like that, the rutting pigs! Sell your soul if you want to, Sue Ellen, but don't ask me to follow you into hell!"

In the end, it was only Sue Ellen, the oldest and wisest of the women whom Derek had "claimed," who believed she was better off with the devil she knew than the devil she didn't.

"It'll be light soon," Lauren said as they stepped out of the cave. "We've got to be back at the hut before dawn."

They hadn't gone forty yards from the cave when they heard a coarse, male shout. The cave had been discovered. Crouching, moving toward the treeline near the shore, Lauren and Sue Ellen watched as pirates, some still carrying torches, but all brandishing long sabers, screamed in wicked triumph, racing toward the cave from all directions.

"God have mercy on them," Sue Ellen whispered, kneeling beside Lauren.

Tears of guilt and frustration burned into Lauren's eyes, and she angrily wiped them away with the back of her hand. "On this island there is no God," she said, parroting Derek's words. "We can't save them now. If we don't hurry back to Derek, we won't even be able to save ourselves."

Chapter 16

Derek watched as the women were paraded past *As the Crow Flies*. It was easy to see that they had suffered greatly since being recaptured by Gregor's men. Derek held the haft of his cutlass, searching the line of women for Lauren.

She's not with them! he thought joyously, but was able to keep the pleasure he felt from showing on his face. *I knew she was too clever to get caught! I bloody well knew it all along!*

He had been on a mad search. Adrenaline had somehow kept him going, although he had gotten no sleep and had eaten very little. Now, seeing the defeated looks of the women, seeing the triumph on Gregor's face, Derek was overwhelmed with fatigue. For now, Lauren would be safe. Gregor's patrols had all come in to celebrate the "great victory" of recapturing the beautiful women.

Derek counted them again: eight. He counted them a third time, then paid closer attention to their faces. Sue Ellen wasn't among them, and this pleased him. She had always seemed like the brightest of all the women he'd kept caged.

"Not even a good word for finding the lost sheep?"

Gregor asked sarcastically as he approached.

It surprised Derek that Gregor used an allusion from the Bible, and it made him wonder what in Gregor's past had turned him into the man he was now. "Thank you," he said with faint conviction. "I was afraid I'd have to leave here empty-handed."

"You'll have your women, all right, but not right away." Gregor smiled crookedly, showing yellowed teeth, his eyes bright and hateful. "No, Englishman, this time you'll have to wait your turn if you want the women for yourself." Gregor moved closer, holding his deadly cutlass, not pointing it at Derek, but nevertheless making his threat very clear. "You got a problem with that, Englishman?"

"Yes, I do," Derek replied calmly, looking down at Gregor, wondering when he would finally have the chance to cross swords with the pirate. "But I won't do anything about it now. Soon enough you won't be working for the Big Man, I'll have the women I need to satisfy my employer's needs, and then—I promise you—we'll find out if you're as skilled with that cutlass as you are at making empty threats." Derek's icy blue eyes narrowed, and he leaned down, his face very close to Gregor's. "You'll find me more sporting competition than the old women you usually challenge. I'll be more difficult to defeat than the captains you've had walk the plank."

For several seconds they just stood and stared into each other's eyes, hating one another, wanting to cross their swords and find out once and for all which of them was the more deadly.

"I can be a patient man," Gregor said at last, taking a half-step away from Derek. The knuckles of his fleshy hand were white as he gripped his cutlass. "I can wait if the waitin' is worth it." Gregor looked toward his men, many of whom were drinking already, surrounding the

196

women they'd captured. "Go back to your dark-haired wench, Englishman. Enjoy her. While you do, remember that there'll come a time when I'm the man who slides between her thighs . . . because I promise you, she won't leave this island until I taste her charms."

Derek laughed with false confidence, though the thought of Gregor and Lauren together nauseated him. Though Gregor did not know it, Lauren was out there somewhere, hiding in the bushes, not knowing where to turn or what to do. She had eluded capture this time, but she couldn't evade them forever. Somehow Derek had to find Lauren before Gregor did.

"Drink your rum," Derek said, turning away from Gregor with distaste. "I've got better things to do than listen to your empty talk."

As soon as Derek was far enough away from *As the Crow Flies,* he doubled back, stepping away from the path and into the trees. He watched Gregor talking to Bones, saying something that clearly did not please the young pirate. Gregor was assigning Bones to sentry duty outside Derek's hut.

"Bloody hell," Derek muttered, turning back toward his hut.

If he didn't get some rest, he'd never have the strength to continue his search for Lauren. And with Gregor and his men celebrating the capture of the escaped women, this was the perfect time to get some sleep, since Lauren would not be in immediate danger.

He was a few feet from his hut when he felt the tingling in the pit of his stomach—the feeling that let him know something was not right.

Believing his instincts, Derek pulled his cutlass and held it defensively. He pivoted slowly, inspecting the surrounding area, searching the vegetation for the danger his intuition warned him was there.

He waited for more than three minutes, just standing, looking, listening. He could feel the powerful presence of someone near, but couldn't place the source of the danger or its exact nature.

And then, in a blinding epiphany of understanding, he realized that Lauren was in the hut, waiting for him to return. He had nothing *logical* to tell him this was so; he had only that which he believed instinctively.

He stepped into the hut, finding Lauren and Sue Ellen huddled in the far corner near his steamer trunk, their expressions hinting at the horrifying situation they had been through.

"Thank God you're alive, you bloody fool," Derek hissed, rushing to Lauren. He tossed the cutlass aside, then reached down and pulled her harshly to her feet. His arms wound tightly around her, crushing her voluptuous form to the muscled surface of his chest. "I was so worried!"

Lauren had expected anger from him, not this. His mouth came down hard, slanting over hers, kissing her with all the fury of a man who had been afraid the woman of his dreams had been nothing more than a fantasy. She pushed against Derek, trying to break the kiss and turn away from him, but he would have none of it. He held her so tight Lauren could hardly breath. Despite her misgivings, despite her doubts, despite even the dampening presence of Sue Ellen only inches away, Lauren was incapable of denying Derek's kisses. The seeping, sensuous inner heat came to life, starting from a point deep within her, creeping outward until the heat tingled even in her toes and the tips of her fingers.

"You beautiful, brilliant fool! I thought you'd left me forever," Derek whispered, breaking the kiss for only a second before claiming Lauren's mouth again.

He traced the outline of her lips with the tip of his tongue, and Lauren moaned softly with approval. Her

198

hands slipped loosely around his waist, her fingertips lightly tracing the line of his ribs through the sheer fabric of his silk shirt. She felt the melting heat of his body and dimly thought how scandalous it was for her to be wearing nothing but Derek's thigh-length blue silk shirt.

The kiss deepened, and just when Lauren was certain that she would pull the buttons off Derek's shirt to free herself from even the mildly restricting clothes she wore, he pushed her away, smiling broadly, and looked down at Sue Ellen, who had watched the entire scene with an expression of incredulous shock.

"How did you get away when everyone else was captured?" Derek asked.

"I followed Lauren's advice. She said the best thing we could do would be to come back here so you could protect us from Gregor and the other pirates."

Derek's blue gaze gleamed with satisfaction as he looked from Sue Ellen to Lauren. Summoning all her effort, Lauren reminded herself that Derek was a white slave trader—a man who profits from the sale of women—and the best that he could ever be was less evil than Gregor and his crew.

"You should be safe here," Derek said. "The men are celebrating now. As long as you stay quiet and away from the door and windows, the sentry will never see you. Later on I can say that I captured you myself."

Sue Ellen's expression hardened. "I'm not going back to some bamboo jail," she whispered, as though the declaration was an oath that would not be broken, even under penalty of death. "I can't go back. I'll lose my mind, don't you see? I can't spend another minute there."

Lauren took Sue Ellen's hand and squeezed it reassuringly. "You won't have to go back. I promised you that, didn't I?"

Sue Ellen smiled back, but there wasn't much faith in the smile. She curled her knees beneath her and sat in the corner of the hut once again, retreating to the one spot in the world where she felt safe.

Lauren allowed Derek to take her by the hand to the far side of the hut where, when whispering, they would have some measure of privacy.

"She must be scared out of her mind," Derek said, his back to the wall, looking over Lauren's shoulder at Sue Ellen. "How did you manage to escape?"

"The guard fell asleep. When he did, I changed into your shirt and went after the women. Most of them wouldn't believe that they were safer with you than on their own, so they refused to return with me. Only Sue Ellen would listen."

"She's the only one who's free right now."

"Not free," Lauren corrected briskly. "She's your captive."

"If I'm so bad, why did *you* come back?" Derek shot back with equal venom, getting tired of fighting everyone, especially Lauren.

She turned away from him. It was ridiculous to think he could be anything but evil! When he first saw her as he stepped into the hut, his blue eyes had literally glowed with happiness; moments like that made Lauren forget what kind of man he really was.

He forced her to face him, pulling her body in so close that her breasts pressed warmly against the iron surface of his chest. "Look at me!" he hissed through clenched teeth. "Do I have to take a riding crop to your backside before you listen to what I tell you?"

Lauren's brown eyes spit flames of unbridled hatred at the words. She defiantly stared up into Derek's taunting gaze, her small hands clenched into angry fists at her sides. "Take a riding crop to me, eh? I guess the notion shouldn't surprise me, considering what kind of man you are!"

Derek chuckled mirthlessly. After all the worry and danger he had lived through since he'd discovered that Lauren had left him, it felt good to have her voluptuous body warm and wriggling in his arms, her round breasts firm against his chest, her special scent filling his senses and making his head spin dizzily.

He felt himself growing erect and knew that he had to put some distance between himself and Lauren soon or she would know the true extent of his happiness at seeing her again.

"Settle down, Lauren," Derek said, forcing the smile from his mouth, though it continued to make his eyes twinkle mischievously. "Sue Ellen needs her rest, and if you'll look, you'll see that she is, at this very moment, sleeping on my—er, *our*—bed."

Lauren looked over her shoulder and groaned. Sue Ellen was stretched out on the mattress, curled up on her side, her face toward the wall. Lauren turned again in Derek's arms, trying unsuccessfully to put some space between them. The heat of Derek's chest felt good against the sensitive tips of her breasts, and that was exactly the kind of *good* that Lauren was now determined to stay away from.

"It's not *our* bed," she said tautly. "It might have been at one time, but it definitely isn't now."

"Oh, really?" Derek arched a blond brow above a dazzling blue eye, smiling mockingly at Lauren. "And you're so spiteful that your nipples aren't hard right now, are you?"

Lauren flushed crimson. She felt the heat suffuse her neck, shoulders, and face, and at that very moment she hated Derek more than she had ever hated anyone.

"Yes!" she hissed, furious with him, and angry with

201

herself for having such a traitorous body. "All right, it's true! But so what? That's got nothing to do with *anything!*"

"Wrong—it's got everything to do with everything," Derek said in his deep voice, his left arm pulling her tighter against him.

His right hand slid past the gentle curve of the small of Lauren's back until he cupped her buttocks, squeezing the firm, muscular flesh through the tails of his own silk shirt. She closed her eyes briefly, stifling a moan of pleasure, knowing in her heart that she craved Derek's touch, and knowing too that it was his touch that stripped her of her better judgment and clouded her ability to distinguish right from wrong.

"Don't," Lauren whispered, turning her face away from him as he tried once again to reclaim her lips in a searing, tongue-touching kiss. "Derek, don't . . . Sue Ellen . . . she's so close."

"She's asleep," Derek replied tersely, the blood racing hot and virile in his veins. "She doesn't matter. Nothing matters right now but you and me and this moment we have together."

He tried to capture her mouth again, and she avoided his kiss by keeping her face turned away. When he grazed the silken arch of her throat and the moist tip of his tongue trailed up to her earlobe, Lauren moaned throatily again, arching within the circle of Derek's arms, shivering as the passion in her soul continued to escalate, fueled by the touches and caresses of the man she should by all rights hate.

"Stop it," Lauren whispered with little conviction when he caught the tender, sensitive lobe of her ear between his lips and sucked it into his mouth. His right hand simultaneously slipped beneath Lauren's shirt-tail, coming up quickly to squeeze her naked buttocks and force her to press intimately against his thigh.

202

"Damn you, Derek, I don't want you to *do* this!"

He chuckled softly, moving his body in a subtle and erotic way that at first Lauren was unaware of until she realized how excited she felt. He kept her pressed tight against him, her legs surrounding one of his, a smooth silk shirttail against moist, heated flesh at the V of her thighs, tingling nipples flattened against sinewy chest muscles.

"I want you now," Derek whispered, nibbling softly at Lauren's earlobe. He reached lower, allowing his fingertips to graze very lightly against the moist entrance to Lauren. Her sigh convinced him that she was not immune to his charms, but he still sought her unqualified capitulation before he could continue. Derek was not, as Lauren suspected, a rapist, and he would never be one.

An inner voice whispered to Lauren, *He's a pirate! He buys and sells women, and if you think any different, you're only fooling yourself!* Another voice whispered, *If you deny him, he'll only force you into it. Better to relent and live to fight another day.*

Lauren closed her eyes and forced herself to think clearly, coherently, to separate the things she knew about Derek from what she suspected, to separate what she wanted to believe from what really was, and to keep the sensual feelings that were coursing through her system from affecting her judgment.

She felt the contact between her and Derek loosen, and as though her arms belonged to someone else, she felt her hands sliding around his neck.

I have the right to feel attractive and wanted. I have that right! she silently declared with much conviction.

"I don't trust you," Lauren whispered, glancing over her shoulder at Sue Ellen, who continued to sleep soundly. "I don't trust you at all."

"We're not talking about trust, my lady," Derek

203

replied, baring his teeth to nip lightly at the smooth flesh of her throat. "All you must know now is that you can trust me to take you to the summit once again, and when you are there, you will know that being in my arms, responding to my touch, is what you were born for."

His arrogance was appalling, but his claim was irrefutable. Lauren *was* confident in Derek's ability to excite her body to a fever pitch. Lauren shifted slightly, spreading her bare feet just a few inches farther apart, and twisted her hips to be at a right angle to Derek. The invitation was subtle, unspoken, and damning, should Lauren continue to deny that she wanted Derek's caresses.

"Tell me you want me to stop and I'll do so at once," Derek whispered, his lips close to Lauren's ear. The fingertips of his left hand traced an oval pattern beneath the silk shirttails against Lauren's taut buttocks; his right hand trailed slowly up and down along the insides of her thighs, always coming close to the apex of Lauren's sensations without ever quite touching the moist, heated petals of her femininity.

"I . . . want . . ." Lauren said before her throat tightened and speaking was impossible.

"What, Lauren?" Derek continued. His fingertips were very high on her thighs, almost touching the tingling entrance. "If you don't tell me, how will I know?"

At that moment she hated him. How would he know? The same way he seemed to know everything about her body—intuitively, instinctively, and with unerring accuracy. She hated his arrogance, she hated his confidence, and she positively loathed her own mercurial moods concerning her body and the things she was capable of feeling.

"I . . . want . . . you . . ." she said, pausing to run the

tip of her tongue around her mouth to moisten her dry lips. ". . . to. . . ."

All she had to do was finish that single sentence, and Derek would have taken his hands from her feverish body and left her in peace. That, anyway, was his promise, and whatever else Derek was, he had promised Lauren that he would not hurt her. Thus far he had been true to his word.

"You want me to *what?*" Derek prodded.

The moment the denial was about to pass between her lips Derek touched her, raising his hand so that his fingertips brushed lightly along the heated length of her femininity, pausing at the top to circle briefly the core of her greatest sensations. And when that happened, denials and protests died soundlessly within Lauren as she sank into sheer pleasure.

Chapter 17

"I should hate you," Lauren whispered, speaking as truthfully as possible under the circumstances.

Derek's hands were touching her from front and back. Lauren turned her head just enough to look toward the mattress through the thick veil of her lashes. Sue Ellen's back was toward her.

"Sue Ellen . . . might wake up . . . and hear us," Lauren said brokenly, not yet willing to completely surrender to the pleasures that Derek so skillfully dispensed.

"Then we must be very quiet, mustn't we?" Derek responded in that faintly superior tone that alternately annoyed and aroused Lauren.

She shivered as a finger, moistened with her own juices, slipped between the puffy petals, easing into her. A moment later Derek inserted a second finger. Lauren caught her lower lip between her teeth, biting down hard to still the quivering moan of ecstasy that welled up from her soul. Her legs trembled as his hand moved up and down, touching her intimately, rubbing and probing with consummate skill. Lauren, still twisted sideways, held loosely onto him, her arms around his neck. Her legs trembled, her knees were weak. She was certain that if she lost her hold of him, she would fall.

She turned her face toward him and was immediately rewarded with the kiss she sought. Parting her lips, she received Derek's tongue. She sucked on it, swirling her tongue against his, drifting deliciously in the kiss and the probing fingers that rubbed against the bud of her pleasure, pushing her slowly and steadily toward Nirvana.

"Derek, this is insanity," Lauren said in a tremulous whisper. "Sue Ellen is right there! Outside. . . . We've got to go *outside!*"

The notion of stopping now was impossible. Lauren could no more stop herself or the passion that flowed in her veins than she could stop the sun from rising or the waves from crashing against the shore.

"We can't go outside. Gregor has put a guard on us. You don't want to have some smelly cretin watching us, do you?"

Lauren shook her head, sending her ebony hair waving about her shoulders. Every nerve in her body was intensely aroused, and now even the contact of her own hair against her skin was delightfully erotic.

She was trapped. She needed Derek, needed him now more than ever before. She could not be outside the hut with him; she did not want to be with him when Sue Ellen was sleeping less than fifteen feet away. She could not give herself over to the pleasure that welled up inside her as long as there was the possibility of Sue Ellen waking and seeing her doing something intimate with him. But the danger that Sue Ellen represented added an erotic element to the encounter, heightening Lauren's excitement.

"I can't make any more decisions," Lauren whispered, turning so that she faced him. "I'm tired of making decisions. I want you, Derek. I know I shouldn't, but I do." She coiled her arms tighter around his neck, pressing herself from head to toe against him. In doing so, she removed the invasive fingers that made it so difficult for her to think coherently. "Kiss me, Derek. Kiss me and do what you will with me. You've got to make the decisions for both of us."

His half-grin was the last thing Lauren saw before she closed her eyes.

Why does he always have to be so calm, she wondered as his warm, exciting lips sealed over her mouth, taking her breath away in a deep, erotic kiss that made it seem as though Lauren's spine was melting.

Derek unbuttoned the silk shirt, smiling to himself when he found it difficult at first, then realizing the problem was that he was unaccustomed to removing a man's shirt from a woman's body.

Be quiet! Be quiet! Be quiet! Lauren thought, mentally chanting it like a mantra as Derek opened the shirt and cupped one luscious breast from the underside, raising it so he could encircle the enlarged nipple with his tongue. When he opened his mouth wide to capture the sensitized crest of her breast, Lauren tossed her head back on her shoulders, hugging Derek's face fiercely to her body.

Lauren hated standing, but she had no option since the floor of the tiny hut was hard-packed earth. Pushing her fingers into Derek's sandy hair, she guided his face from one breast to the other, wanting everything that he could give her, no longer caring who or what he really was, knowing only that the urges of her body were the one reality she cared about at this moment.

"You excite me so," Derek whispered, burying his face between her breasts. "Everything about you is incredible! You drive a man insane with desire!"

Flicking his tongue back and forth over her nipple,

Derek unbuttoned the fly of his breeches. He sprang free, long and hard, almost painfully aroused by the raven-haired woman who had captured his soul in a way he had never dreamed possible.

Lauren, feeling only the warm moisture of the hungry mouth feasting upon her breast, was unaware that Derek had freed his confined manhood. When he straightened, taking his mouth from her breasts, Lauren began to protest. It felt so good that she didn't want him ever to stop. Looking straight into her eyes, Derek took Lauren's hands, raising them to his mouth to kiss her palms, then brought them down to his long, thick arousal.

Again Lauren found herself hesitate in awe and fear. He was magnificently endowed, it was true, but she knew he was also skilled and patient, which made his extraordinary dimensions something to cause only pleasure, not pain.

Curling her fingers around the throbbing shaft of his phallus, Lauren squeezed tightly, eliciting a muted groan of approval from Derek. She brought her hand back and forth slowly, experimentally. The enlarged tip of his masculinity rubbed against her stomach, heating her flesh, making her feel naughty and daring. As she stroked him she studied his face, watching the ever-changing tapestry of passion subtly play across his face.

"What do you want of me?" Lauren whispered, infinitely more in control of her senses now that she was doing the touching, the caressing, the igniting. "Tell me, I'll do anything you want."

The invitation alone was nearly more than Derek could withstand. Forcing himself to remain at least reasonably calm, he took several deep breaths. He took a half-step away from Lauren to give her hands more room, then reached out to cup her breasts, catching the nipples between his forefingers and thumbs.

"Tell me what you want," Lauren continued, feeling bold and powerful as her hands simultaneously twisted around the solid length of Derek's arousal and roamed back and forth over it. "I'll do anything for you . . . anything at all."

"I want you to trust me," Derek replied.

It was not the request that Lauren had hoped for. Her body was at a fever pitch. From the surface of her skin to the marrow of her bones, she was ready and capable of feeling ecstasy. She was willing to do anything for Derek to give him pleasure, to make him feel all the intense emotions that he made her feel. She would do anything at all for Derek . . . anything *except* trust him.

Lauren purred softly, contentedly, twisting her hands over the rigid, pulsating length of Derek's arousal. She could feel his life's blood, hot and lusty, pump through his system, making him almost frighteningly rigid. As Derek toyed with the tips of her breasts, Lauren tried to ignore the warm glow that radiated from her nipples. For once, she would remain as aloof as Derek seemed able to, and see for herself what erotic pleasures came from being in control.

"Tell me," Lauren continued, moving closer to Derek again, brushing the moist tip of his phallus against her stomach as she fondled his constantly burgeoning length, "Tell me what you want, or I'll stop."

Derek looked into Lauren's dark eyes, unable to comprehend the change in her, or how she had turned the tables on him and stolen the control of the seduction from his grasp. In the ebony depths of her eyes he saw confidence, passion, a hunger for danger and excitement that he'd previously glimpsed. His phallus felt swollen way beyond its usual extended dimensions. Her fluttering hands moving over and around his throbbing length steadily heightened Derek's excitement and continued to chip away at the protective icy reserve that Lord Derek York so expertly surrounded himself with.

He placed his hands lightly on her shoulders, his face etched with tension, his eyes glazed as he stared at Lauren's breasts, which swayed gently with the movement of her hands. The smooth heat of her silken flesh against the tip of his manhood was like electricity jolting straight through Derek.

Lauren could feel that he was close to the edge. She worked her hands over him faster, never taking her eyes from his passion-distorted face.

"Oh, no!" Derek gasped, his features strained and taut as molten passion burst forth, racing through the length of him.

"Oh, *yes!*" Lauren responded, working her hands even faster over him as his passion erupted.

Lauren continued to fondle Derek until he caught her wrists in his large hands. His expression was a mixture of surprise, satiation, and unabated sensuality. He touched her face lightly with his fingertips, bending low to brush a quick kiss over her mouth.

"You temptress! Every time I think I know you, I realize I don't know you at all. You're all shadows and light."

Lauren raised up on her tiptoes, first kissing Derek's chin, then his mouth. Her hands felt sticky with Derek's passion, and she wasn't at all certain where she should put her hands or what she should do next. She looked into Derek's eyes, and the unspoken question made him blush. He removed his shirt and handed it to her.

"At least Sue Ellen didn't wake up," Derek said quietly, hitching up his breeches.

Lauren cleaned herself, then tossed his shirt toward

the steamer trunk. When she turned back toward Derek, her ebony eyes were glowing like burning coals. "Sue Ellen is still sleeping," Lauren said in a low, confident whisper. "And you may be satisfied, but I most definitely am not, and until I am, I promise you will not know a moment's tranquility."

Derek chuckled, already feeling himself stir with renewed interest as Lauren took him boldly into her hands. "I love a woman who knows what she wants," Derek said, smiling, sliding the blue shirt off her shoulders. He cupped her heavy breasts in his palms.

I'll have time to regret this later, Lauren thought as Derek's hands firmly kneaded her breasts, heightening the fevered sensations that made her tremble from head to foot. *For now, it's enough that Derek is with me, making me feel so alive!*

In seconds Derek was rigidly aroused. Lauren had been ready for him for quite some time, but she was confused. The dirt floor was wholly unsatisfactory, and Sue Ellen lay sleeping on the only mattress in the hut.

"What are you smiling about?" Lauren asked, not at all pleased with the vaguely humorous expression in Derek's eyes.

"Don't look so nervous, m'lady, I won't leave you to your own devices." Derek reached down to touch Lauren intimately, pleased when he felt she was quite ready for him. "We must be quiet, and careful, but I know exactly what it is you need."

Derek's arrogance offended Lauren, but this was not the time to worry over his manners. Each time she'd been with him, he'd introduced her to ethereal places she'd not even known existed.

He guided her to the steamer trunk, motioning for Lauren to sit on the rounded lid. Derek slipped between her smooth thighs, getting down on his knees.

"Sometimes it's necessary to just make do," Derek

212

said with a half-grin, one hand on Lauren's hip, the other hand guiding his ardent manhood into her. He pushed into her smoothly. "Sweet Lauren, you'll be the death of me yet."

Lauren gripped the sides of the steamer trunk, looking at Derek through her dark, curled lashes, wishing he wasn't so sure of himself, thankful that he really was as skilled as he believed he was.

Chapter 18

Sue Ellen awoke with the eerie sensation that she was not where she should be. Sitting upright, she blinked several times to clear her vision, then focused on the two people lying only a few feet from her on a make-shift mattress of clothes and blankets.

Lauren and Mr. Derek slept in a tangle of arms and legs. Even in sleep, Sue Ellen could tell that they were very much in love. It surprised her that they had allowed her to monopolize the only mattress in the hut, and she wondered if she'd have been so giving had the situation been reversed.

Looking at Mr. Derek, his face calm and peaceful, she wondered what he would be like as a lover. Sue Ellen knew she shouldn't think such things, particularly since it was Mr. Derek's lover who had put herself in such jeopardy to protect her. Just the same, Mr. Derek was the most handsome man she'd ever known, and though he was a flesh-buyer for some faraway Englishman, Sue Ellen sensed there was something else about Mr. Derek that was not evil, something heroic that he kept locked within himself.

At that moment Derek opened his eyes and looked at

Sue Ellen. Correctly guessing that he was naked beneath the thin blanket that covered the couple, Sue Ellen blushed furiously and turned her back to him, mumbling an apology.

Derek smiled to himself, easing out of Lauren's arms. Had last night really happened? It seemed like a dream come true. He had been so afraid for her safety, and when he'd returned to the hut and found her waiting, he'd felt the greatest relief. After Sue Ellen had fallen asleep, he couldn't really believe the magical things that he and Lauren had done to each other, taking each other to the heights of passion repeatedly until both slept the exhausted sleep of love and satiation. No woman had ever driven Derek to such emotional extremes; no woman had ever made him want to make love at every opportunity. Lauren had become the fulcrum of his most extreme emotions. Before he had met Lauren Masters, Derek had believed that lust was the highest expression of his emotional makeup. Now he knew that lust combined with love created a deep passion a hundred times stronger and more consuming.

He dressed quickly, strapping on his dagger and harnessing the saber around his waist. There was much to be accomplished today, and if his guess was correct, Gregor and his men would be in disarray. Aldon Mitchell might even have heard about the women escaping, and there was the chance that he would be angry with Gregor for it. Anything that Derek could do to divide Gregor and Aldon Mitchell would strengthen his position.

He looked at Lauren, sleeping on the thin padding of clothes he had spread out for them in the early hours of the morning. He doubted if she'd been any more comfortable than he'd been sleeping on the hard dirt floor.

Someday he would buy her a mattress a foot thick, one so big they could sleep on it together, stretched out in any direction.

It was a surprising thought for Lord Derek York. He was not a man given to thinking of a woman and long-range goals in the same breath.

Derek knelt and smoothed a lock of ebony hair away from Lauren's eyes. "Wake up, darling," he whispered. "It's morning." When her eyes fluttered open, he smiled, brushing the pad of his thumb over her slender eyebrows, then down over her cheek. "Everything is okay. Sue Ellen is fine. Nobody knows you're here yet. Wake up slowly, darling. There's nothing to worry about."

A sleepy smile crept across Lauren's mouth, making Derek remember how many times he had kissed those lips the night before. Lauren closed her eyes. "Just give me five more minutes."

"Anything you want is yours for the asking, m'lady," Derek said.

To his astonishment, he found he really meant it.

Gregor looked over the rim of his tankard at Derek and wondered once again which of them was the better man with a cutlass.

The verbal bantering between them had been going on for some time in *As the Crow Flies*. Though they often smiled at each other, and even faintly complimented each other on capturing the women who had escaped—or been freed, depending upon whose viewpoint one heard—anyone close enough to hear the undercurrent of hatred in their voices or see the contempt in their eyes would know otherwise.

"I want to meet the Big Man," Derek said, finishing the last of his ale and waving his hand for Mirabell to refill his tankard. "After all the trouble we've been having, and considering the amount of money I'm willing to spend, I've got a right to meet the man who's really in charge of the business."

"I'm the only man you need to know," Gregor replied, and though he smiled, he wanted to cut the Englishman's throat for once again slighting his power and influence. "You ain't meeting the Big Man. It just won't happen."

"Because you say it won't?"

"That's right."

"But I say it has to."

"What you say doesn't count, Englishman." For no other reason than that he loved having power over Derek, Gregor would not introduce him to Aldon Mitchell. "Ain't you figured that one out yet?"

"Apparently not, but then, there are many things I haven't figured out yet." For a moment Derek's gaze met with Gregor and the lust for power in the pirate's eyes was nauseatingly apparent. Mirabell showed up with a pitcher of ale and refilled Derek's glass. She smiled broadly at him, completely missing the fact that Gregor's tankard was long empty of rum. She rubbed her small bosom against Derek's shoulder as she refilled his glass, and though it was intended to look as if the contact was an accident, there wasn't a man in the tavern who'd have believed it. It wasn't until Mirabell returned to her position behind the bar that Derek, in an exaggerated fashion, turned his attention back to Gregor, pointedly reminding the pirate just who was attractive to women . . . and who was not.

"Where were we? Oh, yes . . . I wanted to meet with the Big Man, and you were intent on keeping me from doing that." Derek let his eyes roll from Gregor's face over to Mirabell, then back again, as though it was impossible for him to keep from looking at her. With no small amount of envy, Gregor observed the look Mirabell gave him in return—one of open longing.

"What I suggest is simple," Derek continued in his most professional voice. "Either I meet with the Big Man very soon—tomorrow, in fact—or I'll be satisfied with purchasing Lauren and Sue Ellen. The others have been abused and soiled by you and your men. Their value to my client has consequently been dramatically reduced."

Derek saw that he hadn't quite hooked Gregor yet, so he decided to make a gamble, betting on the pirate's inflated sense of self-worth and his desire to ingratiate himself to the Big Man.

"I'm willing to bet that you've already told the Big Man you've got this buyer who is willing to pay good money for nine women. You'd do that because you want to impress the Big Man—and by the way, I'm going to be very disappointed if the Big Man is not someone of imposing stature. But what will he do if he discovers that his single largest client has decided to take his business elsewhere? You're not the only captain in this sea, you know. I'll grant you, there aren't really many of you in the business of kidnapping white women and selling them, but I'm sure that if I spread enough money around, I could find someone else to fill my requirements soon enough."

"Not in these waters, you wouldn't," Gregor said, his pale eyes flinty with hatred.

Derek smiled crookedly, shrugging his shoulders. "Perhaps . . . perhaps not. As I said, you're not the only captain in these waters, even if you make other captains walk the plank." Derek leaned forward on his elbows, sensing that he finally had Gregor at a disadvantage. "But the Big Man doesn't believe your boasts, and neither do I." Derek suddenly stood, looking down at the red-bearded pirate. "Either I meet the Big Man soon, or I'm gone. I've spent too much time here as it is, and all I've got to show for it is two acceptable women."

"Don't push me too far, you bastard," Gregor whispered.

"Just far enough to get what I want," Derek replied, then turned on his heel and walked out of the tavern, feeling Gregor's heated, contemptuous gaze burn holes in his back.

Derek felt such elation that he had difficulty hiding his joy. He'd guessed that Gregor would brag to the Big Man about all the women he'd sold, and the gamble paid off. Derek could hardly wait to get back to the hut to tell Lauren that very soon he would have the whereabouts of his sister, and then they could all go home.

"Just keep your eyes and ears open," Lauren whispered to Sue Ellen as they stood uneasily outside the tavern. "Derek won't let anything happen to us."

Sue Ellen nodded, but Lauren could tell that she had her doubts.

Lauren, too, had doubts about Derek. It was wrong, she believed, to assume that their long, blissful, climactic night of lovemaking had proved him an honorable man. At the same time, Lauren was certain she'd have sensed Derek's duplicity if he wasn't the man he claimed. Surely, at some point during their lovemaking, Lauren would have been able to tell if he was merely a smoothly seductive man capable of sharing sweet passion. But throughout the long night, with his whispered words of love—not, Lauren remembered, "I love you," but numerous admissions of love for her breasts, her eyes, her mouth, her hair, and everything else about her—she sensed nothing but passion and honesty.

"It's going to be fine," Lauren continued, whispering so the guard, Bones, could not hear her. "Derek will see that you're safe."

Bones came forward, holding a long spear with a lethal-looking brass point on it. "No talking!" he commanded, jabbing the jagged tip of the spear in the air, bringing it dangerously close to Lauren's golden flesh.

"Unless you want that spear shoved up your nose, I suggest you keep your distance," Derek said in a cold, deadly tone as he approached Lauren and Sue Ellen.

Bones eyed Derek warily, then stepped away from the women.

"You mustn't be so abrasive, Derek," Aldon Mitchell said, stepping up beside Derek. "The man is only doing what I pay him to do."

"Of course. But I am protective of the items I purchase. It's like when a man takes the time to train a fine hunting dog. Once a man gets him to take orders and even learn to do what he should do without being told, the dog becomes quite valuable."

Aldon chuckled, nodding his head and patting his protruding stomach. "You're a man after my own heart, Derek. That you are!" Aldon moved closer to Lauren and Sue Ellen, circling them slowly. "So these are the two that caused all the commotion the other night."

"Not both of them," Derek said, "just that one there. The dark-haired one has been with me since we stormed the *Miss Malaki*. I've trained her well."

Aldon nodded, scratching his chin. "So I see. You can see the spirit in her eyes. It's the spirited ones who are hardest to train, but they're the best wenches once they understand they must be subservient to their masters."

Lauren gritted her teeth so hard her jaws ached. *How dared Derek talk like that!* Comparing her to a dog, indeed! It mattered little that Derek had to talk that

220

way for Aldon Mitchell's benefit. It was necessary, perhaps—but did he have to wear such a self-satisfied smile on his face while he did it?

Aldon moved close to Lauren, brushing the backs of his knuckles across her breast through the sheer mitar. She gasped but did not try to defend herself.

"Yes, she's well on her way to being fully trained," Aldon said, nodding in approval. "She doesn't want me to touch her, yet she does nothing to prevent me from doing so." He looked over at Derek, then back to Lauren. "Exquisite body, don't you think?"

"Magnificent," Derek agreed, and though his voice was calm and conversational, Lauren could see the strain showing in his cool blue eyes.

"She'll cost you a shiny crown or two, good man," Aldon said with a short, harsh laugh. "And this one here—she's a sight as well, is she not?" Aldon moved close to Sue Ellen. He cupped her right breast in his hand and squeezed firmly, a lurid grin contorting his face. Sue Ellen closed her eyes, clearly repulsed by the man, and Lauren prayed silently for her newfound friend to have the strength to resist any action that would arouse the evil man's violent instincts.

Lauren looked at Derek, and for a moment their gazes met. *I'll be strong,* Lauren said with her eyes. *But hurry, Derek! Don't let this humiliation go on too long!*

"Shall we begin to talk price?" Derek asked Aldon, accurately reading Lauren.

"I appreciate a man who keeps business ahead of all other interests, no matter how pleasant those diversions might be," the slavemaster replied. "Do you mind if we negotiate in a back parlor somewhere? The stench of taverns has always been distasteful to me, and all this talk has given me a dreadful thirst. I've brought along a very interesting wine that you might find amusing."

221

"Lead the way."

Aldon nodded to Bones, who moved close to Lauren and Sue Ellen. Derek turned hard, questioning eyes on Aldon.

"Business is man's work," Aldon explained. "I find it easier to concentrate without the wenches present. Don't you agree?"

Derek grinned crookedly and nodded, but Lauren could see he wasn't at all happy about being separated from her and Sue Ellen.

Derek settled comfortably into the thickly padded chair in the surprisingly well outfitted bamboo house. He accepted a glass of port from Aldon and sipped it, smiling his approval.

As Aldon sat in the other chair, Derek was thinking that evil this profound and advanced had to be expunged from the earth. The only possible peace there could be with a man the likes of Aldon Mitchell was a Carthaginian Peace—total annihilation. Although Gregor was truly evil, his villainy lacked the sophistication of Aldon's, which was on a far grander scale, and infinitely more reprehensible.

"How many slaves will you be needing?" Aldon asked, swirling the wine around in his glass, sniffing it with a pleased expression.

"Ten to fifteen," Derek answered. "More, if the women are of superior quality." He smiled, his eyes taking on a friendly light. "My employer is a man with very deep pockets and an insatiable appetite. He doesn't mind paying good money to see that his vices are satisfied."

"Precisely the type of man I enjoy doing business with. And his name is . . . ?"

"I didn't give you his name. For rather obvious rea-

sons, he prefers to retain his anonymity." Derek made a
derisive face. "Some people in England and Europe can
be so . . . *provincial* . . . always trying to regulate
everyone else's entertainment."

"I know exactly what you mean. Such annoying
meddling brought me to these islands. Here a man can
indulge in business and pleasure to his heart's content
without anyone looking over his shoulder."

The hypocrisy of Aldon Mitchell's attitude was not
lost on Derek, who found it difficult to resist using his
dagger then and there to put an end to the harem
master's reign of slavery and terror.

"For the two in your possession: I offer a price of
thirty krones for the older one, and one hundred
krones for the spirited one with the eyes of a raven."

Derek was taken by surprise at the currency. He
hadn't expected to use Danish denominations, and he
wasn't entirely sure how the exchange worked out.
Also, the price for Lauren was considerably more than
he had anticipated paying.

"Thirty krones is a fair price for the one, but one
hundred krones is much too high for the other. My
employer has deep pockets, but he didn't make them
deep by spending his money foolishly." Derek leaned
back in his chair and sipped his wine. He had been
through a hundred business meetings not entirely dis-
similar to this one, and he knew that if he showed too
great an interest in acquiring Lauren, her value would
increase and his negotiating position would worsen.
"My employer is particularly fond of blondes . . . pale-
skinned blondes, to be exact. Would you have any to
show me?"

"As a matter of fact, I do."

It was difficult for Derek to contain his excitement.
Could it be that after all this time he was finally about
to find his sister Amanda? When Aldon rose to his feet,

Derek stood a bit too quickly, and he consciously forced himself to produce an outward appearance of nonchalance.

"I have some wenches not far from here," Aldon continued, patting his ample stomach in a satisfied way that greatly annoyed Derek. "I'll have the carriage take us there. You're in no particular hurry to return to that little hut you rented, are you?"

"Not in the least. But when I rented that place, I didn't know there were places such as this that could be rented."

Derek mentally cursed himself for having missed the location of the captured women, and the news that they were being held on the island served to reinforce his fear that he was an outsider to the islands and would always be an outsider, no matter how long or how thoroughly he searched for his kidnapped sister.

Aldon was smiling, nodding his head, obviously pleased that the Englishman appreciated his temporary home away from home.

"I'd have invited you to my home on St. Lucifer, but my privacy is very valuable to me. Privacy . . . it is easily as valuable as health and happiness. If a man hasn't got his privacy, then he really hasn't got anything at all."

Derek followed Aldon outside, thinking the reason Aldon valued his privacy so much was that the things he enjoyed doing the most were things polite society not only frowned upon, but put people in prison for.

"Where's Lauren?" Derek asked casually when they had returned to the entrance of *As the Crow Flies.*

"Lauren? She's the statuesque one with the raven's eyes, correct?"

"Aye."

"I've had Bones put her and the other one up for safe-keeping."

Derek wanted to pursue the issue. He didn't like not knowing where Lauren was, but he could only reply, "Good. She's not entirely trained yet, and I'm still not sure that she won't bolt, given half a chance. Her training will take another couple of weeks. Then she'll be perfect."

Aldon issued a hollow, lifeless chuckle. "You've been sparing the whip, Derek, and that's why she's been taking so long to train! Take a riding crop to her, or lash her bare bottom with your belt, and that'll show her who the master is."

At a snap of Aldon's fingers, a carriage rattled around the side of the public house and stopped before them. It was a small carriage, one not particularly lavish in its appointments, but it was clearly a cut above all other island transportation. Derek complimented Aldon on it while thinking that he wouldn't be caught dead riding in the conveyance if he were in London.

They rattled down a rutted goat trail until they reached a small hut. It looked as if it had at one time been a saloon of some sort. Could it be that Amanda had been this close the whole time? Derek's stomach churned as he thought about his sister living in such squalid conditions, and he knew in his heart that if Amanda was inside and he had the chance to kill Aldon immediately, he'd do it.

Taking a long key from an inside jacket pocket, Aldon opened the huge lock. Only when Derek was standing close to the hut did he notice that the windows were all barred, like those in a prison. He could smell the acrid scent of stale perspiration and fear as soon as the door opened. Derek subtly crossed his hands over his chest and in doing so slipped his right hand inside his jacket, curling his fingers around the haft of the razor-sharp dagger he had strapped to his chest under his left arm.

A dozen women were inside. Mattresses were strewn across the floor for them in what appeared to be Aldon's only nod toward civilized amenities. After a sweeping glance Derek knew that Amanda wasn't there; a second look revealed that none of the women were very young or very attractive.

If Aldon did have Amanda, he wouldn't be keeping her in this squalor—not because he wasn't evil enough to do such a thing, but because he would know that treating an attractive and profitable woman like Amanda shoddily was bad business.

"If this is the best you have to offer, I'm afraid you've been wasting my time," Derek said icily. "Furthermore, if this is the way you treat your merchandise, it's a miracle you've got anything worth selling at all."

A muscle ticked in Derek's jaw. He wanted to do something for the women, but he knew he couldn't, and the impotent rage he felt heightened his disgust for Aldon. Derek turned and walked out of the small hut, the faces of the frightened women etched horribly into his memory.

Derek walked past the carriage, his long legs carrying him quickly back toward *As the Crow Flies.* He had gone thirty yards before Aldon called out for him to stop.

"I was hoping to rid myself of some excess items," Aldon explained, smiling as though all this was nothing other than his usual business practice, that it was Derek who didn't understand the rules of proper business. "Surely a man in your line of work can understand that."

"My time is valuable," Derek said, finding it difficult to rid himself even temporarily of the hideous sight of those women in that small, isolated prison hut. "Now either you show me the best wenches you have to sell, or you can tell me who will have the items I need to round out the order for my client. Give me a name and I promise you'll receive a substantial finder's fee."

The words were not intended to insult Aldon, but they clearly did, and Derek wondered if he had let his anger go too far. After all he'd sacrificed to rescue his sister, the thought that he should fail now was anathema to everything he believed in.

"You work for a wealthy man, Derek, and I understand that. What *you* must understand is that you are not yourself a wealthy man, you only work for one—just as the men who work for me are not wealthy, though they work for a wealthy and powerful man." Aldon's voice dropped to a whisper. "I will provide you with whatever you need. But don't ever insult me by implying that there is someone else in these islands who has more power than I have." Aldon looked deep into Derek's icy blue eyes as they walked. "That would be a fatal mistake."

Derek nodded in acknowledgment. *So his ego really is that overblown,* he thought, not in the least cowed by the threat. *Somehow I've got to make that work against him.*

Aldon Mitchell changed moods abruptly and was once again the charming businessman. He laughed with Derek as they walked with the carriage following them, and he kept up a steady stream of off-color and openly obscene jokes that Derek obligingly laughed at, though he found them anything but humorous.

"Look at this wench," Aldon said as they approached *As the Crow Flies.*

A young blonde woman, dressed in a fine mitar and shikars, stood passively, her hands at her sides, and head bowed.

Aldon moved close to the young woman and twisted a strand of her honey blonde hair round his finger. "She could make your blood run hot, couldn't she?"

"Yes," Derek replied, thinking of Lauren and knowing that this woman failed to compare. "From your private stock?"

"Yes, my friend. Think of her as a temporary loan from me to you, a sign of goodwill among businessmen. I must spend some time with my other pursuits, and the wench will help you spend the time in an entertaining fashion. Very soon I will show you a collection that will satisfy any desire your employer has."

Aldon chuckled, and because he did, Derek laughed softly, but in the back of his mind he was worried about Lauren, and was already wondering why he hadn't seen Bones lately.

Chapter 19

"I don't like this," Lauren said in a whisper, leaning close to Sue Ellen. "I don't like this one little bit."

Derek had been meeting with Aldon Mitchell for little more than thirty minutes when Gregor showed up, smiling broadly, lustfully, as though he'd just been given some news that pleased him enormously. Gregor had Bones with him, and two other sailors from *The Unholy One*. The four men talked quietly among themselves, repeatedly glancing at Lauren and Sue Ellen.

"Don't worry, they won't do anything," Sue Ellen said confidently. "They won't risk defying Mr. Derek's orders. He'll kill all of them if they so much as put a finger on you."

Lauren smiled and nodded, but she wasn't as certain of Derek's influence. Perhaps if Gregor wasn't among the men standing outside the tavern leering at them she'd have agreed, but as it was, the scurrilous captain of the most dangerous pirate ship in the Caribbean was there, and Lauren knew he wanted her.

"Don't look at them," Lauren said under her breath. "Don't give them any reason to talk to us, and we'll be fine."

"Sure. Derek won't let anything bad happen to us,"

Sue Ellen repeated, but this time Lauren could hear the doubt in her voice.

Ten minutes later, the foul-mouthed young boy who acted as Gregor's personal valet came rushing into the village, his face flushed, a devilish gleam in his eye. He whispered something to Gregor, and the pirate's bearded face broke into a broad, lusty grin. He patted the youth on the shoulder heartily, then shooed him away.

"Get ready," Lauren whispered, twisting her knees beneath her so that she could get to her feet quickly if the need arose.

Gregor walked toward her purposefully, his crewmen fanning out behind him. He hooked his thumbs into the broad leather belt that encircled his rotund waist and held up the heavy cutlass he carried.

"On your feet, ladies," Gregor said sarcastically, stepping up very close to Lauren and looking upon her. "It's time to take a little voyage."

"Where to?" Lauren asked as she rose. She received a foul look from Gregor for being bold enough to question him.

"To wherever the hell Cap'n Gregor says you'll go, that's where!" Bones said like a shot.

Lauren looked at Bones, understanding at last why Gregor liked having the skinny sailor around. Bones was a savage sycophant, and he fed Gregor's sense of superiority and power.

Lauren knew she shouldn't speak, but she couldn't remain silent. "We're not supposed to go anywhere," she said in a voice that was much too bold for Gregor to tolerate. "Derek—*Mister* Derek—said he'd whip us if we went anywhere without him."

At first Gregor scowled at Lauren, then his eyes went from her face down to the ample, rounded curves of her

230

bosom, and he laughed and smiled. He made no effort to hide the direction of his gaze or the lust that burned in his soul. Lauren shivered with revulsion as she watched him: she could almost see the machinations of his foul mind clicking over the possibilities. She crossed her arms over her bosom, turning away slightly.

"Don't be shy with ol' Cap'n Gregor," he said, placing a large, dirty hand on her shoulder. "I'm just taking you on a little voyage. You'll be seeing your Englishman soon enough." Gregor caught Lauren's chin between his first finger and thumb, forcing her to look at him as he spoke. "You sparked a fancy in Mr. Mitchell, my dark-eyed lass. He's sent word to me that he wants you taken to his little home on St. Lucifer." Gregor chuckled and released his hold on her chin, letting the tips of his fingers trail over her throat and shoulder before leaving her. "You'll get to know the Big Man real good." He chuckled softly, then continued. "Sometimes the Big Man sends some of his wenches my way before he sells them off. You and me may be . . . *seeing* each other real soon."

"No!" Lauren cried, unable to believe that anything could happen to make it necessary for her to feel Gregor's befouling touch. "I'm not going anywhere until Mr. Derek tells me to."

Sue Ellen had moved to stand beside Lauren, the two forming a unified front against the four battle-hardened men. Gregor was at first shocked that Lauren had the audacity to stand up to him, but then he appeared pleased by it.

"A spirited lass, ain't she, mates? She's a powder keg between the sheets! You can see it just by looking in her eyes!" he said, his eyes burning with a lusty intensity that made Lauren feel as though he was already touch-

231

ing her, defiling her. "That's why the Englishman was so skittish about this one. He knows what a hot-blooded wench she is!"

Bones, one hand portentously close to his own crotch, said, "The Englishman's had her all to hisself, Cap'n Gregor. Would you be willin' to let the rest o' us have a go at her when you're finished?"

Gregor patted Bones's shoulder again, slapping him hard enough so that the younger man was knocked forward a step. "She's as good as yours already, Bones, my good mate! I'll break her in right for you!"

"No, I won't go!" Lauren shouted. She could not believe it was possible for men to have such vile attitudes.

Gregor snapped his fingers and the men fanned out like wolves moving in for the kill. Though Sue Ellen and Lauren fought with all their might, they were quickly hoisted onto the men's shoulders. Lauren kicked and scratched, trying to gouge Bones's eyes out, but she was no match for the vicious little man, and her strength certainly could not compare to Gregor's.

"Fight me, wench!" Gregor taunted, one hand tight over her mouth, the other arm wrapped like a steel band around her waist. "Fight me hard, because that's what makes my blood run hot! I've wanted to taste your charms since I first saw you on the *Miss Malaki!* The Big Man's gotta have you first, but I'm next in line, and when I'm done with you, Bones and the mates are gonna show you what happens to a wench with a fiery tongue!"

Lauren stopped struggling. She closed her eyes as they carried her, trying in vain to block Gregor's words from her ears.

Opening her eyes, she looked at Bones, who held her by the feet. Somehow, she knew in her heart that Bones would be just as bad as Gregor, maybe even worse.

There was something innately cowardly, and therefore savage, about Bones.

"It's been good to finally meet who I'm doing business with," Derek said in conclusion, shaking hands with Aldon Mitchell at the water's edge. "When will I see you again?"

"I've left you some entertainment," Aldon replied, smiling faintly. "She can keep you company until I have a full shipment ready for you. Just be patient until then. A day or two . . . no more than that."

Derek nodded. Another day or two, and then maybe, if luck and the fates and all that was holy was with him, he would have Amanda brought to him, just as he'd planned all along. He'd buy his own sister, then take her away from this Caribbean hell and put her back into the cream of London society, where her adventure would no doubt cause a scandal. But it would also make her the most sought-after debutante in the history of London high society.

Aldon Mitchell got onto the rowboat and six men began rowing him toward St. Lucifer. Derek knew where Aldon lived, of course, but since Aldon had tried to hide the location of his mansion from him, Derek let him believe the secret was still intact.

When Aldon was well out to sea, Derek turned and headed back to his hut with the woman he'd been "given" following close at his heels. He was eager to talk to her in private, to learn what she knew about Aldon Mitchell. Maybe she could confirm that Amanda was alive.

"What's your name?" Derek asked as they walked back to the hut.

"Chantell, my lord."

She spoke with a pronounced French accent and

kept her head bowed. He wanted to tell her that she shouldn't bow to him or to anyone, but he knew that saying such words would only draw suspicion. Glancing occasionally over his shoulder, he wondered how long Chantell had been with Aldon Mitchell. She was extremely attractive, and though her head was bowed, Derek sensed defiance in her.

"You don't have to be afraid of me," Derek said quietly as they weaved their way down the path. "I'm not the kind of man who beats women."

"I will give you no reason to beat me," Chantell replied quietly. "If there is anything you want or need, you must only ask and I will provide it for you."

She's been trained like an obedient dog, Derek thought bitterly. *I wonder what Aldon's done to Amanda. Is she as docile as this one?*

The mental picture of Amanda, who had always been fiery and free spirited, having her head bowed and her spirit broken sent a chill through him. All he had to do was think of his sister being "trained" and he knew that he would not leave the Virgin Islands until this stain on mankind—Aldon Mitchell—had been killed so its poison could infect no one else.

When Derek and Chantell reached the hut, both Lauren and Sue Ellen were gone. Derek's heart began to pound, and his eyes took on a fiery intensity. He knew Gregor was behind this. He *had* to be responsible for Lauren's disappearance. Whether Gregor was acting under Aldon Mitchell's orders had yet to be determined.

"I'll kill that bloody bastard for this!" Derek hissed, already heading back toward *As the Crow Flies,* where he could get a boat to take him to St. Lucifer.

"Master, there's something I must tell you!" Chantell called out, standing in the doorway.

He looked over his shoulder at her. There was some-

234

thing in her tone that told him he should listen to her, even though his every instinct was to rush to Aldon Mitchell as quickly as possible to free Lauren.

"What?" Derek demanded, returning to stand before Chantell, towering over her in an intimidating fashion.

Without looking up into his face, Chantell answered, "I am to be your temporary property in exchange for the one that was taken."

"How do you know this?"

"Master Mitchell instructed me to tell you this when we were alone." Her head still down, Chantell reached behind her neck and began unknotting her mitar. "I am yours to do with as you please, Master."

Derek swore furiously, and Chantell cringed.

"I'm not going to hit you, I said!" Derek snapped, angry that she should be so frightened of him. "And don't take your bloody clothes off!"

"Yes, Master," Chantell whispered, cringing, cowering in the face of Derek's escalating anger.

If there was ever a time in his life when he could kill coldly, yet with anger, it was now. Derek had fought in wars; as a soldier he had killed many men. Then he fought strangers who believed in causes that he did not believe in, fought battles his country said was necessary for him to fight. Now more than ever, his battle with Aldon Mitchell was personal, not only because both his sister and his lover had been kidnapped, but because Aldon Mitchell destroyed women's souls and spirits.

"Stop calling me Master," Derek said, nudging Chantell into the hut. "Listen, you've been to St. Lucifer, haven't you?" She nodded. "You know where he keeps the women, then?"

"I was a part of his harem, Master."

"Would he take Lauren there?"

Chantell eyed Derek suspiciously, not sure what she

should say, clearly afraid of telling Derek too much and then getting into trouble with Aldon Mitchell because of it. But she was also afraid of not being entirely honest with Derek.

"Lauren?" she asked at last.

"The woman you were exchanged for."

"Yes, Master, I believe he would take her to his harem. That is where he kept all the women he owned."

"People can't be owned," Derek replied hotly, his mind whirling, wondering what his next move should be. "Can you draw a map for me so I can find the harem you speak of?"

Chantell finally raised her face, and when she did, Derek could see that there was a world of hatred in her, all of it directed at Aldon Mitchell.

"If you try to steal from Master Mitchell, he will kill you," she said calmly. "The harem is guarded, as is everything he owns."

Derek closed his eyes for a moment, forcing himself to separate anger from logic. Discovering that Lauren had been kidnapped by Aldon Mitchell—or, at least, on his orders—had shaken him deeply.

"You'll find that Aldon Mitchell isn't as invincible as he'd like you to believe." When Chantell turned her face down again, Derek touched her chin, tilting her head back so that he could see into her eyes. "I've been looking for someone . . . a woman who was kidnapped from a boat some time ago . . ."

"It was you who came in the night to St. Lucifer, wasn't it?"

Derek smiled. "Yes."

"Then you are the brother." Chantell's eyes took on a new, defiant hue as she looked at Derek. "Your sister is Amanda, is she not?"

"Yes!"

"She is held at St. Lucifer. It is where Mas—"

Chantell caught herself, and with a look from Derek, continued with building confidence "—where that bastard Mitchell will take your Lauren. If you're going there, you won't need a map. I will show you."

"No, it is better that I work alone."

"I can help you. You don't know the island; I do. You don't know Aldon Mitchell, or what he is like; I do. You would be a fool not to take me with you, and you do not strike me as a fool."

Derek grinned crookedly. "How is it I always find myself with the most stubborn women on this entire bloody damned island?"

Chantell smiled—it was the first genuine smile she'd given Derek—and he knew then that her logic was solid, and that with her along he had a better chance of rescuing Lauren and Amanda.

"It's going to be dangerous," Derek said, his hands resting lightly on her shoulders. "But when it's over, I'll make sure you get the hell away from here. You'll be free, Chantell—I promise you that."

For a moment they simply looked at each other. Finally, Derek turned away from Chantell and said, "You'd better get some rest while you can. There isn't much we can do until sundown, and I can't say when you'll get your next sleep."

Chapter 20

"Cap'n Gregor, sir, we ain't been seein' Jaspar lately."

Gregor leaned back on his chair in *As the Crow Flies* and narrowed his eyes to focus them. After the successful abduction of Lauren Masters, Gregor had given orders that he wasn't to be disturbed by anyone for any reason. Having Bones come up to him now, in direct violation of that order, warned Gregor that the trouble must be considerable.

"He's a drinking fool, Jaspar is," Gregor replied at last. "Tomorrow he'll stagger in here complaining about how he spent the night in a pig trough."

"Maybe you're right," Bones replied, though it was clear he had his doubts. "The last time anyone saw him was when he relieved Dolin on watch of the Englishman."

Gregor scratched his bearded chin, forcing himself to think clearly despite all the rum flowing in his veins. Jaspar *was* a drinking fool, but no moreso than any other man sailing with *The Unholy One*. He'd passed out many times, and he always managed to show up for his morning meal. Not being seen after spending a night watching the Englishman *might* mean that Derek had done something and didn't want anyone to know of it. Jaspar disappeared the night Derek's women escaped. Interrogation of the recaptured women made Gregor believe they'd been set free by a woman, apparently someone from nearby, though that was in doubt since the descriptions given by the women varied considerably.

"Where is the English dog now?"

"In his hut with the wench the Big Man gave him—the French wench with the wild eyes."

Gregor belched, swallowed the last of the rum in his tankard, then rapped his knuckles on the table for Mirabell to give him service. He looked at Bones and made a groaning sound. "The Englishman gets all the best ones, don't he, mate? Maybe later you and me will visit the Englishman's hut and invite ourselves to share in the wench's hospitality, eh?"

Bones completely forgot about his friend Jaspar. The thought of touching Chantell was so stimulating that he ordered a tankard of rum for himself, then sat in silence, thinking only of the French woman, and what he would do to her.

When Mirabell filled Gregor's tankard, he slipped his arm around her slender waist, forcing her onto his lap. She said nothing—no complaints and no wiggling of her bottom against him to let him know that for a price she could be available for the evening.

"Leave me, little wench," Gregor said at last, pushing her to her feet.

He'd drank a great deal, and his thwarted desire for Lauren prevented him from pursuing Mirabell as he might have. He took a hefty gulp of rum and closed his eyes. Tonight . . . tonight he would drink and think. Tomorrow he would figure out what happened to

239

Jaspar, when he could truly let his anger rage against Derek, when he would be out from under Aldon Mitchell's thumb, and most of all, when he could finally feast on Lauren Masters' charms.

Gregor never thought he would pass out—certainly not in *As the Crow Flies*—but he did, right where all his men could see him. Though he wasn't aware of it, the terror he'd worked so hard to inspire in his men began to lessen, and for the first time, the men joked about their captain openly and without fear.

"The Unholy One will be sailing soon," Chantell said, watching Derek's profile as he brought his dagger back and forth over the whetstone, honing the blade to a sharp edge. "A few days ago I was with Mitchell. He said Gregor would soon be bringing us some new friends. Friends . . . that's what Mitchell calls his kidnapped women."

Derek finished with the dagger and began sharpening the cutlass. "That would help. If Gregor's gone and I'm not on *The Unholy One,* it could be to our advantage. Either way, the days are numbered for Gregor and Aldon."

"Good . . . very good."

Derek sheathed his cutlass, then looked at Chantell. In the few hours they had spent together, he'd seen her confidence grow rapidly. She had stopped saying "Master" when she talked to him, and now she carried her head high. He hoped her confidence would continue to grow when they made it to St. Lucifer and she was back in the place she called "hell."

It seemed too easy for Derek. There was no guard watching his hut, which meant he didn't have to kill anyone—at least, not yet—to leave his hut without

Gregor being notified. The previous night, when Derek had gone out looking for Lauren, he'd cut down the sentry with his dagger. Even now, though he knew it had been necessary, Derek could see the look of fear in the man's face and hear the strangled final cry of rage as the dagger plunged in deeply.

The moon was out, but the clouds were gathering in the east, and Derek was able to move swiftly along the pathway through the trees with Chantell in close pursuit. With each step Derek could feel his excitement rising. He knew the false story he'd built for himself wouldn't last much longer, and the moment Gregor no longer believed Derek was a flesh buyer for a wealthy, jaded London businessman, one of the two of them would have to die. But the lie had lasted this long, and if he was able to free Lauren and Amanda tonight, it would no longer be necessary.

Very soon Derek would be back with Lauren, and he'd finally be together with his sister again as well.

"Well, lookee here!"

Derek froze in his tracks, and Chantell bumped into him. In front of them were two young pirates from *The Unholy One*. Derek had seen them before, and he knew they were both inordinately savage, even by the standards of *The Unholy One*. Derek had seen them both kill.

"Hey, Ian, what about the blonde?" the heavier of the two said, his face shiny with sweat, his eyes glazed in a maniacal way as he looked back and forth from Chantell to Derek. "You seen the bitch before?"

"Nope. But I seen the Brit's ugly face too many times!" Ian laughed, running fingers through his long, greasy hair. With his right hand he withdrew a slender-bladed dagger from a sheath hidden at the small of his back. He took a step sideways so that if Derek and

241

Chantell were to continue down the path, they would have to pass between the pirates. "Remember me, Englishman? When we took *Miss Malaki,* I had my sights set on a little whore. You stopped me then." He twisted the dagger slowly in his hand. His tongue lolled wetly around his mouth to moisten his fleshy lips, which already glistened with saliva. "Englishman, why don't you just leave the little filly and take yourself a holiday? Do that and maybe I won't feel like I want to slit your belly open."

Derek withdrew his dagger and cutlass. He was angry with these men for slowing down his progress, but if he was truly honest with himself, he'd realize he was strangely glad an evil excuse for a man like Ian had challenged him. The weeks of comparative inactivity, the inability to do everything he possibly could to destroy Gregor and all his followers, had taken a terrible toll on his conscience.

Lord Derek Leicester York had waited as long as he possibly could. Now it was time for action.

"You want the lady, Ian? What makes you think you're man enough for her?" Derek laughed insultingly, wanting to enrage his adversaries. "She strikes me as more woman than you can handle. She'll eat you alive and spit out the bones."

Chantell moved a step from Derek. She had seen what happened when dangerous men challenged each other, and even though everything about Derek told her he was a skilled fighter, he was outnumbered two to one. No matter how good the Englishman was with his cutlass, Chantell was certain he wasn't good enough to take on two men.

"Don't be a fool," Chantell whispered hotly, knowing full well what her fate would be if Derek failed. "They'll kill you!"

"They'll certainly try," Derek replied, moving forward slowly, a weapon in each hand.

Derek felt the rush of excitement go through him, charging him up, readying him for the battle ahead.

He moved forward cautiously but without fear, like a lion on the prowl, his blue eyes dancing right and left, sizing up Ian and his companion. When the fight was over, either Derek or his enemies would be alive. Perhaps they would all die, but certainly they would not all live.

"Burn in hell," Derek whispered, moving toward Ian while he kept an eye on the other man's movements.

Ian glanced toward his friend before lunging at Derek, coming down hard with his saber in a fierce, brutish attack. Derek blocked the attack with his cutlass, then twisted to the side, away from the silent man's thrust, which Derek guessed—accurately— would immediately follow Ian's.

The pirates attacked with savagery, but with more brute strength and blood lust than with skill and planning. Derek parried Ian's wild, slashing attacks while darting away from the heavier pirate. He continued to back away, drawing the men further away from Chantell. Each time the pirates attacked, their courage and confidence increased; each time Derek blocked or parried a deadly thrust of dagger or saber, he understood just a little more of how his enemies preferred to attack.

The clang of steel filled the still night air. Derek continued to back pedal until the underbrush was thick around him, making quick movement difficult. It was just where Ian was certain he had Derek at a disadvantage that the Englishman did the unexpected.

Darting to his right, Derek disappeared behind a bush for a split second. Since the initial attack, Derek

243

had been backing up, so when he appeared again—this time on the attack—the pirates were caught off guard. He slashed down at the heavyset pirate with his cutlass and lunged forward with his dagger.

The razor-sharp dagger went in to the hilt. The pirate's eyes opened wide, and Derek's face was close enough to smell the man's last breath before his knees buckled and he fell onto his back, his eyes still open.

Derek leapt to the side, stumbling in the underbrush, twisting and rolling, scrambling to his feet a moment later.

"God's bones! You scurvy bastard, you killed me mate!" Ian cried out, standing over his fallen comrade, who lay in a pool of his blood. "You killed me mate!"

With the odds now even, Ian was infinitely less interested in Chantell, or in continuing his fight with Derek. He took several steps away from the corpse at his feet, and though he tried to keep his eyes on his enemy, the dead man drew his gaze like a magnet.

"Stand your ground," Derek said in a low, menacing growl as he advanced slowly toward Ian. The moonlight glittered off the curved blade of his cutlass; blood dripped from his dagger. "Prove you're a man *against* a man . . . even if you are a *little* man."

Ian's lust for Chantell and his desire to revenge the death of his friend were not enough motivation for him to continue the fight.

"You snookered me into that," Ian said quietly, walking back toward the path where the fight had started and where Chantell still stood. "You didn't give me mate a chance."

Derek took several quick, threatening paces toward Ian, which was all the incentive the pirate needed to turn and run as fast as his feet could carry him.

"Come on," Derek said, sheathing his weapons.

"We've wasted more time than we should have."

He started off into the night at an easy, ground-eating trot. Though the deadly fight had lasted less than five minutes, Derek sensed the pirate's death had signaled the death of his own carefully maintained false identity.

Aldon Mitchell was in fine spirits as he went through his master ledger. He'd always had grandiose dreams, but he'd never truly believed he'd acquire so much wealth or so many pretty women. Aldon did not delude himself into believing that he was a handsome man or a charming one. He knew that when he was at St. Thomas or St. Croix and some attractive but poor woman flirted with him it was only because he displayed his wealth and spent it lavishly on such occasions.

Aldon did not care why women paid him attention; it was only important that they did, and that they said the words he wanted to hear.

His old, white-bearded valet stepped up to the bedroom door, holding a silver serving tray. "Master, would you care for another glass of wine?"

Aldon nodded. "Yes. And when you're finished pouring the wine, I'd like you to go see how the wenches are doing. I've brought some new ones in tonight, and the others are preparing them for me now."

"Yes, Master. I will check on the progress immediately."

The old man shuffled away. Aldon sipped his wine and let his mind wander to Lauren, imagining what she must be doing now, and what she would look like when he finally arrived in the opulent pillow room where his entire harem was waiting for him.

Suddenly Derek's face came jarringly into his mind's eye, and Aldon took a heavy swallow of wine. The Englishman had asked too many questions and was not to be trusted. Aldon did not know everything that Derek was up to, but he was definitely more than just a middle-man for a sex-starved, perverted London businessman. The thought of Derek's reaction when he returned to his hut to find Lauren gone brought a smile to Aldon's face.

"English bastard! Thought he had me over a barrel, but I showed him a thing or two!" Aldon said aloud, enjoying the triumphant ring to his voice in the empty room.

He savored the thoughts of Derek's futile anger, rolling the imagined scene over and over in his mind to sample each exquisite nuance of it. Aldon sipped his wine and let the course of his thoughts drift aimlessly. Lauren Masters was at that very moment being prepared for her initiation into his private harem. He was certain she would look magnificent and that his own performance would be nothing less than masterful.

"I should cut your fingers off! I should cut your head off and feed it to the sharks!" Gregor bellowed, his face an even brighter shade of red than his hair.

Ian cowered before him, deathly afraid, occasionally giving a hopeful sideways glance toward Bones, looking for support that never came.

"He attacked us so fast, Cap'n Gregor," Ian continued, his tone high-pitched and whiny. "We was walkin' along, an' the next thing I knew, Mr. Derek's dagger had found its mark. I fought with the Brit, but when he turned tail an' ran, I thought it best to come see you before goin' after 'im."

246

Gregor cursed Ian obscenely, then said, "Do you really think I'd believe such a story? You crossed swords with the Englishman and you're here to tell of it? Not likely, you yellow dog! Not likely at all!"

He turned from Ian and stared out the saloon window. Derek was out in the night with the wench Aldon had given him. Why wasn't he in his hut, doing with the Frenchwoman what any real man would?

The question hounded Gregor, particularly since he didn't like the conclusion he'd come to. The only possible reason for being out with the blonde wench was horribly clear: he intended to go to St. Lucifer. But Gregor was reassured by the knowledge that Derek would have to steal a boat to make the trip. Furthermore, Gregor doubted Derek was up to finding a small island at night—especially with a storm brewing.

"Cap'n Gregor, sir, can I get meself a drink, as long as I'm here an' all?" Ian asked softly, fearfully.

"Yes, yes, yes," Gregor replied, though he'd hardly heard a word that had been said.

The audacity of Derek's move was almost more than Gregor could fathom. Did he actually intend to confront Aldon Mitchell face to face? If not that, then he wanted to steal Lauren away. Either way, it was a bold move for a man who had no friends with him— and very many enemies.

"Get *The Unholy One* ready to sail," Gregor said in a low commanding voice.

"I thought we were settin' sail tomorrow mornin', Cap'n," Bones replied.

"Don't try to think, you fool!" Gregor barked. "Just do as I tell you now, and be quick about it!"

Gregor heard the sound of chairs being knocked over as sailors hustled out of the public house. None of them wanted to be near him when his temper exploded.

With Derek at my side, we could conquer every

island in the Caribbean, Gregor thought sullenly, admiring his enemy's courage and daring, while still finding it foolishly suicidal. *I could have taken over the Big Man's position with no trouble at all with him at my side. Too bad I'll have to kill the Englishman. Tonight.*

Chapter 21

"No, I don't want to go in there," Lauren said, resisting the hands that touched her, that tried to coax her into the high-backed, enamel bathtub.

"You've *got* to," the blonde woman said sympathetically. "Trust me, it's best just to do what you're told. I tried to fight Master Mitchell, and all it got me was the strap!"

Lauren looked at the blonde and smiled softly. She seemed to have come from a good family, and her words carried a faint trace of an English accent.

"What's your name?" Lauren asked, trying to ignore the feminine hands that were unknotting her dirty shikars and mitar.

"Names don't make any difference here," the woman replied. "If Master Mitchell doesn't like your name, he'll change it for you. He's like a god around here. He can do whatever he wants, so you'd better do as he says or you'll get whipped."

The women were all around Lauren, tugging at her shikars and mitar to remove them, some making "tsk! tsk!" sounds as they saw how dirty the soles of her feet were, others inspecting the soiled garments, audibly wondering where she could have gotten such fine silk, and how she could have gotten the garments so dirty and torn.

"Please do as I say," the blonde continued, this time with a touch of impatience and nervousness in her voice. "If you don't get yourself clean, Master Mitchell will get angry, and when he gets angry, he takes it out on all of us."

One of the women in the harem put a hand at the small of Lauren's back and began pushing her toward the tub. Lauren pushed the hand away, and her gaze met with the blonde's. For a moment they just looked into each other's eyes, Lauren realized then that her actions—her *defiance*—could have a direct and painful consequence on the other unfortunate women who had fallen victim to Aldon Mitchell.

Lauren looked at the blonde and wondered how old she was. Sixteen? Seventeen? No more than eighteen, to be sure. Lauren wondered if Derek would find her attractive, whether he preferred blond hair and pale skin to jet black hair and almond skin.

"What's your name?" Lauren asked again, very quietly this time. "Tell me, and I promise I'll bathe."

"It's Amanda. Now, will you please get into the tub? If you're not ready when Master Mitchell comes, we'll all get the strap!"

The name hit Lauren with incredible force. For several seconds she couldn't even breathe. She stood there thunderstruck, looking at the young, attractive girl, realizing now that Derek had been telling the truth all along.

"Lady Amanda York?" Lauren asked, sure of the answer, yet needing to hear it for herself.

At the sound of her name, Amanda froze in place, her mouth slightly open, her lips moving as though to form words, though no words would be spoken.

Since her capture, she had told no one her last name.

Confidence surged within Lauren. She took Amanda's hands in her own and leaned close so that her lips were only an inch from the girl's ear. "Don't worry. Derek is looking for you. He'll find us and set us free."

Amanda squeezed Lauren's hands and replied, "I knew he would come for me!" Crystal tears of relief glistened in her eyes, but suddenly a frightened look came into them, and she whispered, "Don't tell anyone about this! Master Mitchell has spies among us, women who try to curry his favor by telling him what we say and do when he is not with us. You mustn't trust anyone!"

Lauren felt uncomfortable as she was guided into the large tub and women she did not know began to wash her with sponges. She looked into Amanda's eyes and received the subtle, silent reassurance that everything was going as it should, and that she shouldn't be embarrassed.

Amanda took a silver chalice, dipped it into the warm water, and poured it over Lauren's head, wetting the heavy black hair before pouring a smooth soap from another container between her palms.

"You'll like this," Amanda said as she applied the soap to Lauren's hair and began working it into a lather. "It'll make your hair smell wonderful."

Lauren closed her eyes, remembering the last time she'd had someone bathe her, and how erotic it had been. This time, with women touching her, there was nothing erotic about it, but the gentle hands were soothing just the same, easing away her tensions and fears. Amanda's fingers rubbed against her scalp, working the soap deep into her hair, and Lauren sighed wearily, suddenly very tired of running and hiding, of fighting for her life every second of every day.

At last the doubts she had about Derek were

banished once and for all. He really was a good man who wanted only to find and rescue his kidnapped sister.

Lauren felt someone take her by the ankle and raise her foot out of the water. She heard another "tsk! tsk!" and then felt a soapy cloth rubbed along the underside of her foot. A smile creased her mouth. Years ago, how many times had her nanny made similar sounds as she scrubbed her little feet, trying to get them clean for bed, muttering that young ladies ought not run around outside barefoot?

"Make sure we get slippers for her," Lauren heard Amanda say. She wondered who the comment was directed at, but she didn't open her eyes. The warm, soapy water and the soothing massage she was getting muted her fears . . . and her energy. "And get another for the other woman. Her hair's all in tangles, and I don't want to let Master Mitchell see either of them with tangled hair."

"By all means, we mustn't let the Big Man see his personal property with tangled hair!" Lauren muttered sarcastically, her eyes still closed, fatigue pressing down upon her heavily now.

"You stop that!" Amanda hissed, her lips close to Lauren's ear so that none of the other women could hear. "I told you about Master Mitchell's spies, and you'd better listen to me, because if you think I'm not telling the truth, you just keep up that kind of talk and we'll see which one of us gets the strap taken to her!"

Amanda's icy words, laced with fear and remembered pain, stripped away Lauren's fatigue. She pushed herself upright in the tub, then took a large sponge from one of the harem women who was busy trying to clean the sole of her left foot.

"I'll do that," Lauren said sternly, angry with herself. She began running the sponge over herself while

252

Amanda rinsed the soap from her hair. "Let's get this over with, shall we?"

In a sorrowful tone, Amanda whispered, "I'm sorry. I truly am. But unless you do everything Master Mitchell tells you, you'll be punished. I'm only telling you this for your own good. Master Mitchell is a monster who enjoys hurting women. Don't give him any reason to hurt you."

Through teeth clenched in anger, Lauren whispered, "He's not my master!"

Lauren was still in the tub when an old man with a long white beard and a face lined with age stepped into the room. Her heart leaped in her chest at the sight of him—the same man she had run into in Aldon Mitchell's mansion the night she and Derek had broke in!

Lauren twisted in the tub, turning her back to the valet, hiding her face and bosom from him. "He shouldn't be in here!" she said loudly.

One of the harem women replied in a bored tone, "You'll get used to it."

Amanda put a hand on Lauren's shoulder, squeezing firmly, trying to give emotional support, not understanding the real reason Lauren was afraid to show herself to the valet.

To the male intruder, she said, "You have come with a message from the master?"

"No. He sent me here to see how progress is coming on the preparation of his new toys." The old man paid little attention to the fact that all the women in the pillow room were very attractive and half of them were completely naked. "He appears more eager than usual tonight. See to it that he isn't disappointed."

"We will," Amanda said.

When the valet left the room, Lauren breathed a sigh of relief. What would have happened to her if he'd recognized her? It was a question that made her shiver. And how long could she remain in the harem without being recognized?

Hurry, Derek! Lauren thought as she finished with her bath. *Please, hurry back to me!*

Derek sank the oar deep into the water and pulled hard, propelling the outrigger canoe forward. He could hear Chantell's labored breathing, and ten minutes earlier she had complained that the blisters on her hands had now burst. His heart went out to her, but at the same time he couldn't help thinking how strikingly different she was from Lauren—and the comparison wasn't flattering to Chantell. Each time Derek thought of Lauren, he pulled just a little harder on his oar, driven by a power much stronger than himself.

Finding the outrigger canoe had been astonishingly easy. It was the same one Lauren had found the other night. Since he and Lauren had returned the canoe to its original location, the owner probably hadn't even been aware that the canoe had been used. This time, Derek wouldn't be returning the canoe to its owner. Tonight, with Lauren, Sue Ellen, and Chantell with him, he'd try for one of the larger islands. If he could get to one of the major Danish or British colony cities, he'd finally have the sanctioned power he needed to protect the women.

Then he would go after Aldon Mitchell and Gregor . . . with a vengeance.

Derek could smell the approaching storm on the night breeze. It was yet another obstacle in his way to freeing his sister and Lauren, and he silently cursed the skies.

How much longer could Chantell continue to row? He'd seen her stop rowing twice to check her palms, and that probably meant the open blisters were bleeding by now. Though he didn't like to think negatively of her, he silently wished it was Lauren he was going into battle with, not Chantell. With Lauren Masters at his side, he felt more confident than he did alone; with Chantell, he felt burdened. He tried to summon some compassion. After all, Lauren was a woman among women.

"Are you going to make it?" Derek asked quietly.

Chantell simply nodded. She was bone tired, and her body hurt all over in ways she'd never thought possible, but she was free, and she was fighting back against evil people who had done evil things to her. She wouldn't give up, no matter how tired her muscles, nor how sure she was that escape and total freedom were impossible. Somehow she was certain that Derek could play David to Aldon Mitchell's Goliath.

"It's not much further. Another half hour and we'll be on St. Lucifer," Derek said, hoping that Chantell had another thirty minutes of rowing in her.

This was the second time Derek saw the island at night from the sea, and it brought a smile to his lips. If Lauren was here, he'd find her and free her . . . and he'd kill Aldon Mitchell in the process. He knew his way around the island much better now, and having Chantell, he had an insider's knowledge of the workings of Aldon Mitchell's empire.

They beached the canoe, and as before, hid it with palm branches that Derek hacked off with his cutlass. The task took only a few minutes, but Derek's internal clock warned him that time was running out and that he mustn't tarry.

"The main house is in this direction, right?" Derek asked, sheathing his cutlass, nodding toward the

255

mansion he'd broken into a few nights earlier.

"Yes, but the bastard keeps his women in a separate building over there, north of the main house." Chantell smiled to herself, enjoying the fact that she could call Aldon Mitchell "the bastard" now without fear that whoever heard her might try to gain favor by confessing to "the master" what she had said. "There's a road that leads from one building to the other."

Derek thought it over for a moment. His natural inclination was to head in toward Aldon's harem, where Lauren and Amanda would be.

"We're outnumbered," Derek said, as much to himself as to Chantell. "I doubt Aldon's at all worried about me coming after him, but if he is, he'd expect me at the harem. The only way I can get the odds to be more in my favor is to create some kind of diversion, something to distract his attention and divide his forces." He looked at Chantell and asked, "Does he keep guards at the harem?"

"Sometimes yes, sometimes no. It depends on what is happening. Sometimes we were given as gifts to the men for something they'd done, just as I was given to you as a trade for the woman you own."

"I don't own her," Derek snapped angrily, then cursed himself because he'd forgotten all about the horrors that Chantell had already endured. If she made mistakes like thinking a man had the right to own a woman, it was only because she'd been punished for thinking differently. He touched her arm gently, gazing at her through the moonlight. "I'll get you out of this, and in time you'll forget about Aldon Mitchell and everyone here—and this whole bloody mess."

"I'll never forget you," Chantell whispered.

Derek heard the sound of breaking twigs and approaching footsteps. He immediately drew his cutlass, turning toward the sound, his mouth set with grim determination. Just as she had in the previous fight, Chantell moved away from him, not out of fear for her safety, but because she wanted to give him room to move without interference.

The Scotsman approached them, holding a flintlock rifle. He recognized Chantell, but not Derek. This was not entirely surprising, since several mercenaries had been added to the St. Lucifer squad since the break-in several nights earlier.

"What in blazes do you think you're doin' with one of Master Mitchell's whores?" The Scotsman demanded accusingly, jealously. "You ain't been here long enough to be rewarded with her! He'll tell me to cut your privates for this, an' I'll be happy to do it, matey!"

Derek tried to look sheepish, like a man who'd been caught in a tryst with a neighbor's wife. Though he continued to hold his cutlass in his right hand, he made a motion with his empty left hand, as though to signify that every man, now and then, needed what he needed.

"How did you get the wench out, anyway?"

All Derek did was smile. He had no idea what plausible lie he could give the Scotsman.

The mercenary approached slowly, keeping the muzzle of the flintlock pointed at the ground, but holding the weapon in such a way that he could level it on Derek in a flash if necessary. None of this was lost on Derek.

"What's your name, stranger? How long you been with Master Mitchell?"

"Not long. Not long at all."

The Scotsman stopped his approach short of Derek's reach with the cutlass by several feet. He pulled back the hammer of the flintlock, and in the still night air the sound of the mechanism locking into place was threatening and ominous.

"What's wrong, mate?" Derek asked, then quietly

laughed as best he could. "There's no reason to get angry. You want the lady? Fine! Just wait your turn, that's all I'm asking. I'm a reasonable fellow. I know that a man's got his needs. Just let me have a go at her first, then I'm perfectly willing to share."

"You never did give me your name, did you?"

Derek felt his time running out. He groaned, turning halfway round, reacting exactly the way his petulant employees did when he caught them doing something they shouldn't.

"You not going to tell the Big Man about me, are you? God's bones, mate, you know the temper he's got!" Derek complained, but as he did, he swung the cutlass across his body. From the corner of his eye he could see the Scotsman slowly raising the flintlock to his shoulder. "I'm new here! I don't need trouble with—"

The moment the Scotsman got the flintlock to his shoulder, Derek knew he'd run out of time, and that no amount of clever lying would get him out of this mess peacefully. He bent his knees and leaped forward, swinging the cutlass at the same instant in a long, deadly arc toward the muzzle of the flintlock. The echoing boom of the rifle's report made his ears ring, and Derek didn't even hear his cutlass striking the metal barrel of the weapon, knocking it aside, nearly jarring it from the mercenary's grasp.

He dropped the spent rifle and reached for his dagger, but he had badly underestimated Derek's quickness and strength, and that error cost him his life. The Scotsman's hand was on the haft of his dagger when cold steel buried into warm flesh, and his last conscious thought was that this surely must be the man who had caused so much trouble and so many deaths the night before.

After he'd sheathed his cutlass, Derek turned to

Chantell. Her face was pale and her hands trembled. This was the second time that night she'd watched Derek kill, and it was clear such violence was not usual to her.

"Are you still with me?" Derek asked, taking her hands in his own, squeezing them reassuringly. "I need you with me. You know this island much better than I do."

Chantell blinked her eyes and shook her head to clear her muddled thoughts, then nodded. "Don't worry about me," she said in a frightened whisper. "As long as you promise to kill Aldon Mitchell before the night is through, I'll be with you until the end."

Chapter 22

"We've got to be ready with you in an hour," Amanda said softly, dabbing at Lauren's long, wet hair with a thick towel.

Lauren looked at her new friend's reflection in the mirror. It was hard for Lauren to think about the danger she was in, to think about Aldon Mitchell and his rapacious followers. What Lauren needed to know was what Derek was really like, how he had been as a child and as a young man. Lauren knew these questions could wait for another time, since there were much more pressing matters to be taken care of. But for now—at least for the next hour, before Aldon showed up for her and Sue Ellen—Lauren wanted to do nothing but think about the man she had fallen in love with.

"Your hair is so thick," Amanda said matter-of-factly, pushing her fingers through Lauren's damp tresses. "I doubt it'll be dry in time."

For a moment their gazes met through the mirror, and Lauren was surprised to see that Amanda was on the verge of tears.

"What's wrong?" she asked softly, turning on the pillow to face her new friend. "Tell me, Amanda."

Amanda glanced around to make sure none of the other women were paying attention to them, or were close enough to hear what she had to say.

"I feel so bad about this," Amanda began, her voice trembling slightly, her crystal blue eyes filled with sorrow. "I'm a York, after all, and I'm supposed to be able to take care of anything that happens. I can't even get myself out of this mess, much less get you out." Quickly, angrily, she wiped away her tears with the back of her hand. "I feel so helpless. You're important to my brother, and there isn't anything I can do to protect or help you."

Lauren took Amanda's hand and squeezed it, giving her a smile from the heart. "That's not true! Your friendship has already helped me in a dozen different ways, though you don't realize it. Even if you can't get you or me out of here, you've given me advice on how I can make this whole ugly thing more bearable. Can't you see how important this is? Can't you see how proud Derek would be of you?"

Amanda smiled weakly, her lips trembling. "I just wish I could stop . . ."

"I know you do," Lauren said, as unable to speak the whole ugly truth as Amanda. "But we can't stop what's going to happen. It's important that we keep our spirits high, and hope and pray that Derek comes for us soon. He'll come . . . you just wait and see."

"You're right. Derek won't leave us."

Despite the circumstances, Lauren forced a smile to her face and handed Amanda the brush that had been given to them. "Will you please brush my hair again?" she asked, turning again on the pillow so that her back was to Amanda, her legs folded beneath her. "It feels so wonderful."

Amanda began pulling the brush gently through Lauren's long, slightly damp hair.

"Tell me about Derek," Lauren said, an impish light in her dark eyes, studying Amanda's facial expressions through the mirror. "I want to know everything there is to know about him."

"Know everything there is to know about Derek?" Amanda laughed softly. "Nobody knows *that* much. He's always been rather secretive. I think Papa raised him that way. I can't be sure. But Derek never really did talk much—at least about anything other than business."

"Making money is very important to him?" Lauren questioned cautiously.

"No, I don't think so. He chose to talk about business because then he didn't have to talk about himself. That's what I think, anyway." As Amanda spoke, her tone was filled with an emotion that bordered on reverence for her brother. "Derek was never really satisfied. He did so well in school, but it was never enough to satisfy him. I don't think he's ever really been happy."

Lauren didn't want to ask, but she couldn't control her curiosity. "Did he court many women? Was there anyone special?"

Amanda blushed, her pale cheeks darkening attractively. "I shouldn't be telling you those things if you're sweet on each other."

"But you will anyway, won't you? Come on, Amanda, we women have got to stick together. Besides, what well-bred young woman doesn't enjoy a little gossip now and then?"

They both laughed softly, and for a little while it was as though they were getting ready to meet eligible beaux rather than anticipating the arrival of Aldon Mitchell.

"Well, I guess it's fair to say that Derek had many women pursuing him—in a subtle way, of course. With his money and his title and his looks, you could say that there were many women who hoped they'd become Lady York." Amanda picked up a length of pale blue ribbon and slipped it around Lauren's hair, tying it back in a simple but elegant coiffure. "Of course, Derek was always careful, even as a young man. Papa warned us about people and their motives, told us that there would be people who talked sweet to us but really just wanted to get their hands on what we had. I guess it's fair to say that Derek took that to heart."

Lauren felt a tightness in her chest as she listened to Amanda talk about Derek. So he really is a titled English gentleman, she thought with some awe, then corrected herself, smiling. Derek was many things, but she knew for a fact that he wasn't always a perfect gentleman . . . and that was one of the things she loved about him.

"He was careful, then?" Lauren asked, prodding Amanda when she had stopped talking.

"Careful . . . yes, discreet . . . yes, celibate . . . well, I'm afraid my brother has many admirable qualities, but self-denial is not one of them." Amanda leaned close over Lauren's shoulder so that she could whisper directly in her ear. "I remember one night when Papa and Derek were in the library together. It was very late. Derek had just come home and Papa was waiting up for him. Oh! Papa shouted so loud you could have heard him in the next county! Papa said he knew all about what Derek had done with one girl and another. I couldn't believe all the names he said—some were the older sisters of my friends! Then the maid came by and saw me listening at the door and shooed me off to bed again, so I didn't get to hear any more. But after that night I knew my brother did more than just *admire* the ladies."

Lauren felt jealous, then thought about how silly it

was to harbor that useless emotion. She, after all, had been no virgin when she met Derek. But her one act of adolescent stupidity—Richard—could hardly be compared to Derek's romp through the female population of London! Just the same, she wished Derek hadn't "known" so many other women, and she wondered if she would ever be able to keep him interested and happy—sexually and otherwise—in her and her alone.

"Do you have the robe?" Lauren asked, pushing thoughts of Derek and all his damned lovers from her mind.

Rising to her feet, Amanda picked up the gossamer-thin gown. Lauren stood, then bent over at the waist, extending her arms. Amanda helped her put on the gown, and when the soft silk settled down over her, Lauren looked at herself in the mirror and gasped.

The material was so sheer that she could see the outline of her own body through the light blue material. The curves, the highlights, the dark circles of her nipples, and the dark triangular patch at the juncture of her thighs—it was all there to see, only barely obscured by the gown's fine silk.

"Do I have to wear—"

"Master Mitchell demanded it," Amanda cut in quickly, wanting to stop Lauren's protest before it went far enough to travel to the ears of a spy. "It's best to do what he says. He always gets what he wants eventually anyway. If you fight him, you just get hurt for it."

Lauren gritted her teeth, closed her eyes briefly, and prayed for Derek to arrive. *Soon.*

Derek wiped his perspiring brow with his forearm as he crouched in the bushes outside the mansion. He had Chantell at his side, and though he knew that she was very frightened, she had acted courageously so far, and

264

his respect for her had grown dramatically since they'd set foot onto St. Lucifer.

"You're sure Lauren isn't in there?" he asked.

"I can't be sure of anything," Chantell answered, her French accent muted as she whispered. "But in the past, when the bastard brought new women in, he always brought them to the Little House. The only time any of us saw what the Big House looked like inside was when we were all brought there to do cleaning."

"Then Amanda won't be in there, either? She won't be cleaning now?"

Chantell shook her head. Derek looked at her in profile for a moment, wondering how much of her information he could take as gospel truth and how much was just her hopes and wishes. He knew she wanted him to burn the palace to the ground. It was what Derek wanted, too, not simply as an act of revenge, but to help distract Aldon Mitchell's forces while he found Lauren and Amanda and during their subsequent escape.

The Big House, as Chantell called it, did not look as deserted as Derek had hoped. Lamps were lit in several of the rooms, and occasionally he saw someone— perhaps one of Mitchell's servants—walk past a window. The activity suggested that something of importance was about to happen, or had just happened, and self-doubt tore into Derek as he wondered whether his sister and his love would ever be safe and free from the pernicious evil of Aldon Mitchell.

He was thinking that one of the upstairs rooms would be a good place to start the fire when activity at the large double front doors drew his attention, causing him to crouch a little lower behind the foliage surrounding the mansion.

Derek's heart leaped in his chest when he recognized the rotund form of Aldon Mitchell stepping through the doorway accompanied by two burly, dangerous-looking men. With a wave of his hand Aldon sent one of the men running. The bodyguard returned within seconds with a mule-drawn carriage.

"Think they're going to the harem?" Derek asked, his lips touching Chantell's ear as he whispered.

"We'll see which direction the carriage goes," Chantell answered. "He's got the look to him, though—the bad look he gets when he wants a woman."

Derek took Chantell's hand in his and squeezed it. "He'll never see another sunrise."

The carriage headed off at an easy pace down the rutted road. With a glance toward Chantell, Derek learned that Aldon was headed in the direction of the harem house.

"Stay here," Derek whispered as soon as the carriage had disappeared from view. "Don't move until I come back. If you hear any shooting, or if the place is burning and I'm not back, you're on your own—understand?"

Chantell nodded. Derek patted her cheek, then stepped out of the shadows, moving toward Aldon Mitchell's palatial mansion with murder in his eyes.

Three minutes later flames had lighted two upstairs bedrooms. One man lay dead, a saber still in his hand, his last thought that he'd never really believed the Englishman could move that swiftly.

An old woman with hair the color of snow stepped out of a downstairs room. She met Derek's gaze and froze. Though her first reaction had been one of fear, after a moment she had cool resignation in her expression.

"I won't hurt you," Derek said calmly, knowing that the fire would take at least five minutes to engulf the upper floor of the mansion before moving downward to the ground floor. "Get your family and get out."

The woman looked at him impassively, seeing Derek as just another European master who would command respect.

"Do you speak English?" Derek asked, disconcerted by the old woman's implacable countenance. "Do you understand what I'm telling you?" The old woman nodded. "The Big Man will be dead by morning," he said.

The old woman smiled and nodded before turning away from Derek to retrieve her children and grandchildren. She did not know what the future held for her and her family, but if Aldon Mitchell was dead, it had to be better than the past and present.

The seconds seemed to tick by slowly for Derek, but he knew that that was only because his mind was moving so very, very fast. He made his way through the last two rooms downstairs, checking for women and children, herding the innocent victims of Aldon Mitchell's greed out into the comparative safety of the night.

Derek was at the front door when another guard attacked him, howling with rage, rushing forward with a long cutlass raised above his head. The man was naked from the waist up, and his breeches were partly open. Behind him a young woman stood in a doorway, a thin sheet wrapped tightly around her, her tear-stained face almost void of expression as she watched the carnage unfolding.

The man, like so many of his ilk, attacked with blind fury, brute force, and no forethought. He crossed swords with Derek once, and the sound of metal meeting metal still rang in his ears when the Englishman's dagger buried deep into his fleshy stomach.

When Derek looked back at the young woman wrapped in the sheet, she gave an enigmatic smile, used a corner of the sheet to wipe the tears from her face, then followed the others out of the mansion. If Derek had any fears that she was the pirate's willing lover, it was banished by the woman's Mona Lisa smile.

Outside, the chaos was just beginning. The matires were running in all directions as parents gathered children and did a quick head count. Derek knew the fire had not spread so quickly that people would be trapped inside.

Derek found Chantell crouching in the shadows, the smooth planes of her face highlighted by the eerie glow of the burning mansion. Her eyes held a strange, mesmerized look.

"Time to go," Derek said, his voice harsh. He grabbed Chantell by the arm and hauled her to her feet, shaking her hard to mentally bring her back from wherever she had gone. "I need your help, Chantell! God's bones, don't have the vapors on me now!"

Chantell very slowly turned her face away from the burning mansion toward Derek. She spoke several words in French, stopped herself, then began again in faintly broken English. "You really can stop that bastard Mitchell, can't you? You can burn his home . . . you can kill him . . ."

"Only with your help," Derek said, lying, wanting Chantell's help but not needing it. He shook her again and watched the glaze clear from her eyes. "Lead the way! Lead me to the bastard!"

Chantell quickly began jogging down the rutted pathway toward the harem house, with Derek close at her side.

The bodyguard pulled the carriage to a halt, then leaped to the ground to open the half-door for Aldon Mitchell. The portly despot was attired in his finest white jacket trimmed in gold lace brocade, and in breeches that were considerably tighter in the thighs than they had been when he'd first had them made. His stockings were new and a brilliant white, and the buckle shoes were shiny. Although the clothes no longer fit him any too well, Aldon felt attractive in them. But it was a relief to know that he would soon be out of them.

The white-bearded valet was waiting at the front door, looking a bit worried, but not so much so that Aldon should have any concern that his demands hadn't all been met.

"Master . . . we await you," the valet said solemnly, bowing as deeply as his old bones would allow. Aldon slid past into the dimly lighted building.

Without a sideways glance, Aldon went directly to the pillow room, drawn by what he knew was waiting for him there. Aldon had personally selected the clothes he wanted for Lauren and Sue Ellen, and just thinking about what they would look like made his palms sweaty and his silk shirt stick wetly to his underarms.

The door to the room was open slightly, and when Aldon hit the door with his open palm, it swung round on its hinges, banging loudly against the wall. Eight women all gasped in unison at the sound. Aldon smiled, stifled his chuckle of pleasure at seeing their collective fear, then said, "Wenches! So good to see you all again! I trust you have all met our new friends, Lauren and Sue Ellen."

Lauren held her ground, her hands loose at her sides, her shoulders square, her chin held high. Amanda had warned her that Aldon enjoyed exploiting any weakness in others. If Lauren tried to hide her near nudity, Aldon Mitchell would most assuredly flaunt her emotional discomfort in front of the others and do everything within his power to make her feel helpless and insignificant.

"My God! Dear God in heaven!" Aldon cursed in a hushed whisper when he finally picked out Lauren standing behind Amanda and several other women.

The women parted and Lauren held her breath. In her heart, she knew that this whole charade was being played out because she and Sue Ellen were there. The way Aldon looked at her, his eyes trailing slowly, greedily up and down her, made Lauren feel sick to her stomach.

"*Very* nice," Aldon said, drawling out the first word theatrically. He casually pushed women aside so that he could walk slowly around Lauren. For only a second, while he was directly behind her, Lauren closed her eyes and summoned all the courage she had. Aldon came to a stop in front of her and casually reached out to take a lock of her silky ebony hair between his fingers. "Even better than I had hoped for . . . so much better. . . ."

Words failed Aldon, but Lauren was in no way complimented by his appreciation. The sheer night rail, though covering her from neck to ankles, made her feel more naked than if she wore nothing at all. The gauzy, see-through silk, though loose and flowing, seemed to conform perfectly to every part of her, from the gentle curve of her hips to the taunt, full swell of her breasts. Lauren saw the sweat beaded on Aldon's forehead and upper lip, and disgust for him grew. Aldon had yet to touch her; he hadn't made her touch him yet—but his hands were already trembling and clammy. Though she had little real ability to make any kind of comparison, Lauren could tell instinctively that Aldon was ineffectual and clumsy in bed, selfish and short-

270

winded. Seeing him in his new light made him seem much less threatening.

Aldon circled Lauren slowly three times, never touching her, knowing that when he finally did, his excitement would be so great that he could not postpone his own culmination for more than just a few seconds.

He turned his attention to Sue Ellen. She was beautiful, to be sure, but she wasn't Lauren. She lacked the spine-melting beauty of the dark-haired, voluptuous young woman from Virginia, and because she wasn't quite so attractive, quite so stimulating, Aldon concentrated on her. It might make it possible for him to contain his excitement a bit longer.

"You're both quite extraordinary," he said softly to himself, not wanting any response from the women. "I can see why that damned Englishman wanted you both for himself." Aldon scratched his freshly shaved chin, circling Sue Ellen slowly, enjoying both what he could see of her through the sheer night rail and what the see-through silk concealed. "Did he train you well?"

Lauren wanted to scream. *Train? Like a dog or a horse?* If she had Derek's deadly dagger at that moment, she'd have plunged it gladly into Aldon's heart, even if it would mean her own death at the hands of his bodyguards. The sacrifice—her life for Aldon's—would be worth it if she could prevent another woman from suffering the humiliating fate that she now was forced to live through.

Aldon touched the side of Lauren's face with his fingertips. She did not flinch at his touch, and she kept her gaze lowered, just as Amanda told her would be safest.

"Perhaps he did train you after all," Aldon said, letting his fingertips slide upward over an ebony,

271

arching eyebrow. He felt his excitement rising swiftly—dangerously so—and he turned away from Lauren again, concentrating on Sue Ellen until he was sure his self-control, such as it was, could be maintained.

Aldon reached out to cup Sue Ellen's breasts in his hands, rubbing the tips with his thumbs, touching her through the cool silk of the night rail. He studied her face as his fingers manipulated her, wanting to see a positive reaction, but not really expecting one. Sue Ellen, with her gaze directed at the floor, gave no outward sign that she was being touched at all.

"Did he touch you like this?" Aldon asked, an edge to his voice.

It pleased him when women responded to his touch. He didn't care if they responded with passion or with revulsion—so long as they responded, he was happy and excited. Sue Ellen's aloofness made Aldon feel oddly powerless, which deflated the mild erection that he had managed.

"Answer me, you wench!" he hissed, his face close to Sue Ellen's, his fingers catching the tips of her breasts to squeeze harder than necessary. "Did that English dog touch you like this?"

Sue Ellen raised her eyes briefly. She looked straight into Aldon's gaze and said quietly, truthfully, "No, he did not touch me like that. He didn't touch me at all."

Aldon chuckled, at first thinking Sue Ellen was lying to him. For her lies, she'd get the strap. But then, almost as soon as he'd decided that Sue Ellen deserved a solid whipping, he realized that she *was* telling the truth. Could it be that Derek preferred men to women? If that was the case, he would be the perfect buyer for a London businessman who hungered for virgins. It would be as good as having a eunuch guarding the harem.

Aldon started to laugh. He took his hands away from Sue Ellen, feeling strong and powerful once more. His slumbering phallus twitched and began coming to life again as Aldon, now secure in his power over these women, imagined them both helpless against him, and virgins as well.

"My sweets!" he cooed, walking around Sue Ellen and Lauren to feast his eyes on them. He squeezed Sue Ellen's buttocks, chuckling softly, feeling his excitement rising, making him feel powerful, invincible, masculine. "This is going to be a night you will always remember. Tonight I am going to teach you everything there is to know, everything you must learn if you are to give pleasure to a man. Tonight, my sweets . . ." He leaned close to Lauren, inhaling the natural fragrance of her body, his lips brushing against the arch of her neck. "Tonight I am going to give you what you need."

Lauren was glad Aldon was standing behind her, because then she knew that he couldn't see the smile that flitted across her face. Aldon Mitchell giving her what she needed? That overweight, overbearing, egotistical jackass teaching her how to please a man? After having made love to Lord Derek York, it was a completely ludicrous notion that she could feel anything besides revulsion at the hands of any other man. She ached to tell Aldon as much, to see the horror on his face when he realized that he was an ugly, fat, pathetic—

"You find something humorous?" Aldon asked, the words interrupting her thoughts as he leaned in close to Lauren, his nose nearly touching hers. "Or perhaps it is just the thought of my touch that makes you smile?"

Lauren had no idea what the right response was. Though she knew that she should fear Aldon Mitchell, his strutting and parading, his boasts and false bravado, it all just seemed too ludicrous to take seriously.

"Well?" Aldon demanded.

The humor ended when Aldon placed his hand on Lauren's hip, touching her through the sheer silk. He was a strutting peacock, but at the moment he was a strutting peacock with power over her. The smile vanished from Lauren's face, and a cool, faintly resentful expression clouded her dark eyes and changed the line of her mouth.

"Or is it that you don't think I can teach you anything? Is that it, my little wench?" Aldon chuckled. His hand slid up from Lauren's hip, moving up her side, inching slowly toward her breast. "If that's what you think, you're in for a real treat. I'm going to teach you things that I don't teach to all my other little whores." He took several steps away from Lauren and Sue Ellen. "Get on your knees," he said, his eyes thinning to slits. "Take my clothes off, my sweets. I'm going to teach you to—"

The door to the pillow room swung open and banged against the wall, just as it had before, but this time it wasn't Aldon Mitchell trying to make a dramatic and frightening entrance. It was the broad-shouldered, tall Belgian bodyguard, and he wasn't trying to be theatrical.

"It is on fire! Master, it is all on fire!" the bodyguard shouted.

The vision of seeing Aldon coldly execute his friend was still fresh in the bodyguard's memory. He knew the price one paid for failure, and though the Big House burning had nothing to do with him whatsoever, he was certain he'd get the blame.

"What is on fire?" Aldon demanded, the veins in his neck showing. The bulge in his breeches, at best

274

unimpressive, embarrassed Aldon horribly, now that there was another man in the pillow room.

"The Big House!" the bodyguard blurted out, his face draining of blood, certain that he, too, would be summarily executed at Aldon Mitchell's vicious whim.

Lauren glanced over at Sue Ellen, then at Amanda, and in those looks they asked each other the same question: *Is it Derek?*

"Get my carriage!" Aldon shouted as he rushed past the Dane. "Lock the doors! These wenches will pay dearly for this night!"

Someone had to pay for any inconvenience in Aldon Mitchell's life, and he always made sure his slaves were the ones that paid the price.

Chapter 23

"Put your backs to it, you yellow dogs!" Gregor screamed, standing in the aft of the rowboat as the sweaty sailors strained at the oars.

Twenty minutes earlier, Gregor had been calling to his "good mates" to put everything they had into their work. With the rapid approach of the storm, Gregor was now calling them dogs, cowards, and worse.

How far away was St. Lucifer? Seven miles? More? Less? It was difficult to guess, and with the overcast skies, Gregor had no stars to guide him. This would be one of those Caribbean storms that blows in with little warning, hits with ferocious intensity, and is gone almost as quickly as it arrived.

Gregor could feel the storm on the wind. To the east the sky looked almost purple. This was not a night to be out on the sea, particularly not in a rowboat, and for the hundredth time that night he cursed the Englishman's soul. Though Gregor knew the waters near St. Lucifer better than any man alive, there were still a dozen barely submerged rocks that could rip a hole clean through the strongest hull, and only in the daylight could he be certain of his exact position. Gregor had left *The Unholy One* what he had hoped was a safe distance out to sea.

His men were tired, he knew. But Gregor also knew that his reputation and possibly his life were at stake. He didn't know exactly what Derek's motive was in going to St. Lucifer, but whatever it was, it wouldn't look good for Gregor.

And then he saw the fire, and all of his worst fears took on a new reality.

"There can be no God in heaven," Gregor whispered, squinting his eyes to see what at first was just a glow in the dark.

The closer they got to St. Lucifer, the more Gregor could see. The fire had engulfed the Big House and many of the surrounding trees. There was no doubt in Gregor's mind that the entire mansion was in flames and that Derek had set the fire. To the west, where the harem house was, Gregor could see no glow of fire.

Part of him wanted to have his men turn the rowboat around and return to *The Unholy One*. He could sail back to the island and sit the storm out in *As the Crow Flies* in relative comfort and safety. Maybe Mirabell might even find him a little more handsome, now that Derek was no longer around. Returning to the tavern where he was master of his fate seemed so much better than pushing on to St. Lucifer, where he would have to face Aldon Mitchell and discover the full extent of the damage caused by Derek.

Never before had Gregor been quite so vividly aware of his own cowardice. He looked at his men straining at the oars and thought how they would never know the reason—the real reason, that is—for his having them turn the boat around to return to their ship. Perhaps then they'd never know that the thought of facing Aldon Mitchell after his house had burned to the ground made Gregor feel empty and nauseated. They'd never know that any man brave enough, crazy enough, or just plain angry enough to attack a man like Aldon Mitchell—as Derek had—was too much of an enemy for Gregor to challenge willingly.

The closer they got to St. Lucifer, the brighter the fire became. A reddish-orange glow filled the sky above where the Big House was—or had been. Not even the surrounding trees that usually kept Aldon's palatial estate hidden from the water could hide the devastating effects of the fire.

"That crazy English bastard's done it," Gregor whispered, shaking his head in amazement.

He could hear some of the men talking about the fire. If he turned around now, they would all know he was afraid of meeting up with Aldon or Derek or both; he could no longer use the approaching storm as an excuse.

"Put your backs into it, you stinking dogs! Tonight we'll find out what you're really made of!"

The young, foolish, bloodthirsty sailors, led by Bones, cheered enthusiastically, but all Gregor could think about was how young they were, and what kind of opponent Derek must be if he would even consider going against Aldon Mitchell single-handedly.

The door slammed shut, and the iron bar locking it was thrown. Lauren looked at Amanda and whispered, "It's got to be him."

"Who?" other women asked, crowding around Lauren and Amanda, eager to learn all they could.

Amanda tried once again to warn Lauren about talking too much in front of the other women; captivity had taught her that spies are everywhere, and that

278

no one can be trusted. Lauren didn't care . . . she was certain that before the night was through, Derek would set them all free.

"A good man," Lauren said simply, rushing to the barred window. "He's come to rescue us!"

"How do you know?" another woman asked, her voice filled with condescending suspicion.

"I can feel it in my bones, in my soul," Lauren replied without looking at her accuser.

Amanda said quietly, "If she had a soul, maybe she would know what you mean."

Shouts echoed through the night. The women huddled near the window, their faces pressed against the restraining iron bars, their eyes desperately searching the night for any sign of a rescuer. They were still pressed together, nearly a dozen exquisitely beautiful women, when the locking bar was thrown from the door and Lord Derek Leicester York stepped inside. His navy silk shirt was torn open to the waist, and a bloody slash across his chest dripped blood across his flat, rock-solid stomach. He had a cutlass in one hand and a dagger in the other, and his cold blue eyes burned with the intensity of the fight.

"Derek!" Lauren shouted, pushing her way through the crowd of women, launching herself at the man she loved more than life itself.

Derek, still holding a weapon in each hand, opened his arms and let Lauren leap inside them, pressing herself against him, searching for his mouth. He kissed her only briefly, his eyes still searching the room for enemies.

"Aldon's not here. He's taken his men to the Big House," Lauren said, pressing her face into the nape of his neck, inhaling deeply to catch the distinct, comforting scent of him, secure at last that everything

279

would be all right, now that he was there.

Derek eased himself away from her, and only then did Lauren realize that he had a long, clean cut across his chest, and that her night rail, once pristine, was now matted with blood and sticking to her.

"You're hurt!" she cried.

"It's not as bad as it looks," Derek said, somewhat distractedly.

Amanda York, standing near the window with her face in her hands, was crying sobs of joy, looking at her older brother over the tips of her fingers. She wanted to rush to him, to take him into her arms and squeeze him tightly, but she still did not truly believe, deep within her heart, that it really was him. Too many things had happened to her since the last time she'd seen him for her to believe that her trauma was really nearing an end.

Lauren stepped away from Derek, following the line of his gaze until she saw Amanda. Tears sprang into her eyes as she saw the love that was there between brother and sister, clear and undisguised.

"I'm here now," Derek said softly, opening his arms for Amanda, though he continued to hold his weapons. "I'm going to take you away from all this."

Just as Lauren had, Amanda rushed into Derek's arms, throwing her arms around his neck and holding him as if she would never let him go. Watching, Lauren remembered the doubts she'd had about Derek, thought of all the times she'd questioned whether the story about Amanda was really true or just a clever ruse to hide his villainy, and she felt guilty at her mistrust.

"You're bleeding," Amanda said, echoing Lauren, her tears still streaming from her blue eyes, which Lauren now noticed were exactly the same color as Derek's.

"We'll take care of it later," Derek said, gently pushing himself out of his sister's grasp. "Right now we've got to get out of here before anyone comes back."

Derek looked at Lauren, his eyes going from her face down to her bosom, and her heart sank. *He didn't touch me!* Lauren wanted to scream, but she knew it would do no good—not now, anyway. Seeing her in the thin night rail was all the evidence he needed to believe that she had been violated by Aldon Mitchell.

"It's going to be a bad storm," Derek said, his right arm around Lauren's waist. He was giving the women a few minutes to catch their breath before continuing. Where exactly they were going, he didn't know, but since it was away from the mansion, he figured it was the right direction.

"Bad enough to keep Aldon and his men pinned down?" Lauren asked.

Derek shook his head, wanting to lie and say something comforting to Lauren.

"If Aldon's pinned down, then we're pinned down, too," Derek said after a moment, still searching the night sky. "This is a small island. It won't take Aldon long to find us, if he's got a big enough hunting party." He looked at Amanda, who was breathing deeply, but who still appeared to have plenty of energy left. Several of the women did not look as if they could trek much further, at least not at the pace Derek had set for them. "We've got to get off this island, even if we do get caught in the storm. I'd rather fight the storm than Aldon and his men."

Lauren looked at the knife wound across Derek's chest again. It wasn't terribly deep, but it was long, and he had lost a lot of blood. She reached up to touch his cheek with her palm, drawing his gaze down to her own.

"He didn't touch me," she whispered.

"Of course not," he replied, and Lauren knew he thought she was lying.

The island was not as deserted as Derek had first thought. When they came across a small village, they were able to get some clothes for the women—well-worn shikars and mitars, mostly, but also a cotton shirt and a cheap cotton dress that had been cast away by someone or stolen by Gregor's men. Derek thanked the villagers profusely in French, Spanish, English, and German, though few of them actually understood any of what he said. The only thing that did bring forth a response from them was the name "Mitchell" and the pantomimed gestures to indicate that the Big House was burning.

"Put this on," Derek said, handing Lauren the dress he'd acquired. He handed Amanda a shikars and a cotton shirt. "Not exactly fashionable, but at least you won't catch your death of cold."

Lauren removed the bloodstained night rail and pulled the dress over her head. Death of cold? Not likely. Even with the storm whipping up the wind, it had to be at least seventy-five degrees out. She buttoned up the dress. *I can't make him believe that Aldon didn't touch me, even if it is the truth. I can't make him believe anything at all . . . if he doesn't want to believe it. . . .*

They trudged on, moving in what was sometimes an aimless way, searching for a boat, for anything that would offer Derek and the women some measure of protection against their unseen pursuers. The fire, Derek hoped, had bought them some time, but that time would be running out quickly. Unless he could find a way of getting himself and the women off St. Lucifer, burning the Big House would have been only a vengeful act, a reprieve, that wouldn't change the end result one whit.

An hour later they found a boat. It was tied to a dock that looked to be in such bad repair that Derek was afraid to let all the women walk on it at the same time.

"Stay here while I look it over," Derek told Lauren and Amanda.

He took a moment to study the faces of the women who had followed him through the Caribbean jungle. Many of them were nearly dead on their feet. Chantell was so tired that she had lain on her back in the sand, arms and legs outstretched as she gulped in air. Sue Ellen was on her knees, her head down, her thick hair now matted with perspiration and clinging to her forehead and temples.

It's me that Aldon wants, Derek thought as he studied the women, attempting to guess how much strength each of them had left. *He won't really care about the women now. He'll want revenge, and that means they're in more danger with me than without me.*

The boat was in bad shape. Apparently it was still being used, but Derek could see that it had already been patched and repaired several times, and given his druthers, would be patched in several more places before he'd want to use it. But Derek wasn't given his druthers, and if he was certain of anything, it was that ten people in the boat would sink it to the seafloor.

Which of the women would he take with him, and who would be left behind?

Even pondering the question made Derek feel hollow inside. He couldn't meet the questioning gazes of the women when he returned to shore.

"The boat isn't taking in water, but it isn't in good condition. It's not safe," he said softly, to no one in particular. "It'll never handle all of us. Not for long, anyway."

"What does that mean?" Lauren asked.

She knew that if Derek had to make a decision as to who'd go and who'd stay, he'd deny himself and give someone else the opportunity for freedom. In this respect, she understood Derek better than he did himself. She wanted to stay with him no matter what.

"I don't know yet."

Chantell said softly, "I'll stay." All eyes turned to her, knowing what her sacrifice meant. "What difference does it make? I've been with that bastard so long now, no man will ever want me again. I might as well stay."

"You're wrong, Chantell—as wrong as you can be," Derek replied softly, wanting to quash all the negative thoughts the attractive young woman from France had about herself, damning himself softly because he knew he couldn't.

A dark-haired young woman, her eyes bright and fierce, stepped forward, challenging everyone. "I'm not staying. I'm not staying for anyone, and I hope to God I never have a man touch me again as long as I live!"

With that first affirmation, a half dozen others followed in quick succession. Derek tried to explain that the boat was not in good shape, that it had been patched several times, and that there was absolutely no way of knowing for certain how much weight it could hold or how long it would remain afloat.

"There's a storm coming," Derek said, looking at the women in what was left of the moonlight, seeing their scanty clothing and feeling their desperation. "What's going to happen to you if you get caught out there in the storm? Are any of you experienced sailors? Will any of you know what to do?"

"He just wants the boat for himself!" the first woman shot back, turning to the others who had demanded passage. "He wants it for his family, that's all!" She turned to Amanda, her eyes cold and bitter, and whispered, "You thought you could get away with that, didn't you? You were always a selfish little bitch, Amanda! I'm *glad* Master Mitchell took the strap to you!"

Lauren didn't say anything, but she'd have bet her inheritance that she'd just discovered who the spy in the harem was.

Derek tried to talk the women out of using the boat as they clambered hastily aboard. The more he thought about it, the more convinced he was that booking passage on that boat was a one-way trip. The women, egged on by their new and particularly selfish leader, were more and more convinced that Derek only wanted the boat for himself when he tried to talk them out of leaving on it.

"You'll never make it," Derek said quietly, so quietly that the women pushing off of the small dock could not hear him.

Lauren slipped her hand inside Derek's, wanting to touch him, to give him comfort. But she doubted she could, and when he didn't squeeze her hand, she was convinced of it.

"It's not your fault," she whispered. "They were determined to go. You can't protect people from themselves, no matter how hard you try."

Derek looked down at Lauren briefly, then turned his gaze away. He seemed to have trouble looking at her for very long, and this seemed to tear at her very soul.

"I seem to have trouble protecting anyone lately," he said, then pulled away from her. "We've got to keep moving," he told the women who had remained with him. "I don't know what's ahead for us, but I do know that the moment we stop, we'll lose ground to Aldon and his men."

He did not say that they had only a few hours of darkness left. As soon as the sun came up, the odds of their being found would heighten considerably, and the odds of their continued freedom would become considerably worse.

Aldon turned away from the fire, pushed back by the intensity of the heat. The flames rose fifty feet in the air or more, engulfing everything. The crackling sound of burning wood and the small explosions of tree sap bubbling and bursting within the trunks of living trees filled the night air.

"I want them all killed," Aldon said with surprising calm. He looked over at Gregor, who stood beside him, then down at Bones. "Do you hear me? I want them all killed. Not just the Englishman—everyone. The women. Everyone."

Gregor was relieved that the blame for this was not being leveled at him, and he was more than happy to agree to handle the assassinations personally.

"Don't you want us to bring some of the women back for you?" Bones asked. To him, killing attractive women seemed a horrible waste.

"No, you fool!" Aldon bellowed, his calm suddenly shattered. "Don't you realize what's happened? That God damned English bastard burned down my home and set my property free! They were women—just god-damn wenches—and he burned down my house for them! I want them killed! I want them slaughtered! I want an example made of them so that you and everyone else in these seas will know what happens to people who oppose me!"

Gregor looked at Aldon Mitchell as he ranted, thinking that the Big Man really wasn't so big after all, nor nearly so implacable as he wanted his underlings to believe.

Chapter 24

The wind was rapidly becoming stronger, and Derek could smell rain in the air. Part of him blessed the rapidly approaching storm; it would certainly make it more difficult for Aldon's soldiers to follow them. But, it would also make it dangerous to be on the water. The second boat they found appeared to be very seaworthy and was small enough to be sailed easily, yet large enough to carry himself and the women.

"This is my plan," Derek said, gathering the women in a circle around him. "I want to head west for St. Thomas tonight. I've no way of knowing how severe this bloody storm is going to be, but I'm willing to bet it'll be a bad one. Being on the water when it hits won't be the safest place to ride it out. But the wind is blowing west, so we have a chance."

Amanda, like her brother, had grown up studying the trade wind charts for the family's various shipping interests, and she added, "Yes. If the storm does hit, and hits hard, it'll actually help us, because it'll push us toward St. Thomas."

Derek smiled. "That's right. Once we get to St. Thomas, there are several cities where we can find refuge. Aldon Mitchell is a power around St. Lucifer only because these islands are more or less uninhabited. On St. Thomas, there is a government, legal agencies, *laws* . . . you can't be a self-proclaimed god in a civilized society."

Chantell squared her shoulders and said, "I'm with you wherever you go."

"Me, too!" Sue Ellen added quickly.

Lauren and Amanda exchanged glances. Amanda was accustomed to seeing this kind of adulation for her brother, but Lauren was not, and it was particularly difficult when Derek hadn't given her many comforting words since first seeing her in the scandalous night rail provided by Aldon Mitchell.

They pushed off with Derek at the helm. Moments after setting sail for St. Thomas, they heard the harsh cry of the boat's owner cursing them. Derek's teeth were white in the dark night as he smiled, and Lauren cursed softly to herself, wishing he would turn his smile on her once again, just as he had when they were together in the little grass hut with the dirt floor where she'd let her passion for him flow freely.

The outrigger was deep in the water as the small sailboat keeled over so far to starboard Derek was certain Sue Ellen would get thrown out. Straining at the rudder, Derek battled the storm with all his strength and sailing skills he possessed.

The storm had hit with jarring force, just as he'd predicted. He'd suspected it would be a bad storm, but he had grossly underestimated it.

First the wind hit, buffeting the little sailboard around with such force that Derek dropped the sails. Hardly had he gotten the sails down when the wave swells heightened to twenty-five feet. And the rain came down in sheets, threatening to fill the boat.

Lauren and Chantell bailed as quickly as they could with the two buckets aboard, but for each bucket of water they tossed over the side, two buckets rained in.

Had it been an English sailboat of similar size, Derek was certain the boat would have capsized and sank. The outrigger prevented the boat from capsizing a dozen times, and though he needed all his mental and physical energy to fight the storm, Lord Derek York was too much of an entrepreneur to resist calculating the profit of bringing this innovation to the Europeans.

As the first hour of the storm passed into the second and then the third, with overcast skies that allowed no starlight, Derek lost track of the direction the winds and the waves were carrying them. If it was due west, that was wonderful; if it wasn't, he didn't much care. All he wanted now was to stay alive through the storm. In the morning he could figure out where they were by the location of the sun.

The women continued valiantly battling the storm, even though they were all soaked to the bone and achingly tired. Chantell and Amanda had gotten seasick, and only the ready availability of fresh rainwater kept them from becoming dehydrated.

A huge wave, coming from behind, lifted the sailboat high, then tossed it back to the sea as though it and its inhabitants weighed nothing at all. Gallons of water filled the boat, and Lauren attacked the water with renewed energy, tossing out bucket after bucket.

Derek watched Lauren feverishly bailing water, her ebony hair flying this way and that, clinging to her like a skullcap, spread out over her shoulders. The wet cotton dress clung to her figure, hiding nothing, and Derek remembered how she'd first looked when he'd entered the harem, and how he hated Aldon Mitchell because he knew that the bastard had seen Lauren this way.

Had he done more than just look at Lauren? And what about Amanda? She, too, had been obscenely attired, yet that hadn't bothered Derek quite so much as seeing Lauren that way. He felt guilty for this strange distinction.

What if Lauren was pregnant? Derek could never know if the child was his or Aldon's. Could he live with the question of whose child Lauren had given birth to? Every time he touched her, would he wonder just a little if she felt his touch, or Aldon's?

Derek wasn't worried that Lauren had gotten aroused when she was with Aldon—it was ludicrous to think she would. But would the memory of Aldon's touch cloud her thoughts and make it impossible for her to feel pleasure at Derek's touch?

Dear God, Derek thought as he watched Lauren straining against the weight of a water-filled bucket, *she's got more courage than any five men!*

A wave came crashing over the stern, slamming Derek into the rudder paddle and forcing the breath from his lungs. He wiped the saltwater from his eyes and, as he did every time the sailboat was hit by such a wave, rapidly checked the women to make sure they were still in the boat.

Lauren was looking at him as she kneeled near the edge of the boat, the bucket in her hands. Their eyes met and held. She didn't have to speak to ask the question: Have feelings changed between us?

Derek knew it was wrong to look away. He knew it would send the wrong message to her. But he couldn't keep looking into her dark, questioning eyes. When he gathered his resolve and looked back at her, wanting to tell her without words that he loved her and would always love her, no matter what had happened or what would happen in their lives, Lauren was again busy bailing out water.

With effort he turned his attention away from Lauren and to his sister. Amanda was ghostly pale. She had been the first to get seasick, and as the storm raged on, she showed no signs of getting over it soon. Though she did not want to fill her stomach with anything, Derek urged her to take mouthfuls of rainwater when she could.

She's strong. Mother and Father would be proud of her. When she gets back to London, she'll be the toast of the town and everyone will hear of her exploits.

Even as Derek thought this, he realized that there were some exploits Amanda would not be able to talk about, and that before his task in the Virgin Islands was complete, he'd have to rid the world of Aldon Mitchell, Gregor, and as many of the pirates from *The Unholy One* as possible.

Another violently capricious wave picked up the sailboat and tossed it back to sea. Sue Ellen, who had nearly been thrown out before, ended up on the edge of the boat. She'd have fallen overboard if Lauren hadn't grabbed her by the ankle and kept her in.

"The storm won't last much longer!" Derek shouted, trying to be heard above the roaring wind and crashing waves. He actually had no way of knowing how much longer the storm would last. "Just be strong! We'll get through this!"

Lauren looked at Derek, and once again the questions in her dark eyes were easy for him to read. *Yes,* she asked him, *we'll live through this night, but will our love live through it as well?*

Derek squinted, his eyes red and swollen from the saltwater, and tried to see into the impenetrable, rain-filled night. His chest was bruised from being tossed by countless waves into the rudder paddle. The gash on his chest had stopped bleeding, but the smooth edges of the wound were white and puffy, and the blood that had coagulated to form a protective scab over the wound had been washed away.

He could hardly see Chantell, who had taken up a position at the bow. Sue Ellen had struggled mightily, but she was on her side on the floor of the boat, on the verge of blacking out from dehydration and exhaustion. Chantell was still able occasionally to toss a bucket of water out of the boat. Lauren continued to bail with all her might.

"Can you see—" Derek began, shouting over the din of the storm.

His words were cut short when the bow of the sailboat was ripped apart by rocks. Derek was thrown against the boat's rudder paddle, and he heard the sound of wood breaking—echoed by the distinct sound of his own ribs cracking. His last conscious thought was one of rage and frustration that he had failed—failed to bring his sister back to London, failed to save the other women, and most of all, failed to let Lauren know all she really meant to him.

"If you don't find them, you're as good as dead," Aldon Mitchell said quietly to Gregor as they stood on the beach. *The Unholy One* was anchored out a safe distance to sea, waiting for its captain and crewmen to return. "And if you don't come back here, I'll find you. These waters aren't big enough for both of us to be in control, Gregor—remember that. You'll own the waters and I'll own the land . . . but only as long as I let you live."

For a long moment the two men stood quietly staring into each other's eyes, the volatile hatred between them now plain. Gregor would have killed anyone else for speaking that way. But Aldon Mitchell evoked such numbing fear that Gregor accepted the threat silently and without challenge.

"I'll find the bastard and all his bitches," Gregor replied. "If the sea ain't swallowed them up, I'll find them."

"Try St. Thomas. That's where you first met the Englishman. If the storm hasn't killed him, that's where it will have taken him."

Just then Bones stepped forward, clearing his throat to draw attention to himself and warn his superiors that they were no longer alone.

"What?" Gregor growled.

"Cap'n Gregor, sir, a local said he tried to stop the Englishman from stealing his boat. Said he only had four wenches with him."

Gregor chewed his lip in thought. He didn't trust the local people to tell the truth, but it didn't seem likely that the man would willingly give his boat to Derek. "Question him some more. He's probably lying. All the locals lie whenever they can."

"I did question him some more, Cap'n. I can't question him no more."

"Why?"

"'Cause he ain't got no tongue no more," Bones replied, and it was clear that he was having a difficult time keeping the smile from his face. "He got his tongue cut out after he talked all he could. Then he got his belly slit open."

Gregor made a waving motion with his hand and Bones disappeared quickly, certain that he had pleased both Captain Gregor and the Big Man.

When they were alone again, Aldon said, "I've got most of the constables and politicians on St. Thomas in my pocket. I've been paying them all good money to stay out of my business. But I haven't bought all of them yet, and that means Derek can still cause us the kind of trouble that could get us hanged. Think of that, Gregor—think of that a *long time*. Think about what it'll feel like to have a rope around your neck."

Aldon Mitchell turned from the pirate captain and headed back to his empty harem house, which was now all he had left. He did not have a single slave left to take his anger out on.

Derek was the first to awaken. He was slumped over the broken rudder paddle of the stolen, shipwrecked sailboat. His side hurt like hell, and he was certain he had more than a few broken ribs.

Soon the sun would come up over the eastern horizon. The first pink rays were just now brightening the skyline. The sea was calm and almost serene. It took several seconds for Derek to collect his senses and clear his vision.

The four women were still in the boat. Derek pushed himself to his feet and went to Lauren first. She was on her side, her head on her left arm, shivering slightly, unconscious. Derek smoothed wet hair away from her forehead. She felt cold and clammy. He felt for a pulse at her throat and found it quickly. The beat was strong and steady, and Derek smiled.

"The strongest woman I've ever known," Derek said softly.

He stepped over Lauren and went to Amanda. Even unconscious, she clutched the bucket that she'd used to bail water. There was a deep bruise on her left cheek that was dark and ugly against her pale skin, but other than that, she appeared to be unharmed. Her pulse was even, though not terribly strong.

Derek looked up from his sister to examine his surroundings for the first time since regaining consciousness. The sailboat had slammed into huge rocks fifty yards from the shore of what he hoped was St. Thomas. The boulders—two of them—had completely ripped apart the hull of the boat, but the saving grace was that they had also pinned the shattered vessel between them. That quirk of fate was all that had saved the passengers.

Derek turned his attention to Chantell and Sue Ellen. Chantell, who had been at the bow when they'd struck the rocks, had broken her right arm in the collision. Derek was almost certain of his diagnosis, judging by how swollen her normally slender arm was. If she was to maintain use of the limb, he'd have to get her to a doctor quickly. He had seen what happened to people once gangrene set in, and he couldn't imagine such a fate for Chantell.

Sue Ellen, aside from a substantial assortment of bruises and cuts, appeared to have survived the crash well, even though she was unconscious when the boat struck the rocks.

"It's a bloody miracle we all didn't die," Derek said softly.

From behind him, Lauren said, "What makes you so sure we didn't?"

Derek rushed to her, stepping around the shattered remains of the hull. He knelt beside her, taking her face lightly between his palms to look deep into her eyes. His concern for Lauren made him forget his own broken ribs. "How do you feel? Do you hurt anywhere?"

"I hurt *everywhere*," Lauren said, then pushed Derek's hands away.

She turned her eyes from him. She didn't need to think about his suspicions, and his tender concern only reminded her of how differently he saw her since her capture by Aldon Mitchell.

"Where are we?" Lauren asked, looking around. She saw the shore just fifty yards away and gasped. "We were *this* close and didn't make it?" she exclaimed.

"We're lucky we're not all dead," Derek reminded her.

Lauren, with a groan from aching, abused muscles, pushed to her feet. "I suppose that's true, but just the same, it seems if God was going to put something in our path during the storm, it would have been considerably kinder if he'd put that soft, sandy shore instead of those rocks."

Lauren's attitude told Derek she wasn't hiding any injury from him in an attempt to be brave. Pure relief washed through him like laudanum, taking away his pain and quelling the fears that had been too intense for him to dwell on for very long.

With a little help, Sue Ellen regained consciousness. Only then did Derek discover that her left knee was massively swollen. She was able to get to her feet and remain standing, but she'd need help walking because the injured knee could bear no weight at all.

"Get me to shore, if you can, then go on without me," Sue Ellen said gamely to the collection of battered castaways aboard the remains of the fishing boat. "When you find a village, you can send someone for me."

"No," Derek said with authority, causing all the women to look at him questioningly. "We've gone this far together, we can go all the way. I'll help you walk. If leaning on me isn't good enough, I'll carry you."

Lauren and Amanda, who knew Derek best, exchanged looks. When he got in a mood like this, it was best to do what he said. He looked at each woman in turn, almost challenging each one to defy him, to say that even *he* did not have the strength—not after all that had transpired during the past twenty-four hours—to carry Sue Ellen to the nearest village.

297

"Find whatever will float to help you get to shore," Derek said, looking to the east, from where they'd sailed. Far off, the morning sky was a deep, azure blue. He recognized the signs—another storm was brewing. It would take hours to reach St. Thomas, but as surely as the sun would rise, the storm would build in intensity in twelve or fifteen hours, and when it reached the island, it would cause havoc and damage to its inhabitants.

They collected what they could, finding those items that would float, then as a group made it to shore. Derek's ribs were only cracked, he suspected, not broken. He spit and was relieved to see that his saliva was clear and free of blood. If he'd broken any ribs, he most assuredly would have brought up blood from his lungs.

Once ashore, Derek looked back out to sea. He could not see *The Unholy One,* or any other ship for that matter, but he knew that somewhere out there, Aldon Mitchell was on his way. The logical move would be to get to the nearest inhabited, civilized island. But if Derek knew this, so did Aldon Mitchell.

"We beat the bloody bastard," Derek whispered, turning back to the women.

"He's still alive," Chantell said in a whisper, cradling her broken arm in her lap. "You promised."

"He's alive for now. As soon as we get you and Sue Ellen to a doctor, and we find a hotel, Aldon Mitchell's reign will come to a suitably unsavory end."

Lauren closed her eyes and looked away from him. Though she wanted Aldon Mitchell dead—he was a man she felt did not deserve to live—she wished it was another man who would take on the responsibility of hunting the madman down. The Lord Derek York *she* wanted to know—to love—would not pursue a man like an assassin pursuing a victim.

298

"We'd better get moving," Derek said, his gaze only briefly meeting Lauren's, where he saw disapproval in her eyes. "He'll come after us, and I want to be able to tell the constable our side of the story before he does."

Arm in arm, those able to walk helping those who had difficulty, they headed away from the shore dotted with the remains of what had once been a sailboat.

"The Fates are smiling," Amanda whispered, looking around the small but spotlessly clean office.

"For a change," Lauren replied. Then, not wanting to be too pessimistic, especially since the prognoses for both Sue Ellen's knee and Chantell's arm were favorable, she added, "The worst is behind us. It'll be easier from here on."

The five shipwrecked travelers had found a narrow, rutted road and followed it for less than a mile when they came upon a two-story white wooden building with European-fashioned windows. A sign outside proudly proclaimed it to be the residence and office of Dr. Willard Williams.

The doctor was an aging, accommodating, competent man. After Derek had slipped one of his few remaining gold coins into the doctor's pocket, Williams inspected the wounds on Chantell and Sue Ellen and stated that both women should remain with him for several days to ensure that infection did not set in.

"Whatever you think is best," Derek had said.

Once the worst of the injuries had been attended to, Dr. Williams insisted on checking Lauren, Amanda, and Derek. A discreet man, he did not question what Derek was doing with four women, or how they had been injured, but the look in his eye indicated that he most definitely did not approve.

"Where are we?" Derek asked at last, when the

299

immediate need for medical attention had been satisfied. Dr. Williams gave him a strange look. "What island, I mean? We were on a boat. There was trouble," Derek ambiguously explained.

"St. Thomas." The elderly doctor eyed Derek as though he was personally responsible for everyone's injuries, and possibly even the cause of the storm. He did not like seeing women get injured, and particularly not when there were so many women with just one man.

"Doctor, perhaps you'd know where I could find hotel rooms for myself and my . . ." Derek wasn't sure what he should call Lauren and Amanda. Nothing seemed quite suitable, and after a moment he concluded with, "friends."

"There are several fine hotels," the doctor replied, peering over the rims of his rather thick spectacles, silently communicating his disapproval of Derek's being with two scantily clad women. "Of course, accommodations will cost you. And you'll have to get some better clothes for the ladies. There are women in town who make dresses for the rich European women. See them for what you need." The doctor fixed Derek with a wizened glare. "What has happened here, young man, is between you and me." He pulled Derek aside behind a pull curtain so they could talk man to man. "If I were in your shoes, I'd be very careful of who I talked to. This island is a good place to live. I like my neighbors who were born on this island, and those who were born elsewhere. But I can tell you this: no one will sit idly by while one man keeps four mistresses simultaneously!"

"Dr. Williams, good sir, you're getting the wrong impression. It's not like—"

"Do not interrupt me, young man!" the doctor said sternly, raising a finger and waggling it under Derek's

300

nose. "I say this only for your own good. Take the two with you and leave the other two here with me. I'll take care of them."

Derek wanted to explain that he did not have four mistresses, but he knew that no amount of explanation would satisfy the bighearted but meddlesome doctor. Dr. Williams would believe what he believed, and nothing Derek could say would change that.

"Thank you, Doctor," Derek said at last, clasping the man's hand firmly. "I appreciate everything you've done for me."

Again faintly scolding, the doctor replied under his breath, "I do it for the young ladies, not for you, young man!" Their gazes met. "The village is just down this road. You'll find two hotels on this street, and there's another one closer to the seaside."

"There's a constable in the village?"

"Of course there is. We're not barbarians."

Lauren, Derek, and Amanda said quick good-byes to Chantell and Sue Ellen, then left the small clinic with renewed spirits and energy, sure that the worst of their troubles were behind them.

Chapter 25

Feeling freedom and safety so close, the three covered the remaining distance quickly. The women chatted happily, and Derek remained silent, appearing pleased.

"A bath with lots and lots of soap," Lauren said. She ran fingers through her thick hair and grimaced at its grimy state. "And then I want a steak. A beefsteak *this thick!*" She held forefinger and thumb three inches apart.

"Me, too!" Amanda piped up. "I've eaten enough fish this past month to last a lifetime."

"And wine," Lauren continued as they walked. "Icy cold, and from a good year."

Amanda made a happy moaning sound, adding, "Champagne with fresh strawberries and blueberries! Derek, remember how Mama and Papa would take bowls of berries and champagne into the bedroom, then not come out all day?"

Derek smiled crookedly. His gaze slipped from his sister over to Lauren in her coarse cotton dress. Their gazes held, and in his mind a voice whispered hauntingly, *Had Aldon forced her to sleep with him?*

He turned away from Lauren, not wanting her to read his thoughts, yet certain she already had. It wasn't fair of him, he knew, to judge Lauren by her past. He certainly didn't want to be judged by *his* past. It was especially wrong of him to consider what she had done with another man, if she had had no choice but to do what that man had forced her to do. In Derek's coldly logical mind, this all made perfect sense, but it wasn't his logical mind that was ruling him just then, it was his emotions, green and jealous, that were eating away at his insides.

The city, like many others Derek had seen on St. Thomas and St. Croix, expanded slowly from a business center, with roads following a few main arteries in all directions. They found the shanty huts of the unskilled laborers and dockworkers first, then passed houses made of wood and brick, mud and mortar, closer to the center of town. Finally they came to the beating heart of the city, with its taverns and gambling halls, its hotels and restaurants, its merchants and its hawkers and criers.

The constable's office was directly across the main street from a hotel, and seeing the hotel—which had recently been whitewashed and looked extraordinarily inviting to the exhausted travelers—made the fatigue that Derek had held deep within suddenly rise to the surface, flooding through every muscle in his body.

The street was crowded with people—many sailors, but also businessmen and women dressed in fine clothes. Just the sight of a normal city atmosphere, with business and commerce that did not involve the buying and selling of women, cheered and rejuvenated Derek, reminding him of the pleasures that awaited him back in London.

They stepped into the constable's office, Derek

303

leading the way. A young man in his twenties, the early makings of a pot belly curling over his belt, turned his bored gaze away from his game of solitaire.

"Can I help you with something?" he asked, his words oddly tinged with an American southern accent.

"I have something to report," Derek replied. His immediate reaction to the young man was a mixture of disdain and suspicion. "Is your superior here?"

"The lieutenant ain't on duty during the day. I'm in charge now, so why don't you tell me whatever it is you've got to say?"

The constable's appraising gaze went from Derek to Amanda and Lauren. Derek saw undisguised lust in the man's eyes, and it was not easy for him to resist lifting the constable out of his chair and teaching him some manners.

"When does the lieutenant come on duty?"

"Six."

"I'll come back then."

The constable began to say something, but Derek didn't stick around to hear it. He didn't like the young man's attitude at all, and with such delicate matters it was best to tell as few people as possible. Besides, Derek did not care for dealing with underlings, particularly unprofessional underlings with undeserved attitudes of superiority.

They crossed the street to the hotel. Derek pulled his small leather money purse from his belt and checked the contents: he had three gold coins, enough for a couple weeks' lodging for the three of them, along with clothes and food, but not very much more.

He lightly placed his hand at the small of Lauren's back as she passed in front of him to enter the hotel, and he felt her stiffen. *She's frightened of my touch,* he thought bitterly, cursing Aldon Mitchell for putting that fear into the heart of the woman he loved. *Even though I want her desperately—now more than ever—if I love her I must give her time to recover from what's happened, from all that she's been forced to do. I've got to give her time.*

"I'll need two rooms," Derek instructed the small, goateed man behind the hotel's front desk. "One for myself and one for my . . . sisters."

The hotelier cast a sideways glance at Lauren, with her midnight black hair, then at Amanda, with her honey blonde hair, and only his professionalism prevented him from smiling lasciviously. The sexual perversions people wished to engage in were none of his business, and the gold coin Derek slipped into his hand convinced him he'd made the right decision.

Constable Jonas Liebermann wasn't completely sure he had finally grabbed the brass ring in the merry-go-round of life, but the possibility was certainly there, and he wasn't about to let such an opportunity pass him without a good looking-over.

It had been three years since Jonas had taken the job of constable, when he was hired by the lieutenant, who was on Aldon Mitchell's payroll. Jonas, too, was getting paid secretly by Aldon, accepting money in return for relaying salient information concerning ship movements and cargo. His pay as constable wasn't much, and it wouldn't cover his expenses for liquor and women without the added income from Aldon Mitchell.

What galled him most of all was that the lieutenant, who spent most of his time in the local brothels and public houses, got two or three times as much money from Aldon. Whenever Jonas learned something that might be of value to Aldon, he told the lieutenant, who then passed the information along. Aldon always paid for the information, but Jonas was certain the lieutenant was not giving him as much money as he pocketed himself.

But this time it was going to be different. This time he wasn't going to say a word to the lieutenant about the three new people in town, even if the lieutenant did return from St. Croix, where he was on his monthly visit to his wife and four children.

Jonas stepped into the doorway of the office and studied the sky. There would be another storm tonight. Maybe the lieutenant wouldn't make it back to St. Thomas that evening. The longer he was away, the better Jonas's chances were of selling his information directly to Aldon Mitchell. There was only one question remaining: how to get a boat out to Aldon Mitchell's island mansion without alerting everyone else in the city who was also on Mitchell's payroll.

Jonas smiled and returned to his game of solitaire. The storm would give him time to think. He'd figure out some way of making the most of the situation. Although the storm prevented him from alerting Aldon Mitchell, it also prevented the Englishman and his women from leaving St. Thomas . . . and as long as Jonas was the law in the village, the Englishman wasn't going anywhere.

The hotel was much more lavish than Lauren had first imagined. The beds were elevated on solid wooden frames, and the mattresses were stuffed with goose down. Lauren flopped face down on the bed and sighed, closing her eyes for what seemed like the first time in months.

"I could sleep for a week," she said, her words muffled against the light cotton blankets.

"So could I," Amanda added. "But before I do, I'm taking a bath. The saltwater makes my skin itch after a while. My skin's so fair."

Lauren rolled over, then sat up. *Yes,* she thought, *you've got fair, delicate skin. Pale skin, just like your brother's. Is that what he's looking for in a woman? Am I good enough to make love to, but not good enough to be shown to his family?*

Since rescuing her from Aldon Mitchell's harem, Derek had been polite with Lauren, but he certainly hadn't been warm and affectionate. He hadn't given her any more consideration than Sue Ellen or Chantell, and that was something Lauren couldn't deny.

There was a knock on the door between the two rooms. Derek said through the door, "The bath is being brought into my room. You two can bathe first, and I'll go buy us some clothes. Will you be all right without me?"

Amanda laughed softly. "Darling brother of mine, we ladies aren't nearly so helpless as you think! Run along now, but do hurry back." Amanda turned away from the door, looking at Lauren. "Derek is so protective—he always has been. Maybe that's why he's always been so special to me." She shrugged her slender shoulders. "You can bathe first."

Lauren knew Amanda was only being polite, that she really was eager to bathe. Lauren was just as eager to wash herself clean of all that had happened over the past few days, but she said, "No, you bathe first. If you don't mind, I need a few minutes alone to think."

"Of course," Amanda replied. "I understand perfectly."

But in truth, she didn't understand at all. What was

307

bothering Lauren most wasn't what had happened with Aldon Mitchell; it was what *wasn't* happening with Lord Derek York.

She felt the hand at her shoulder, but she pulled away from it. She didn't want anything but the feel of the cool Virginia grass against her bare feet, the breeze in her waist-length, jet-black hair, and the overwhelming sense of freedom and security that surrounded her when she was on her own land, running free, without a care or a responsibility in the world.

"Lauren, wake up," Amanda said, shaking the sleeping woman again. "Your bath is ready, and your dinner will get cold. There'll be plenty of time to sleep later, but you'll never get your strength back if you don't eat."

Pulling out of sleep was like trying to run in waist-deep water. With great disappointment, Lauren realized that she was not a little girl, she was not at home in Virginia, she was not playing tag with her sisters.

She looked at Amanda and smiled dreamily. "I must have fallen asleep."

"You fell asleep two hours ago. Derek didn't have the heart to wake you, so we just let you sleep."

Lauren sat up, pushing the hair away from her face. She didn't like to look Amanda directly in the eyes because her eyes were precisely the same color as Derek's. "If you're hungry, go ahead and eat. I'll be there as soon as I can." Lauren inhaled and caught the mouthwatering aroma of broiled meat. The scent wasn't exactly beef, but it was delicious to the senses just the same. "What's that? I'm famished!"

"Hurry up and bathe now," Amanda said laughingly, taking Lauren by the arm and literally pulling her to her feet. "Bathe first, then eat. You don't want to be in the tub when Derek returns!"

Lauren was curious about where Derek had gone, but she asked no questions. If Derek wanted her to know, he'd have told her, and judging by all he'd said to her since taking her from the harem, he was no longer interested in including her in much of his life.

The soapy water was warm and felt heavenly. Lauren did not take the leisurely bath she had envisioned, but she had no complaints when she was finished. Her body and hair were clean and smelled of fresh soap, and the new clothes Derek had purchased, though perhaps not of the latest Paris fashion, were clean and comfortable. It was especially nice to have pantalets, a chemise, and petticoats after having gone without them for so long.

When she returned to the room she shared with Amanda, she found Derek still had not returned. It was disconcerting not to know where he had gone, or what he was doing, and though she tried to dismiss her fears—Derek was, after all, quite capable of taking care of himself—she couldn't help worrying.

"It's lamb, with some kind of sauce I've never heard of," Amanda said as Lauren sat down to her food. "Derek ordered it. It's quite spicy, so you might want to be a little careful at first."

The food was more highly spiced than Lauren was accustomed to, but she was so hungry that she ate avariciously of the meat and bread, and drank freely of the accompanying cool wine.

"You've no idea how good this tastes," Lauren said, nibbling at her buttered potatoes, savoring each morsel.

"Yes I do. I was just as hungry as you. And if you stop to think about it, I was in captivity much longer."

Amanda turned her face away for a moment, as though she wished she hadn't brought up the subject of captivity. "But that's all behind us now, isn't it? Thanks to Derek . . ."

"Yes, it's all behind us," Lauren replied. She turned her attention back to her plate, not because she was still terribly hungry, but because the mention of Derek's name made her feel uncomfortable.

As if on cue, the adjoining door opened and Derek stepped in, looking more handsome than Lauren ever had seen him. His suit was charcoal gray, with black stripes around the cuffs and along the sleeves. His breeches were snowy white, tucked into knee-high black riding boots made in the finest English fashion. His white shirt was worn open at the throat, framing his tanned face in stark and appealing contrast. He crossed his feet at the ankle and leaned against the door.

"Good evening, ladies," he said rakishly, a half-grin playing with his sensuous mouth, a twinkling light in his blue eyes. "I trust my time away has been well spent by both of you."

"It has indeed!" Amanda said, her face beaming at her brother's entrance. "We've both bathed, and I've been trying on everything that you've bought for me. Oh, Derek, how did you know exactly the right things to get?"

"You like them, then?"

"I adore them! I love everything you bought!"

Derek turned his gaze slowly toward Lauren, obviously seeking her approval for what he'd purchased. Though she wanted to thank him—whatever had transpired between them did not change the fact that he had spent a considerable amount of money on clothes for her—she couldn't force anything more than lukewarm enthusiasm to the surface.

"The clothes are very nice," she said at last. "Thank you very much."

"Well, you can't get any tidier than that," Derek murmured sardonically. His smoothly cultured tone bespoke a quality private education and the hint of irony that comes only to those who have spent too much time in the most elite society.

Amanda and Derek exchanged a quick look, then she hastily excused herself and left the room, conveniently ignoring the stern glare Lauren gave her.

"Did you plan that?" Lauren asked after the door had closed behind Amanda. To Lauren's dismay, her voice held a faintly shrill edge, and did not sound at all like her.

"With Amanda? Heavens, no!" Derek said, crossing his arms over his broad chest once again, leaning against the wall. "No need to plan such things when we can easily have an entire conversation with just a look when necessary. We've always been that way. It's almost as if we can read each other's minds."

"How nice for you," Lauren replied, this time making no attempt to hide her sarcasm.

She realized that what was suddenly bothering her was not Derek's behavior—since the escape he'd done absolutely nothing to let her know that she meant something special to him—but rather his attitude. Just as he'd set out from London to do, just as he'd promised Lauren and himself he would, he'd found Amanda and freed her, against considerable, daunting odds. For Lauren, who had known great fear, it was as though Derek was impervious to danger. The unspoken assumption was that because *he* could laugh in the face of fear, anyone who couldn't was somehow less than he. Whether Derek intended this or Lauren simply conjured the feelings up in her own heart really didn't

311

matter. She believed it was so, and believing made it so.

"What's wrong? Have I said something to offend you?"

Lauren had serious doubts concerning Derek's forthrightness. "Nothing is wrong, and you haven't said anything to offend me."

Derek looked at Lauren, thinking her the most beautiful woman in the world. He had taken great pleasure in picking out clothes for her, and it had allowed him to fulfill a secret fantasy to see her dressed in European fashions. Her thick, ebony hair was freshly washed and brushed out over her shoulders, free of any restraints.

"I should have bought a ribbon for your hair," Derek said softly, almost in a whisper. He had promised himself he would leave Lauren alone, but seeing her now made his resolve begin to slip. "I suppose it's just as well. You have such beautiful hair, it would be a shame to restrain it in any way."

Lauren rose from her chair and went to the window overlooking the bustling city. Why was he doing this to her now? When Amanda was near, he'd treated her like a stranger. Was he afraid to let his own sister know what he felt for Lauren? Or was he perhaps embarrassed by her?

She heard the soft click of his bootheels against the wooden floor. Such soft footsteps for such a big man, she thought, not turning around.

"Are you quite all right?" Derek asked, standing in the center of the room, looking at Lauren's back.

He knew that if he moved any closer, her allure and his ravenous hunger for her would be too great to deny.

Seconds ticked by and still Lauren didn't answer. Derek was certain that she had been through hell in Aldon Mitchell's arms, and he was torn between wanting to hold and comfort her, and wanting to take her into his arms to carry them both into a world of ecstasy they could only share with each other, a sensual place safe and inviolate in a violent and calloused world.

"I can't help you unless you talk to me," Derek said in a whisper. "I really do want to help."

"I don't need your help."

"Have you always been so stubborn, so independent?"

Lauren wheeled around, her dark eyes blazing. His sarcastic tone might or might not have been imagined, but she was going to confront it just the same. "Who do you think you are?" she demanded. "What I think and what I feel are none of your business!" Derek took a step back. Lauren did not realize she had closed the distance between them by taking long strides. "What do you care, anyway? You think Aldon Mitchell had his way with me, don't you?"

Derek's brows knitted together. He was thoroughly confused about what had suddenly fired her anger, and he was entirely unaccustomed to having anyone—and certainly never a woman—challenge him like this.

"Why, Derek?" Lauren asked, pointing a finger at him accusingly. "Why couldn't you show me any kindness at all when Sue Ellen and Chantell were with us? Why haven't you shown me any kindness in front of your sister? Are you ashamed of me? Is that it?"

"*Ashamed of you?*" Derek repeated, confounded. The question seemed so absurd it made him smile, which only inflamed Lauren's rising anger. "That's insane!"

Lauren was breathing deeply, her breasts rising and falling, straining against the tight bodice of her gown. She had recently spent so much time wearing a mitar that the gown's décolletage seemed constraining, and the friction against her breasts was oddly arousing. It had to be the gown, Lauren told herself . . . it certainly

313

couldn't have anything to do with the close proximity of Derek!

"Now I'm insane, am I?" Lauren said, much more quietly than before. "You're a real charmer, Derek York . . . or should I be formal now and call you *Lord* York?"

"What's this all about? You're angry with me, and I'd like to bloody well know why!"

She was so close all Derek needed to do was reach out and take her into his arms . . . but he did not. Just seeing her face flushed with excitement, her bosom straining against the blue, lace-trimmed décolletage above the dramatic curve of her waist and hips, sent his blood racing, and he could hear his pulse in his ears.

"You treated me no different than Chantell or Sue Ellen when you rescued us," she said softly. Lauren's shoulders slumped slightly, and as she finally confessed her fear, it was like wind coming out of a sail, deflating her, slowing her anger to a gentler intensity. "I wanted to know that I'm not like the others to you. When you looked at me at Mitchell's and saw me in that night rail . . . I could see the disappointment in your eyes. Since then you haven't looked at me the same way, you haven't touched me, you haven't . . . I used to see the desire in your eyes, shining within you. It bothered me, but it also excited me . . . in a way, I guess . . . a little bit."

"It excited you more than a little bit, I guess," Derek said in the low, growling whisper that Lauren had learned to love. He moved closer, placing his hands lightly on her hips. "And if I didn't look at you the same way, it was because I was trying to protect you from *me*. I didn't want to be just another randy male to you, disregarding your thoughts and feelings while I worshipped your body."

Lauren's sensuous, full-lipped mouth curled upward

in a smile as understanding finally dawned on her. "I doubt you could ever be *just anything.*" She placed her hands over Derek's, pressing them more firmly against her hips. There were a thousand things she wanted to say, and a thousand things she wanted to hear, but for now, just feeling Derek's touch was good enough. "I was so afraid that you wouldn't want to touch me any more. You see, Aldon never—"

"Even if he had, do you think it would have changed my feelings for you?"

Lauren, who had been staring at Derek's chest, let her gaze drop. She did not want to look into his eyes, knowing that if she did, her sense of judgment would once again be swept away.

"Yes," she said finally. "I do think it would. Men are . . . men are just that way. Possessive."

Derek slid his hands around Lauren to pull her in close, one hand moving down to curl around the upper curve of her buttocks, the other roaming to the middle of her back, pulling her in so that he could feel the firmness of her breasts against his chest.

"I'm possessive of you, all right," he said, the rumbling timbre of his voice deep and intimate, an audible caress to Lauren's tantalized senses. "I can't stand the thought of anyone ever touching you. But I'm not like most men, m'lady. It is what happens in your heart that matters to me." Derek's right hand slipped upward to move lightly over the swell of her breast, his forefinger tapping the spot over her heart. "Here is what counts," he said, and then his hand closed over her breast. Hot waves of pleasure blossomed within Lauren with such astonishing speed that all she could do was issue a small, startled gasp and tilt her face up to Derek, her lips moist, parted and inviting, and wait for his kiss.

Chapter 26

Derek thrust his tongue between her lips, and Lauren happily accepted it. She leaned into him, her hands sliding beneath his linen jacket to feel the sinewy muscles of his stomach through his frilly silk shirt.

"I was so afraid!" Lauren gasped when the kiss finally broke. "Afraid you'd never want me again!"

"You sweet, beautiful fool!"

Lauren realized almost after the fact that she was pulling at Derek's belt, fighting to open it. Her behavior was shamefully brazen, passionately demanding—and she didn't care! After all she had been through, whatever inhibitions and restrictions society set on her could all be damned! She had Derek with her, and though he could not say that he loved her, she could feel his love in his touch and see it in his eyes, and that was all that really mattered.

His strong fingers pressed deeply into the plush mound of her breast, touching her through the gown, but that wasn't good enough for Lauren. Frantically, she slipped her fingertips into the décolletage and pulled down hard, stretching the exquisite fabric beyond what any tailor had intended. She heard the telltale sound of threads giving way to greater strength, and then her breasts sprang free, her nipples hard and extended, tingling madly, aching for attention, for the sensual skill that she knew Derek possessed.

"Kiss me!" Lauren cried out, her hands shaking so badly she couldn't unbuckle Derek's belt.

His mouth slanted down over hers, his kiss hard and frantic. Lauren parted her lips, sliding her tongue deep into Derek's mouth to taste and explore. She leaned into Derek, forcing her breasts into his palms, trembling from head to toe at the frightening escalation and intensity of her own passion. She pulled hard at Derek's belt, irrationally choosing strength over skill, knocking them both off balance and nearly sending them toppling to the floor.

Derek rolled her nipples between forefingers and thumbs as he drew Lauren's tongue even deeper into his mouth. The bed was only a few steps away. All he needed to do was take Lauren into his arms and carry her that far, and then they wouldn't have to stumble around, standing up, trying frantically to remove each other's clothes. Unfortunately, Derek didn't think he could take the time to carry Lauren that far. His erection strained like steel against the tight fabric of his breeches, and he knew he'd never have the patience to pull off his knee-high boots, which were new and a little on the tight side.

Her breasts filled his hands. Derek kissed the sweet arch of her throat, then bent even further and captured the blunt, tingling crest of her breast between his lips, his tongue in skilled motion on her aroused flesh. Lauren cried out her pleasure, hugging Derek's face tightly to her bosom with one hand while still trying vainly to unbuckle his belt with the other.

Lauren heard the throaty, sensual cry of ecstasy, but it took a moment or two before she realized that she'd made the sound herself. Was it possible that anything could feel this good? Was it possible for a woman to want a man as much as she wanted Derek?

The warmth of his mouth on the aroused tip of her breast, his tongue and lips tantalizing her with exquisite skill, heightened sensations all through Lauren's voluptuous, trembling body. In a dim corner of her mind she was vaguely aware of her frustration at being unable to find sufficient skills to perform the simple function of unfastening Derek's belt. The task required only a moment of conscious thought, she sensed, but that moment was more than she could summon, especially when Derek's mouth was working its magic on her breast and his hand was slowly pushing up her dress and petticoats, his strong fingers kneading the smooth muscles of her calf and thigh through the silk stocking.

Lauren pushed her fingers through Derek's sandy hair, guiding his avaricious mouth from the tip of one breast to the other. He was doubled over, and she was still holding tightly onto the end of his belt. *He must be uncomfortable,* she thought, the odd, discordant concern so out of place with everything else she was feeling. *We should go to the bed. We can lie down there. . . .*

What few conscious thoughts Lauren had vanished like smoke in a windstorm when Derek's hand moved higher, above the frilly top of her stocking and the garter, and his fingers pressed firmly, intimately against her, touching her through her pantalets. The pressure made a heat like molten lava pour through her veins, and Lauren cried out as she was gripped by sensations so intensely pleasurable they were almost painful.

"The bed!" Derek commanded, straightening himself, taking his mouth from Lauren's tempting breasts, pushing her in his haste.

Nobody had ever pushed Lauren without being reprimanded, but if there was another person in the world whose needs were as great as Derek's at that moment, it was Lauren. She nearly ran to the bed, throwing herself on it, turning in midair to land on her back. Her décolletage was still pulled below her breasts, and as she bounced briefly on the goosedown mattress, her dress slid up over her knees, bunching at her thighs.

"It's madness to want you this much," Derek hissed, getting on the bed, hovering over Lauren briefly, like a predator about to pounce, his hands on the mattress at either side of Lauren's head.

She was looking straight into his eyes when she finally managed his belt. When his breeches burst open, his manhood sprang out, filling her hands. Lauren made a cooing sound deep in her throat, running her fingers experimentally over the fiery length of him.

"So big," she whispered, spreading her thighs to accommodate Derek's lean hips.

He leaned down to kiss her, their lips only lightly touching, their tongues darting speedily from mouth to mouth. As Lauren stroked Derek's arousal, he feverishly unknotted the drawstring of her pantalets and pulled them down her legs.

"The dress," he whispered, a hand sliding under Lauren to where a string of pearl buttons ran down her spine.

"Later," Lauren shot back, shocking herself at her own boldness and impatience.

Where she got the strength to move Derek the way she did, Lauren would never know. Taking him by the shoulders, turning and twisting, she nearly tossed him onto his back, then straddled his hips and his raging maleness with her silk-sheathed thighs.

"I need you now," Lauren whispered, guiding Derek as she settled down upon him, opening joyously to enclose him.

"Now . . . and always!" Derek cried out, cupping Lauren's heavy breasts as the slick wetness of her enveloped him.

The lovemaking was frantic, very nearly selfish on both her part and his—quick, satisfying, and primal. Afterward, Derek lovingly undressed Lauren, slowly removing each item of clothing, explaining where he had bought it and what his other options had been, making a game of the disrobing.

"Just close your eyes," Derek whispered, tracing Lauren's eyebrows with the tip of his finger. "You know, I was in Australia, and they have something they throw in the air that comes back to them. It's shaped somewhat like your eyebrows. Did anyone ever tell you that before?"

Lauren giggled softly at the nonsense love talk, keeping her eyes closed. "No, but then I've never known anyone who's been to Australia."

"I've been to many places—all around the world, actually," Derek continued, his forefinger now tracing the bridge of Lauren's nose, then moving around her mouth and down her chin. "I'm going to show you the world, m'lady. Show you all the interesting things there are to see . . . *feel* all the interesting things there are to feel."

Derek's tone was conversational, as though he was giving a casual acquaintance a travelog, but as he cradled Lauren's head in the crook of his left arm, his right hand was slowly roaming her body, the tips of his fingers now circling the enlarged tip of her breast.

"Have you ever been to London? Beautiful city,

that—I don't think there's another quite like it in all the world."

Lauren was being slowly, irrevocably driven out of her mind with a bizarre kind of controlled passion that was different than anything Derek had taught her before. When she felt the tip of Derek's middle finger circling her navel, then traveling lower, she was hungry with anticipation for the passion she would soon feel—again.

Why is he taking so long? her passion-addled brain demanded, though she lacked the boldness simply to demand that Derek dispense with the preliminaries and caress her body with the dazzling skill she knew he possessed.

It took a while for Lauren to realize that the leisurely progress of Derek's hand was by design, not out of casual indifference to what he was doing. His control over himself allowed him to have control over the seduction, and in the hazy recesses of her consciousness she realized that there was nothing more stimulating than a man in control of himself and his surroundings.

His fingertips brushed over the tightly curled, small triangular thatch of hair at the juncture of her thighs. Lauren unconsciously held her breath, her trembling lower lip caught between even white teeth as she waited with agonized anticipation for that first blissful moment of contact . . . which didn't come.

Something is wrong, she thought dizzily, her ripely voluptuous body trembling slightly in Derek's arms. *He's stopped!*

"What . . . what are you . . . doing?" she managed to ask after quite some time had passed. She looked up into Derek's cool blue eyes and saw the infuriating laughter in his gaze and the faint curling of his lush, sensual mouth. "You stopped!"

He nodded. Wordlessly, he set his hand in motion again, his fingertips lightly caressing Lauren's inner thighs, moving away and then coming toward the apex of all her sensations, always getting tantalizingly close—maddeningly close—before sliding away once more.

"Tell me what you want," he said, his voice a deep, resonant purr that spoke of confidence and an innate sensuality that made Lauren tremble just at the sound of it. "Tell me, and I'll take you where you want to go."

"Derek, don't play with me now!" Lauren replied in a kind of frantic whisper she was certain did not sound like her at all.

"Play with you? My darling Lauren, what we are doing is far too serious to call playing. Nothing in this world is quite so serious as satisfaction. Without satisfaction, life is not worth living." He chuckled softly, and when the tips of his fingers very nearly brushed against Lauren's moist entrance, she quickly gulped in air and held her breath. "See how important it is? It even makes you stop breathing. Satisfaction is what we live for, my darling. Now please, do us both a favor and tell me what it is you want so that we may continue."

"I want you!" Lauren said, her dark eyes glazed with passion involuntarily held in check. "I need you, Derek! I need you now!"

What bothered Lauren most was that she was telling the absolute truth. What was going through her now was not mere wanting—it was a blood need she was quite convinced she would die of if Derek did not soon bring her to the heights of sensual culmination.

"I'm aware of that," Derek continued, still in the strangely conversational tone that could be so annoying and yet erotic at the same time. "But you still haven't told me what you want me to *do*."

322

Lauren could not take another second in Derek's arms without him touching her. She simply could not wait another moment, no matter how deliciously different this new concept of delayed erotic gratification was. Grabbing him by the wrist, she pulled his hand up between her thighs.

"Touch me!" she cried out.

The liquid fire of completion swept through Lauren with startling speed. Derek's probing fingers had hardly begun their tantalizing assault when he dipped his head down to feast once again on her responsive nipples. The combined sensations, working in conjunction with all the other feelings and emotions that Derek had made Lauren experience, were much more than she could take. She arched her back, her mouth pursing in a silent scream of ecstasy, as shuddering waves of physical emotion burned through her.

Later, weak and sated, she lay in Derek's arms, wondering how on earth Derek could ever have learned to do the things he did. Half asleep, Lauren snuggled in closer to Derek's chest, inhaling to smell his special scent, listening to the wind buffeting the windows and the rain lashing angrily at the world outside.

All that turmoil, all of nature's angry emotions, were outside. They couldn't touch Lauren now—not when she was in Derek's arms and they were sharing a bed. Aldon Mitchell, Gregor, Bones . . . all the ugliness and evil in the world seemed wonderfully far away.

She felt Derek's eyes upon her as he idly twirled a lock of her silky hair around his forefinger. Earlier, she would have been uncomfortable at his scrutiny, afraid that he was seeing some flaw in her, or wondering how long he had to stay with her until he could politely excuse himself, now that his passion was spent.

"I think you should know," Derek said slowly,

propping himself up on one elbow to look down at Lauren, who was on the threshhold of sleep, "that I am quite in love with you."

Lauren smiled sleepily, turning her head on Derek's arm to look up into his eyes. She had never even dared think he would confess his love for her. Showing her his love, she had thought, was as much as he was capable of. Warm tears of joy glistened in her eyes, and she blinked them back, knowing of Derek's disapproval of tears—even tears of happiness.

"Say it again," she said.

Derek grinned, clearing his throat theatrically and solemnly, like an actor about to go onstage. "Lauren Masters, I am in love with you. I never thought I'd love anyone the way I love you. If I never knew what love was before, never knew what it could be, it's only because I hadn't met you. Only then did I realize what I was capable of feeling."

Tears trickled from the corners of Lauren's eyes. "For a man who has said very little on the subject, you're doing fine now."

"Should I stop?"

"Don't stop," Lauren said, her palm resting lightly against Derek's freshly shaven cheek. "Don't ever stop telling me how much you love me, and I'll never stop telling you how much I love you. We'll tell each other all the time so that we'll never forget. Promise me that."

Derek dipped his head down to taste Lauren's lips, kissing her quickly. "I love you, m'lady," he whispered, kissing her softly between the words. "I will always love you."

The storm had loosened a shutter, making it bang against the side of the hotel. Outside their room, Derek could hear someone shouting to have it battened down.

"We don't have storms like this very often in

England," Derek said quietly. "I just know you'll love it there."

"Oh?"

"Well, if you're going to be my wife, you should be in London with me."

If Lauren had not been lying down, she would have fallen down. In the course of twenty-four hours she had been rescued from a harem, weathered a catastrophic storm, been shipwrecked, been ensconced in a fine hotel, been given beautiful new clothes, learned that the man she loved was also in love with her and was quite willing to say so . . . and if that wasn't enough, she was also being proposed to.

"Derek . . . what are you . . . ?"

"Do you want me to get down on one knee? I will, if it's necessary."

"No—I just want you to say the words."

Derek took Lauren's hand in his, kissed the back of her hand softly, and then, looking into her eyes, stated, "Lauren, I am in love with you, and I believe I will always be in love with you because I know I'll never find anyone nearly as fascinating as you are. My life will not be complete until you are in it—formally and forever. Will you, Lauren Masters, marry me?"

"Yes," Lauren whispered in response as warm tears sprang anew into her eyes. She wrapped her arms around Derek's neck, hugging him close. "Yes, my darling, yes!"

Chapter 27

Renaldo, at age thirteen, could not be sure exactly what this news would bring him, but he was certain it would be enough to buy food for his entire family. And his father would be so proud of him!

The wreckage of the sailboat was, by itself, neither unusual nor valuable to Renaldo. In the warm and turbulent Caribbean waters, small sailboats were often shattered against the rocks—particularly when storms came, as they had the past two nights. And the arrival of strangers in town was not particularly unusual, since the village was a common port for many shipping lines. But foreigners without luggage or belongings who bought fine clothing with gold coins, along with the recently discovered boat wreckage—and the sudden arrival of both the Big Man and Captain Gregor to St. Thomas at the same time—that was information the constable would surely pay good money for!

Renaldo's tiny brown knuckles again rapped against the weatherbeaten door. He could see Jonas lying on the cot inside the cell, which doubled as his living quarters. Jonas was snoring softly, and Renaldo knew better than to rush in to shake him awake. The last time he'd done that, Jonas had booted him in the backside hard enough to lift his feet clean off the ground.

He hit the door again, hard enough to make his knuckles ache, and finally Jonas groaned and rolled onto his side.

"Mr. Jonas! Mr. Jonas! I have something very special for you!"

Jonas blinked his eyes several times, then pushed himself to a sitting position. His tongue felt furry; his eyes felt dry. Part of him wanted to take the peasant boy by the throat and toss him around a bit for waking him, but in the past Renaldo had come up with several interesting and profitable bits of information, so Jonas was inclined to withhold the reaction, at least temporarily.

"You'd better have a damn good reason for wakin' me, boy," Jonas growled. He rolled his head on his shoulders, trying to work the stiffness from his body. Why were mornings getting worse all the time?

"I do, Mr. Jonas! Only the best for you, Mr. Jonas!" Renaldo's small, dark face beamed with excitement and just a touch of nervousness. The news he had would be worthless in an hour, maybe less. "Big news for you, Mr. Jonas!"

Jonas finally allowed the peasant boy to enter, and after a coin had changed hands, Renaldo told of the Big Man coming with Captain Gregor, and of the vicious little man, Bones. Jonas, though certainly no intellectual giant, was sage enough to realize the potential for profit—made even easier by the fact that the Big Man was coming right to his doorstep!

"Run along, boy," Jonas said, pushing the young peasant toward the door. "And don't say a word of this to anyone else, or I'll boot you good. Understand me?"

"Yes, Mr. Jonas, yes!" Renaldo replied, the coin he'd earned clutched tightly in his tiny hand.

The caw of a tropical bird of unknown origin woke

Lauren. She smiled sleepily, her head resting on Derek's arm. Through the night they had slept together, Derek's arm wrapped protectively around her.

Could there ever be a contentment quite like this one? Lauren mused. To wake up beside the man she loved, warm and safe, and secure . . . it was the most gentle, loving feeling Lauren had ever known, and it gave her a deep sense of inner peace.

She rolled toward him and lightly placed her hand against his stomach. He breathed slowly in his sleep. His sandy hair was mussed, giving him a comfortably rumpled look that Lauren found delightful.

Memories of last night's lovemaking came back, and Lauren blushed with embarrassment. Had she really been so abandoned in Derek's arms? In all the times she had made love with Derek, never before had she been so demanding in her desires. How many times had Derek taken her to the edge of sensual oblivion and then beyond? Four times, maybe five? He'd done it with his hands, with his mouth, and with his seemingly tireless manhood thrusting deeply inside her.

Lauren closed her eyes, thinking of all she had done the previous night, and wondering what Derek thought of her now. Surely he couldn't think less of her because of her abandon—if it hadn't been for him, she wouldn't have even known she was capable of such sensations!

And even more pleasing than the memories of lovemaking were memories of Derek's proposal. Once he pushed through his hesitation in saying "I love you," he became a changed man. He told her over and over that he loved her, that he would always love her, and that as soon as it was humanly and legally possible, he would marry her.

"I'll talk to your father," Derek had said between episodes of intense lovemaking. "He'll understand that

328

I love you very much, and that we simply *must* get married immediately. From what you've told me, he's a man who'll understand."

"I also know that my father's a protective man who'd want to skin you alive if he knew what we'd done!" Lauren giggled, pressing herself a little more firmly against his side. "But don't worry, I won't let Father hurt you. I'll just tell him that I'm a compromised woman now, and unless he wants my reputation sullied forever, he'll allow the wedding within the week." Lauren laughed again. "Now you can't back out or he really *will* kill you."

They laughed together after that, and somewhere during their laughter the passion blossomed anew. They made love with an almost childlike innocence, two young people being naughty and defying their parents.

Lauren sighed, remembering it all, and thinking about all the wonderful nights to come that she would enjoy with Lord Derek York. And once she became his wife, what would she be? Would she be titled at all? *Lady York?* Lauren smiled. She liked the sound of that! *Lady Lauren York.*

The warmth of Derek's naked body beside her seemed to have changed. No longer was it comforting—now it was stimulating; and no longer was Lauren satisfied to dwell on memories of last night's adventures, she wanted to create new adventures—daylight adventures.

With an impish grin, Lauren pulled away from Derek to look at him, and eased the thin sheet down his body. To her surprise she noticed that in sleep Derek was fully aroused, and a series of tiny tremors raced up and down her spine.

The cut along Derek's ribs appeared to be healing nicely. During their lovemaking, Lauren had forgotten

329

herself and scratched his chest, causing him to grimace in agony. They had then removed the bandage to see if the wound had been reopened. Seeing that it hadn't, they resumed their lovemaking, with Lauren being a bit more careful of how she touched Derek, and much more curious concerning what it would take to make her future husband *not* want to make love.

She pulled the sheet lower on his body, her eyes taking in the lean, sinewy strength of him. The outline of each rib was clearly visible, and even though he was relaxed in sleep, she could see the muscles in his stomach, a crisscrossing structure of solid strength.

He's beautiful, Lauren thought, her eyes moving slowly over him. For the first time in her life she was consciously impressed by a man's beauty, and visually drinking in Derek's masculinity now made her feel rather naughty, as though she really shouldn't find a man's body at all pleasing to her feminine senses.

Very slowly, with just the tip of her forefinger, she pushed the sheet lower on his body, edging it closer to the rising column of flesh that tented the cloth. Her fingertips were just inches from Derek's manhood when she heard his slightly startled intake of breath. She recoiled from him, afraid she had been too forward.

"I didn't mean to wake you," she whispered, turning her face slowly toward Derek, hesitating, afraid she would see disapproval in his eyes.

"Don't apologize," he said in a husky, sensual whisper. "It's wonderful to wake up with you beside me." He touched the side of her face lightly with his fingertips, brushing the pad of his thumb over Lauren's lips. After a moment, Derek slid his long fingers into Lauren's satiny hair at the nape of her neck. "And don't stop," he murmured, kicking the sheet down to his knees.

Lauren curled her fingers around the hard, throbbing shaft. The solid flesh seemed to have a life of its own, pulsating vibrantly in her palm. She squeezed tightly, testing its steely strength.

"Don't stop, Lauren," Derek repeated, his blue eyes burning with a passionate intensity that thrilled her.

Hesitantly at first, unsure of herself and what was expected of her, she brought her hand up and down. She slithered lower on the bed. Derek's hand at the back of her neck gave gentle guidance, and when she kissed him, the deep, satisfied groan of pleasure reassured her and gave her confidence. She flicked her tongue lightly over the enflamed tip, and Derek flinched as though jolted with electricity.

"Deeper," he whispered.

She took him between her lips, and Derek began moaning softly, lost in the throes of the pleasure Lauren provided.

Derek stood at the balcony, overlooking the awakening city below. He held a steaming cup of coffee in one hand and a muffin liberally slathered with butter in the other. The morning breeze was cool and refreshing against his naked body.

"Don't you think you should put something on?" Lauren asked, sitting cross-legged. Though she was naked, Lauren was perfectly at ease and completely unembarrassed.

Derek turned away from the balcony. He had placed a small throw rug over the railing to hide himself just in case any early morning busybody decided to look up. Lauren's smirk delighted him.

"You look like the cat that just ate the canary," he said, shaking his head in amazement.

"Me, sir? Surely you have me confused with someone else!" Lauren said, placing a hand to her bosom and rolling her eyes in a caricature of innocence. But then her grin resurfaced and she dramatically let her gaze roam up and down Derek's naked body.

"You've got to be kidding!" Derek said with a laugh, accurately reading his fiancée's thoughts. "After last night and this morning—you're *still* not satisfied?"

"It's not that I'm not satisfied, darling. In fact, you always satisfy me . . . that's why I've become rather— oh, shall we call it, *enthusiastic?*"

"Shall we call it greedy?" Derek replied.

He turned to set his coffee cup on the railing, intent on proving to Lauren that he could take her to that magical land once more. Across the street, in front of the constable's office, he saw Aldon Mitchell, Gregor, Bones, and Jonas Liebermann standing in a circle, talking intently.

"Bloody hell!" Derek whispered through clenched teeth.

He watched as Jonas separated himself from the group. Jonas was nodding his head, leading the group, and when he jerked his thumb in the direction of the hotel, Derek knew that Aldon Mitchell's long tentacles of power and influence reached as far as this small stretch of St. Thomas.

"We've got to go!" Derek said, pulling on his breeches. "Hurry and get dressed! I'm going to get Amanda up!"

"What's wrong? Derek, you're scaring me!"

"Aldon Mitchell's down there with Gregor, and the constable is leading them here."

Ninety seconds of thinly controlled panic followed as Derek, Amanda, and Lauren, wearing some of their clothes and carrying others, rushed from their rooms and down the hallway. They rounded the corner of the stairway leading to the rear entrance just as Jonas set foot on the second floor, with Aldon and Gregor close at his heels.

They stopped at the rear door, tugging on clothes, pulling on shoes and boots, fastening buttons and tying laces.

"How could he know?" Lauren asked, finishing with the last of her buttons.

"Spread enough money around and you can find out everything that happens," Derek replied.

In his haste he had taken his prized dagger with the shoulder sheath but had left behind his cutlass. His mind was working rapidly, sorting out possible avenues of action. Outnumbered, and with the additional handicap of having two women with him, all he could do was run. He slipped the dagger into the sheath below his left arm, then pulled on his waistcoat.

"Don't run," he said as they stepped outside. "Just walk nice and easy, and don't draw attention to yourself."

Derek, Lauren, and Amanda disappeared down back alleys and side streets, continually moving further away from the hotel until they finally abandoned the city altogether. As the jungle again swallowed them, covering their escape, Derek wondered how far the women could go before they could run no further, and what would happen when that time came.

Chapter 28

Gregor was sweating profusely, and hating with greater vehemence and broader scope than ever.

He hated physical exertion, especially on such a hot and muggy day. Each step he took reminded him of the key focus of his hatred—the English bastard who was the cause of all his troubles. The English bastard, and the dark-haired American wench . . . yes, he would make them both pay for all the trouble they'd caused him.

Bones walked several steps ahead. Much more slender than Gregor, he was much less bothered by the heat and strength-sapping labor of trekking through a thick jungle. Behind Gregor were ten of his finest and most savage sailors.

"Mates, stop!" Gregor called out, trying hard to not pant as he spoke to them. He smiled lasciviously for their benefit. "The Big Man says we're to kill them all and bring their heads back in a bag. Well, the way I see it, the Big Man has been giving orders too damned long already!" There was a murmur of approval from the men which encouraged Gregor. "So this is what we're going to do—we'll kill that bastard Englishman and we'll kill him slow! And when we're done with him, the women will be ours! Makes no damned sense to kill two lovelies like that—not when we're strong men with strong needs!" It was more than just a murmur of approval this time. As Gregor continued, the plan forming in his mind as he talked, he realized there was no turning back now. He had been a slave to Aldon Mitchell's vast wealth too long—too long, and for far too little. "We'll take the wenches for ourselves."

"But what about Master Mitchell, Cap'n Gregor?" Bones asked, his eyes narrowed in concentration. He had seen men suffer for confronting Aldon Mitchell, and he didn't want to face the Big Man's wrath unless it was absolutely necessary.

"Master Mitchell?" Gregor asked sarcastically. "That slimy landlubber ain't *my* master." Gregor withdrew his dagger and touched the tip of the blade with his thumb as though testing its sharpness. "Why do we need him? Why should he profit from our hard labor? We're the ones who storm the ships, we're the ones who get the gold and the jewels and the money. Why should the Big Man in his fancy white clothes get money *we've* earned?" Gregor laughed menacingly. "I'll cut Aldon Mitchell's throat from ear to ear, *then* we'll see who's the master!"

This time Gregor received a roar of approval. Now he knew his men would follow him endlessly through the jungle and wouldn't stop searching until they'd captured the blonde and the brunette, and until Derek was dead. There was no turning back for the men, or for Gregor, and with a freshness to his step, he continued on, tracking the fugitives with renewed vigor.

*   *   *

Amanda was crying softly. The tears dribbled down her pale cheeks as she pushed on, struggling to maintain the pace that Derek set.

"Are you all right?" Lauren asked in a whisper, not wanting to alert Derek, who, at the lead, had hardly looked back since they'd left the village.

Amanda nodded, tried to smile courageously but failed, then wiped the tears angrily from her eyes.

"Derek, we need to rest a minute," Lauren said. "I'm exhausted. I just need a few minutes." It seemed better to put the blame on herself than on Amanda.

Derek gave Lauren a compassionate look and nodded. "I'll backtrack some and see how far behind they are." He turned and disappeared into the jungle.

Alone with Amanda and able to talk freely, Lauren said, "Now you can tell me what's wrong."

The courage and strength that Amanda had drawn upon for the past hour vanished. Her slender shoulders began to shudder, then she buried her face in her hands and wept. Lauren sat beside her, putting an arm around her comfortingly.

"That's all right," Lauren whispered, stroking Amanda's hair as the teenager cried. "You'll feel better if you cry. This has been very difficult for everyone."

"I thought it was over when we were in the hotel," Amanda said, her tears gradually subsiding. "I really thought we were free at last, but they'll always be after us . . . always!"

"No, they won't. This terrible situation will all be behind us soon. Derek will get us out of this."

Amanda shook her head slowly, sadly. "Not this time. Not me, anyway."

"What are you talking about? Derek would never leave you behind. You're the reason he's here!"

Amanda pulled up her dress slightly. One glance told Lauren all she needed to know.

"My God!" she gasped. Amanda's right ankle was purple and swollen, her dainty foot now looking grotesque inside the new shoe. "When did that happen?"

"About a half hour ago," Amanda answered, wincing as she wiggled her toes inside the shoe. "I slipped, and at first it didn't seem too bad, but as we went on, it hurt more and more." She turned her gaze to Lauren, and in a tremulous voice whispered, "I can't go on much further. You'll have to go on without me."

At that moment Derek returned, and though Amanda quickly moved her skirts, he saw that she was hiding something. Without a word he knelt and checked her ankle.

"Can you put any weight on it at all?" Derek asked, holding his sister's foot gently in his hands.

"Some, but not much. It's hurting worse all the time."

"I can believe that."

"I'm sorry . . . I'm so sorry."

Derek looked at Amanda and smiled confidently, patting her cheek. "No need to apologize, and don't worry about a thing. We've gone too far to fail now. We'll all get out of this."

For a moment Derek thought of Sue Ellen and Chantell, whom he'd left with the doctor. He hoped they were safe and figured they would be, considering the physician's rather paternal interest in their welfare.

"How far behind us are they?" Lauren asked.

"Twenty minutes ago I caught a glimpse of them when we were rounding that valley. If they haven't gained any ground, I'd say they're about thirty or forty minutes behind us."

Amanda started crying again, the tears silently falling from her big blue eyes. "I'll slow you down," she whispered. "You'll both get caught because of me."

"None of us is going to get caught by anybody," Derek said, a hard edge to his voice. He grabbed his sister by the arm and hauled her to her feet. Turning, he crouched, putting his arms out, indicating he wanted Amanda to leap up on his back. "Just like when we were kids," he said as he hooked his arms around her legs. "Remember how we used to play horsey?"

"And you were always such a *good* horsey," Amanda replied with a forced giggle, despite the pain and the danger.

Lauren walked behind them, watching Derek carefully. She loved him, and she knew that he was in extraordinary physical condition. She also knew he could not possibly carry Amanda and keep up a pace fast enough to elude their pursuers.

If they were going to escape, something had to change. Lauren just didn't know what it was yet.

"They rested here for a bit, Cap'n," Bones said, pointing to the trampled grass. "They gotta be gettin' awful tired."

"I'll cut my own throat before I'll believe that a man with two wenches can outdistance us, eh, mates?" Gregor replied. The men all cheered at his bravado, but he could see the sweat rolling down their faces. He pulled a bottle of rum from inside his tunic and took a big swig before passing the bottle to Bones. "Have a chug and pass it along. It's the last taste of rum you'll have until we've got the wenches in our beds and the Englishman is feeding the fishes!"

The rum was finished in a minute or two, and then the men pushed on, slowly and relentlessly closing the distance between themselves and their prey, able now to envision the pleasures that would be theirs once they captured the women.

Lauren took Derek's dagger and hacked off another strip of cloth from the hem of her dress. The cloth was needed to wrap Amanda's ankle to keep the swelling down, and getting rid of the very bottom of her skirt also made it easier for Lauren to move.

Derek had taken off his waistcoat and tossed it beneath some bushes. If Gregor and the others found it, then so be it. His silk shirt was sticking to his lean torso like a second skin, soaked through with perspiration, and his breath was coming in ragged gulps.

He can't last much longer, Lauren thought as she finished with her dress, then caught up with Derek again. She tucked his dagger back in its sheath for him so that he wouldn't have to take his hands from Amanda's legs.

On three different occasions in the past hour they had either heard their hunters or seen them. If Derek had any thoughts of an open confrontation with the crew of *The Unholy One,* he abandoned them when he saw the number of men—with Gregor in the lead—now chasing them.

Seeing Bones was especially disturbing to Lauren; Derek had told her how savage the slender pirate could be.

They reached the crest of a hill and before them stretched the Caribbean Sea, looking as cool and inviting as anything Lauren had ever seen.

"A boat," she said, mostly to herself. "We've got to find a boat."

Derek stopped at the crest and let Amanda down. She carefully balanced on one foot, keeping the weight off her injured ankle, and said nothing.

"If only I knew this island better," Derek said, wiping sweat from his face. "Mitchell can't have bought everyone *everywhere*. We could find an honest constable . . . if only I knew where to go."

The sound of men's voices caught their attention, and as one they crouched low and listened carefully. The boom of Gregor's thunderous voice sent a shiver through Lauren.

"They're not five minutes behind us," Lauren said, voicing what the other two already knew.

"Get on," Derek said to Amanda, turning his back to her. "We've got to keep moving."

Lauren's plan was still forming in her mind when she rushed forward to stand directly in front of Derek as he held Amanda on his back.

"I love you," Lauren said in a breathy rush of words. She pulled his dagger from its sheath, then rose up on her toes to kiss Derek's mouth. "Come back for me as soon as you can."

Derek never had a chance to stop her. Lauren wheeled away and sprinted into the clearing, toward the shore. He watched in silent horror as she ran in the opposite direction, her long, powerful legs propelling her.

She was fifty yards away when they heard the first shout. The men of *The Unholy One,* like howling wolves running down a deer, screamed to each other, breaking into the clearing as fast as they could in pursuit. Gregor, the heaviest of them, followed behind, secure in the knowledge that it didn't matter who caught her—he would be the first to have her.

"You fool," Derek whispered, watching Lauren until she moved away from the shore and disappeared into the trees. "You sweet, beautiful fool."

Derek turned away, knowing there was nothing he could do to undo what Lauren had done. He had to get Amanda to safety, then return for Lauren as quickly as possible, heavily armed and laden with money to buy the mercenaries to fight and destroy Gregor and Aldon Mitchell and anyone else foolish enough to stand between himself and Lauren Masters.

Run like a fox, my love, Derek thought as he carried his sister away from the men who no longer pursued them, *and I will pray that the hounds do not catch you.*

Chapter 29

Michael Masters sipped his morning coffee and read the newspaper, though the news held only half his concentration. He was still thinking about what the sailor had told him the previous day, a farfetched story about white slavery and men owning entire islands where they lived as gods—no laws governing them, no one stopping them.

The story seemed unbelievable, but still. . . .

Sharon, Michael's wife, sat beside him. Though he'd refused to tell her what he'd heard about the current state of affairs in the Virgin Islands, Sharon had been able to tell that something was bothering her husband. With a little investigating, she was able to hear the same story Michael had heard.

"What are you going to do?" she asked, studying her husband's profile as she blew softly on her coffee to cool it.

"About what?" Michael replied.

For a moment their eyes met and held. They had been married too long and knew each other too well for Michael to pretend he didn't fully understand his wife's question. He smiled, acknowledging the futility of trying to deceive his perceptive wife.

"I'm not sure yet. Part of me wants to outfit a ship

and sail down there right away. But if I do that, I'll lose all the connections to the area I have while I'm here."

Sharon reached over, placing her small hand lightly over Michael's larger, callused one. "Lauren is a strong and capable girl. She'll be all right."

Michael nodded, then turned his attention back to the newspaper, not so that he could read the print, but so that he could focus his eyes on something while his mind considered all the possible avenues of action he could take to locate his wayward daughter.

Michael and Sharon had just finished their breakfast when Ida, the family nanny and housekeeper, stepped into the breakfast nook.

"Mr. Michael, there's a gentleman here to see you. An English gentleman, by the sound of him. Says his name is Lord Derek York."

Michael and Sharon again exchanged questioning looks.

"Lord York, you say?" Sharon asked.

"Yes, ma'am. Seems a real gentleman, too."

Michael's mouth quirked into a crooked grin. "Now I know why that name sounds familiar—we've done shipping for the Yorks of London in the past. Sharon, remember two years ago, when we wanted to get started in England, and we set up that temporary partnership with York Unlimited?"

Sharon smiled, nodding. "Yes, but as I recall, they had some very stubborn people working for them."

Ida chuckled, muttering, "There's plenty of stubborn folk working for this family *too,* missy!"

"I know I should see him, but I'm just not up to dealing with another salesman today," Michael said. "Ida, please set up an appointment for me to meet him later in the week, and I'll gladly see him then."

"Yes, sir," Ida replied, disappearing through the batwing doors.

She'd hardly been gone a minute when Michael and

Sharon heard her high, sharp cry of anger and alarm, followed with "You can't go in there!" Lord Derek York burst into the breakfast nook, his icy eyes spitting daggers of anger.

"I'm really bloody damned sorry to disturb your breakfast, but I know where Lauren is, and I would bloody goddamn appreciate a little help in getting her back, because I happen to be in love with her! Now are you going to help me or not?"

Lauren curled her toes around the edge of the rock to get a better grip on it. She raised her spear slowly and carefully, not wanting to draw attention to herself. Tied securely to the end of the spear was the dagger she had taken from Derek just before leading Gregor's men on a wild chase through the jungle.

Wait, she told herself consciously. *Be patient, then strike with everything you've got!*

Every muscle in her body tensed, and then, when the time was right, she launched the spear.

Her aim was perfect, hitting the fish just behind the gills, severing the spine. It was a clean kill, and Lauren leaped into the water to retrieve the spear, and her dinner. She carried the fish out of the water quickly because it was bleeding, and blood drew sharks.

In the past two months, since she had been fending for herself after running away from Derek and Amanda on St. Thomas, Lauren had learned patience, how to hunt and fish, and a hundred other things that she had never before thought important.

For the first couple of weeks, she had often gone hungry. Her haste to satisfy her appetite had caused her to miss fish that swam close to shore on the small, otherwise uninhabited island not far from St. Thomas.

Lauren soon learned that patience really was a virtue, and hunger a good teacher.

She cleaned the fish right there on the rocks, throwing the entrails back into the sea for smaller fish to eat. She had learned that nothing should be wasted. Finished, she washed her hands and arms, then put her dress back on.

She looked around the island briefly, studying the treeline, thinking that some day she would see a sign of another person. It just didn't seem possible that this island, which was so beautiful it had looked like paradise when Lauren had spotted it from the canoe she'd stolen on St. Thomas, would not have anyone living on it.

The reason there were no people, Lauren had later discovered, was simple: there was no freshwater. She had learned to satisfy her thirst by drinking the milk from coconuts, and catching whatever rainwater she could.

I'm lonely, Lauren thought suddenly.

It was a simple mental declaration of the way things were; it wasn't a particularly sad realization. *I miss Derek. I've just got to be strong and wait for the day when he finds me. He's looking for me now. I just know he is.*

Carrying the fish, which would feed her for two or three days, she headed back to the cave that had been sheltering her from the wind and the rain.

What she did not know was that she was no longer alone on the tiny island.

"Listen to me. If you load up an armada and go down there in full force, you'll never find *The Unholy One,* and you'll never find Lauren."

Derek put his hands on his hips, looking into Michael's eyes. For a moment, Derek wondered if it had been a sound idea to come to Virginia and involve Lauren's father in her rescue. The moment Derek had explained what had happened to her, Michael wanted to load up his fastest ships with men and weapons and storm the entire Virgin Islands. Derek argued forcibly that to act so overtly would make their intentions too visible to Gregor.

Michael's mouth was pressed into a thin, harsh line. He was a man of action, not a man given to waiting for the right moment to act. Derek sensed this, but he also sensed that if he could appeal to Michael's better judgment and logic, he could make Lauren's father understand the best course of action to take against a man like Gregor.

"Unless you've been there, you'll never really understand what the islands are like," Derek said, sitting on the edge of a leather wingbacked chair in Michael's study. "There are something like a hundred islands, most uninhabited, all treacherous to those who don't know the area. Unless you're familiar with the seas, you're a dead man. At least, you will be if you try to trap Gregor in those waters. He knows every inch of them. He knows every sandbar, every submerged rock. That's why he's never been caught. Whenever the Queen sends ships after him, he leads them in circles around the islands, knowing that if he just keeps moving long enough, he can lead his pursuers into rocks and onto sandbars."

Michael nibbled on his lower lip. The young man's logic was arguable, but sound. Michael, who liked pushing the odds of nature, could see that Derek was honestly concerned with Lauren's safety and welfare, and that a cautious, surreptitious approach to finding Lauren was the best kind. He didn't *like* the fact that an all-out assault wasn't the best strategy, but he accepted it.

"Let's just suppose you're right for a minute," Michael said. His dark eyes, fiercely focused, reminded

346

Derek of Lauren's. "We go down there—you and me and a few of my best men. We take enough money with us to buy the people who need to be bribed and impress the people who need to be impressed. But that still doesn't mean we'll find Lauren, does it?"

"No, it doesn't."

The two men looked long and hard into each other's eyes. They did not trust each other, but they both loved Lauren.

"We don't know if Lauren has been able to stay clear of Gregor and Aldon all this time." Michael paused to roll a cigarette and light it. He exhaled with a grateful sigh. "Has she been captured? If so, is she still on St. Lucifer, or has she been taken to another island? So many questions . . . yet you're convinced a quiet approach will work better than a show of strength." Michael shook his head, as though in disagreement with himself rather than with Derek. "I hope to hell you're right. Every inclination in my bones tells me to find the best mercenaries money can buy, load up my fastest ships, and head down there immediately. Give me twenty minutes alone with one of the men from *The Unholy One,* and I assure you, I'll know everything that man knows about Gregor, Aldon Mitchell, and any white slavery operation operating in the Virgin Islands."

Derek quickly looked away, suppressing a smile. For a dozen different reasons, he respected Lauren's father as much as he respected his own.

"If it would have helped to use muscle against Gregor, you've got to believe I would have." Derek looked away a moment, wondering if Michael thought him a coward. "I had to consider the safety of my sister," he continued after a moment. "Amanda was the reason I went down there. I never expected to meet a woman like Lauren . . . not ever in my life, and certainly not under those conditions." He looked straight into Michael's dark eyes. "I never thought I would know a love as complete as the one I feel for your daughter. I'll do whatever it takes to get her back. If I suggest stealth over strength, it's not because I'm cowardly, it's because I love Lauren."

Michael smiled the first real smile since Derek had charged into his house hours earlier. "Very well, then, we'll do this your way. Amanda will be safe here. I've got several good men in my employ who know how to handle themselves in difficult situations, and when it's all over with, how to keep their mouths shut."

"Then they are doubly valuable," Derek said.

"Collecting doubly valuable salaries, but they're worth every penny," Michael said wryly, and with no small amount of pride. "Now let's figure out what we'll need to take. I want to set sail no later than sunrise."

Derek looked at Lauren's father. He felt the sudden acceleration of his own heart. "Agreed," he said.

Tajeen squeezed her hands into tight fists and nibbled on her lower lip. She had information she was certain Gregor would find valuable. Everyone had heard about how Gregor had offered a huge sum of money—jewels as well as gold coins—for anyone giving him information concerning the whereabouts of a dark-haired American woman.

It had been more than a week since Tajeen had seen the woman. At first she was not sure that the naked woman spearfishing was the one Gregor sought, but the more Tajeen thought about it, the more certain she became. Now she worried how she would explain to Gregor her delay in relaying the news.

Like most everyone in the neighboring islands, Tajeen had witnessed Gregor's terrible wrath. When angered, he could be ruthless, and could take pleasure in inflicting pain.

Wiping her moist palms on her shabby shikars, Tajeen combed her hair with her fingers. She could hear the revelry going on inside *As the Crow Flies,* and she knew she would find Gregor inside. With any luck, the mean, thin man named Bones would not be with him. Several months earlier, Tajeen had run into Bones on one of the paths leading to the small village where her family lived. Bones had caught her, but Tajeen had escaped, and if she hadn't been so fleet-footed, Bones would have done more than just touch her.

I don't ever want to feel his hands upon me again, Tajeen thought, her courage quickly fading. But she knew she must continue into the tavern, even if it would put her in danger. *My family needs the money. With the money this will bring, we can all go far away from Gregor and Bones and the Big Man and everyone else who brings suffering to us!*

She stepped closer to *As the Crow Flies,* her heart hammering against her ribs. Briefly Tajeen thought about the American woman and wondered what would happen to her once Gregor captured her. Though she tried not to think about it, a horrible realization flooded through her. She could only guess at what hideous plans Gregor had for the American woman.

Think about your family! she thought, admonishing herself for letting her sympathies become divided when she was so close to acquiring the money necessary to take herself and her family far away from this island and the hell it represented.

Bones was sweating, but he smiled as he led the small expedition of men. Under other circumstances he'd have been angry that Gregor had made him row to an unnamed island, but since it was to search for the dark-eyed American wench, and since Gregor had promised that he would be second in line to have the woman, the additional work was more than welcome.

"She's here somewhere," Bones said quietly, mostly to himself, though he had four men surrounding him as he knelt near the remains of a small campfire. "This fire is only a day or two old."

The men fanned out, searching for more clues that might tell them where Lauren was, or if she was still on the island.

He studied the dried fish scales on the ground, all that remained of a large fish that had been caught and cleaned. Bones smiled, hoping Lauren had been eating well. He didn't want her to lose her figure from lack of food. When he had her, he wanted her looking her best.

What she looked like after he passed her down to the next in line wasn't any of his concern.

One of the men called out, and Bones came running. On the ground, partially hidden by vegetation, were the remains of a coconut, stripped of most of its rich white meat. The pirate handed a shell fragment to Bones. He touched the white, inner surface of the coconut . . . and smiled broadly.

"It's not dried out yet," he said in a whisper. His insides tightened at the thought of having Lauren's thrashing body beneath his, and with effort he pushed the thought away—temporarily. "She's got to be close, mates! Fan out, and don't bruise her when you catch her! Gregor wants the wench lookin' like a mermaid princess!"

With quiet determination the men combed the heavily forested island, searching for more clues as to the whereabouts of an American woman so beautiful that she'd become the object of all their fantasies.

It wasn't long before another shout rang out through the trees.

350

"Here! She's here!"

Bones took off at a dead run toward the sound of the voice, feeling a sudden and strange fullness in his loins at the first sight of long, jet black hair and flying feet beneath a ragged-looking European dress.

Lauren felt the sand give way beneath her bare feet, and she cursed softly under her breath. *Why now?* she thought, too frightened to look over her shoulder to see if the sweaty-faced pirates who chased her with such lusty zeal were gaining ground.

She heard one of the men shouting, saying something to the leader. *At least it isn't Gregor,* thought Lauren with small satisfaction.

Her satisfaction was short lived when she heard Bones's name shouted. The only person in the world who adored cruelty and sadism more than Gregor was his right-hand man, Bones.

During the time she'd spent on the island she'd become acquainted with many of its quirks, nooks, game trails, and ravines. This information made it possible for Lauren to put ground between herself and the human wolfpack pursuing her—at least initially.

She led them deeper into the island, away from the ocean, where ground could be covered quickly and visibility was poor. In the thick undergrowth one was lucky to see fifty feet in any given direction. The sound of breaking and bending branches, of angry curses and startled cries, was never far behind Lauren as she led the pirates toward the center of the small island, constantly moving inward with the gentle natural elevation of the island's geography.

The dress was difficult to run in, and Lauren almost wished that she wore nothing at all. As it was, she needed to pull up the skirt to give her legs sufficient room to move.

She led the men higher, into land that she herself did not know well. The higher Lauren moved, the more damp the ground became. The recent rains had left the grass slippery, and twice Lauren fell hard to her knees. If luck and the fates and all that was holy was with her, she would lead the men high into the trees, then double back toward the water, where she hoped to lose them by making good distance when the land was clear and sandy.

In land now completely unfamiliar to her she saw a game trail that seemed to disappear almost straight into a thicket of trees. Knowing that the trail had to lead somewhere, Lauren raised her skirts and followed it at an easy dogtrot. Bones and his men were fifty yards behind her now, and they were slowly but steadily losing ground. Lauren prayed that this trail would be the one that would allow her to lose them once and for all.

The trail took a sharp turn, then without warning, opened out onto the sea. The craggy edge of the cliff went almost straight down for about three hundred feet. Lauren tried to stop, but she'd been running so fast and her bare feet were so wet that she began to slide. Somehow she managed to grab onto a low-hanging branch before toppling over the cliff to the rocks far below.

"My God!" she gasped, peering down at the crashing waves, her heart hammering against her ribs from the exertion and from the nearness of her own death.

She had never really liked heights, and looking down now gave her a queasy feeling in the pit of her stomach.

Don't think about it! Don't let the fear paralyze you!

Lauren grit her teeth in frustration, angry at the delay. Each second that passed allowed Bones and the others to get closer . . . and time was running out.

Still holding the lifesaving branch, Lauren studied the trail as it followed the edge of the cliff. Whatever animals used it, they had to be sure-footed and fairly small. The narrow trail followed the side of the cliff and was heavily overgrown with trees and vegetation. Whether there was room enough for a person to walk on it was doubtful—exactly the reason Lauren knew she had to take it.

Lauren crouched low, very nearly getting down on her hands and knees, and crept along the path. She could hear the men behind her, very close now, stopping at the juncture where she'd stood just a minute ago, wondering just as she had which direction to take.

With her weight on the balls of her feet, Lauren lost her footing. She came down hard on one knee, her right foot sliding over the edge of the cliff. She grabbed handfuls of the coarse, long grass, and that alone kept her from sliding into the abyss. Slowly, feeling herself again close to death, she brought up her right leg until her knee was pressed into the wet grass and she was once again balanced on the trail.

She could not say what prompted her to look out to sea at that terrified moment. It was a feeling—nothing more than a feeling that started in the pit of her stomach and made her react without being consciously aware of it.

The three ships were little more than specks in the distance, three specks sailing in a triangular formation, two double-masted vessels and the lead ship, triple-masted, and considerably larger than the others.

Lauren squinted, straining to see better. The ships were so far away, yet there was something familiar about them—something so familiar that not even the nearness of her hunters could prevent her from sparing precious seconds to concentrate on the miniscule flags they sailed under. Blue and white flags, it seemed.

Masters Enterprises!

The realization was so powerful that Lauren nearly

shouted with happiness. They were the ships of Masters Enterprises, and that had to mean that Derek had gone to her father, and together they had come back for her!

I knew he would come! I knew Derek wouldn't leave me here!

Lauren got up onto the balls of her feet, feeling more confident than she had in weeks, and continued on along the slippery, narrow game trail.

She had put less than thirty yards between herself and the point where the trail emptied out onto the sea when a hideous, triumphant cry echoed through the afternoon air. Lauren was sickened by the sounds of savagery and lust and primal emotions.

"Here! Bones, she's here! I've found the wench!"

Lauren tried to look over her shoulder. It was a mistake—she lost her tenuous balance. Her feet slipped out from beneath her and she landed on her backside, sliding over the edge, her feet searching frantically in midair for footing that was not there. She grabbed the brown, coarse grass with both hands, hoping it had the strength to stop her downward progression. The slow, hideous tearing sound of the ropy grass giving way to her weight, blade by blade, was the worst sound she had ever heard. Twisting, Lauren clung to the cliff's edge, her cheek pressed against the grass that moments earlier she had stood upon.

Desperately she caught fresh handfuls of grass, and this time she managed to grab enough to stop her slow, inch-by-horrid-inch descent over the edge.

I don't want to die, she thought, terrified.

Somehow the idea surprised Lauren. There had been times, alone on the island, when she truly did not care whether she lived or died. But now, with Derek so close—with the ships within sight—she had something to live for again.

354

The men were closer, but Lauren did not look. She was able to maintain her position, but she could not pull herself back onto the path to escape.

All I have to do is let go now, and they'll never touch me. I'll never know the horror of their hands on me. Just a few seconds in the air, then I'll hit the rocks below, and that will be the end of it all. They'll never have the chance to touch me . . . and neither will Derek.

She had to hold onto life . . . to hold on until Derek could rescue her. She owed herself and Derek that much. Whatever horrors Bones and Gregor and even Aldon Mitchell could inflict upon her, they could not be enough to extinguish her will to live—not when she had Derek's vow of love, not when she knew he'd come back for her. As long as she lived, he'd continue to search for her and succeed in freeing her.

"Come on, you bastards," Lauren hissed as the pirates edged closer. "Help me up, and don't drop me. I don't want to end up splattered on the rocks."

She heard Bones chuckle and say, from a safe distance, "She's being damned good about this, ain't she, mates?"

The pirate caught Lauren's wrist, and he hoisted her onto the trail easily.

"Gregor's been waiting for you," the pirate said, openly leering at Lauren as he guided her back to firm ground. "He's been waitin' for a long time, and he ain't waitin' much longer."

Chapter 30

"What do you see?" Michael asked, standing so close to Derek that their shoulders were nearly touching.

"A boat. Just a boat. I can't tell who is in it, or how many people there are." Derek squinted into the powerful telescope, trying to see better.

Derek felt the empty burn in his stomach, the dull, despairing ache that hadn't left him since the moment he'd watched Lauren run into the clearing, leading Bones and his foul crew away from himself and Amanda. Would he soon have her back in his arms?

Pushing his doubts aside, Derek collapsed the telescope, which was taken up instantly by a sailor. Derek hadn't had to ask for assistance, it was simply given; and he knew that Michael Masters had chosen his crew well.

"All the men have been versed on the story they are to give," Michael said quietly, reassuringly. He caught Derek's gaze, and for an extended moment the two men just looked into each other's eyes, giving and receiving strength.

"We can go straight to St. Lucifer, or we can try the safest course by investigating *As the Crow Flies.*" Derek looked out to sea, studying the boats that moved near the shore. "If she's been captured, she's probably on St. Lucifer. I burned down the mansion, but that's where Aldon Mitchell reigns over his dominion—and it isn't likely that he's changed. If she's been able to remain free, Mitchell and Gregor will still be looking for her, and we'll find them—sooner or later—in *As the Crow Flies.*"

There was another pause. Finally Derek said, "I say we go to the tavern. Lauren's so damned stubborn and smart I'm willing to bet she's eluded Gregor this long."

Michael just smiled and nodded, then turned to see to other duties. He prayed with all he held dear that Derek's guess would prove accurate.

"You're a dung heap, Bones," Lauren whispered, her dark eyes flinty with contempt.

Bones just looked at Lauren, hating her, wanting to hurt her, wanting to teach her a lesson. He couldn't, of course. He couldn't rip off her clothes and rape her, like he desperately wanted to; he couldn't even slap her. He couldn't do anything until Gregor had had his fill of Lauren, and then passed her along to him.

"Talk brave, wench," Bones whispered, his eyes thin, angry slits, the tension showing in his gaunt face and along the cords in his scrawny neck. "You ain't going to be with Cap'n Gregor always. When he's done with you, he's giving you to me. Then we'll see what brave words you got."

Lauren knew she shouldn't taunt a man as vicious as Bones. She knew she shouldn't—and she knew she couldn't stop herself. She smiled smugly as they made their way toward *As the Crow Flies.* Part of her hoped she could make Bones so angry he'd strike her, maybe bruising her. Then, just maybe, Gregor wouldn't want her. But that wasn't likely. It was more probable that he'd retaliate against Bones—but even that would be a victory.

"It'll be a relief to be with a *little* man like you after being with a *big* man like Derek." She laughed derisively, her eyes mocking Bones. "I suppose that being with you will be like being with . . . nothing at all."

Bones wheeled around to face Lauren, his hand on the haft of his dagger. The column of pirates came to a quick halt.

"Don't do it," one man said. He was one of the older pirates, and his blood did not burn quite so hotly as that of the younger ones. "She's taunting you, boy, cain't you see that? Don't let her get inside your skin." He chuckled wryly. "Soon enough you'll be inside o' hers."

Bones hit Lauren in the shoulder with the heel of his palm, knocking her halfway around. "Get movin'," he hissed through clenched teeth. "Cap'n Gregor's got something special for you, he has! Tomorrow you won't think everything is so damned funny!"

Lauren walked, closing her eyes briefly. This was the moment she'd dreaded during those long, sleepless nights in her cave on the small, lonely island: being surrounded by a contingent of men led by Bones, and brought to the foul public house where Gregor awaited her.

She recognized some of the men who'd come to gawk. Word had gotten out that she'd been captured. Bones was congratulated, like a conqueror coming home after slaying the undefeatable enemy. Men slapped him on the back and gave him hearty good cheer . . . and Lauren knew that these were not actually "men," more like animals who could look and talk like men, but were too savage, too barbaric, too primitive to deserve that distinction.

When she entered the clearing, which constituted the main street for the small village where *As the Crow Flies* was at the center, Lauren had twenty men surrounding her, most of them saying disgusting things about what they would like to do to her, all of them too frightened of Gregor and his vicious temper ever to go so far as to touch her.

The crowd parted as though divided by some huge, invisible hand, and Lauren stopped walking.

Gregor stood framed in the tavern doorway, his face flushed crimson with liquor and excitement and almost completely obscured by his red beard and unkempt curly hair. His eyes raked Lauren up and down, devouring her, taking her in as though he had never seen her before.

Revulsion welled up inside her, and for a moment she wondered if she'd done the right thing by allowing herself to be captured by Bones instead of taking the suicidal plunge from the cliff. Her death would have been swift and painless.

The crowd moved away from Lauren, giving Gregor room to walk around her slowly, inspecting her as a buyer would inspect a prized brood mare.

"Very good," he said softly, drawling the first word out. "And not a mark on her . . . at least, not one that I can see. You've done well, Bones. You'll be rewarded for this, I promise you."

Lauren stood quietly, hands at her sides, hating the feel of Gregor's hot gaze upon her. She was living her worst nightmare, and the reality of it was far more horrible than the vague fears that had chased away the comfort of sleep during her weeks of hiding.

In the two months Lauren had spent without seeing Gregor, she could tell that he had changed—and not for the better. His eyes were yellow, and though he'd never been particularly fastidious, his grooming had become markedly worse. A malodorous air hung about him—his clothes were soiled and torn, his beard grown ragged. He looked like a man haunted by demons who had been drunk for two months. Looks didn't lie.

He stepped up close to Lauren. His eyes seemed to have just a moment of difficulty focusing as he peered down Lauren's full bosom, handily displayed, for she was missing two buttons of her bodice.

"You wench," he said in a soft, deadly whisper, "have you any idea how much trouble you've caused me?"

Lauren smiled crookedly, putting on her best brave face. "I can guess. You look as if you've been dead for the past two months . . . or maybe you've just been dead drunk."

Gregor smiled then, laughing softly and cruelly. "Time hasn't taken the spunk out of you, has it? What happened to your English friend, eh? He up and leave you behind?" Gregor said, softly enough so that not many of the other pirates could hear the conversation. "How does it feel, little one, eh? How's it feel to be the one who gets set aside and left behind?"

"I wouldn't know." Lauren squared her shoulders. There was a strange new desperation to Gregor, and though it made him seem less strong, it also made him seem more dangerous. "I haven't been left behind. Derek will be back for me . . . you just wait and see."

Gregor laughed loudly, turning to his men. "Have you heard that, mates? She says the bastard Englishman is coming back for her! The thought of it has me quivering in me boots, it does! What about you, mates?"

"Quiverin', Cap'n Gregor!" Bones shouted. "Quiverin' like a baby, I am!"

When Gregor turned back to Lauren, his yellowish eyes were sharper, more focused—and more vicious. His gaze locked with Lauren's, and without breaking

360

his gaze he took a swallow from a bottle of rum. He wiped his mouth with the back of his hand, belched, then reached for Lauren's hair. She slapped his hand to block his touch, which obviously pleased him.

"You don't like my touch, eh, wench? You only want to be pawed by that Englishman, is that it?" Seemingly oblivious to the thirty men surrounding them, Gregor rubbed his crotch. "Maybe I oughta take you right now, right here in the dirt!" he hissed, spraying droplets of spittle as he spoke the foul, feverish words. "Maybe I oughta take you now, then let all the others have you, one after the other!"

Lauren looked straight into Gregor's eyes, and from a deep well of courage she had not known she possessed, she whispered with conviction, "Derek is going to kill you."

The flat, calm certainty of her statement caught Gregor off guard and visibly shook him. Time froze. Gregor and Lauren looked at each other, both knowing the truth in her words.

"We'll see, eh?" Gregor said at last, though it did not really break the silence that had enveloped them and the lusty-eyed men who hoped they'd soon get their turn between the thighs of the voluptuous—and courageous—American woman.

For the benefit of his men, Gregor leered at Lauren, his eyes widening as he visually devoured her breasts before he disdainfully met her gaze again. He moved very close to Lauren—close enough so that when he whispered, only she could hear him.

"Maybe that English bastard will kill me, you wench. But he won't kill me before I have my way with you. That's the way the wind is blowing, and you just gotta know that you can't change the course of the storm." Gregor raised his hands slowly to cup her breasts from the underside without ever breaking the hold of his eyes upon hers. His fingers pressed lightly into the firm swells as his face cracked into a crooked grin. "And maybe he won't kill me after all."

The fatality that Lauren had seen flash briefly in Gregor's eyes told her that this was a man who was not afraid to die—a man who, in fact, was contemptuous of all life, including his own. She knew then that nothing Derek could do to him would repay him sufficiently for what he intended to do to her.

"For once you're right," Lauren whispered, fighting to ignore the dirty, callused hands on her breasts and the rum-laced breath that assailed her. "Derek might not kill you . . . because you'll already be dead."

Gregor laughed softly at Lauren's bravado, and when he did, he closed his eyes for just a second. That was the opening that Lauren needed, and she didn't hesitate to take it.

In a blur of deadly intent she pulled Gregor's dagger from the sheath at his waist. She stabbed at his big belly, driving the knife straight forward. Gregor instinctively curled his elbows inward, protecting his middle. The dagger sliced cleanly through his forearm, and blood fountained from deep wounds in his arm.

Gregor howled in pain, and before Lauren could withdraw the dagger to stab him again, this time in a lethal place, Bones was upon her, catching her wrist and wrestling her to the ground. Lauren cursed herself—if she hadn't pulled her arm back so far to strike with all her might, she wouldn't have given Gregor the opportunity to defend himself.

"You bitch! I'll kill you for this!" Gregor hissed, his face a red mask of rage as he clutched his profusely bleeding arm.

While several pirates held Lauren to the ground, Bones helped Gregor bind the wounds on his arm with a tight cloth.

"You're bleedin' pretty bad, Cap'n," Bones said,

putting yet another strip of cloth around his arm to help soak up the blood that had not yet stopped seeping through the bandages.

Gregor had been cut before, but never had he lost quite this much blood, and despite the false aura of confidence that he tried to maintain, he was scared to the core of his soul. He felt lightheaded, and the tips of his fingers and toes felt numb.

"Put the bitch somewhere safe," Gregor said to Bones. His voice was weak and lifeless. "I'll have her later. She ain't going nowhere anyway. I've got time."

"Aye, Cap'n Gregor!" Bones replied, sensing his leader's sudden vulnerability. Bones wondered what would happen to him if Gregor died. He knew that other men aboard *The Unholy One* disliked him and tolerated him only because he'd ingratiated himself to Gregor.

Lauren was carried kicking and screaming to a small bamboo pen used to hold geese. She was thrown inside, and two men were assigned to keep a watch over her.

"You cut the cap'n bad," Bones whispered, kneeling beside the cage to look straight into Lauren's dark, frightened eyes. "But he'll get his strength back quick, and when he does, he's gonna take you *hard.*" Bones licked his lips lustfully. "You shoulda killed him. All you did was make him angry, and that's the worst thing you can do with Cap'n Gregor."

Bones started laughing then, a high-pitched, animal sound of sadistic glee. He was still laughing as he walked away from Lauren, leaving her behind with her two sullen guards. Lauren watched him leave and felt a shiver ripple through her. Bones was right: merely wounding Gregor was the worst thing she could possibly have done.

They paddled quietly through the dark water. There

363

was no need for conversation. All six men knew exactly what was expected of them when they reached shore.

Derek was in the lead, with Michael next. The small armada that had stormed out of Virginia had been left behind. Derek had successfully argued that fewer men would be needed to investigate St. Lucifer, and the smaller complement would help maintain the secrecy that had so far been their ally.

The V-shaped hull of the craft hit the sandy shore with a soft crunching sound. Derek leaped out, flintlock pistols tucked into the wide belt that surrounded his waist, his deadly curved cutlass on his left hip.

"Over there is where the mansion used to be," Derek explained, pointing in the direction of the Big House. "If Aldon Mitchell is still on the island, my guess is that he's staying in the harem house."

The small band trotted along the beach to the narrow trail that cut through the trees. Though Derek had been on this trail only once before, he remembered every tree, every turn.

The harem house was lit inside, and there were guards near the surrounding treeline and near the front and back doors.

Michael and Derek split up, moving through the trees. They would wait three minutes, then make their move through the clearing to the men who guarded the front entrance.

Taking his cutlass from its sheath, Derek paused at the edge of the treeline, studying the guard.

His black-clad body invisible in the shadows, Derek finally stepped out of the trees. Even his sandy-blond hair was mostly hidden under a black wool knit cap. He held the cutlass behind him so that the pale moonlight would not reflect off its polished, razor-sharp blade.

The guard saw Derek when fifteen feet still separated them. It was at that point that the guard made a fatal move. Rather than running and screaming, alerting fellow guards so that he was not the only man fighting Derek, the guard reached for the flintlock rifle.

He was still trying to thumb back the hammer and sight it on the onrushing young man dressed in black when cold, razor-sharp steel met with soft belly flesh. He was looking into Derek's eyes when he died.

Derek set the corpse down against the building, propping it up so that the guard appeared to be sleeping. He inspected the flintlock. Judging by the corrosion of the firing mechanism, it was questionable whether the weapon would have fired even if the guard had been able to pull the trigger. A good soldier would have kept his weapon in perfect condition. Derek's contempt for Aldon Mitchell, and everything associated with him, grew another notch.

Derek was the first to enter the harem house. Another guard stepped into the entrance area, munching on a piece of fruit. He looked at Derek, confusion in his eyes. By the time the guard recognized Derek, his fate was sealed. Derek caught the corpse before it fell to the floor, easing the body down silently. He heard footsteps.

Derek looked up, clutching the haft of his cutlass, ready to kill again if necessary. It was Michael Masters, flanked by his men. Lauren's father gave the corpse on the floor a disapproving look, then nodded appreciatively at Derek.

"It's an ugly business," he whispered.

Derek nodded, hating the carnage as much as any man would, yet knowing that there was no other course of action to take if Lauren was to be rescued.

Standing outside the doors to the pillow room, Derek paused to steel his courage. He was not afraid for his own life, but for what he might find. What would he do if Lauren, abused and now hateful of men, was sickened by the sight of him?

Don't think about that now! he cautioned himself.

Pushing the doors open wide, he burst into the room, cutlass in one hand, flintlock pistol in the other. Aldon Mitchell was sitting behind an old, scarred table, hunched over a ledger, quill in hand. When he looked at Derek, his lips began quivering, and almost immediately his entire body began to shake violently.

"Where is she?" Derek asked, temporarily ignoring the frightened, kneeling women he strode past.

Aldon just looked at Derek, then at Michael Masters, then at the grim-faced sailors who were moving through the room, checking to see if any of the women needed medical attention.

"Who?" Aldon asked, his voice quivering. Instantly the tip of Derek's cutlass was at his throat. "I-I-I don't know! Please, please, please don't hurt me! I'm begging you!" Aldon wailed. He pushed himself out of the chair and dropped to his knees, clenching his hands together as though in prayer. "I didn't mean to hurt anyone! I didn't!"

Derek and Michael, standing shoulder to shoulder, just looked at the kneeling man, sickened by what they saw. Like so many self-appointed demigods, Aldon Mitchell lacked any true courage.

"The American woman . . . where's Lauren?" Derek repeated, the point of his cutlass against Aldon's jugular vein.

"S-She's with Gregor. I haven't seen her yet! . . . I swear to God! A boat arrived here not two hours ago to tell me he'd just caught her after searching for two months!"

"That's a lie," Derek said, adding an ounce of pressure behind the cutlass, drawing a drop of blood. Aldon made a squealing sound that wasn't entirely human, though the pain couldn't have been enough to warrant such a response.

"It's true, I tell you!" Aldon screamed. "Take the

wenches, if you want! Take them all! I'll get you more right away if you'll just let me live! I'll get you dozens of wenches!"

Derek might have let Aldon Mitchell live. Killing a kneeling man who begged for his life was not something Derek found manly or courageous. But Aldon's continuing refusal to understand the inherent evil of kidnapping women and making them into slaves convinced the English nobleman of what had to be done.

"So Gregor has Lauren now?" Derek asked.

Aldon nodded his head vigorously. "She stabbed him! That's what I was told." Aldon tossed his hand to the side in a sweeping motion, indicating the six women who knelt, frightened, on the pillows in the room. "Take the wenches with you. I'll get you more right away. The finest women in all the world. And trained! They'll be trained by me personally, and they'll do anything you want! Anything at all!"

Derek turned his back on Aldon Mitchell. He looked at the women and said quietly, "There are boats to take you to the United States, if that's where you want to go. Don't worry, he'll never hurt you again." To one of the soldiers who stood in the room, he said, "This man is responsible for kidnapping Lauren Masters. I think you know what should be done."

Derek and Michael left the room. A moment later the soldier followed them, leaving the corpse of Aldon Mitchell behind.

Chapter 31

"It won't be long now," Derek said, leaning back so that he could look at Michael as he spoke. "I know where Gregor stays on the island. We'll find Lauren there."

Michael nodded, saying nothing. Derek could tell that the level of inhumanity was shocking to the sophisticated American businessman. Derek wondered, too, if Michael was unhappy that he had ordered Aldon Mitchell's execution. He hoped not, but he also knew with absolute certainty that he had made the right decision.

Feeling Michael's gaze on him, Derek asked, "Is something wrong?"

"No. You made the just and proper decision with that monster," Michael said, accurately reading Derek's thoughts. "Sometimes in life, you've got to make the hard decision." Michael patted Derek's shoulder briefly. "We'll get her back, and you'll have my blessing to marry her."

For the first time in weeks, Derek's face creased into a wide, honest smile. "To tell you the truth, I was a little worried about asking for your blessing."

"Now all you'll have to do is get Lauren to agree with

it," Michael said, reflecting Derek's smile. "I've learned that anytime I think something is right, she's against it. She's the most stubborn woman I've ever met."

Derek nodded, saying, "That's one of the reasons why I love her."

Looking up at the stars, Derek could hardly wait to reach *As the Crow Flies*. As the sailors rowed on, he wondered how many of the men in the boat—himself included—would be alive in the morning.

The sound of drums and fiddle, of laughing men and dancing women, had been ringing through the early dusk for an hour when Bones arrived at the goose cage for Lauren.

"You shoulda killed him," Bones said, smiling broadly as he unhooked the cage door. "Cap'n Gregor is in fine spirits, an' he's looking forward to seein' you again!"

Lauren crawled out of the cage and didn't complain when Bones grabbed her by the upper arm and hauled her to her feet with much greater force than was necessary. She glared at him, and that brought forth another fit of cackling, unamused laughter.

"Come on, little wench, there's a party going on, and you're the guest of honor."

If Bones hadn't had four men with him, Lauren would have given serious consideration to attacking the slender man physically. But there were too many crewmen from *The Unholy One* for her to successfully defend herself and escape.

As she walked on, her senses were razor sharp, and she was confident she'd think of some way to escape before Gregor could follow through on his foul threats.

A huge fire had been set ablaze outside *As the Crow Flies*. Thirty men and a handful of women surrounded

369

the fire, many of them drinking, all of them laughing. It surprised Lauren to see so many women present, and she wondered whether the women there ever worried about being the "wench" for which a similar party would be thrown in her "honor."

There was only one chair set near the fire—a big, high-backed chair that had been stolen from a captain's chambers aboard a ship that had fallen under the cannons of *The Unholy One*. Gregor sat there, his hands resting lightly on the thickly padded arms. The bandage around his forearm was very thick, but it was snowy white, despite Lauren's desperate hopes to see signs that his wound was still bleeding.

Gregor smiled at Lauren as she was brought closer. A cheer went up among the pirates. Wineskins were raised and glasses filled. Foul toasts were uttered and glasses emptied. Lauren was half pushed, half pulled by the pirates and Bones until she was brought close to Gregor and forced to her knees.

Suddenly the revelry ended and a hush fell over the crowd.

"As you can see, I have regained my manly strength," Gregor said, looking at Lauren kneeling before him, but speaking in a booming voice for the benefit of the people surrounding the fire. "I should almost thank you for cutting me. It was only a minor cut, and it gave us time to prepare this celebration." He looked away from Lauren to the men and women who hung on his every word. "Isn't that right?"

A cheer went up from the crowd, shocking Lauren. It was hard for her to believe there could be so many people in one place who showed such contempt for life and for common laws of decency.

"Continue!" Gregor shouted. The drum and fiddle began again, and he was no longer the center of attention.

370

Lauren could feel everyone's eyes upon her. She occasionally looked away from Gregor, and when she matched gazes with the women, she sometimes saw sympathy, but more often she saw nothing but resignation. These women accepted the debauchery of the men around them without judging it one way or another. Lauren knew she could never live her life that way, no matter what happened to her.

When Lauren shifted positions slightly, sitting rather than kneeling on the ground, Bones rushed forward. In the foulest language she'd ever heard, he warned her that if she did anything like that again, he'd personally cut the soles of her feet with his dagger. The prospect of forcing himself upon her, she realized, had pushed Bones over the edge of insanity. She hastily moved her knees beneath her once again, turning away from Bones, appalled at what she had seen in the depths of his eyes.

Gregor gave her a sadistic, leering smile and said, "I want them all to see you, to look at you. I want to show them all that *I* am the power on this island—the *only* power. When I've finished proving myself to these people, I'll have them take your clothes off, so every man and woman will know what is mine." He chuckled softly, his eyes raking over the kneeling woman's body, imagining once again what she would look like naked. "And only after I have proved to everyone here that I always get whatever I want, only then will I take you away from all this and teach you what it's like to have a *real* man between your thighs."

Lauren noticed that Gregor was not drinking. His eyes were clear and bright, perhaps only faintly tinged with yellow from previous excesses. She had cut him, but true to his word, Gregor had recovered quickly. She noticed, too, that this night he wore no dagger at his waist. Gregor had made that mistake once before,

371

and he wasn't going to let it happen again. Whatever violence was needed to subdue her would come from Bones and the other pirates who had been assigned to watch over her during the celebration.

Hurry, Derek! Please hurry, Lauren thought, frightened that her time was running out, and that there was nothing she or Derek or her father and all his millions could do to change the inexorable course of events.

The fire blazed, sending flames skyward ten feet and more, and Lauren had difficulty keeping her eyes away from it. It mesmerized her and made her brain function sluggishly. Tonight, if she was to have any chance of escape, she would need all her mental and physical strength.

Lauren surreptitiously searched for weaknesses she could use to her advantage, but she found few. Gregor continued to sit in his overstuffed chair, which looked out of place on the Caribbean island. He leaned back regally, sipping from a glass that Lauren suspected did not contain rum. She had also spotted at least four men who had been assigned to guard her from a distance. They hadn't been difficult to spot; they were the only ones who were not drinking, dancing, smiling, and fondling the serving girls.

Though she was unbound, she had no chance of escape, but was forced to kneel beside Gregor like some well-trained dog at her master's feet.

She felt his eyes upon her and looked up at him, not at all surprised to meet his gaze. Gregor's eyes were dark, intense, hateful, and filled with lust. He smiled crookedly, showing yellowed teeth.

"Tonight, all your running will end," Gregor said, speaking just loud enough to be heard over the drum and the fiddle. "What happened to all your big talk, wench? I thought you were the one who always had so much to say, who always kept her chin up."

He laughed. Lauren felt tears burn in her eyes. She turned her face down, hating the sound of Gregor's laughter. She searched within herself for the courage to defy Gregor, to fight him to the bitter, hateful, inevitable end. Despair swept through her, and a single tear slipped down her cheek. She wiped it away quickly, angrily.

She wouldn't beg. She wouldn't beg for mercy from Gregor or from Bones or from any of the human monsters that sailed aboard *The Unholy One*. They could take her, perhaps, and there might not be anything she could do about it. But she wouldn't let them break her spirit, no matter how bleak, or brutal, or hopeless things became. She just had to hang on long enough for Derek, because he had returned for her. He had come back for her, and when he found her, he would once again make everything all right in her world.

The music stopped abruptly.

Lauren looked at the crowd. The faces were flushed with liquor and exertion and excitement. They were waiting for the "big event" to happen, and Lauren knew that *she* was that Big Event. She did not see a single face that expressed any sympathy to her plight—not even among the women.

Lauren finally looked at Gregor. He was still seated, his right arm raised, his palm to the crowd. His left arm, the one with the thick bandage around the forearm that Lauren had wounded, remained resting on the chair. She wondered how much pain he was in, and if she could possibly hurt his injury enough to make him not want to defile her.

Gregor snapped his fingers. Two of the men who'd been keeping watch on her rushed forward. Lauren's heart thudded furiously within her chest, her eyes darting right and left like a frightened, trapped rabbit's.

Gregor snapped his fingers a second time. The two

guards grabbed Lauren by the arms and hauled her brutishly to her feet. With a grin on his face, Bones moved forward, his eyes almost glowing with demonic satisfaction and anticipation.

"Take your damned hands off me," Lauren hissed through clenched teeth, trying to pull her arms from the grasp of the guards. They continued gripping her tightly, their hands around her wrists, holding her arms apart.

Bones slipped around Lauren, moving behind her. She heard Gregor snap his fingers once again, and she was turned so that she faced the crowd, her back now to Gregor. A murmur went through the crowd of revelers, and Lauren looked into their flushed, excited faces, and thought, *This can't be happening to me. Derek would never let this happen to me.*

Remaining seated, like a king addressing his dutiful and loyal subjects, Gregor spoke to the crowd in a low, menacing tone.

"We are all aware of the trouble this wench has caused. She has insulted me and defied me. She even drew my blood, stabbing me with my own knife. She thought she could defy me and get away with it, and this—what you will see tonight—is what happens to wenches who don't obey me!"

Another murmur went through the crowd.

Lauren felt hands at her hips. She tried looking over her shoulder, but the men holding her arms pulled with even greater strength, jerking hard on her limbs. Lauren winced in pain but did not cry out. The chuckle of approval she heard came from Bones, who had begun to touch her.

"You're a pig," Lauren said, unable to see Bones, but feeling his hands on her hips moving slowly up her sides.

"And you're a beauty," Bones replied, his hands now near Lauren's underarms, touching her through the ragged dress, inching very slowly toward the torn décolletage and the heavy mounds of her breasts. "You're a real beauty, and you're going to make the cap'n *real* happy."

His hands went over her breasts, the fingers curling inside the loose décolletage. Lauren swallowed her contempt, hating the feel of Bones's hands on her breasts, unable to believe that so many people could be so fascinated at what was happening.

"What should I have Bones do?" Gregor asked in a voice that was booming, authoritative, and charismatic.

As one, the crowd began chanting, "Rip! Rip! Rip it off! Rip! Rip! Rip it off!"

She heard Bones's chuckle and closed her eyes. She could not look into the sickening faces of the crowd as her clothes were being torn from her.

And then, just as she was certain Bones was going to tear the bodice of her dress apart to expose her breasts to the crowd, gunshots rang out through the night air.

It took a split second for Lauren to realize exactly what had happened. She opened her eyes and saw some men in the crowd falling to their knees, dropping whatever they were holding, and throwing their arms over their heads in defense. The women, who somehow seemed to know that they weren't the object of the attack, remained standing. The two men who had been holding Lauren's wrists to render her defenseless against Bones crumpled to the ground, each man clutching his chest.

"What the hell?" Bones mumbled, his brain sluggish from all the rum he'd consumed during the celebration.

Gregor, who hadn't dulled his senses with alcohol, reacted immediately, spinning out and away from the overstuffed chair a moment before a bullet punched a hole through the plush upholstery.

Lauren also reacted quickly, spinning on her heel, her small hands clutched together in a double fist. She swung blindly but effectively. Her fists smacked hard against Bones's jaw, twisting him halfway around and dropping him to his knees. For good measure, she raised her fists high over her head, then brought them crashing down against the back of his head with such force she thought she might have broken several bones in her hand. The stunned Bones crashed face first into the ground, groaning, nearly unconscious, mumbling incoherent threats at her.

Lauren turned back toward the treeline just in time to see Derek leap over a fallen pirate, his long, curved cutlass in his left hand, a flintlock pistol in his right. Their eyes met for only a moment, and then a pirate rushed toward Derek, holding a cutlass out in front of him like a lance.

In that instant, Lauren's heart stopped beating. But Derek easily sidestepped the rush, tripping the pirate and then skillfully dispatching him with the cutlass.

She rushed to Derek, oblivious to the carnage and violence surrounding them, needing desperately to feel him and assure herself that he was really here and not a fantasy she'd conjured up to help her through the hideous times with Gregor and Bones and all the other pirates from *The Unholy One*.

Derek spread his arms, and Lauren launched herself into them, throwing her arms around his neck, holding him fiercely, her tears now shed gladly, happily, because Lord Derek York had come back for her, and from this point forward nothing could ever separate them again.

She was still holding Derek, her face buried in his neck, when she heard the familiar, scolding voice of her father. "This is not the time, Lauren!"

With her arms still around Derek, Lauren looked

over her shoulder at her father's handsome face and screamed joyously, "Papa!"

"Not now!" Michael shouted.

Lauren realized the gravity of the situation a second later, when her father fired a shot that seemed directed at Derek. A harsh cry of pain was followed immediately by a body falling to the ground just behind him.

"I love you!" Lauren said, taking just one more second to look into Derek's eyes before releasing him.

All around her the battle raged. Though the men with Derek and Michael were outnumbered, they were highly trained, skilled soldiers, which more than made up for the imbalance of manpower. Though Lauren, her confidence now soaring, wanted to get into the fight herself, an incredibly large man whom Derek addressed as Hugo was assigned to protect her. Lauren was pulled through the mêlée by the giant Hugo, who, without the slightest display of emotion, killed two pirates who appeared to threaten Lauren.

With a grim, fierce look in his eyes, Derek crossed swords with a pirate whose face he recognized but whose name he could not remember. The contest was short lived when Derek used a move he'd been taught years before, while at Eton: he feinted to his left, waited for the pirate's lunge, backed away from it, then leaped forward just behind the attack. His cutlass cut deep, just beneath the pirate's outstretched arm; the man was dead before he hit the ground.

Derek moved away from the fire, away from the center of fighting. Now that Lauren was safe, the unfinished business Derek had with Gregor had to be resolved. It wasn't enough just to free Lauren and bring her back with him to London or Virginia, or wherever in the world she wanted to live. Derek had made a promise to himself that he would expunge all evidence of Gregor's existence so that no man loving a woman as much as Derek loved Lauren would ever go through the heartache he had endured.

Derek moved into the trees, slowing his stride, feeling all his senses tingling with anticipation of this final confrontation with the man he had put up with for so long in order to ensure his sister's freedom.

"Come on and show yourself," Derek said, his eyes narrowed to slits as he peered into the shadows, knowing Gregor had gone this way. "You always said you wanted to cross swords with me. Now's your chance."

He continued moving forward, deeper into the forest, clutching his cutlass and pistol. His intuition told him Gregor was close.

"Judgment day, Gregor," Derek said, much more quietly this time, his warrior instinct telling him the enemy was very close. "It's time you paid for everything you've done."

"Not goddamned likely."

Gregor stepped into the clearing, a huge saber in his hand. Even in the darkness his eyes were glittery bright, and Derek knew, as he had known all along, that this was a formidable enemy, an equal in many ways, and that unless he fought flawlessly, he might never live to marry Lauren.

Though they were still several feet apart, they began circling each other, sizing each other up, even though they had both done so a hundred times in the past.

Derek looked into Gregor's eyes, part of him hoping that he would see the dull glow of alcohol which would inhibit his reflexes. But another part of Derek wanted Gregor to be at his best. It was time for retribution, time to find out exactly what Gregor was made of, time to put an end to their battle for dominance.

The grin on Gregor's face vanished. Whatever humor there was in this final battle also vanished when the reality of death, perhaps seconds away, insinuated itself.

"We've waited a long time for this," Gregor said, circling slowly, studying Derek as though his life depended upon it. "You've been wantin' a piece of me, Englishman, and I've been wantin' a piece of you." He chuckled, spotted what he thought was an opening near Derek's left hip, then lunged for it, thrusting his cutlass forward in a stabbing move. Derek parried the thrust, stepping out of reach in the same instant. Gregor chuckled.

"You're quick, Englishman, real quick. But you're fightin' on your heels! You're runnin' from me, and you'll never taste victory by runnin'."

With a lesser opponent, Derek might have allowed himself to be drawn into this boastful banter, but with Gregor—a man who had killed many and whose tricks numbered even more—he did not trust himself to be so cavalier.

Gregor lunged again, this time aiming for a vulnerable spot on Derek's right knee. Again Derek parried the strike as he danced back out of harm's way . . . but this time Derek learned something valuable: Gregor attacked with the intention of merely wounding him, not of delivering a quick, deadly strike. A jab to the knee, then a slice in the forearm, followed by a slash to his thigh . . . eventually such injuries would cause sufficient blood loss to sap Derek's strength, leaving him open to Gregor's final thrust.

"Cat got your tongue?" Gregor asked. He raised his cutlass high above his head and lunged forward, bringing his silver blade down with enormous strength.

Derek had no choice but to match swords with Gregor, and even though he successfully blocked the slashing attack, he was knocked back several steps. Gregor's enormous strength and his added weight

379

advantage were factors Derek knew he had to overcome if he was to win.

He had hardly regained his balance when Gregor attacked again in precisely the same manner. The brute force of his second assault forced Derek to take three more steps back, moving away from the small clearing, nearly stumbling in the low undergrowth of vegetation beside the trail. Leaping, Derek moved back into the clearing a second later before Gregor could attack again. A smile of appreciation crossed Derek's lips.

"You're more sophisticated than I thought," Derek said with the respect of one warrior for another. Gregor had intended to drive Derek into the undergrowth, where he wouldn't be as agile in the tangled jungle floor, and where Gregor's greater strength would prove an advantage. Gregor was not, as Derek had sometimes suspected, merely a brute monster going in for the quick kill. He was quite capable of planning his assault many moves in advance.

They circled, the clang of blade against blade ringing through the night air. Sweat trickled down Derek's spine as he parried and thrust, studying Gregor while searching for a weakness he could exploit.

The circling stopped and their eyes met. Derek whispered, "How does it feel to be a dead man?"

Gregor attacked, and just as he had in the previous attacks, his left arm slipped away from his body as his right, carrying the heavy cutlass, swung in for the kill. Derek took a long step back, hesitating a fraction of a second to allow the deadly cutlass to cut harmlessly through the air just beneath his chin. As the blade sliced past him, Derek leaped forward, his body angled sideways to make a smaller target, and thrust at Gregor just beneath the left arm, at the single fatal opening that Gregor allowed him. It was all Derek needed.

Steel met with flesh and bone. Gregor looked

straight at Derek, his eyes registering shock and rage. He raised his cutlass, but before he could bring it down against Derek's skull, the cutlass fell from his numb fingers.

"Bastard Englishman," Gregor whispered.

With a hard pull, Derek removed the blade from Gregor's chest. He felt neither elation nor sympathy. Something that was evil on this earth was just seconds away from death. A rabid dog had been dealt with swiftly, and with finality.

Gregor reached for the cutlass in the dirt at his feet. When he leaned over, he lost his balance and went face first into the ground.

He was dead a moment later, his lifeless eyes staring hatefully at the English lord who had ended his reign of terror in the Caribbean Sea.

"It's over," Derek said softly to himself, looking down at the corpse. "It's finally over."

He turned and headed back toward the clearing, where the last of the fighting was winding up. A strange, weary elation swept over him as he thought about Lauren and the glory of having her once again in his arms, and how they would be together now and for all time.

Lauren leaned back until she felt Derek's chest against her shoulder. She looked up at him and was caught for the hundredth time by the perfection of his profile. He slipped an arm around her shoulders, and together they looked out to sea.

"Nervous?" he asked.

Lauren shrugged. "A little, I suppose. You'll be there with me." She twisted the wedding ring around her finger.

"You're nervous. Whenever you get nervous you

start twisting your wedding ring around and around."

"I'm not used to it yet. I haven't been wearing it very long."

Derek smiled at the excuse.

Lauren looked at her wedding ring and at the hand that wore it. The ring was a little tighter now than it had been three months earlier, when Derek had placed it on her finger during their wedding ceremony. She placed her right hand on her stomach. Though she couldn't feel anything move inside yet, she knew she was pregnant with Derek's child.

Would their child be a son? If so, she wanted him to look just like his father.

Lauren looked up again. A breeze ruffled Derek's hair, and Lauren felt a tightness in her chest and a tingling deep within her.

What would Derek think when she told him she was expecting their first child? Lauren had suspected for a week now that she was pregnant, but she hadn't told Derek because she was afraid that if he knew, he would cancel their plans to move to London. She knew how eager he was to return home. It had been many months since he'd been there—nearly a year—and she hadn't wanted to allow anything to postpone the voyage.

"What are you thinking about?" Lauren asked quietly, resting her head against Derek's hard chest again.

"Our family."

"Don't worry, I'll charm your father. He'll approve of me," Lauren said with much more conviction than she felt. In truth, she was petrified of meeting her formidable father-in-law.

"Not Father. I'm talking about *our* family . . . you and me and baby makes three." He squeezed Lauren's shoulder, hugging her a little closer to his chest. The

382

breeze was cool, and Lauren did not like being cold. "We'll have a beautiful child . . . I just know it. And I hope the baby's a girl and she looks just like her mother."

A smile tugged at Lauren's mouth. "How did you know? I always thought husbands were the last to find out."

Derek's smile broadened. "I didn't know, actually—not until this moment. I was guessing, and you confirmed my suspicion."

Lauren grinned. She never could keep secrets from Derek, and now she understood that there was no reason for her to have been apprehensive about Derek's reaction to her pregnancy.

"I love you," Derek said quietly, hugging Lauren just a little bit harder. "I love you for a thousand reasons, but right now, knowing that you're going to make me a father, I love you more than ever . . . more than I ever dreamed it was possible to love anyone."

Lauren felt tears of joy pool in the depths of her eyes, but she refused to shed them. Though Derek was more able to accept open displays of emotion now than when she'd first met him, he still was not entirely comfortable with her tears—even if they were tears of happiness.

"We'll take the east wing at home," Derek continued. "And though we'll be living at York Manor with Father, you won't have to worry about having enough privacy. There are forty-two rooms in the manor." He kissed the top of Lauren's head, pausing a moment to inhale deeply, breathing in the sweet scent of her. "As soon as we get home, we'll get started on the nursery. You can have it any way you want it."

Lauren tried to speak, but emotion choked off her words. Instead, she turned within the circle of Derek's embrace, slipped her arms around his narrow waist, and hugged him close, pressing her cheek against his chest. It would be a good life, she knew, so long as she had Derek at her side.

She hoped her child was a son, for Derek's sake, but she also knew that their first child would not be their last. Their love would endure through the rigors of parenthood and the occasional strains of marriage, and with it all, their love would produce many children. Lauren was certain of it.